RUSSIAN SCIENCE FICTION

RUSSIAN
SCIENCE
FICTION

★ AN ANTHOLOGY ★

COMPILED AND EDITED
WITH AN INTRODUCTION BY
ROBERT MAGIDOFF
Director, Russian Program, New York University

TRANSLATED BY
DORIS JOHNSON
Assistant Professor of Russian, Purdue University

NEW YORK UNIVERSITY PRESS

CONTENTS

Introduction

SCIENCE fiction became an important branch of Russian literature only during the Soviet period. The several literary works describing future civilizations, or life on other planets, which appeared in pre-revolutionary Russia were utopias concentrating on social relationships, rather than science fiction. The first such utopian novel was written in 1783 (but not published until 1807) by Prince Mikhail Shcherbatov. In his *Land of Ofiriya* he described the kind of moderately democratic country which he had hoped feudal Russia would become after political and agrarian reforms.

Prince Vladimir Odoyevsky's *Morning Star* (1840) contained some vague references to air travel, color photography, automobiles, and hybridization of plants, but here, too, the emphasis was on social structure, more particularly on a society dominated by scholars, scientists, and poets. Similarly, the revolutionary critic, Nikolay Chernishevsky, in his famous novel *What Is To Be Done?*, published in 1863, made a passing reference to buildings of metal and glass and the abundance of food, but was really interested in a new society based on socialistic relationships, atheism, and free love. (The reference here is to the chapter entitled 'The Fourth Dream of Vera Pavlovna.')

Jules Verne and H. G. Wells captured the imagination of millions of Russian readers between the appearance of *What Is to be Done?* and the next major book in this genre, A. Bogdanov's *The Red Star* (1908). Nevertheless, the latter also concentrated on the social, rather than scientific and technological, aspects of life on Mars, where most of the action takes place. The Martians have developed a society of 'complete freedom', where men achieve longevity through blood transfusions, but in the end voluntarily take their own lives in magnificently appointed suicide palaces, so as not to detract from the 'life of ecstasy' prevailing on the planet. Bogdanov, incidentally, was a physician who in 1926 organized the State Institute of Blood Transfusion, and died as a result of an unsuccessful experiment performed on himself. A member of the Bolshevik

Party since 1905, he predicted in his novel that 'inevitable terror' and 'barbaric patriotism' would accompany the building of socialism.

The early works of Soviet science fiction continued the trend of concentration on social and political problems at the expense of scientific and technical fantasy. Four works of that period merit attention: *We* by Eugene Zamyatin (1920), *The Fatal Eggs* by Mikhail Bulgakov (1927–28), and Alexey Tolstoy's *Aelita* (1923) and *Engineer Garin's Hyperboloid* (1926). The first two were savage satires on the emerging Soviet regime, depicting it as cruel and totalitarian. *We*, yet to be published in Russia, was smuggled out of the country, to make its first appearance in the United States in 1924. *The Fatal Eggs*, overlooked by the censor, was suppressed immediately upon publication.

Count Alexey Tolstoy left Russia after the revolution, but returned and wrote, in addition to other works, two science fiction novels praising the Bolshevik regime. The hero of *Aelita* is an iron-willed demobilized Red Army soldier who, upon reaching Mars, leads a revolution against the oppressors. One of the characters in the book is an American, the sympathetically depicted journalist Archibald Skyles. In the next novel, however, Tolstoy is anti-West, as well as pro-Soviet.

Despite his ideological conformity, Tolstoy was too complex a writer to serve as a model for the coming generation of Soviet science-fiction writers. This distinction belongs to Alexander Belyaev (1884–1942), who is rightfully considered the father of Soviet science fiction and its leading representative until World War II. While it is true that he borrowed much from Alexey Tolstoy, he owes even more to Jules Verne and H. G. Wells. Most of the action in Belyaev's works takes place outside of the U.S.S.R. and most of the protagonists are non-Russians. His characters, modeled after those in Verne and Wells, with an occasional borrowing from Dickens, are wooden and stereotyped.

There is no originality, no humor, and no character development —only a skillful and at times almost poetic popularization of technology and science. Belyaev's *Invisible Light*, included in this collection, is a good example. It also contains a characteristic dogmatic depiction of capitalist society as one plagued by unemployment, exploiting the have-nots, and breeding revolution. In this society, every technological or scientific breakthrough merely increases the monstrous power of the exploiters. In the Soviet Union, on the other hand, judging from his books in which the action takes place in Russia, inventions are always made for the benefit of mankind.

World War II put an end to the hegemony of Belyaev and his imitators, and brought to the forefront what might be termed the

Yefremov school, after Professor Ivan Yefremov. There is still no clean-cut break with dogmatism: the West is still presented as predatory and decaying, and Soviet society as a near-paradise. But the emphasis has shifted.

The new emphasis, while not neglecting ideology, is increasingly pedagogical, and aims at stimulating and channeling scientific creativity and the curiosity of the young generation, firing its imagination with unlimited prospects for the conquest of nature and for its transformation. The reader is exposed to a boundless faith in man and in his power to control nature and to place it at his service. For example, in Nemtsov's *Shadow Under the Earth*, a Soviet scientist invents an instrument that can 'see' through anything, including soil, leading to fabulous discoveries of minerals. In *The Soaring Poplar* by G. Gurevich, trees are made to grow with miraculous speed and to bring new life to desert areas. The philosophy of this trend is explicitly formulated in a brief passage from Gurevich's book:

Man stands at the basis of everything. We write in books on agricultural technology: 'To grow a plant, four things are needed— moisture, light, warmth and food.' But this is not so. What is needed is the fifth factor—man.

Some works of Soviet science fiction belonging to this category inadvertently reveal the shabbiness and deprivations in the average Soviet citizen's day-to-day existence, and their limiting impact on his dreams. *The Magic Shoes*, included in this volume, is a case in point. Another example is A. Palei's *Tausen's Island*, where the breeding of gigantic sheep revolutionizes animal husbandry.

Along with the glorification of man the creator and transformer, there is a marked tendency ever since the fifties toward a new humanism in Soviet science fiction, relating man to the communist society he lives in, and idealizing both. Everyone works for the common good, even to the point of self-sacrifice, like the hero of one of our stories, *The Astronaut*. According to this trend, the socialist environment has changed man's very nature, replacing fear, distrust, and hostility with openness, kindness, and generosity.

These virtues belong also to the creatures inhabiting outer space, but not to those who have had the misfortune to live under capitalism, as the reader of *Cor Serpentis* will learn.

A major theme in Soviet science fiction, as in all Soviet literature, is the glorification of teamwork, of what the Russians term collective effort. In it lies, they claim, the secret of creative accomplishment and of the selflessness that changes man from a creature distorted by the individualism rampant in capitalist society into a proud citizen of the harmonious world of socialism.

Besides its comparative excellence as a literary work, Dudintsev's *A New Year's Fairy Tale* is also significant in that it does not support this creed: its hero, although he belongs to a team of scientists, shares his work on a miraculous invention only with the woman he loves. Singlehandedly, he brings a priceless gift to humanity, moved solely by his compassion for suffering men, and inspired only by the creative urge within himself. True, when he is on the verge of death toward the end, his colleagues complete his noble task, but the general tenor of the story does not suggest that this last-minute collective effort is any substitute for the creative spark within the individual.

Soviet science fiction-writers concentrate chiefly on the novel. There are comparatively few short stories, and these are scattered in magazines and occasional collections which are not readily available in this country. The compiler is thus left largely to the mercies of chance and of the Soviet bureaucrats who decide what may, and what may not, be exported from the U.S.S.R. To make this anthology more representative, three stories were included in translations, not altogether adequate, that had been done in Moscow. Efforts to obtain the original versions were unsuccessful.

Robert Magidoff

Notes on the Authors

ALEXANDER BELYAEV (1884-1942), author of 'Invisible Light', became a legend during his lifetime. Although confined to his bed with tuberculosis of the spine, he studied law, music, and science, and wrote indefatigably. Among his most popular science-fiction works are *The Amphibian*, *Professor Dowell's Head*, *A Jump Into Nothingness*, and *The Last Man from Atlantis*.

VICTOR SAPARIN (1905-), author of 'The Magic Shoes' and a journalist by profession, is the editor of the Soviet geographical magazine, *Around the World*. He differs from the majority of Soviet science-fiction writers in that he writes of subjects which lend themselves to down-to-earth treatment.

E. ZELIKOVICH, author of 'A Dangerous Invention', is a present-day Soviet science-fiction writer. No other information about him is available. 'A Dangerous Invention' has been somewhat condensed by the omission of verbose passages, but the text has not been altered.

VADIM OKHOTNIKOV, author of 'The Fiction Machines'—no information available.

IVAN YEFREMOV (1907–), author of 'Shadows of the Past' and 'Cor Serpentis (The Heart of the Serpent)', is a professor of geology who combines fossil hunting with writing, and who is the acknowledged dean of Soviet science-fiction writers. In addition to numerous short stories, he has several novels to his credit, including the very popular *The Land of Foam*, about ancient Egypt and Greece, and *Andromeda*, where the scene is set in the year four thousand.

MIKHAIL VASILYEV (1920-), author of 'Flying Flowers', is a trained engineer who is at present the science and technology editor of *Komsomolskaya Pravda*, the Communist youth daily in Moscow. Vasilyev writes science-fiction short stories, as well as popular science books, such as *Space Travel*, *Man and Energy* and *Reports from the 21st Century* (the last in collaboration with S. Gushchev).

13

Because the Russian original of 'Flying Flowers' is not obtainable in the United States, we are presenting it as it appeared in a Soviet collection, *Destination: Amaltheia*, translated by Leonid Kolesnikov.

ANATOLY DNIEPROV (1919-   ), author of 'The Maxwell Equations', is a distinguished Soviet physicist engaged in research in the laboratories of the U.S.S.R. Academy of Sciences. His main preoccupation in his science fiction (and possibly in his research) is with cybernetics.

Because the Russian original of 'The Maxwell Equations' is not obtainable in the United States, we are presenting it as it appeared in a Soviet collection, *Destination: Amaltheia*, translated by Leonid Kolesnikov.

VALENTINA ZHURAVLEVA (1933-   ), author of 'The Astronaut', is the youngest and one of the most popular writers of science fiction in present-day Russia. A doctor by profession, she draws her material mainly from the fields of medicine and biochemistry.

Because the Russian original of 'The Astronaut' is not obtainable in the United States, we are presenting it as it appeared in a Soviet collection, *Destination: Amaltheia*, translated by Leonid Kolesnikov.

VLADIMIR DUDINTSEV, author of 'A New Year's Fairy Tale', is one of the 'angry young men' of the post-Stalin period in Soviet literature. He gained world fame in 1957 with the publication of *Not By Bread Alone*, a novel in which he called for intellectual independence and attacked Soviet bureaucracy. Brutal criticism by Communist ideologists silenced him until 1960 when, in 'A New Year's Fairy Tale,' he once more raised his voice in defense of the sacred spark of creativity within the individual.

KONSTANTIN TSIOLKOVSKY (1857-1935), author of 'The Moon', was one of the leading Russian theoretical scientists and inventors. As far back as 1903 (in a study entitled 'Investigation of Cosmic Spaces'), he worked out the theory of rocket flight, and demonstrated the possibility of rocket devices for interplanetary communication. The Russians claim for him the distinction of being 'the father of modern rocketry.'

Since Tsiolkovsky's work lay predominantly in science and technology, rather than in writing, 'On the Moon' has an awkwardness that is reflected in the translation. The story is included, however, as an example of early Russian efforts in science fiction.

Russian Science Fiction

Part One

Invisible Light

BY ALEXANDER BELYAEV

'WELL, one can plainly see that Viroval is a great doctor.'

'He must be, if even the totally blind can see it.'

'How do you know I'm totally blind?' The patient turned to the stranger sitting beside him.

'Oh, your clear blue eyes don't fool me. They're as lifeless as a doll's.' Laughing quietly, the stranger added, 'Besides, I moved my finger right in front of your nose, and you didn't even blink.'

'That was nice of you,' the blind man smiled bitterly, and nervously smoothed his already well-groomed chestnut hair. 'Yes, I'm blind, and said "one can plainly see" out of old habit. But you don't need eyes to recognize wealth and distinction. The best section of the city. A private house. Smell of roses at the entrance; broad staircase; doorman. The aroma of expensive perfume in the vestibule. Footmen, attendants, secretaries. A high, fixed fee. Preliminary examination by assistants. Soft rugs under one's feet, armchairs upholstered in silk, the pleasant odor in this reception room.'

'A remarkable psychological preparation,' the stranger remarked quietly, his yellowed face wrinkling in an ironic smile. He swiftly examined Viroval's luxurious reception room as if to check the blind man's observations. The armchairs were all occupied by patients, many of whom wore dark glasses or bandages on their eyes and expressions of expectation, anxiety or hope on their faces.

'But you have only recently lost your sight. How did it happen?' he addressed the blind man again.

'What makes you think it was recent?' The blind man raised his brows in surprise.

'Men who are blind from birth have different habits. Apparently your optic nerve was affected. Necrosis, perhaps the result of a very unpleasant, unmentionable disease. . .'

The blind man's cheeks, forehead, even his chin flushed red. He frowned.

'Nothing of the kind!' He spoke rapidly and indignantly, without turning his head toward the stranger. 'I'm an electrician. I was working in an experimental laboratory of the Universal Electric Company assembling new ultraviolet lamps. . .'

'The rest of the story is obvious. I thought so. Excellent!' The stranger rubbed his hands, leaned toward the blind man and whispered: 'Give up this charlatan Viroval. You could get just as much help from a shoemaker. Viroval will deceive you until he has taken your last dollar. Then he'll announce that he's done everything possible. And in his own way he'll be right, since no specialist in the world would be able to extract another cent from you. Do you have much money? What do you live on?'

'You must take me for a fool,' the blind man answered with obvious aversion. 'But even a blind fool can see through you. You're an agent for some other doctor.'

The stranger laughed noiselessly, his face gathered into wrinkles.

'You've guessed it. I'm a doctor's agent. My name is Kruse.'

'And the doctor's name?'

'Also Kruse.'

'The same name?'

'More than that,' Kruse snickered. 'I'm my own agent. Dr Kruse at your service. May I know your name?'

The blind man hesitated, then answered reluctantly:

'Dubel.'

'Delighted to meet you.' Kruse touched the blind man's elbow in a friendly manner. 'I know what you think of me, Mr Dubel. In this city of hucksters and speculators, thousands of doctors fight one another for patients, resorting to the foulest means, to trickery and deceit. But not a single doctor has yet lowered himself so far as to personally make the rounds of other doctors' waiting rooms, slander his competitors, and recruit patients for himself. That's just what you were thinking, isn't it, Mr Dubel?'

'Let's assume I was,' the blind man said drily. 'What then?'

'Then I have the honor to inform you that you are mistaken, Mr Dubel.'

'You'll have a hard time convincing me,' the blind man retorted.

'We'll see!' Kruse exclaimed, and continued in an undertone: 'We'll see. I'll advance an argument for which you'll have no answer. Listen. I'm a unique kind of doctor. I don't take money for treatment. Moreover, I support my patients at my own expense.'

The blind man's eyebrows quivered.

'Charity?' he asked quietly.

'Not quite,' Kruse answered. 'I'll be frank with you, Mr Dubel, hoping that you'll repay me in kind. Your turn is coming up soon— I'll be brief. My parents left me a considerable fortune, and I can permit myself the luxury of carrying out scientific research according to my own taste, in my own home, where I have a small clinic and a well-equipped laboratory. Patients like you interest me.'

'What are you suggesting?' Dubel interrupted impatiently.

'For the moment, nothing,' Kruse smiled wryly. 'My time will come, after Viroval has taken your last cent. But I must know how long that will be. Believe me, I'm not interested in your money.'

Dubel sighed:

'I don't have much. My accident was written up in the newspapers, and became quite well known. The company had to give me a year's salary to kill the publicity. This was a great victory. In these days even healthy workers don't have that much security.'

'How much longer will your money last?'

'About four months.'

'And then?'

Dubel shrugged.

'I'm not in the habit of looking ahead.'

'Yes, yes, you are right. Looking ahead is becoming increasingly difficult, even for those who can see,' Kruse rejoined. 'Four months. Hm. . . . We'll assume that Dr Viroval will shorten that time considerably. And then you not only won't be able to afford treatment, you won't even have enough to live on. Excellent! When that happens, come to see me.'

Dubel didn't have a chance to answer.

'Number 48!' a nurse in a starched white uniform announced.

The blind man rose. The nurse came up to him, took him by the hand, and led him into the office. Kruse began to leaf through the magazines lying on a round varnished table.

A few minutes later Dubel came out of the office happy and excited. Kruse hurried to him.

'Let me drive you home. Well, how did it go? Viroval, of course, promised to restore your sight?'

'Yes,' Dubel answered.

'Naturally. It couldn't be otherwise.' Kruse sniggered. 'He really will restore your sight . . . in one sense. You asked what I can promise you. That will depend on you. I will bend every effort to restoring your sight completely. But first you must do me one service. . . . Oh, don't be afraid. A small scientific experiment which will, in any case, take you out of the gloom of blindness.'

'What does that mean? That I'll be able to distinguish light from darkness? But Viroval promises to restore my vision completely.'

'Well, there you have it! I knew it was too soon to discuss the matter with you. My time has not yet arrived.'

When they reached the house where Dubel lived, Kruse said:

'Now I know where you live. Let me give you my card; it has my address. I hope to see you in about three months.'

'And I hope to see you, to see you with my own eyes, if only to prove to you that Viroval . . .'

'Is not a fraud, but a worker of miracles?' Kruse laughed, and slammed the door of his car. 'We'll see, we'll see!'

Without answering, the blind man crossed the sidewalk confidently and disappeared into the house.

Now Dubel was again sitting in an automobile, this time a taxi. He had just enough money left to pay the driver. The streetcar bells, the noise of the crowd, had faded into the distance. There was a sensation of warmth on his skin, as though the sun's rays were exerting a light pressure. Apparently there were no tall houses that would have provided shade on this quiet street. The odor of young green, of earth and spring. Dubel pictured to himself cottages surrounded by gardens and flower beds. Only the occasional rustle of tires disturbed the quiet. The cars probably belonged to people living there. Kruse must really be a rich man if he lived on such a street.

The taxi stopped.

'We're here?' Dubel asked.

'Yes,' the driver answered. 'I'll take you up to the house.'

The yard smelled of flowers. Sand crunched under one's feet.

'Careful, there's a staircase,' the driver warned.

'Thanks. I can make it now.'

Dubel paid the driver and climbed the staircase. He pushed open a door at the top of the stairs and entered a cool hallway.

'You've come to see Dr Kruse?' a woman's voice asked.

'Yes. Please tell him that Dubel is here. He'll know.'

A small warm hand touched Dubel's.

'I'll take you to the drawing room.'

By the variety of odors and the changes in temperature and in the sounds reflected from the walls, Dubel guessed that his companion was leading him through several rooms, large and small, sunlit and gloomy, furnished and unfurnished. A strange house, and a strange procedure—leading patients through the whole house.

A door creaked, and Kruse's familiar voice called out:

'Whom have we here? Well—Mr Dubel! You may go, Irene.'

Kruse's cold, dry hand replaced the woman's. Taking a few more steps, Dubel detected the strong, mixed odor of medicines and heard the ring of glass, porcelain and steel. Someone was apparently putting away instruments and glassware.

'So you've come, Mr Dubel,' Kruse said cheerfully. 'Sit right here in this armchair. . . . But how long has it been since we saw each other? Two months, if I'm not mistaken. Yes, just two months. My respected colleague, Dr Viroval, cleaned your pockets even sooner than I predicted. I think it's unnecessary to ask whether you can see me?'

Dubel stood with his head bent.

'Well, old fellow, don't be down-hearted,' Kruse gave a crackling laugh. 'You aren't sorry you came?'

'Exactly what do you want from me?' Dubel asked.

'I'll tell you in all frankness,' Kruse answered. 'I've been looking for a person like you. I will treat you free of charge, even support you at my own expense, and will make every effort to restore your vision completely at the expiration of our term of agreement.'

'What kind of agreement?' Dubel asked suspiciously.

'We will, of course, conclude a written agreement,' Kruse sniggered. 'I have to guarantee my own interests. I have an invention which must be tested. There will be an operation which involves some risk for you. If the experiment succeeds then you, even though blind, will see things which no one else in the world has ever seen. Once I have patented my discovery, I promise to do everything in my power to restore your vision.'

'You mean I have only to give my consent?'

'Quite right, Mr Dubel. Your position is hopeless. Where can you go from here? Onto the street to become a beggar?'

'At least explain what will happen to me after the operation!' the blind man exclaimed irritably.

'Oh, if the experiment succeeds, then . . . I think . . . I am sure . . . that after the operation you will be able to see electric currents, magnetic fields, radio waves, in a word, any movement of electrons. Incredible things! How? It's very simple.'

Pacing up and down the room, Kruse continued as if he were delivering a lecture:

'You know that every organ reacts to external stimuli in its own specific way. A light tap on the ear, and you will hear noise. Pressure applied to the eyeball produces a sensation of light. As the saying goes, you will see sparks before your eyes. In other words, the organ of sight reacts with sensations of light not only to light itself, but also to mechanical, thermal, or electrical stimuli.

'I have constructed a small device, an electronoscope, something like an insulated galvanoscope, only of infinitely greater sensitivity. Its conductors—very fine silver wires—are attached to the optic nerve which should then react with a sensation of light to the current in my apparatus. So far, it's all very simple.

'The difficulty lies in connecting the inert mechanism of the electronoscope to a living organ of sight, and in enabling you to perceive three-dimensional light sensations. In all probability your optic nerve has not been completely destroyed. But it won't be easy to find the best point of contact. We will resort to an operation only if it is absolutely necessary. It may not be, since electric currents can also reach the optic nerve through contiguous nerves, muscles, and blood vessels. That's the underlying theory. I'll explain the details if you decide . . .'

'I've already decided,' Dubel answered with a gesture of resignation. 'I have nothing to lose. Experiment as much as you like. You can even chisel through my skull if necessary.'

'Fine! Excellent! Now at least you have an aim in life. To see what no other person in the world has yet seen! Such an opportunity doesn't fall into everyone's lap.'

'And out of all this something may just possibly also drop into your lap,' Dubel said caustically.

'Good publicity, nothing more. Publicity which will help me drive all his patients away from Viroval,' Kruse answered with a smug laugh.

'Darkness. Black as soot, and deep as a chasm. But that's not true: utter darkness has no dimensions. I can't tell whether the darkness stretching before me would be measured in kilometers or centimeters, whether I am surrounded by emptiness or by objects on all sides. They don't exist for me unless I touch them or bump my head. . . .'

Dubel fell silent.

He lay stretched out on a bed in a large white room. His head and eyes were tightly bandaged. Kruse sat in an armchair near the bed smoking a cigar.

'Tell me, doctor, why are you breathing so heavily?' Dubel asked.

'I don't know. Probably my heart playing tricks. From excitement. . . . Yes, I'm excited, Mr Dubel. I am probably more excited than you. . . . Why haven't you seen anything? You've been lying there for a long time.'

'Wait!' Dubel exclaimed suddenly, and raised himself a little on the bed.

'Lie down! Lie down!' Kruse pushed Dubel's head back on the pillow.

'Wait! It seems to me . . . I see . . .'

'Finally!' Kruse spoke in a sharp whisper. 'What do you see?'

'I see,' Dubel answered excitedly, '. . . it seems to me . . . if it's not just an optical illusion. Do blind people have optical illusions?'

'Yes. Well? Well? What do you see?' Kruse exclaimed, fidgeting in his chair.

But Dubel didn't answer. His face was pale and strained, as if he were listening to something. Stepping carefully, Kruse went to the door and pressed the electric bell. When the nurse appeared, he gave orders quietly, as if he were afraid of disturbing Dubel's reverie.

'Quick . . . nitroglycerine . . . I'm having an attack.'

'Doctor! Dr Kruse! Yes, yes, I see . . . the darkness has come alive!' Dubel spoke as if in a delirium. 'Clouds of light are passing through. . . .'

'What color?' Kruse croaked, breathing hoarsely.

'White . . . although at the edge of the darkness it seems to be a very pale blue. The light comes and goes rhythmically, like waves.'

'Waves!' Kruse wheezed. 'Damn! All I would need would be to die at this moment. . . . Give it to me! Give it to me at once!' he ordered as the nurse came in. He drained the medicine in one quick gulp, closed his eyes, and leaned back in the chair. The croaking noises became less frequent and not so loud.

'The light comes in short bursts, then in long ones,' Dubel described the visions.

'That could be the telegraph,' Kruse guessed. 'Well, I feel better now, much better. I'm listening!'

'It's amazing. I see more light . . . spots, points, arcs, rings, waves, narrow vibrating rays that intersect one another, fuse, separate. . . .A honeycomb of light. Patterns. . . . It's impossible to distinguish them all.'

'Remarkable! Incredible!' Kruse was overjoyed by the success-ful results of his experiment. 'You can't distinguish them because you aren't used to the apparatus yet, and you can't separate currents of different strengths. No wonder you feel as though you were engulfed in a chaos of light. But you'll soon get used to it, and you'll be able to separate currents of any intensity. Well, don't stop now, my friend! What else do you see?'

'The darkness is gone completely,' Dubel went on. 'Everything is full of light. Light of varying strength and of different colors— light blue, red, green, violet, dark blue. A spot of light the size of an apple just flared up here on the left. Bluish rays are emanating from it like a tiny sun.'

'What can it be?' Kruse exclaimed, leaping from his chair. 'You see that? Impossible! That's a sunbeam which lit up the polished door knob. But you couldn't possibly see that!'

'I don't see a knob. I see only a little ball of light with bluish rays coming from it.'

'But how? Why? What rays?'

'I think I know the answer, Dr Kruse. The energy in the sunbeam has begun to pull electrons away from the metallic surface of the knob.'

'Yes. Yes! Yes! You're right, absolutely right. Why didn't I think of that at once? Well, let's experiment. You cannot, of course, see the wires of the electric lamp? No. Now I'll turn on the light. The current is moving, and . . .'

'And I can see the electric wire. A shining line passes along the ceiling,' Dubel· pointed, and Kruse nodded his head affirmatively, 'along the wall. . . .There's a current leak in the corner; you'll have to call a repairman. . . .Then the wire passes through a series of rooms, down to the first floor, and out into the street. I can also see the burning light bulb. Right there. Only I don't see the bulb itself, but streams of electrons from an incandescent filament.'

'Thermal emission—the Edison effect,' Kruse nodded.

'And you know what, Dr Kruse?' Dubel added gaily. 'I see something even more interesting than the Edison effect. I can see it even without turning my head. Please come up to the bed. That's it. Your head is right here, And your heart is here?'

'Quite right. My word! Can you really . . . can you really see the electric currents radiating from my brain and heart? But, after all, what's so surprising about that? Every cell in our bodies carries out complicated chemical reactions which are accompanied by electrical phenomena. But the heart, and especially the brain, are veritable generators.'

'There's a soft purple light coming from your brain. It gets brighter when you're thinking intensely. And when you get excited, your heart bursts into flame,' Dubel said.

'You're a treasure, Dubel! Pure gold! A priceless gift to science. A galvanometer can't describe what it sees. I'm proud of myself . . . and of you, Dubel. Tonight we'll drive around the city, and you'll tell me everything you see.'

A new world opened before Dubel. The evening when Kruse drove him around the city was etched forever in Dubel's memory. That first evening was sheer magic.

Dubel saw light wherever there was electric current. And where is electricity not present in a large city? Dubel saw the high tension flashes given off by automobile generators. Streetcar motors rolled along the streets like wheels of Chinese fireworks, throwing out showers of sparks—electrons. The streetcar cables hung along the streets like incandescent ropes, surrounded by such powerful magnetic fields that the whole street was bathed in light. Dubel saw, or rather guessed, that the current from the overhead cable ran under the roof of the car to the regulator on the front platform, then under the floor .into the iron frame of the car, into the axle, the wheels, the rails, the underground cable. A multitude of cables shone brightly underground. Here and there they were broken, and Dubel saw distinctly how the bluish, forked streaks leaked out into the ground. Behind him, on the outskirts of the city, he saw whole cascades of fire. One of the city's many electric plants was located there. Its powerful generators were spewing out these fiery cascades.

It was fascinating to watch the tall buildings. Dubel didn't see the walls. He saw only the brightly shining, complex network of the electric light conductors, and the weaker glow of telephone wires, the gleaming skeleton of the skyscrapers. Dubel could identify several buildings by these skeletons. Here and there shaggy clusters of light from motors were visible.

The whole atmosphere was filled with scattered light from radio waves. Torrents, rivers of light poured from the city right up to the stars, connecting heaven and earth. This was the action of cosmic rays breaking loose electrons from the entrails of the sun, and magnetic currents from the earth itself.

'Many a scientist would let his eyes be plucked out for the privilege of seeing all this!' Kruse exclaimed exultantly, listening to Dubel's description. 'By the way, be prepared, Dubel. Tomorrow reporters from the big newspapers are going to interview you, and day after tomorrow I will show you off at a scientific conference.'

Kruse's invention created a sensation. For several days running all the newspapers tried to outdo one another in reporting it, and Kruse bathed in a glow of fame. They interviewed Dubel constantly and took many pictures. After that he began to receive business offers.

The War Department suggested using Dubel to intercept enemy radiograms in time of war. Dubel saw radio waves as a series of light flashes of varying duration. He was superior to a radio receiving station because he did not have to be adjusted to the length of the wave. He saw them all, long and short.

One leading electrical firm offered him a job controlling current leakages in underground cables and detecting the so-called migratory currents which damage underground cables and various metal structures. The firm estimated that a living apparatus—Dubel—would cost much less than repairmen and technicians equipped with conventional devices for locating current leaks.

Finally, the Universal Electric Company made him an offer. They wanted him to serve as a live apparatus for experimental work in the company's scientific laboratory. They were investigating various systems of cathode tubes and lamps, oscillographs, and instruments radiating ultraviolet, roentgen, and gamma rays. Here they studied the whole gamut of electromagnetic oscillations, and carried out experiments on the bombardment of atomic nuclei and on the properties of cosmic rays. A living apparatus like Dubel could, of course, be very useful in experiments on invisible rays.

Kruse permitted Dubel to accept the offer of the Universal Electric Company.

'But you will live with me as before,' Kruse said. 'It will be more convenient for me. Our agreement is, of course, still in effect. I haven't yet completed all my experiments on you.'

Dubel was a wage-earner once more.

At 8:00 in the morning he was already sitting in a laboratory which smelled of ozone, rubber, and certain acids. Whether the experiments were conducted in the daytime or at night, by lamplight or in total darkness, Dubel was always surrounded by his iridescent world of balls, rings, clouds, streaks, and stars. Machines droned, hummed, and crackled, and Dubel saw streams of electrons being torn away and bent or broken in their flight under the influence of ingenious barriers, meshes, and traps. Dubel described and described, described everything he saw. Two stenographers took down his words.

Completely unexpected findings were recorded; Dubel saw light phenomena which no scientist could have predicted. When a gigantic electromagnetic installation, bigger and heavier than a locomotive, was set in action, Dubel reported:

'Phew! It's enough to blind a person! The magnetic field is filling one whole section of the city with bright light; its extreme limits go far beyond the outskirts of the city. Why, I can see clean through the whole city. I see the city's electrical skeleton on all sides at the same time. I can even see you, gentlemen. Electrons surround me like a shining swarm of bees. Mr Lardner has sparks pouring from his nose; Mr Lamott's head reminds me of the head of Medusa the Gorgon, in flames. I can see all the metallic objects clearly; they are burning as if they were incandescent, and they're all interconnected by shining threads.'

With Dubel's help, several scientific problems were solved which otherwise would have remained a mystery. The company appreciated him and paid him well.

'I can consider myself extremely fortunate for a blind man, but nonetheless people who can see are far happier than I,' he told Kruse. The doctor listened to reports of his work every day, and based his attempts to perfect his own apparatus on them.

Then the day came when Kruse said:

'Mr Dubel, today the term of our agreement expires. I must keep my part of the bargain—to restore your normal vision. But then you will lose your ability to see the movement of electrons. This gave you a tremendous advantage in life.'

'Nothing doing! The advantage of being a living machine! I'm not interested. I've had enough. I want to see, I want to be a normal person, not a walking, talking galvanoscope.'

'It's entirely up to you,' Kruse sneered. 'If that's your decision, let's begin the course of treatment.'

28

The happiest day in Dubel's life finally arrived. He saw Kruse's yellow, wrinkled face and the young but spiteful face of the nurse who assisted him. He saw raindrops on the window panes, the gray clouds of autumn, yellow leaves. Nature had not bothered to greet the return of Dubel's sight with gayer colors. But this was a small matter. When there are eyes, they will find gay colors.

Kruse and Dubel looked at each other silently for a while. Then Dubel shook Kruse's hand warmly.

'I don't know how to thank you. . . .'

'There's no reason to thank me. My reward is in the success of my work. So I am not a charlatan, not a Viroval. By restoring your sight I have proved this to everyone. I hope his reception room will soon be empty. . . . But enough about me. Now you are a seeing, normal person, Dubel. I envy you your health, your physical strength, and . . . what do you intend to do now?'

'I can take a hint. I'm not your patient any more, and should therefore not burden you with my presence. Today I'll move to a hotel; then I'll find myself an apartment and a job.'

'Well, I wish you luck, Dubel.'

A month passed.

One day Kruse was called downstairs to the entrance hall. There stood Dubel, in an overcoat with the collar turned up, hat in hand. Streams of rain flowed onto the parquet floor from the brim of his hat. Dubel looked thin and exhausted.

'Dr Kruse,' Dubel said, 'I came to thank you again. You restored my sight. I have begun to see clearly . . .'

'Perhaps you'd better tell me whether you've succeeded in finding work?'

'Work?' Dubel laughed sardonically. 'I have begun to see clearly, Dr Kruse. I see twice as well as I did before. And I'm asking you . . . to blind me. Make me blind forever. I want to see nothing but the movement of electrons.'

'Voluntarily subject yourself to blindness? But that's monstrous!' Kruse exclaimed.

'I have no alternative. I don't want to starve.'

'No, I won't do it; I most emphatically refuse!' Kruse answered angrily. 'What do you think I am? Anyway, you're too late. Yes. I introduced certain changes in the construction of the electronoscope, patented it, and sold the patent to the Universal Electric Company. Now anyone can see electric currents. The company has no further need of such clear-sighted blind men as you were, Dubel.'

Dubel put on his damp hat in silence and stared at his strong young hands.

'All right,' he said, looking straight at Kruse. 'At least these are

good enough to smash this hellish way of life! Goodbye, Dr Kruse!'
He left, slamming the door behind him.

The rain passed, and the sun shone brightly in the blue autumn
sky.

The Magic Shoes

BY VICTOR SAPARIN

IT all begin over nothing. When Petya was putting on his shoe, his mother noticed his sock peeping out from a round hole as big as a penny. There was another 'penny,' somewhat larger, on the sole of his other shoe. This was no surprise to Petya; he had known for a long time that right shoes wear out faster than left shoes.

But the discovery astounded his mother.

'Just think, Ivan Ivanovich,' she addressed a visitor from another city who happened to be in the kitchen. 'Shoes simply burn up on this boy's feet. I bought these a month ago. Did you ever see the like of him?'

Ivan Ivanovich put the tea kettle on the kitchen table and inspected Petya carefully.

'He's an ordinary boy,' he said calmly. 'No different from other little boys.'

'No different!' Petya's mother threw up her hands. 'Where have you ever seen such a boy? He'll be the death of me! He wears shoes out faster than I can buy them.'

'I was just like that.' Ivan Ivanovich tried to reassure Petya's mother. He lifted the tea kettle to the faucet. 'And it worked out all right. I even managed to become a professor. It's just that he's very active.'

'But shoes are made for normal children,' Petya's mother retorted. 'There's no special footwear for fidgets.'

'That, incidentally, is a shame,' Ivan Ivanovich became serious. 'It's too bad they don't make such footwear. They make special sports shoes—football shoes, for example—and no one blames football players for running a lot. It's just as natural for boys to run, and they ought to provide them with special footwear too.'

'I would like to see the shoes,' the mother shook her head incredulously, 'that he wouldn't wear out in a month. It would be a miracle.'

Petya snorted, deeply hurt. After all, was it his fault he was so active? What was he supposed to do, sit with his feet tied? Instead

31

of analyzing the situation scientifically, as the professor had done, his mother just scolded Petya for every hole. As if he wore them out on purpose.

Ivan Ivanovich set the kettle on the stove and was already heading towards the door. He stopped on the threshold and looked back at Petya again, as if he were calculating something.

'I'll send you some magic shoes,' he said simply. 'The boy seems to be cut out for them, if everything you say about him is true. There's just one condition: let him do anything he wants to do in them. Most important, let him wear them every day. Don't worry, Antonina Ignatievna, he'll never wear out my shoes.'

Petya's mother, overcoming her irritation, began to laugh. Ivan Ivanovich was so amusing!

'If they really are magic . . .'

Petya was sure that Ivan Ivanovich had said this just to calm his mother. And he certainly didn't look like a magician, if it came to that. He didn't wear a turban, as the circus magicians did, and he had neither a special piercing stare nor highly significant hand movements. An ordinary person in a gray jacket, wearing glasses and a grizzly, wedge-shaped goatee. No different from Uncle Seryozha, the shoemaker on the second floor. You couldn't even tell that he had been an active little boy.

About two weeks after Ivan Ivanovich left for his faraway city, a package arrived from him.

Petya expected to see some kind of superboots with very thick soles, metal spikes, and horseshoes on the heels, like the mountain-climbing boots he had been admiring in a store window. But the package contained very ordinary brown shoes of very simple cut.

Petya tried them on; they fitted perfectly.

'That's just like him,' mother said. 'Ivan Ivanovich is a very intelligent man, but he doesn't know that you have to allow a margin for growth in children's shoes. And he thought they'd last a long time! All right, wear them. You'll have to take care of them, but you'll outgrow them just the same. And I promised . . .'

From the very first time that Petya put on the shoes, strange things began to happen. Strangest of all was the fact that, contrary to all the laws of nature, nothing happened to them.

At first Petya walked very carefully, as if they really were magic shoes that might play mean tricks on him. But he gradually got used to the new shoes and stopped thinking about them. He ran around the yard as before, and played soccer just as recklessly.

One evening, when Petya got into bed, his mother picked up the shoes and began to inspect them.

'Surely they must be worn out by now,' she muttered, raising the shoes to the light. 'No, they're not. Imagine! The soles are like new. That means you can take care of them if you want to.'

That evening she kissed Petya good-night with special tenderness. But the little boy had a vague feeling that he hadn't exactly deserved such praise.

'Of course,' he reassured himself, falling asleep, 'a lot depends on the kind of shoes you have. Marya Petrovna keeps complaining that her slippers always wear out on one side. It wouldn't be fair to blame it all on me.'

Marya Petrovna lived in an apartment across the hall. She was well known for her skeptical attitude toward everything in the world except herself. As for little boys, she had long ago and for all time classified them, active or inactive, as fundamentally loathsome creatures.

So when Antonina Ignatievna praised Petya for wearing his shoes carefully, she dashed his mother's hopes at once.

'You'll see, Marya Petrovna! They really are magic,' Petya's mother said. 'Or else this isn't the Petya I know. He's been wearing them every day for almost six months, and there isn't a worn spot on them anywhere.'

'I don't see anything special about that,' Marya Petrovna declared, looking at the soles. 'They're crepe rubbers. See, it's rough and blistered. There's no wear and tear. But it's not healthy; rubber can give you rheumatism.'

'But crepe soles let air through,' Petya's mother objected.

'However you look at it, it's still rubber,' Marya Petrovna cut her off.

'They can't be rubber,' Antonina Ignatievna contradicted. 'They're too light. Try them!'

Marya Petrovna reluctantly held the shoes for a while.

'They weigh almost nothing.' She spoke as if this were a serious deficiency. 'If you ask me, it's a fraud.'

'Why a fraud?'

'Very simple. Don't you know how crepe rubber is made? They blow bubbles in the rubber. Well, they just let more bubbles into these; that's why they're so light.'

She set the shoes on the floor and wiped her fingers.

Petya's mother knew that crepe rubber wasn't made that way at all, but Marya Petrovna had the last word, as always.

Month after month went by. The shoes held up as if they really were magic. Antonina Ignatievna was already beginning to regard them with some misgivings. She knew, of course, that the professor was no Mephistopheles, just an ordinary person. But there was something supernatural about his gift. It wasn't merely a question of the unbelievable durability of the shoes. Other peculiarities came to light.

Once she noticed a scratch on the toe of the left shoe. Obviously Petya had knocked against something when the children were playing in the yard. But the scratch disappeared; not a trace of it remained.

And how was she to explain the fact that the shoes always looked brand-new, even though Petya never cleaned them?

Finally, although the shoes had been a perfect fit months ago, they hadn't become the least bit tight. True, leather shoes do stretch. But the fact remained that the shoes looked as if they had just come from the store.

Marya Petrovna, who loved to instruct everyone, read Petya's mother this lecture:

'You're really spoiling that boy! Holidays, workdays, every day in new shoes! You could have spent the money for something else. You'll be sorry enough later on!'

'For heaven's sake!' Antonina Ignatievna objected at last (only to regret it later). 'He's been wearing the same pair for a whole year!'

'What? Do you take me for a fool?' Marya Petrovna was offended. 'You don't want to admit it? Oh, these doting mothers! They go crazy over their children. I don't know what they wouldn't do for them. It just spoils them.'

After this, Marya Petrovna began to call Antonina Ignatievna a desperate liar, and to say that first of all she was completely unfit to bring up her son; that, secondly, she was without question insane; and that, thirdly, she bought 'her Petenka' new shoes every month while she herself wore old ones for a whole year.

Poor Antonina Ignatievna tried to explain things to Marya Petrovna, but, after all, what could she say?

These shoes complicated Antonina Ignatievna's life unbelievably. If she told people the truth, no one would believe her. To 'admit' that she bought Petya new shoes every month would be awkward.

When two more months had passed and nothing changed, Antonina Ignatievna became really alarmed.

'I'll tell you what,' she said to Petya one fine day. 'Let's put these shoes away—let them rest for a while. Put on your old ones.'

She gave Petya his old shoes, the same ones that had started all the trouble in the first place. Uncle Seryozha resoled them.

'It's a good thing we bought them a size large,' she said. 'You'll have to wear them even if they pinch a little. I'll put these in the cupboard.'

Was she trying to convince herself that Petya had learned to take care of his shoes? Or had the indestructible shoes simply begun to frighten her? It would be difficult to say what she had in mind. But she sighed with relief when Petya put on his ordinary, non-magical shoes.

They felt heavy to Petya; in the past year he had gotten used to shoes so light that he could hardly feel them on his feet.

He soon wore through the soles, and Antonina Ignatievna had to take them to the shoemaker again. So the active little boy was just as active as before. Their durability had nothing to do with Petya. But Antonina Ignatievna stubbornly sent the old shoes to be repaired again and again, until finally Uncle Seryozha said:

'Now they're not good for anything. Buy the little fellow a new pair.'

Buy a new pair? When there was a practically new pair in the cupboard?

Reluctantly, Antonina Ignatievna opened the drawer where she had put the shoes. She hadn't even looked at them for several months.

'Clean them,' she sighed as she gave the shoes to Petya. 'Try them on. Have you outgrown them?'

Petya took the shoes: they shone, as before, with refreshing brightness, and they fitted his feet perfectly, just as they had when Petya put them on for the first time.

This didn't disturb Antonina Ignatievna at all. She had already become accustomed to surprises of this kind. Something else troubled her. She remembered very well that the soles had been slightly scratched when she put the shoes away. At the time this had made her very happy; the scratches and abrasions attested to the ordinariness of the shoes, and showed that they, too, were subject to natural forces. Strange! She was overjoyed by the very thing that had once upset her so. The trouble had started in the first place because of worn-out soles!

But now, turning the soles of the shoes to the light, she saw an unmarred crepe surface.

A still stranger discovery, the strangest of all, was made when she looked at the soles from the side.

The poor woman put on her glasses, took them off, put them on again. But no, it wasn't her imagination. The soles really were thicker than before. She had always wondered why Petya didn't wear out such thin soles!

Antonina Ignatievna was afraid even to consider the only explanation which occurred to her. Could there really be such a thing in the world as shoes that grow?

She didn't want to give Petya these growing shoes, and at the same time she didn't know what else to do with them. Maybe she should simply throw them away.

The problem solved itself. Petya had no need of shoes at that time; he got sick. Fortunately, it was only a mild case of grippe, but he had to stay in bed for nearly a week. However, the remarkable shoes were not idle during that time. Word about the magic shoes spread throughout the neighbourhood and Petya's friends, who also got scolded by their mothers for wearing out their shoes, asked to borrow them to play soccer. They were little bothered by the fact that their durability didn't have a scientific explanation. On the contrary, their imaginations ran all the wilder. They advanced the most improbable theories, firmly believing in the unlimited possibilities of technological development. Some of them, the smallest, who had not yet outgrown fairy tales, were convinced that the 'professor's shoes' really were magic.

The young soccer players took turns wearing Petya's shoes. In the heat of the game knees and elbows were sometimes bruised, but the shoes were undamaged; they withstood even this test. It seemed that no power on earth could conquer them.

With this Antonina Ignatievna could stand it no longer. She got Ivan Ivanovich's address from her neighbor and wrote him a letter.

She received the following answer:

. . . Yes, they grow! And this is no miracle, dear Antonina Ignatievna. I can understand your surprise, and I'll try to explain everything.

Why do they grow? There are certain plants, called epiphytes, which live in air instead of in the soil. They don't have roots: they can live on fences without touching the ground, or even on a telegraph wire. What do they live on? Not on telegrams, if you'll pardon the witticism. They take everything they need for growth from the air. Air, of course, always contains moisture and mineral dust. These plants are well adapted to such 'airy' food.

After several years of research, we have succeeded in making these tiny vegetable organisms grow in large colonies, like coral. They form a solid mass, durable, light and flexible, like rubber except that they are porous. Their leaves are in every way as good as leather, and they have one property which no leather possesses —they grow. Remember how the leather shrank in Balzac's story? Our 'leather,' on the contrary, is constantly getting larger, because it is alive. The plant organisms multiply quickly, and take their food from the air. We have prepared a leather for the soles which grows especially fast, since this part of the shoe wears out much faster than the uppers. Besides, the sole is better fed than other parts of the shoe. It comes in contact with the ground, where there are more minerals and more moisture. This contributes to the more rapid restoration of the leather of the soles. The naked eye can't perceive this growth. If you hadn't put the boots in a cupboard for four months, you would probably never have learned that they are growing along with Petya.

Of course, growing shoes have their own disadvantages. They can't be stored very long; their size would change. If an adult bought shoes to fit, he would soon discover that they had grown to be too large for him. Therefore, for adults' footwear the leather can be used only in the soles. But this isn't bad: the postmen, policemen, and other people of 'walking professions' who are testing our shoes are very grateful.

Children's shoes are another matter; they can be made entirely of growing leather. We think that we have completely solved the problem of making shoes which can be worn continuously for several years. Under laboratory conditions we have already subjected many pairs to artificial wear and tear equivalent to five years of normal wear. But it is one thing to test shoes in a laboratory and quite another to put them into actual use. For this reason I will be very interested to know how Petya's shoes are holding up. If it isn't too much trouble, please write me at least twice a year. We have many schoolboys testing our shoes. But Petya's are from the very first lot, and information about them will be especially helpful. I wrote you two letters, but must have gotten the address wrong.

For these experiments we select boys who are especially lively. But this doesn't mean that our shoes can be treated any way you like. On the contrary, they require good care.

In testing bicycles, we force them to perform under the most severe conditions. But during normal use one has to observe all the rules of maintenance. Our shoes are designed for adults who walk a lot or for children who run a lot, but not for the careless. Make this clear to Petya. Taking proper care of a thing will double its life span. If Petya wants to become a champion shoe-wearer—not in the sense that he wears out footwear faster than anyone else, but a real champion, setting a record for long wear—he must observe the simple rules which I have enclosed in this letter. I will be very anxious to know how long our shoes will hold up under normal wear. Please write.

P.S. A few days ago our first experimental factory went into operation. Now 'magic' shoes are already being produced on the assembly line.

A week later Petya went to the movies and saw in a newsreel 'self-restoring soles,' as the narrator called them, being produced in an experimental factory.

'There are self-sharpening knives,' the narrator said, 'and self-winding watches—watches for absent-minded people. And now we have soles which don't wear out. You will see them grow right before your eyes.'

The audience saw large shallow vats, where very tiny plant organisms which looked under the microscope like little yellow stars were being grown in a nutrient medium.

The audience could see them growing together to form a fine film that floated freely. The film gradually became thicker.

'The material becomes thicker and thicker,' the narrator said, 'as the micro-organisms continue to grow. Now the "leather" is ready to be cut.'

In the cutting section automatic machine tools stamped out thousands of soles of various sizes from the artificial 'hides.'

'But the sole will continue to grow,' the narrator explained.

And everyone saw an enormous sole, filling the whole screen. Photographed by the time-lapse technique, the sole increased in thickness right before the eyes.

'Actually this took two months,' the voice continued. 'The sole increased by an amount equal to the loss during constant walking. Most important, it will never stop growing, like the mushrooms which some of you probably raise. You can wear out the uppers, but the soles—never.'

'Well,' Antonina Ignatievna sighed with relief when they returned home. 'Now everything is clear.'

She met Marya Petrovna fearlessly.

'Go see the movie,' she advised her neighbor. 'It shows how Petya's shoes are made. Then you will finally believe that I don't buy him new ones every month.'

'Well, you know,' Marya Petrovna objected, 'they have all kinds of tricks in the movies. I have a nephew studying in the institute of cinematography. There they give a special lecture called "Optical Illusions." '

'But these shoes are real,' Petya's mother retorted, and moved her son closer to Marya Petrovna. 'And so is Petya. He's not an optical Illusions".'

'Nevertheless,' Marya Petrovna flung out without looking at Petya, 'little boys are all cheats. And your boy is no exception. I can't understand why you make such a fuss over him! So they made him some kind of special shoes. He could have worn ordinary ones.'

Only then did Antonina Ignatievna understand that she would never prove anything to Marya Petrovna, and that she had worried in vain about her opinion.

And the shoes? Petya is wearing them to this day.

A Dangerous Invention

BY E. ZELIKOVICH

MY cousin, Peter Mikhailovich Goryunov, is famous in our city. We schoolboys love him very much—he has an inexhaustible supply of remarkable stories. They are always stories about ordinary, everyday things, and he can tell one on any subject you choose. His stories always have some kind of trick: he may surprise you, or confuse you, or recount thrilling adventures.

One day during our last school holiday my friends and I were rather bored. We took down a stack of old magazines and were just getting ready to dust them off when Peter came in.

We assaulted him at once, demanding a story.

'A story? About what?' he asked.

'About dust,' one of my friends blurted out suddenly.

'Yes, yes! About dust, Peter Mikhailovich,' everyone chimed in.

'Well then, let it be about dust,' he agreed. 'What kind of a story shall it be?'

Each boy had his own suggestion, and each one tried to drown out his companions. The upshot of it all was that we wanted a story about dust that would be adventuresome, scientific, amusing and serious, fantastic and true to life.

'That's quite a tall order,' Peter complained. 'For such a story you'll have to wait a few days.'

True to his word, Peter returned in a week and read us this story.

I. KOLYAA'S NEW APARTMENT

Not long ago, Kolya Rheostatov graduated from an electromechanics institute. He dreamed of further study, of inventions, of working like a fiend, when suddenly—tuberculosis. Now he sits in the doctor's office, pale, thin, and coughing hoarsely.

'You can't imagine,' the doctor told him, 'what a terrible menace dust is. Construction dust, road dust, soot from factories. All this pollutes our lungs and causes respiratory diseases. Civilized man must fight a continuing war against dust.'

'What will happen to me?' Kolya asked timidly. 'Will I really die from it?'

'Oh, well,' the doctor smiled. 'Your case isn't quite that serious. Take care of yourself; go live in the country. It's springtime. Rent a room in the village of Spotless. I've already sent scores of patients there; it's a fine place. Just keep away from dusty roads. Good luck!'

On his next free day Kolya set out for Spotless. He wandered through the village looking for a room, but everything was already taken. Suddenly a strange-looking cottage at the edge of the village attracted his attention. Rather, it wasn't the cottage itself, but the roof, that was strange—there was a large gray fir tree growing on it. High-tension wires led up to the cottage.

'What could that be?' Kolya wondered. 'I'll go have a look.'

A stout woman answered the door.

'Do you have a room for rent?'

'Sh . . . ,' the woman hissed. 'Not so loud—the professor's home. I'll rent you a room, but the professor mustn't find out.'

Kolya looked at the room and came to a whispered agreement with the landlady. On the way out they passed a closed door bearing a small sign : 'Do not enter, and do not knock.'

So he had found a room. Kolya was delighted. Forgetting the housekeeper's warning, he asked in a loud voice :

'Do you have much dust here? The doctor ordered me . . .'

Kolya never finished the sentence. The door with the stern inscription crashed open, and a small frail old man with an enormous shock of gray hair darted headlong out of the mysterious room.

'The devil take you all,' he shouted, enunciating each word clearly, 'and your conversations about dust!'

'Professor Snorkle!' the landlady broke in reproachfully.

But the old man was beside himself, and went on shouting :

'For three weeks I've been struggling to determine the coefficient of adhesiveness of the troposphere, and this ceaseless, idiotic chatter about dust . . .'

'Professor Snorkle!' the landlady repeated emphatically.

The old man became even more furious. His little black eyes blinked and darted restlessly under the thick gray brows.

'This is unbearable! This is the fifth idiot who's been here today with his nonsense about dust! Get out!' he screamed, and stepped forward threateningly.

Without thinking, Kolya seized the old man and flung him backwards. Then he dashed outside and set out running, coughing as he went. Repugnance boiled inside him.

'Young man! Young man! Wait!' the landlady shouted, running after him.

Kolya stopped. Breathing heavily, the stout woman ran up to him and began to speak disconnectedly:

'Young man! Don't be angry. He's not always like that, but he's been terribly nervous lately. He works day and night, looking for some kind of 'ficient. He's gone out of his mind . . .'

Kolya listened without saying anything.

'Today he's driven five people away. You've rented the room, so go ahead and move in. You won't find another one anywhere. I don't need the money—he pays well—but it's frightening to be alone with him in the house. He keeps talking to himself. "I'll find the 'ficient," he says, "and I'll make all mankind happy." '

'Marya Ivanovna!' a shout was heard, and a shock of gray hair appeared in the window. 'Marya Ivanovna! Come here and bring that young man with you.'

'Let's go,' Marya Ivanovna whispered, seizing Kolya's hand.

Kolya went back to the house.

'Please come into the laboratory,' the old man addressed Kolya without looking at him.

Kolya entered the mysterious room with the inscription: 'Do not enter and do not knock.'

'Sit down.' The old man spoke without raising his head.

Kolya sat down and looked around. Utter chaos reigned in the laboratory: furniture out of place; a bookcase overturned; pieces of wood, sawdust, scraps of tin and wire littered the floor; the chairs were heaped up with bottles, scattered instruments, rags, beakers, retorts, boxes; a row of shelves contained a large number of test tubes and vials filled with dust-colored powder.

The dark beamed ceiling was almost hidden by a maze of wires; near one wall there was a marble slab with switches and electrical equipment. In one corner stood an enormous installation resembling a radio station. A tall column leading from it disappeared through an opening in the ceiling.

The old man sat down too, leaning against the back of the chair. He fixed a sharp, searching gaze on Kolya. Kolya was upset. He was preparing his defense, when the old man burst out laughing suddenly.

'Ha, ha, ha! How adroitly . . . ho, ho, ho . . . you grabbed me! Ha, ha, ha!'

He laughed loud and long, his head shaking, his whole body quivering. Kolya got alarmed: this was a madman!

Suddenly the old man became serious.

'Here's the thing, young man,' he said sternly, getting up. 'I decided to let you stay because otherwise I would never be rid of these summer tramps and their conversations about dust. I have studied it for thirty years, and it bores me. So this constant chatter about dust irritates me. Anyway, I need an electromechanic.'

'How did you know?' Kolya was surprised.

'It's written on your face. Well, well, don't be frightened, I'm joking. I heard you talking to the landlady. I like you: an energetic young man who doesn't hesitate to assault a great inventor, professor at three universities and an active member of eleven scientific societies. That's no mean accomplishment! Let's be friends!' The old man stretched out his hand to Kolya.

Kolya got up in embarrassment, stretched out his hand, and said hoarsely:

'Kolya Rheostatov.'

'Snorkle,' the old man introduced himself. 'Doctor of philosophy, of medical and mathematical sciences, the world's greatest expert on dust. Now look at this.'

The professor seized Kolya's hand and dragged him to the shelves filled with test tubes.

'I have here quite a few samples of the earth's dust. This one,' he pointed to a yellowish powder, 'is from the Chinese province of Honan; this one is from French Morocco; this one from Calcutta. These are samples of the best types of Australian dust.'

Kolya didn't know what to make of it all. But the mad old man continued to display his strange treasures. Before Kolya's eyes flashed vials of dust from Kamchatka, Mexico, Sweden, Canada, Ireland, the Azores, Abyssinia, from meteorites, cosmic dust.

'I will destroy all this dust!' the professor announced in a tone which brooked no contradiction. 'I will heap benefits on mankind. They will raise a monument to me. I will cure you of tuberculosis.'

'How did you know?'

'It's written on your face. But,' the professor added gloomily, 'first I must determine the coefficient of adhesiveness of the air. I must know what wave length the oscillator should be tuned to. Otherwise there would be a disaster. Here it is—the result of my life's work!'

Kolya turned toward the enormous installation in the corner.

'One turn of the switch,' the old man went on, 'and Professor Snorkle's powerful waves will pierce the earth's atmosphere and produce a miracle.'

Kolya's head spun from everything he had seen and heard. 'A madman,' he thought. 'But perhaps not—who knows?' His stomach was growling; he was ravenously hungry. Suddenly it seemed to Kolya that this nonsense was only a dream. He pinched himself.

'Oh, it's real!' the professor exclaimed, as if he had understood the gesture. 'You see before you the greatest invention of our time! . . . But you're probably starved . . .'

'He's a mind reader!' Kolya decided.

The professor clapped his hands: 'Marya Ivanovna!'

The door opened slightly and the landlady's head appeared. An expression of fear was frozen on her face.

'Lunch for two!'

II. THE REVOLT OF THE SUMMER RESIDENTS

Kolya moved into the cottage. He learned that the fir tree on the roof was really a very delicate electrical system, and that Professor Snorkle was the finest of men.

Many vacationers lived in Spotless. Most of them had tuberculosis and had settled there on the advice of the same doctor. Professor Snorkle's short temper was well known to all of them. Some had learned of it through personal experience. They hated the old man, and called him 'Rusty Vacuum Cleaner'.

The summer residents usually gathered on the croquet field after supper. When Kolya first came there, they surrounded him on all sides and bombarded him with questions and with various expressions of sympathy. They were quite eloquent in their denunciation of the old professor.

'How did you manage to get a room there?' the locksmith Screwchev marvelled.

'It must be hard to live with such a barbarian,' the electrical engineer Switchkin sympathized.

'He's completely insane!' exclaimed the telegraphist Ampersky.

'A beast,' the electrician Resistov growled.

Kolya felt it was his duty to defend the old man.

'You're wrong, my friends,' he said. 'Professor Snorkle is not at all like that. I thought so myself at first. But he's not insane, just odd. He's very brilliant. He's constructed a machine to annihilate dust. I saw it myself.'

'Then why doesn't he put it to use?' one of the group asked.

'Because he must first determine the coefficient of adhesiveness of air,' Kolya answered. 'Otherwise, he says, there will be a disaster.'

Laughter broke out on all sides.

'My friends,' Screwchev said sharply, 'this is all nonsense. If such a machine exists, it should be put to use right away. Why should we die from dust while he's looking for his coefficient? Suppose he doesn't find it for another ten years?'

'That's right! Absolutely right!' the others agreed.

'In my opinion,' Screwchev continued, 'we should use force if necessary to start the machine. Are you with me?'

'Yes! Yes!' voices resounded on all sides.

'And Rheostatov will have to help us. After all, he has tuberculosis too,' Screwchev continued.

Kolya had no answer to this. The vacationers' unexpected attack
put him at a complete loss. He went home in dismay, but decided to
say nothing to the professor for the time being.

Several days later, the professor told Kolya:

'Tomorrow morning I'm leaving for a week in the Caucasus. I
have to collect a few samples of dust from the Middle Ages, to
study changes in sedimentation over the centuries. I leave the
laboratory in your hands. The summer residents are plotting something, so keep your eyes open.'

'Should I tell him?' the thought flashed into Kolya's mind. 'No,
nonsense. It's not important. He'll either laugh at me or get upset.
He won't leave, and will kick up a row in the whole village.'

The professor couldn't have left at a more inopportune time.
Kolya was uneasy. That night he had trouble sleeping, and developed
a slight fever.

'You've grown thin overnight,' the professor said next morning
at breakfast. 'There's something on your mind. Of course your
personal affairs are no concern of mine. But I'm afraid,' he added
meaningfully, 'that they may not be personal . . .'

Kolya coughed into his fist and answered firmly:

'They're personal, Professor Snorkle. It will pass. Don't worry;
I'll take good care of the laboratory.'

The professor pressed Kolya's hand and got into the car. It
quickly picked up speed and disappeared into the thick forest.

Screwchev stood by the garden hedge watching the professor leave.
Kolya pretended not to notice him and went into the house. He
didn't go to the croquet field that day. He should have.

'Friends!' Screwchev addressed the vacationers. 'Rusty Vacuum
Cleaner has gone. It's time to act. But I don't trust Rheostatov. We'll
have to trick him and the landlady out of the house. Then we'll
start the machine. It should go off all right. Let's try. It can't do any
harm. What do we have to lose? Nothing! If it doesn't work, we'll
just switch off the current and that will be the end of it.'

Just then everyone turned toward the road. Dr Leucocytov was
approaching, that same doctor who had treated Kolya and the
other summer residents.

'How did you get here, doctor? What brings you?' Questions
came from all sides. 'You're just in time!'

'Didn't you know that I own a cottage here?' the doctor replied.
'I spend one or two months in Spotless every year. I'm a tubercular
myself.'

They immediately told the doctor all about their project.

44

'You underestimate Professor Snorkle,' he said. 'I know him : he's a first-rate scientist and without doubt an inventor of genius.'

Ashamed, the vacationers fell silent.

'And I know his machine,' the doctor continued. 'It has been ready for a long time. You wonder why he hasn't put it to use? Unfortunately, he is not only a medical man and a physicist, but also a philosopher. He doesn't think the dust should be completely removed from the atmosphere; he is afraid something might happen. I don't agree with him. I am interested only in the medical aspects, and I think the dust should be removed completely.'

The patients agreed noisily.

'I met him at the station today and expressed my view quite frankly. I asked him : "How would you react if I switched on the oscillator while you're gone, Professor Snorkle?" He answered with a very amiable smile : "You will be responsible for all the consequences." So I have decided to take this responsibility upon myself.'

The doctor's last words were greeted with a wild burst of applause.

'It's true,' the doctor said, 'that breaking into a person's house is a criminal action. But Snorkle will forgive us this small liberty. It's nothing more than a joke, an experiment. Well, let's prepare a little "anti-dust surprise" for him. Are you with me?'

The doctor's suggestion was accepted enthusiastically, unanimously, and without debate. The conspirators decided that the doctor would lure Kolya and Marya Ivanovna out of the house on some pretext. In their absence Switchkin and three others would turn on the fabulous invention of Professor Snorkle.

III. THE MACHINE IS STARTED

'We are doing wrong,' Screwchev said, removing the hinges of the lock, 'I know that. But a great invention belongs to society, and is not the private possession of a headstrong inventor.'

'Especially,' Resistov interjected, 'since a scientist, Dr Leucocytov, completely approves our decision.'

'The main thing,' Ampersky added, 'is that we are not acting from personal, mercenary aims, but for the good of society.'

'Cut the philosophy,' Switchkin broke in curtly. 'It's too late for moralizing. Let's get it over with. We might be seen.'

A minute later the four plotters were facing the mysterious machine. They quickly inspected it and got acquainted with the electrical system. There was some specialized equipment that they couldn't understand, but everything seemed to be in good working condition. In the center of the control panel there was a scale graduated from 0 to 100 per cent.

'Let's be cautious,' Switchkin said. 'We'll set the needle on zero before we switch on the current. Then we can bring it to 100% gradually.'

They set the needle on zero. When it came to turning the switch, they all looked at one another; no one wanted to do it. Switchkin suggested drawing lots. The job fell to Resistov.

'He's an electrician,' Screwchev said. 'It's right up his alley.'

Resistov approached the control panel and quickly threw the switch.

Kolya and Marya Ivanovna were visiting the doctor, and sat peacefully drinking tea.

'But I don't agree with him,' the doctor was saying. 'It's clear to me that his arguments are not valid. So we decided to arrange a little experiment in your absence . . .'

The doctor looked at his watch.

Kolya was stunned. He understood at once, and leaped from his chair. Colliding with people and furniture, he set off running.

Confusion reigned in the sitting room.

'What's the matter with him? What happened? Stop! Wait! Kolya!' they shouted after him.

They chased him, accompanied by several barking dogs.

Kolya ran without looking back. His heart was pounding furiously; he got a stitch in his side. He stopped from time to time to cough, then immediately ran on.

It was getting dark. The horizon was covered with a dense shroud of leaden clouds.

'The Lord only knows what they may be doing!' Kolya thought with horror.

He had reached the end of the village. A plot of grass came into view and, at the edge of the forest, the familiar little house with the slender fir tree on its roof. Everything seemed to be in order.

His pursuers began to overtake Kolya. One of the dogs seized him by the trousers.

Just then the fir tree on the roof flared up, lighting the whole area with a violet light. A milky blue radiance hung in the air. Suddenly there was a deafening explosion. The earth trembled.

Kolya fell. It seemed to him that heaven and earth had come together.

The lights went out in Professor Snorkle's laboratory. The oscillator hummed so loudly it was painful to hear it. The apparatus, the floor, the walls, the ceiling—everything—shook. Test tubes and vials fell from the shelves. The whole house seemed to be whirling into space, ready to fall apart any minute under the impact.

Switchkin was the first to come to his senses.

'Turn off the switch!' he shouted wildly.

Blinded by the unexpected onslaught of darkness and by the violet light in the windows, Resistov couldn't find the switch handle. He was afraid to grope for it, lest he be struck by the current.

The unbearable noise continued. The ringing and clanging, the crackling and whining of the oscillator, and the terrifying violet radiance outside were horrifying.

'Matches! Matches! Who has matches?' Switchkin howled at the top of his lungs.

Ampersky and Screwchev pulled out matches and tried to light them. They struck one after another with frantic motions, but the sulfur flared up and died immediately.

'Stop!' Switchkin commanded hoarsely. 'Get closer to the panel!' Pushing Resistov aside, he rushed up to do it himself.

'Light several matches at once!'

On the second flash Switchkin saw the switch, seized it and pulled with all his might.

The noise stopped immediately. The lights came on; the violet radiance dimmed.

No one said a word. They couldn't look at each other. Finally, squinting from the light, they looked up. Switchkin was still clutching the switch handle; Ampersky and Screwchev were holding matches ready to strike; Resistov's lower jaw hung down.

'Now we've done it,' Switchkin said gloomily. 'We won't get away with this!'

The dogs abandoned Kolya and rushed off howling. People stood motionless until the fir tree stopped blazing, the violet radiance grew dim, and the rumbling and roaring ceased. Then they ran to Kolya. Blood was streaming from his throat. They lifted him up carefully and carried him home.

After a moment the doctor and the other conspirators entered Marya Ivanovna's house. They were covered with dirt from head to toe. Dirt flowed from their faces, hands and clothing. But they were so upset they didn't even notice.

Kolya came to in his own room. He leaped from the bed and staggered to the laboratory. Caught red-handed at the scene of the crime, the 'experimenters' stood pale and dishevelled, their faces downcast.

'Who gave you the right to break in here?' Kolya demanded.

'We were acting for the good of . . . ,' Ampersky whimpered. 'We didn't think . . .'

'You didn't think?' Kolya echoed. 'Just what did you think? That you understand the professor's inventions better than he does? That he's a fool, and you are smart? You especially should be ashamed,

Switchkin. You're an engineer; you should have understood . . .'

'I did understand,' Switchkin answered dully, 'but, unfortunately, too late.'

The four hapless benefactors of humanity left the laboratory like whipped dogs. But Dr Leucocytov stayed by Kolya's bed all night, careful not to say a word which would remind the patient of what had happened.

Dawn was breaking. The young geologist Diabasov woke up trembling from the cold and piercing dampness.

'Why is it so cold, Professor Snorkle?'

'I can't understand it,' the professor answered, shivering under a thin blanket.

Sunlight began to appear on the walls. Diabasov went out on the balcony.

'Professor Snorkle!' he exclaimed. 'What an odd color in the east!'

It was a pale violet dawn.

'And look at the sky,' the professor said.

The sky did look peculiar; it was the same dark blue color everywhere.

The sun wasn't red, as it usually is at dawn, but bright gold. It was sharply outlined in the blue dawn; its rays did not spread out into the sky.

The professor threw an overcoat over his pajamas and went out to join Diabasov.

'Did you notice that?' he asked, pointing into space.

The balcony, neighboring houses, trees and streets were covered with a thick layer of some moist, dirty substance.

About an hour passed. It quickly got warm, then hot, then scorching.

Flinging knapsacks over their shoulders, the professor and Diabasov set out on an expedition. Outside the city limits a car passed them. Diabasov jumped aside and automatically covered his eyes to protect them from the whirlwind of dust. But surprisingly enough, the car didn't raise any dust, although there was a thick layer of it on the road. The car seemed to be moving through a puddle, splashing fine drops of water which immediately settled heavily. Not a trace of dust was visible above the road; the air remained crystal clear.

Diabasov looked at the departing automobile in amazement.

'What does this mean? What do you . . . ? but what's the matter, Professor Snorkle?'

The professor stood without taking his eyes from the road, pale and blinking nervously. Suddenly he started running headlong back to the city. Diabasov took off after him.

'Professor Snorkle! Where are you going?'

That morning the inhabitants of the little provincial city witnessed an unusual spectacle: a little old man rushed along the street at top speed, flinging piles of dust about. He had lost his hat, and his thick shock of gray hair flew in the wind. A young man rushed after him. A crowd of small boys followed them both, whistling and shouting.

'Terrible. . . . Those idiots set it on zero. . . . I thought he was joking. . . ' the professor mumbled incoherently.

'I d-don't understand a th-thing!'

'You don't have to. . . . The adhesiveness is completely destroyed. . . . A chain reaction. . . . No power on earth can stop it now.'

The professor paid no attention to the little boys and the startled inhabitants staring after him with open mouths. He ran past the hotel and finally reached the railroad station.

There was a long line standing by the ticket counter.

'A ticket north!' the professor shouted from the threshold.

But as it turned out there wasn't an express train until evening. The professor dropped onto a bench completely exhausted.

IV. THE PROFESSOR RETURNS

In the village of Spotless they talked of nothing all day except the events of the preceding evening. People wandered about the village in groups and went from house to house telling one another the most improbable fables.

And, indeed, something evil was taking place in nature. Her green disappeared; the trees and grass were covered with a thick layer of dirt. Gray scum lay on the ponds. But the air was transparent as crystal.

The professor arrived in Spotless two days later. Jumping out of the car, he ran immediately to the laboratory.

'Just as I thought!' He was in despair. 'The indicator is on zero. What shall we do now?'

He listened to Kolya's report and ordered him to summon everyone who had taken part. Half an hour later a column of summer residents filed into Marya Ivanovna's garden, led by Kolya and the doctor.

'You can't imagine,' the professor addressed them, 'what you have done. If the whole earth were covered with gun-powder, and you had set a match to it, the disaster would not have been as great as the one you have precipitated by turning that switch.'

The professor paused, then went on :

'Our monstrous guilt before humanity depresses me infinitely. The tragedy arises because it is not in my power to restore the atmosphere to its normal condition. But in the last analysis, the guilt is all mine. I should not have locked myself inside the laboratory. I ought to have acquainted society with my work, and forewarned of the dangers inherent in this seemingly harmless experiment on the removal of dust. I did not, and now we see the result.'

Everyone was shaken by the professor's words, and by his unexpected magnanimity. The doctor and Switchkin wanted to drop through the earth.

'Now a terrible ordeal awaits all of us,' the professor continued. 'Now I will do what I should have done long ago; I will explain to you my work on the elimination of dust.

'I have given thirty years of my life to the struggle against dust. Why? You will be surprised to learn that a cubic centimeter of air in a large city contains millions of dust particles. Or, rather, it did until yesterday. Usually these myriads of insignificant particles are invisible. But if you remember watching slanting sun beams, you will know that I'm not exaggerating. With each intake of breath we draw about five hundred cubic centimeters of air into our lungs, containing hundreds of millions of dust particles.

'Atmospheric dust is made up of very fine particles of stone, clay, soot, and microbes. Microbes of tuberculosis, tetanus, malignant anthrax, and typhoid fever can be carried in the air for a long time and can infect people and animals with terrible diseases.

'Cities have many good methods for fighting dust : street-washing, paving, green plants, smoke filters. These methods are being applied on a larger and larger scale, and the air of our cities has gradually become cleaner and healthier. But this requires a great and constant effort. So I sought a way of destroying dust with practically no expenditure of labor, rapidly and simultaneously throughout the globe. I found the way and you, unfortunately, put it into practice. Unfortunately because dust also has an enormous positive significance in the life of nature. You will soon learn about this from your own bitter experience.

'To destroy dust in the literal sense of the word is, of course, impossible. I therefore took a different approach. I decided to decrease the adhesiveness of air. What is adhesiveness? You know that your foot gets stuck in mud; your hand in dough. But for tiny dust particles even air is adhesive enough : it resists their movement and keeps them suspended just as wet clay holds back a man's foot.

'So I reached the conclusion that it was necessary to decrease the adhesiveness of air, so that the heaviest and most harmful dust particles would precipitate.

'But the whole question lay in the extent to which the adhesiveness of air should be decreased. This had to be calculated with exceptional accuracy. I worked on it for two whole years. But you switched on the oscillator without waiting for the results of my work. As if that weren't enough, you set the indicator on zero, completely destroying the air's adhesiveness. Now every bit of dust has settled on the ground, like iron filings. From now on not a single speck of dust can float in the atmosphere.

'The worst feature of this is the chain reaction. This has an analogy with fire. One spark is enough to burn down a whole village; the flame will spread by itself. It's the same here. The reaction started by my apparatus is just such a chain reaction. In a few seconds it embraced the whole earth's atmosphere.

'You can see for yourselves what has happened. The air has lost its milkiness because there is no more dust to disperse the sun's rays. Now the sky above us will be forever dark blue. The play of colors at dawn and at sunset has disappeared. I'll tell you why. When the sun is on the horizon, its light rays must pass through a much thicker layer of air than at noon, and the dust contained in the air holds back part of the blue and violet rays and lets through the orange and red. This explains the magnificent colors at sunrise and sunset, especially in the city's smoky, dusty atmosphere. Now that is gone forever.

'But this is nothing compared with what lies ahead.'

'What are we going to do now?' Screwchev spoke almost in a whisper.

'We must find a way to restore the adhesiveness of air. I will work like a fiend. You can probably help too.'

Everyone, greatly alarmed, surrounded the professor and began telling him what they could do.

V. THE GREAT DISASTER

The worldwide disaster predicted by the professor crept in imperceptibly, insidious as a slow-acting poison. Despite the crystal clearness of the air, it became more stifling with each day. The dark blue cloudless sky with the unchanging bright sun very soon began to bore the inhabitants of Spotless.

Gentle rains disappeared completely from the world. They were replaced by less frequent, raging torrents pouring down in bright sunlight. In some areas they occurred fairly often, but were completely absent in Spotless and many other places. Each downpour caused terrible destruction and ended in a flood. Despite this, many rivers in the plains began to dry up.

The scorching heat was unbearable. The increasing humidity turned the world into an enormous steam bath. When people moved, they were quickly drenched with perspiration which brought no relief. Even the wind did not help: the sweat only came faster.

Stifling hot days alternated with cold nights. The unbelievable stuffiness was replaced by a no less unpleasant dampness that pierced to the bone and made everyone seek refuge indoors. During the night the ground and everything on it was drenched with moisture, as after a hard rain. When daylight came, this moisture quickly dried up, and the unbearably oppressive heat again held sway.

The plants reacted strangely. They seemed to have fallen into a stupor: their growth stopped completely. The least hardy grew sickly and died from unknown causes. Nothing helped; neither watering, nor transplanting, nor fertilizer. The agronomists coined a new term for this phenomenon: 'Wet drought.' An unparalleled crop failure threatened the world.

Following these dreadful phenomena, the old professor muttered bitterly:

'Yes, yes, I expected this. . . .It had to happen. Nature is obeying her laws to the letter.'

That year not a single tree bore fruit, not a single bush gave berries, not one plant bore seeds. Cereal grains formed no ears, cones didn't grow on the pines and firs, there were no potatoes.

Things became worse every day. It was getting more and more difficult to live, to work, even to breathe. Toward the end of the summer the air became so humid that people looked as though they had just been dragged from a pond. In the shade water flowed from them continually. Clothing was soaked with it, and stuck to the body. There were no dry objects in the shade; everything was wet and loathsome.

People began to hate the burning sun moving in the dark blue cloudless sky. Despite the heat and humidity, they had to stay inside with the windows closed. They kept stoves and kerosine lamps burning. This was the only way to keep the air relatively dry.

The professor was tremendously depressed. One thought obsessed him: 'What if we aren't able to restore the adhesiveness? What if it is impossible?'

In Marya Ivanovna's house work proceeded feverishly day and night. Experiment followed experiment. The doctor, Switchkin, and the other culprits worked in a frenzy, trying to expiate their guilt.

The changes occurring throughout the world inspired horror. And it was all so unexpected, incomprehensible.

'Professor Snorkle,' the doctor once said quietly. 'We are amazed at the tragic accuracy with which life supports your predictions. Our crime is great; we are stunned by the unexpected consequences of our action. But to be honest, there is much that we don't understand. The heat, the stuffiness, the humidity, the destruction of plants. Is this really all because of . . . dust?'

'Yes,' the professor answered hoarsely. 'All this is due to the absence of dust. If you doubt it, let me remind you of a principle from physics.'

The participants in the fateful experiment prepared to listen.

'You see the problem?' the professor said. 'As you probably know, there is always water vapor in the air. The higher the temperature of the air, the more vapor it can hold. At plus 20 degrees, one cubic meter of air can hold a maximum of 17.12 grams of water vapor. The air is then saturated to the limit. If it becomes supersaturated, condensation takes place. But vapor has to condense on something, on some object in contact with the air.

'Water evaporated from the ground, rivers and oceans used to rise to the colder layers of the atmosphere and condense on dust particles. Each speck of dust was coated with a very fine droplet of water, invisible to the naked eye. These drops formed clouds and mist. In clouds the droplets merged into bigger and bigger drops and fell as rain.

'Now there are no longer any dust particles in the atmosphere on which water vapor could condense. Therefore there are no more clouds or rain. The air now is heavily supersaturated with water vapor. The air can now hold four times as much vapor as before. When anything comes in contact with this supersaturated air, the water vapor condenses on it greedily. That's why we are always wet. We not only perspire, we are constantly condensing atmospheric moisture on our bodies. The wind doesn't increase the evaporation of moisture from the body, thereby cooling us, as it did before. Just the reverse; it merely brings us new masses of supersaturated air.

'When the amount of water vapor in the air exceeds certain limits, the vapor immediately condenses, like an explosion. So we have catastrophic downpours in some areas. They are brought mainly by warm winds from the south. Because there are no such downpours on the plains, their rivers are drying up. But mountain rivers overflow in devastating torrents because the supersaturated air condenses on the mountain surfaces.

'Clouds and dust envelop our planet like a blanket, and the air never gets too hot or too cold. Now the air is crystal clear. So in the daytime we have scorching heat, and at night it is cold, because of increased heat loss from the ground.

'All this is oppressive, unbearable. But one could still become adjusted to it if it were necessary. The destruction of vegetation is much worse.

'You think this is because of the lack of rainfall? Not at all. The question is more complicated. Formerly the surfaces of the leaves continually gave off moisture, and fresh moisture entered the plants from the soil, together with the nutritive salts dissolved in it. But now the evaporation of moisture from plants has stopped; the air is already supersaturated. Plants therefore cannot draw more moisture from the soil, and consequently do not receive the indispensable minerals. Finally, since the air is supersaturated with vapor, it holds back that part of the sun's rays which help plants metabolize carbon dioxide and build starch.

'Summer is drawing to a close, and if we are not able to restore the adhesiveness of air by the end of September, all vegetation will inevitably perish, and with it the animals and all of us,' the professor concluded stiffly.

His every word affected his audience like the blow of a hammer.

VI. PROFESSOR SNORKLE'S LAST INVENTION

It was the morning of September 29.

In the laboratory preparations for the next experiment had been completed.

'Close the windows tight!' the professor ordered. 'Now let's have the current.'

He approached one of the meters and slowly began to advance the needle along the scale to the right. A hum was heard; the miniature fir tree standing on the table began to emit a blue light.

The professor continued to advance the needle. The hum increased, the blue light dimmed and soon went out altogether. The air in the room had somehow changed. The professor sniffed experimentally and quickly advanced the needle to zero. Then he looked around and smiled for the first time that summer.

'Get everyone in here,' he said. 'And bring pans of dust. It would be best to heat it, and seal it hermetically.'

Everyone gathered in the laboratory.

'Put out the lamps and open the windows wide,' the professor ordered.

Three people rushed to comply. As soon as the windows were opened the laboratory was filled with moist stuffy air and everyone was soon soaked to the skin.

Kolya and Screwchev brought a pan of dust.

'Turn on the light!' the professor shouted. 'Close the doors and windows tight again.'

When this was done he took a handful of dust and threw it up in the air. It all fell to the floor immediately.

'The switch!'

Kolya turned the handle. The professor advanced the needle along the scale until the flashing of the fir tree dimmed. The air changed again. Everyone stood motionless. The professor perched on the table and began throwing dust in small handfuls as high as he could. Most of it began to settle slowly, but some of it hung in the air, forming a little cloud. The room filled with mist. There was a soft freshness in the air. It became easier to breathe. The professor threw a few more handfuls of dust and everyone's clothing began to dry out. Then he leaped from the table with shining eyes and asked everyone:

'Do you understand?'

Loud applause answered him.

'Today the world will be saved,' the professor said. 'The waves of "VV-147" are at work.'

It took about an hour to hook up the apparatus "VV-147" to the large oscillator. Kolya, Screwchev, Resistov and Ampersky worked like fiends. Switchkin checked each connection with infinite, finicking care.

'Look outside,' the professor said when everything was ready.

Everyone rushed to the windows. The pitiless sun shone in the dark blue cloudless sky.

A hum was heard. It increased gradually, changing to a booming roar. The wind raised dust from the earth. A light mist appeared in the atmosphere. The sun began to grow dimmer. It became cloudy for the first time that summer.

The old professor advanced the needle along the scale by scarcely perceptible degrees. Nature obediently followed his directions.

The roar grew louder and the wind grew stronger, raising whole clouds of dust into space. The sky was covered with a solid dark gray shroud and the sun disappeared.

The needle crept further and further to the right. Then the professor stopped it and went to the window.

The wind had turned into a hurricane. Dust impregnated the atmosphere; the sky took on a leaden color. Soon they had to turn on the electric lights. Dull claps of thunder mingled with the powerful hum of the oscillator. The first large rain drops hammered on the roof. To people exhausted by suffering, they sounded like a symphony.

Impenetrable darkness advanced upon the windows, and the thunderstorm burst—the hardest thunderstorm in the history of

Spotless. Water spilled from the sky in solid sheets; blinding lightning tore the sky asunder; the cottage shook from ceaseless crashes of thunder and from raging water.

'Get away from the windows, my friends,' the professor said in a loud voice. 'I would like to say a few words.'

Everyone sat down. The professor had to shout to make himself heard.

'Friends,' he began, 'the task has been accomplished, although it has cost us all a great deal. Now we can remove dust from the earth's atmosphere at any time and to any extent. We will be able to clean the air periodically of harmful dust.'

Taking the switch handle, the professor continued:

'By one turn of this hand—'

The sentence was cut short. There was a terrible flash in the room and a simultaneous sharp clap of thunder. The lights dimmed for a moment. The professor was frozen into immobility, leaning against his offspring—the huge oscillator. Blinded by the flash, no one noticed right away that his clothing and the shock of gray hair were on fire.

'He's been struck!' Kolya screamed, turning pale. He rushed up to the burning professor.

But he had barely touched him when the body of Professor Snorkle crumbled into ashes.

The Fiction Machines

BY VADIM OKHOTNIKOV

I'VE had an itch to become a writer for as long as I can remember.

My literary friends were rather skeptical: 'You think it's easy? Go ahead and try. It's not like inventing a machine, where you can figure everything out mathematically, and see right away what has to be done. In literary work there are too many imponderables.'

'Figure this one out,' a famous writer told me. 'I rewrite my material twenty-five times! Do you understand—twenty-five times!'

'Nonsense!' I replied haughtily. 'For example, my memoirs would make fascinating reading. It's just a matter of sitting down and writing.'

The moment I faced a sheet of blank paper I began to change my mind.

'Actually, it's not so easy,' I thought. 'How should I start?'

For some reason, mathematical formulae kept appearing on the paper. Or, failing that, abstracts of my latest research, entitled: 'On the Problem of Pseudo-parametric Resonance in Four-terminal Networks in Circuits Under Transient Conditions.'

Somewhere in the depths of my consciousness the obscure word 'plot' kept cropping up.

'What should I write about?' I asked myself. 'They say there's such a thing in literature as artistic form. What does that mean? You just have to begin somewhere; there's nothing to it. Let me think: form!'

Finally I decided to start writing.

'My reminiscences, dear friends, concerning . . .'

That's as far as I got. A drop of ink trickled off my helpless pen, forming a good-sized blotch on the manuscript.

'Confound it!' I exclaimed. 'No one could write with such an abominable pen! Creativity demands a maximum of comfort. For example, why should I have to keep dipping the pen in an inkwell? This distracts me from the creative process. And then this blotch . . . What I need is an automatic pen—a very modern, special fountain pen. Strange I didn't think of it sooner.'

I spent several days constructing a highly perfected fountain pen. The product of my efforts held enough ink to write *War and Peace*. Well satisfied, I again sat down at the desk :
'My reminiscences, dear friends, concerning . . .' I rattled off.
I got no further this time, either. When I first picked up the pen I was sure the words would flow smoothly and freely. But while I was writing this little phrase, my thoughts overtook the pen, got entangled somehow, and came out as an incredible mishmash.
'My mind is faster than my hand. I haven't had enough practice,' I decided. 'It's all right for these professionals. All they do is write.'
Suddenly a brilliant idea popped into my head. I was delighted. Of course! How simple! Other writers would burst with envy. I'll build a special machine!
I pictured the machine in my mind vividly. A highly perfected sound-recording apparatus. I would walk around the room and expound my reminiscences aloud. A sensitive microphone would pick up my uninhibited speech; the apparatus would record it. The room would be quiet; nothing would distract my attention. A typist or stenographer couldn't begin to compare with it. The machine wouldn't make mistakes or interrupt with questions. After all, an outsider would impede the free flight of my thoughts.

Nearly a month went by while I was designing and constructing this highly perfected dictograph. True, it turned out to be rather cumbersome—took up the whole desk—but it was extraordinarily convenient.
The sound is recorded on magnetic tape. The mere flick of a switch reverses the instrument, and the words I have just spoken resound from a loudspeaker. If I don't like a particular turn of speech, or if a thought is somewhat muddled, I just press another switch and the awkward phrases are erased. Then I repeat the sentence in an improved version.
I should also mention that, whenever I want it, light, inspiring music from another loudspeaker creates an appropriate creative mood.
The stenographer types the recorded speech in my absence, and hands me the finished manuscript.
The first practical application of my new device was very successful. I had spoken, as it seemed to me, with exceptional eloquence. Pacing around the room, I beat myself on the chest, and even shed a few tears when I had finished. I was sure I had created a work of genius beyond expectations.

Imagine my disappointment when I saw the typed copy of my dictation! I was appalled.

'You haven't typed it correctly!' I complained to the typist. 'First of all, the punctuation marks aren't in the right place. Look at this: "My reminiscences dear. Comrades concerning . . ." It's absurd.'

The typist left, upset and very offended. I was in a horrible mood for the rest of the day. I had to correct the mistakes with an ordinary pen. But the proud inventor's spirit is not so easily vanquished. My imagination was already at work on another, still more perfect machine. Unquestionably, any such limitation as a touchy and capricious typist could have no part in it.

That evening the author S. visited me. He is well-known for his heated participation in any debate on the question of writing techniques, despite the fact that he himself has written almost nothing.

'Well, how's it going? Are you writing?' he asked sternly.

'Certainly!' I answered unconcernedly. 'I'm doing quite well, thank you.'

S. spent the whole evening discussing a new theory of prose and lambasting a new approach to plot development cooked up by the writer Sh. For my part, I proved that contemporary men of letters do not have a proper scientific approach to the physical techniques of the writing process. Neither of us understood a thing the other was saying, but we were both well satisfied with ourselves.

'I would like to give you this recording machine,' I offered as he was leaving. 'It will be a great help to you.'

The writer looked dubiously at the complicated device, but accepted it.

'Good. Thank you. I'll try to make use of it,' he said uncertainly.

The new device took three months to build. Strictly speaking, you couldn't call it a device. It was a complicated installation that occupied half the room.

Huge metal cupboards housed the cumbersome sound analyzers. Each letter had its corresponding sound filter. You just had to pronounce each letter in front of a microphone; the apparatus immediately set the corresponding key of the typewriter in action. You could speak at any speed and watch the printed text creeping out of the machine before your very eyes.

From the scientific and technological point of view this was a revolutionary device. But—again a 'but' appeared.

I remember with what enthusiasm I set about dictating, spurred on by the cheerful clatter of the automatic key-board. Everything went beautifully, right up to the moment when I read the first printed sheet.

This is what I saw:

'My remunisenses deer frends consurnen . . .'

At first I was paralyzed with exasperation. My machine couldn't spell! How could this be? Only then did it dawn on me that the fault lay not with the machine, but with human beings, who spell words quite differently from the way they pronounce them. For example, we often do pronounce the letter 'c' as an 's.' The machine didn't bother with such trifles. It printed everything honestly, just as it heard it, and made no corrections.

It took two more months to perfect the machine. True, it now occupied practically the whole room, but as compensation it printed everything correctly.

I won't go into the details of my disenchantment with this machine. The opus which it helped to create seemed to me extremely muddled and completely lacking in talent.

'Obviously I can't express my ideas clearly and graphically in words. I don't have the gift.' I was forced to this discomforting conclusion.

I had no doubt at all about the ideas themselves. They were nothing short of brilliance. I could feel them boiling in my head, bursting out of me—and becoming pale and lifeless when twisted around my unwieldy and uncooperative tongue.

The decision to build still another, superperfected device came to me just as the writer G. dropped in for a visit. G. had written an enormous number of works which for some reason no one wanted to read.

'Well, how's it going? Are you working?' he asked affectionately. 'I hear you've already written a lot.'

'I'm not doing too badly,' I answered gloomily.

'Very interesting,' G. continued. 'Too bad I don't have time; I would have read . . . As a matter of fact, I've come to you on business. You gave S. a dictograph. Just imagine, the publishing houses are swamped with his manuscripts! Can't you help me get hold of such a gadget? Build me one, I beg you!'

Instead of answering, I took him by the arm and led him to the room where my latest model was set up.

'I'll give you one even better than the machine S. has,' I mumbled on the way. 'It prints just from the sound of your voice. Take it; it's in my way.'

At the sight of the monstrous aggregation, G. turned several shades paler.

'But can I set all this up in the shed on my country place?' he asked hesitantly, obviously intimidated by the dimensions of the cupboards.

'You can,' I said decisively. 'I'll even give you a truck to transport it, and send the men to move it. Just take it!'

Six months of feverish work passed. The new machine is finally ready, the most highly perfected writing machine imaginable.

It's a real wonder. It combines the latest achievements of radio-technology, telemechanics, automation, and electrophysiology. Altogether it takes up three rooms.

The author sits in a special, comfortable armchair. It's true he looks a little strange, something like a man condemned to the electric chair. He wears a metallic cap with little curls of wire extending from it. Conducting wires are also attached to his hands and feet.

The principle behind the new machine is extraordinarily simple. It is well known that our organism generates weak electric currents which wander all over the body. The currents from each organ have properties specific to that organ. Medicine has already adapted devices for recording the electric signals generated by the action of the heart. Research on the nervous system based on electrophysiological currents has also been carried on for a long time.

I can claim credit only for the fact that I was able to decode the minute signals generated by our thought processes. It was somewhat difficult to transform them into a system of strong electrical impulses, but that is all in the past. Fourteen cupboards, filled with 125 electronic lamps, solved the problem in splendid fashion. My thoughts were easily transformed into a legible text printed on a typewriter.

For a long time I couldn't bring myself to exploit the possibilities of this unlimited creative power. I waited for inspiration. That moment finally arrived. . . . The metal arm-bands were firmly attached; the electric cap crowned my carefully shaven head. The signals indicated that all eleven laboratory assistants were in their places. I could begin.

I pressed the starting button with a trembling hand. . . .

The text obtained with the thought-printing machine I studied in detail while stretched out on my bed, where I had collapsed from over-exertion and from the effects of the new failure.

Here is the text which danced before my inflamed eyes:

'My reminiscences . . . my reminiscences . . . What if the current goes dead? . . . Actually, what reminiscences am I going to write about? No, I'd better begin this way: "Gazing at the blue Black Sea" . . . That's no good. . . . I wonder why they call it Black. Every time I've seen it, it was blue. . . . Strange. . . . How should I describe it then? . . . "Gazing at the Black Sea, which at that moment was blue . . . and which . . ." This idiotic cap is pinching my head! . . . I'll have to improve on it. . . . So what the deuce am I going to do with this blue Black Sea?'

I gave the thought-printing apparatus to the dramatist N. Lately public opinion had been accusing this author of creative stagnation. He defended himself by saying that he often saw whole plays in his dreams, but could never remember them when he woke up.

My machine helped him considerably.

The doctors diagnosed my case as extreme exhaustion.

'You simply must take a three-month rest in the country,' they told me. 'You have done truly monumental work! An enormous achievement! The entire medical world is astounded. . . . Your device for recording thoughts . . .'

Obviously they didn't understand what was troubling me. It wasn't the two years of uninterrupted work. It was the cruelty of failure that had undermined my health. I wanted to be a writer! Only for this had I built my complicated machines.

All my inventions turned out to be remarkably useful. Other men of letters used the dictographs and printing machines to good advantage. G., the author of innumerable unread books, so increased his output that he began to disgust even himself, and suddenly quit writing. The thought-recording machine found wide application in medicine and in communicating with deaf-mutes. A remarkable drama appeared on the stage, a product of one of the playwright N's dreams.

But I did not become a writer.

'Why?' was the question that tormented me. 'Yes, why, why, why?'

I gave myself up to long and sorrowful reflection. One day, strolling along the shore of a small lake, I saw a beautiful goose-quill lying on the ground.

'Not so very long ago, people wrote with this primitive device,' I thought. 'The level of technology at that time was pathetic. I wonder just how they did it?'

I picked up the quill and set out for the summer-house where I whittled it into the shape of a pen. At my request, paper and ink were brought in.

At first I drew a few misshapen figures; then I tried to write.

'Yes,' I thought, 'it actually does write. After all, it was with just such a pen that Pushkin, Lermontov, Gogol, Shakespeare, and Dante wrote. And it didn't turn out too badly. But something went wrong in my case. And with such perfect facilities! Suppose I tried using this pen?'

I doggedly set about writing and covered page after page. Thus this short narrative was born, written and rewritten thirty-six times during my vacation. Perhaps you think I wrote it with a goosequill pen? No, with an ordinary fountain pen.

Part Two

Shadows of the Past

BY IVAN YEFREMOV

'WELL! You're finally here—late as usual!' the professor exclaimed cheerfully as Sergei Pavlovich Nikitin strode into his office. Nikitin, a paleontologist, was quite young, but his discoveries had already attracted much attention. 'I had visitors today. From the Agricultural Exhibition. Two eminent shepherds from the eastern steppes. They brought a gift, a token of their respect for science. Look, a huge golden musk-melon. . . . Smell it! Let's have a taste of it—to our shepherds' health.'

'Did you call me just for that, Vasily Petrovich?'

'You are very impatient, young man! Over there, on the left . . .'

Nikitin walked quickly to a little table in the corner. Eight smooth, dark-brown fragments of large fossil bones lay systematically arranged on gray cardboard. The paleontologist seized a bone, tapped it with his fingernail, turned it over. He scrutinized in turn each piece of heavy, solid bone, impregnated with silicon and iron.

Long years of experience enabled him at once to supply mentally the missing parts of the bones, and by their characteristic shape to visualize the complete skeleton of the extinct animal.

'Everything is clear, Vasily Petrovich. This dark polished coating on the bones is desert pigment, which means your shepherds found them right on the surface. They're dinosaurs, Vasily Petrovich, and very well preserved! The first such find in the Soviet Union. We should reward the shepherds in some way.'

'You mean a bonus? My dear boy, they're richer than all of us! All they wanted was to know whether they could do anything else for us. No, this is pure interest in science. They're coming again tomorrow, to meet you and bring another gift of some kind. Well, let's cut the melon and talk this thing over.'

Holding a chunk of the fragrant melon, Nikitin stood before a huge map on the office wall. He stooped to examine the lower left-hand corner covered with tiny dots denoting menacing desert sands. The old scientist leaned out of his armchair to follow Nikitin's finger.

'The field of dinosaur bones is roughly here,' Nikitin pointed, 'two

67

hundred miles from the source of the Talda Sai, near the Bissekta wells. We'll have to travel toward the Layila hills and then over rocky desert and some steppe land.'

Blinding sunlight, reflected from white walls, made Nikitin squint with pain as he walked through the spacious yard of the freight station covered with a soft carpet of yellow dust.

The three brand-new trucks were already lined up by the edge of the road, waiting for the director. Their white canvas tops curved upwards; a reddish dust had already powdered the shining gray paint. As if laughing at the heat and dust, clear water gurgled past the large stones of the irrigation ditch at the side of the road, and the running motors of the trucks hummed quietly in tune to it.

Nikitin got into the cabin of the first truck and slammed the door. Dust rose in a slanting golden pillar. The trucks entered a city of white houses and green avenues scattered along the northern slope of the sun-scorched hills.

Returning from a late conference, Nikitin walked slowly along the whispering irrigation ditch. It was quite dark under the thick foliage of the trees.

Directly ahead of him a young girl in a white dress slipped out of the shadows, leaped the ditch and walked down the road. Her bare, sunburned feet almost blended with the soil and because of this she seemed to be floating in the air. Thick black braids, sharply outlined against the white material, lay heavily on her back, their fluffy ends reaching almost to her knees.

Nikitin stopped and, looking at the quickly receding figure, was lost in thought for a moment. Then he strode on more rapidly and soon reached the large wooden gate of the house which sheltered the expedition.

In the big yard illuminated by electricity Nikitin saw the members of his expedition gathered around the trucks. They were all laughing at something; even the grumpy senior driver was grinning good-naturedly.

Marusya, the dark-eyed laboratory assistant who had recently been elected Party organizer, rushed up to Nikitin.

'Where did you disappear to, Sergei Pavlovich? We decided to hold a meeting, and couldn't find you. We waited and waited, and somehow it started all by itself.'

'Quite a lively meeting!' Nikitin smiled.

'It's all because of the trucks' names,' Marusya explained.

'What names?'

'You see, we decided to start a competition among the truck crews. And Martin Martinovich suggested naming each truck, to make things easier.'

'And what are they?'

Martin Martinovich, an elderly Latvian in round glasses, the expedition's specialist in excavations, broke into the conversation:

'We called yours Lightning, and the other two Destroyer and Dinosaur.'

A loud honking resounded in the street and the headlights of a black limousine flashed on and then off again at the gate. Nikitin went to meet the secretary of the Regional Party Committee, whom he had seen before on business concerning the expedition.

The secretary looked around. 'Quite a nice set-up you have here. When do you leave?'

'Day after tomorrow.'

'That's fine, Comrade Nikitin. I have a request. . . .' The secretary paused. 'I've come straight from a conference. It seems there's an asphalt deposit quite close to Bissekta. It must be investigated; my geologists insist. . . . In short, you'll have to take along someone from the Geological Board.'

Nikitin frowned apprehensively. The secretary took him by the arm, and they both walked to the edge of the yard.

'All set?'

'Yes, Sergei Pavlovich. We can start loading.'

'You work with Martin Martinovich. Fuel and instruments go on our Lightning; fuel, lumber and camping equipment on the Dinosaur; water, provisions and rubber on the Destroyer.'

The sultry breath of day burst through the low open door. Nikitin was throwing the papers which littered the table into a briefcase. He was in a hurry to get to the telegraph office.

'May I come in?' a gentle feminine voice called from the yard.

A shapely silhouette appeared in the blinding rectangle of the open door. A blazing halo outlined the white dress. Peering into the half-darkness, the newcomer stooped a little, and Nikitin caught sight of yesterday's black braids.

A vague premonition of happiness made Nikitin's heart beat faster. The visitor was carrying a small suitcase. He rose to meet her, and the introductions were made.

'Miriam . . . What's your last name?' he asked.

'Nurgalieva. But Miriam is enough,' the girl smiled.

'And it doesn't frighten you, Miriam, that this trip will be a long and difficult one?'

Her dark eyes flashed with mischief:

'No, it doesn't frighten me. Your expedition is so well-equipped. Yesterday the dispatcher told me this trip will be a real vacation.'

'Fine.' Nikitin shook her hand. 'Choose whichever truck you like.'

'If it's all right, I'd like to go on the Destroyer with Marusya,' the girl requested.

'You women! Already plotting!' the paleontologist laughed, as he walked out into the yard with Miriam. 'Actually,' he added, 'we've met before. Yesterday evening, on Engels Street.'

He nodded and walked toward the gate. Puzzled, the girl watched him go.

The trucks went swaying and bumping along the roadless gray steppe overgrown with wormwood and scorched by blazing sun. The bleached, cloudless sky, monotonous and uninteresting, seemed to be pressing down on the plain. For four days the motors had been humming smoothly. Despite the slow speed, the white city and the railroad were two hundred and fifty miles behind them—two hundred and fifty miles of tall sand dunes alternating with rocky hills, flat wormwood steppe, and pale yellow salt marshes.

Gears gnashed in protest. Motors droned. Steering wheels slipped in the perspiring, weary hands of the drivers. Exhaust fumes flew into the boundless steppe in a dove-colored haze.

Just once, late in the evening, they saw the friendly glow of lights, from a sulphur factory behind the hills. After that there was nothing except the round felt nomad tents, man's temporary dwelling-place in a region where only the desert is eternal.

Beyond the factory they travelled for long hours without a stop, taking advantage of the bright moon and the last stretch of usable road. The clay steppe, smooth and barren, shone like a myriad of tiny lakes in the moonlight, and the trucks picked up speed on its firm surface. At night the steppe seemed both friendly and mysterious.

Nikitin gave the order to stop for the night only when the trucks again started to pitch and sway, raising thick dust on the uneven surface of powdery clay.

Electric lights wired to the trucks lit the camp brightly. Feet plunged into the dusty soil as into deep snow. In places the brittle stalks of some kind of dried grass protruded.

Ahead, barely visible behind a veil of moonlight, lay the Layila hills—the border of the rocky, waterless desert in which the cemetery of fossil monsters lay hidden.

Behind endless rows of hills bestrewn with gray crushed stone the sense of isolation was especially strong. Lost beyond countless bendings, turnings, ascents and descents, the world seemed to exist no longer. The gray trucks passed the hills and came out on a broad lifeless plain covered by a thin layer of fine sand. The air above the desert trembled in hot shimmering streams which blocked the forbidding landscape from view.

The members of the expedition began to see alluring azure lakes, marvellous forest groves, and snow-capped mountain ridges flashing in the distance. At times, white, foamy sea waves seemed to advance toward the blunt noses of the trucks, only to recede and be replaced by rows of white houses shaded by dense foliage much like the city they had left far to the south, beyond the sands. The trucks themselves lost their severe, distinct outlines, spreading out to improbable lengths or towering in the air like huge elephants.

It was growing dark. The tall blue and green towers of a new phantom castle flashed in the scarlet rays of the setting sun and disappeared for the last time.

Here one could travel even at night. The Lightning, raising pillars of dust, its powerful headlights shining far ahead into the plain, continued to lead the column. The Dinosaur and Destroyer dropped behind so as not to be submerged in its dust.

The monotonous drone of the motor made one sleepy. Nikitin dozed off sitting beside the driver, but was soon awakened by the Dinosaur's strident honking behind them. The Lightning stopped, and the other two trucks drove up slowly.

'What's the matter?' Nikitin asked.

'I just can't drive, chief,' the Dinosaur's driver answered, shamefaced. 'These damned mirages!'

'What are you talking about?'

'It's true, Sergei Pavlovich,' Martin Martinovich confirmed the driver's statement. 'In the daytime the mirages seem far away, but now they're right under our noses. It's unbearable!'

'I'm not having any trouble,' the senior driver put in scornfully.

'You were driving in front, Vladimir,' the other driver replied. 'We have to follow in your dust. The headlights shine on it, and we see all kinds of weird things. We can't go on.'

'Nonsense!' the senior driver answered angrily. 'I know dust can produce mirages, but to say you can't drive because of them—'

'Try it yourself. I'll go first!' The Dinosaur's driver was offended.

'All right, go ahead,' the senior driver agreed sullenly.

They got back into the trucks and started the motors. The Dinosaur, its canvas top swaying, passed the Lightning slowly and, picking up speed, disappeared in a cloud of dust. The Lightning's driver waited until the dust had settled and started out after it.

His curiosity aroused, Nikitin rubbed the windshield and stared out at the road. For a few miles they saw nothing, and the driver began to snort derisively, grumbling to himself. Attention began to relax. Suddenly the driver turned the wheel sharply and the truck veered to one side. An enormous hole, bordered with white tile, yawned right in front of them. Nikitin rubbed his eyes in amazement. In the whirling spots of dust tall houses rose along both sides of the corridor cut through by the headlights. They seemed so real that Nikitin shuddered. The hot-tempered driver began to swear.

The houses disappeared, replaced by a pattern of black and yellow stripes. The road split open, leaving a black cleft. Clenching his teeth, the driver clutched the steering wheel and tried to overcome the optical illusion. A few minutes later an incredibly steep arched bridge loomed into view, so real that Nikitin turned to the driver in alarm. But he had already applied the brakes.

Behind them the Destroyer honked persistently. Stopping the truck, the driver smoked a cigarette, washed his eyes, opened the window, and then drove stubbornly on. New phantoms again rose from the dust, close at hand, real and terrifying. Tension mounted. The Lightning braked and swerved in its attempts to avoid non-existent obstacles. Finally, the driver groaned, spat, stopped the truck, and signalled his defeat to the Dinosaur. When the dust settled, the Destroyer, which had stopped long ago, joined them.

As soon as they pulled up to camp, the mad phantom world disappeared. Night stretched the horizon to a black infinity. Huge stars shone tranquilly, and their familiar, unchanging constellations were a reassuring sight. But during the day, in the roar of the motors and the swaying of the trucks, the flashing fantastic visions multiplied till everything began to seem unreal.

When suddenly the first black contours of the Arkarla hills rose from behind the irridescent border of the latest mirage, Nikitin was overjoyed. For a long time they seemed no taller than the radiator caps, then they began to grow rapidly till they completely covered the north-western horizon. The guide pointed to a mountain scarred by innumerable fissures, its steep front slope trapezoidal in shape. The Lightning made straight for it, traveling at low speed, and the ground again became rough as the billows of stone rose higher and higher.

Finally, lurching wildly, the Lightning rounded a turn with brakes squealing, and the truck slowly descended to the broad plain of an ancient depression between the mountains.

On the western side dark cliffs jutted menacingly; the steep slopes of the eastern hills were bright red sandstone. Two eagles circled slowly high above the plain.

The guide directed the expedition northward along the red cliffs. There, where the dark and the red hills met, they should find the source of the ancient Bissekta wells.

The smooth surface of the plain was in some places furrowed by erosion and abundantly strewn with smooth pebbles covered with desert pigment. The pebbles gave to the soil an unnaturally dark color, forming a background for the crystals of transparent gypsum which sparkled in the sun like myriads of tiny lights.

'Stop!' Nikitin shouted suddenly. He jumped from the truck quickly, his assistants piling out after him. They too had seen the fossils.

On the left two large petrified treetrunks lay at angles to one another. Their coniferous wood and traces of knots stood out clearly in the bright sun. Enormous bones with dark glistening surfaces were scattered all around the trunks.

The excitement of the explorers mounted as they discovered more and more treasures.

Extremely well-preserved bones of gigantic sauria covered most of the plain. The paleontologists rushed off in all directions. Their enthusiasm infected the drivers and the workmen, and they too participated in the search, astonished at the extraordinary spectacle.

Not all the bones lay free on the surface; many were still buried in the dark sandstone. Bones jutted out everywhere in the gullies and towered in large heaps on the hills.

The shepherds had been quite right—they had discovered a graveyard of unheard-of dimensions, containing the remains of thousands of gigantic extinct animals.

This scorching, lifeless plain choked with enormous bones created a strange impression. Ancient legends came to mind—legends about battling giant dragons, about immense graves of monsters, about hordes of mammoths destroyed in floods. The origin of these legends was now obvious; they were undoubtedly based on similar discoveries of mountains of enormous bones.

'You haven't reached it yet?'
'No, Sergei Pavlovich.'
'Then dig deeper.'
'We can't. We've hit rock.'
'Rock!'

Nikitin threw down his notebook, leaped up, and rushed to the spring. When he saw that Martin Martinovich was right, his heart sank. Hiding his anxiety, Nikitin slowly left the camp and went up into the mountains to think the thing through in solitude.

The crushing discovery had come on their second day in the valley: The spring wouldn't yield enough water for the expedition. Perhaps it would have sufficed for two or three nomads and their camels, but not for the men and trucks of a large expedition. The source might have been good a hundred years ago, but it had since dried up, and they had to begin using the emergency supply. But what about water for the return trip? They would have to drop everything and travel 125 miles to the east where there were good wells. But if they did that, there wouldn't be enough fuel for the trip to the home base.

Stunned by this unexpected blow, Nikitin keenly felt his helplessness before unpitying nature. What could he, and all his splendidly equipped expedition, do without water? Where would they get it here in the scorching hills, supplied only by the tiny stream of an ancient well?

Attempts to revive the source led to nothing. Could this unforeseen misfortune really disrupt an expedition so carefully planned, rob it of success, force it to risk human lives?

Engrossed in his discomforting thoughts, Nikitin trudged mechanically on. He was walking along a small gorge cut deep into the saddle-shaped mountain. Stifling heat from the scorched black rocks poured over him. Nikitin stopped and suddenly saw Miriam.

She was sitting cross-legged on a rock, her slender waist bent. There was an open notebook on her knees, and she was so deep in thought that she didn't notice Nikitin. The heavy braids seemed to be weighing down her head, which was turned toward the hazy open spaces. It suddenly struck Nikitin that the girl's pose and her whole being were in curious harmony with the surrounding nature. For the first time he felt that Miriam was a true child of her native land; her deep-rooted strength was hidden under a mask of external calm. Nikitin stood stock-still, not wanting to disturb her.

A country of scorching lifeless expanses where nothing comes easily. Only the stubborn labor of many generations can conquer pitiless nature. Here it was impossible to break through in a gust of passionate energy. One had to move forward slowly, patiently, and steadfastly, always prepared to struggle against new difficulties, suppressing by an act of will the universal hunger for miraculous, sudden happiness.

Sensing Nikitin's presence, the girl turned around, then jumped up and came to meet him, looking searchingly into his eyes.

'What's wrong, Sergei Pavlovich?' She spoke slowly as always. There was a note of genuine concern in her voice.

In an impulse of frankness, he told Miriam about the impending crisis. She said nothing until they had almost reached the camp. Then she spoke, half-embarrassed, and as if she were talking to herself:

'I heard that last year at the Dyurt-Kyr works they increased the water pressure . . .' Miriam paused, '. . . by dynamiting. If we only had . . .'

'We do have it!' Nikitin exclaimed. 'Blow up the outlet of the spring! It doesn't always work, but . . . It completely slipped my mind. We'll try it right away!' He became more cheerful and quickened his steps. 'We'll risk the largest charge.'

A thunderous explosion shook the lifeless mountains. A tall column of dust rose above the well, and a few seconds later there was a terrible roar in the mountains as if an avalanche had broken loose. All the expedition members rushed to the well and silently began to examine the debris and to dig clear the outlet of the spring. The camp became still quieter when Nikitin and Miriam began to measure the water flow. The expedition's chief straightened up suddenly.

'Thanks, Miriam.' He seized the girl's hand and squeezed it firmly.

'Hurrah for Miriam!' everyone shouted.

The girl rushed to find refuge behind the senior driver's back. He, squaring his powerful shoulders, pronounced threateningly:

'Lay off!'

'How's your work on the asphalt going, Miriam?' Nikitin asked with a smile.

'It's a very interesting deposit, Sergei Pavlovich. Only it isn't asphalt, but a special very hard rosin.'

'Show it to me tomorrow. Right now why don't you come and see what we've accomplished?'

Little mounds of dug-up earth covered the plain. Joiner's glue bubbled over the campfire. Martin Martinovich, stripped to the waist and black from the sun, was diligently immersing brittle bones in the glue. Several people were working near the middle of the plain on a large rectangular area with deep ditches dug all around it. Its surface layer had already been removed. Two workers picked gingerly at the crumbly sandstone with large knives, dividing the clod into three parts. Marusya had just finished cleaning the skull, and was pouring shellac over the damaged parts.

Nikitin led Miriam up to the clod of sandstone. She looked in amazement at the skeleton of an enormous saurian spread out on its surface. It lay on its side, its long tail coiled under and its huge hind paws crossed. The vertebrae, ribs, even the blunt hoofs—every bone —had been carefully numbered.

The base of the monster's skull, about two yards long, flared into an enormous bony collar studded with blunt spikes. Two long slanting horns protruded above the eye sockets; a third horn crowned the snout which ended in an enormous beak.

'That's a triceratops, a three-horned herbivorous dinosaur, very well armed against predators,' Nikitin explained. 'The skeleton was preserved intact. We'll divide it into three parts, set it in strong frames,' the paleontologist pointed to a pile of girders, 'and pour in plaster of Paris. We'll transport them in heavy blocks and remove the plaster of Paris back at the laboratory.'

'What were the predatory animals like, if these creatures needed such terrible weapons against them?' Miriam asked.

'Predatory animals?' the paleontologist exclaimed. 'Well, here's an example.' He picked up a flat tooth about six inches long with serrated edges. 'This belonged to a tyrannosaur, king of the saurians, a giant who walked on his hind paws. . . . We'll soon be moving the excavations to the foot of the mountains,' the scientist went on. 'Martin Martinovich just found three skeletons of armoured dinosaurs there. Spiked armour, real tanks, only, unlike modern tanks, they don't have offensive weapons. For the herbivorous animal could only defend itself passively. It might hide behind armour or stick out its horns, but did not itself attack.'

Before they reached the eastern gorge, Miriam turned to the left and led Nikitin along the foot of the mountain among scattered heaps of stone.

Before them rose a solid wall of reddish-black rock. It was split, as if by the blow of a giant sword, by a narrow passage. Towers of stone flanked this cleft on both sides. High overhead, projections of rock overhung the passage.

The gorge was straight as a rifle barrel and nearly as smooth. Soon Miriam and Nikitin came to a small open valley, locked in on all sides by steep cliffs. The side opposite the entrance curved in a smooth semicircle, from the center of which an enormous cube of solid brown sandstone jutted out. The foot of the cube was drowned in a heap of flat pieces of sandstone that had apparently crumbled off only recently. A huge black mirror shone on one side of the cube. The paleontologist looked around in perplexity.

'This is the deposit of asphalt,' Miriam said quietly, 'or, rather, solidified rosin. It lies in even layers through the solid iron-bearing sandstone, probably deposited by the wind, like the ancient sand dunes. When we blew up the spring these rocks crumbled off and revealed a fresh stratum of petrified rosin. Its smooth surface hasn't yet been damaged by weather and shines like a mirror.'

'When do you think the rosin and sandstone were deposited?' the paleontologist asked quickly.

'At about the same time as the dinosaur bones,' Miriam replied. 'All the deposits accumulated here in the valleys of these ancient mountains have remained almost inviolable.'

Nikitin nodded in approval and sat down on the coarse, crunching sand. The girl settled down opposite him in her favourite cross-legged pose.

It was extraordinarily quiet, and not quite so hot, in the closed-in valley. Dry grasses growing on the floor of this natural mountain hall tinkled faintly, like little crystal bells in the distance. For the first time in his life Nikitin heard their mournful, rustling call. He looked at Miriam in amazement. The girl bent her head and put her finger to her lips. Soon infrequent, immeasurably distant notes of the same low tone were interwoven with this whispering, ghostly ringing—the voices of the brushwood at the foot of the mountains.

Lulled by this barely audible music of the hushed desert, Nikitin was lost in thought. The grasses were calling them to peer into the very heart of nature. They spoke of those mysteries which usually escape our consciousness, blunted as it is by deep-rooted habit, and which are laid bare only at rare moments.

It occurred to Nikitin that nature is infinitely richer than all our ideas about her. But her wealth of knowledge is never bestowed as a gift. Man can approach her hidden mysteries only in close communication and in constant struggle with nature, and only with a pure heart, which alone can respond to her melodies like a finely tuned musical instrument.

Nikitin raised his head slowly and saw Miriam looking straight at him. The paleontologist got to his feet awkwardly and, in a voice which seemed to him harsh, drowned out the delicate song of the grass:

'It's time to go, Miriam.'

The girl got up silently.

On leaving, Nikitin surveyed the peaceful little valley with pleasure.

'Why didn't you tell me about this lovely spot sooner?' he said reproachfully.

'You were too busy,' Miriam answered quietly.

'Tomorrow we'll move the camp to the foot of the mountain,' Nikitin decided. 'Then it will be right alongside the main excavations.'

With a confident rakish blow Martin Martinovich drove the last nail into a long box.

'That does it, Sergei Pavlovich,' he exclaimed cheerfully, wiping his sweaty face.

'Finished,' Nikitin responded. 'Tomorrow we'll rest and load up, and start for home in the evening. We can't stay here any longer.'

'Sergei Pavlovich,' Marusya broke in, 'you've been promising for a long time to tell us about these . . .' she pointed to the boxes lying all around, '. . . creatures, and we never had time. Why not today? It's only three o'clock.'

'All right. After dinner we'll go to the little valley and talk,' Nikitin agreed.

Everyone listened attentively as Nikitin spoke. He told the fourteen members of the expedition how, in the most ancient eras of the development of life on earth, the animal organism was perfected, slowly, through millions of generations. How at times fantastic four-legged amphibians and reptiles appeared. How in the struggle for existence the less perfect and less mobile types gradually died out; the cruel broom of natural selection swept through the endless flow of generations, at times brushing aside all the weak and unfit.

At the beginning of the Mezozoic era, about one hundred fifty million years ago, reptiles were scattered everywhere on the ancient continents and became the progenitors of the most perfect of all animals—the mammals, who developed under the stern conditions prevailing at the end of the Paleozoic era. But soon the comparatively harsh dry climate became warm and humid, and a wealth of lush vegetation covered the earth. Such conditions were easier, more favorable, and an era of enormous reptiles began. They ruled dry land, sea, and air, reaching incredible sizes and numbers.

The gigantic herbivorates had monstrous horns or an armour of bony spikes and shields for defense against predators. Others, lacking such protection, hid in the water near the shores of lagoons or lakes. They measured 80 feet in length and weighed sixty tons. Winged sauria ruled the air: of all the flying animals they had the broadest wingspread.

Predatory animals walked on their hind legs, balancing themselves on their thick tails. Their front paws became weak, almost useless, appendages. Enormous heads with large sharp teeth served as weapons of attack. These were monstrous tridactyls, twenty-five feet tall—brainless fighting machines of terrible strength and ruthless ferocity.

Amid these giant sauria lived the ancient mammals—tiny creatures resembling a hedgehog or rat. Under the favorable conditions of the Mezozoic era the sauria nearly stamped out that progressive group of animals. From this point of view the Mezozoic was an era of dark reaction which lasted about one hundred million years and impeded the progress of the animal world.

But then climatic conditions and vegetation began to change, and the enormous sauria were in for a bad time. The herbivorous giants needed abundant and easily assimilable food, and the changes in vegetation were a catastrophe both for them and for the gigantic predators. The natural balance of the animal kingdom was destroyed; the reptiles began to die out, and the mammals to flourish. They became the lords of the earth and finally gave rise to man.

'Try to imagine for a moment the endless chain of mindless generations which passed through these hundreds of millions of years,' the paleontologist concluded. 'The whole inconceivable number of the victims of natural selection along the blind path of evolution.'

Nikitin fell silent. No one else spoke. High in the already darkening sky an eagle screeched. Nikitin smiled pensively and said :

'Yes, the greatness of paleontology lies in its immense perspective of time. In this respect only astronomy compares with it. But paleontology has one very weak side, tormenting for those who aspire to fuller knowledge. I mean the dearth of our working materials. Only an infinitesimal number of the extinct animals has been preserved in the earth's crust, and those only as fragments. Our excavations yield nothing but bones. True, we can use them to restore the complete external form of the animals, but only within certain limits. Worst of all, we will never have detailed information about the animal's inner structure, or be able to see it as it was alive. By the same token we will never be able to check the accuracy of our theories or to correct mistakes. Physical laws are incontrovertible, and the virtue of human reason lies in looking them straight in the face, without being deluded by fairy tales.'

Profound melancholy resounded in Nikitin's voice and communicated itself to the others. The paleontologist got up abruptly :

'Never mind. You neophytes can turn to the free and powerful imagination of our fiction writers. Not limited to narrow, accurate facts, they resurrect the extinct animal world vividly and convincingly. I can recommend "The Lost World" by Conan Doyle and "The Struggle for Fire" by Rosny Aîné, my favorite author. He can captivate even a paleontologist with the power of his imagination, with his marvellous descriptions of the ancient world, with his recreation of the shadows of the past.' Carried away by his subject, the paleontologist began to quote :

' "A hazy shadow of the past merged with the deep twilight and an ominous red mist swirled over the plain . . ." '

Marusya's muffled scream made Nikitin stop speaking and turn around. His heart stood still and he froze on the spot.

Above the dark slab of petrified rosin, rising from somewhere in its depths, appeared a gigantic gray-green phantom. An enormous dinosaur towering thirty feet above the heads of the stupefied spectators hung motionless in the air over the upper edge of a rocky precipice.

The monster carried its hump-nosed head high; large eyes stared dully and sombrely into the distance; a wide lipless mouth bared a long row of fangs bent inward. The dinosaur's back, slightly humped, ended in an incredibly powerful tail which supported him from behind. The enormous hind legs, bent at the joints, were no less powerful than the tail. Large as pillars, they were supported by three toes spread wide apart and armed with gigantic hooked nails.

On the front part of the trunk bent toward the ground, two clawed front paws, very small compared with the huge trunk and head, dangled awkwardly and helplessly.

Though the black cliffs shone through the phantom, the finest details of its body could be distinguished. The monster's back, studded with fine bony scales, its rough skin overhung with heavy folds, a strange protuberance on the throat, the great bulging muscles, even the wide violet stripes along the sides—all this lent the vision amazing reality. Every member of the expedition stood mute and entranced, eyes glued to the gigantic shadow which seemed real and ghostly at one and the same time.

A few minutes passed and the light changed slightly. The motionless phantom began to melt away and finally disappeared. Nothing remained except the dark mirror, which had lost its blue overtones and now shone dully like copper. Everyone sighed audibly. Nikitin licked his parched lips.

For a long time no one could utter a word. The appearance of the incredible phantom monster had destroyed all their conceptions of the world molded by education and everyday experience. They realized that something extraordinary had burst without warning into their lives. Most shaken of all was Nikitin. The scientist was accustomed to analyzing and explaining nature's riddles, but for the moment no reasonable explanation occurred to him.

Everyone was lost in speculation. The camp buzzed late into the night, until Nikitin finally calmed them down by saying that there was nothing strange about seeing the specter of a monstrous tyrannosaur in that land of mirages.

They were checking the truck motors before setting out. A bluish haze hovered over the brown pebbles of the plain. Nikitin looked at his watch and set out in haste for the narrow gorge.

The black mirror stared at him from its indifferent depths. The place had lost its former quietness; the noise of the motors carried from behind the rocky walls. A vague feeling as of something uprooted and lost forever gripped Nikitin. He was waiting for yesterday's phantom, but he waited in vain. He must have mistaken the time of its appearance and come too late.

Angry at his own negligence, he stood for a long time before the pile of rocks at the foot of the mirror. Sand crunched behind him—Miriam was approaching rapidly.

'Martin Martinovich says we're ready to leave. I offered to come and get you. . . .I wanted to have one more look . . .' out of breath, she spoke jerkily and rapidly.

'I'm coming right away,' the paleontologist answered irresolutely. He fell silent, then added: 'Wait, Miriam!'

The girl moved forward compliantly and also stared into the black mirror.

'What are you going to do when we get back, Miriam?' Nikitin asked suddenly.

'Work. Study,' the girl answered briefly. 'And you?'

'I'll work too—on these dinosaurs, and I'll think . . .' the scientist faltered and ended too sharply: 'about you!'

Miriam lowered her head and for a moment made no reply. Then she said: 'If I were you, I'd think of nothing but solving the riddle of the phantom dinosaur. That was no mirage.'

'I know it wasn't a mirage!' Nikitin said dejectedly. 'But I'm only a paleontologist. If I were a physicist . . .'

Nikitin broke off abruptly and went up closer to the slab of petrified rosin. For a long time he stared at its mute surface and an almost unbearable savage yearning filled him. For a brief moment the impenetrable curtain of time had been lifted. Out of all mankind, only he and his companions had been permitted a look into the past. And he alone had sufficient knowledge and scientific experience. Miriam was right. He had to solve this mystery of nature.

Suddenly he thought he saw silvery shadows floating up from the black depths of the mirror. He began to concentrate, his eyes and his attention drawn taut. The discontinuous parts quickly merged into a hazy but complete image, like a badly developed photograph. The figure of yesterday's tyrannosaur appeared, inverted and greatly reduced in size, in the center of the black mirror. On the left he saw a grove of enormous trees, and in the background the vaguest outline of mountain tops.

Whipping out his notebook, Nikitin called Miriam and began to draw the ghostly image. They both stared fixedly at the silvery-gray shadows, but the picture became no sharper. Soon spots of light began to dance before their straining eyes, and the black mirror again became blank.

Nikitin had to force himself to leave this place of mystery, for he knew he should stay a few more days to watch the mirror.

By a rare whim of fate he had come face to face with a truly remarkable phenomenon. Very soon, perhaps in a few days, sun and wind would demolish the smooth rosin surface and the riddle would remain unsolved forever. It was his duty as a scientist, the very meaning of his existence, to capture what had been revealed to him by chance and give it to all mankind.

But he would have to abandon this miraculous window into the past here in the remote, forbidding mountains. He had no more time. It was dangerous to postpone their departure. As it was they had worked till the last possible moment completing the excavations. The difficult return trip with overloaded trucks lay ahead.

Risk lives entrusted to him for the sake of a half-mad, inexplicable vision? No, he couldn't do it.

Nikitin returned to the trucks almost at a run. Coming up to the Lightning, he again caught sight of Miriam. She was standing motionless by the Destroyer, staring at the entrance to the gorge. This was the last impression which he took with him from the mystifying Arkarla mountains.

'Let's go!' he shouted, and slammed the door of the truck. He began to watch the sparks of gypsum flashing under the truck wheels in the valley of the dinosaurs.

A cold, gloomy light was fading rapidly in the leaden sky. Through the storm-windows Nikitin saw the black snow-covered roof of a neighboring house. Smoke rose from its chimney and was torn away in sharp gusts of wind.

He pushed his book aside and straightened up in his armchair, gripped by deep melancholy.

His stubborn mind, the mind of a scientist, refused to surrender, but the bitter consciousness of failure was already maturing within him.

Nikitin remembered sadly how only his irreproachable reputation as a scientist had saved him from open ridicule, even from a suspicion of insanity. The physicists to whom he turned for help reacted with puzzled humor—they knew all about optical illusions, mirages, and hallucinations. Putting himself in their place, Nikitin couldn't blame them.

Even back in the graveyard of the dinosaurs, Nikitin had understood that the smooth surface of black rosin had preserved a kind of photograph, and that this photograph had been projected into the air in some inexplicable way. But how could there be a photograph without silver bromide plate, without developing and fixing? Ordinary scattered light does not produce images. There would have to be a camera—some kind of dark chamber with a narrow aperture through which light rays could cast an inverted image of anything within focal length. But the image of the tyrannosaur in the black mirror *had* been inverted!

To solve such a mystery would require extraordinary dedication, a passionate effort of mind and will geared to accomplishing a single aim. Inspiration was needed, but here, in his present humdrum existence, inspiration was an infrequent visitor. Moreover, the episode 2,500 miles beyond the steppe and torrid sands, seemed to be slipping further and further away. Could he really convince anyone, could he himself really believe in the ghostly vision of the country of mirages, here in the pale and sober light of a cold winter evening? And Miriam . . . hadn't Miriam also gone out of his life like a fleeting mirage?

Nikitin closed his eyes. In a moment the darkened window, the snow and the cold had disappeared, and a whole series of pictures flashed through his mind.

Blinding white walls, dark green foliage pierced through with burning gold, the murmuring irrigation ditch, clouds of copper dust . . .

Again the trucks swayed, motors hummed evenly, and blue chains of fantastic mirages filled the shimmering hot air. Through the haze of this fantastic elusive world on the boundless scorched plain Miriam's face stood out more and more distinctly. Nikitin leaped from his armchair, nearly upsetting it.

'Why didn't I realize. . . Why didn't I tell her?' he asked himself, pacing the floor. 'But it's not too late. I can write, or even go to her.'

Nikitin was excited; some powerful force was pushing him to an immediate decision. He would go to her, tell her everything. Right away.

He made a clumsy movement and knocked against a dinosaur vertebra lying near the edge of the table. The heavy bone crashed to the floor and broke into several pieces. The paleontologist came to his senses and stooped to pick up the scattered fragments. He was ashamed, as if an outsider had been spying on his most cherished dreams. Nikitin looked around hurriedly and the familiar surroundings once again took possession of him. This was his world, peaceful, simple and clear, if at times perhaps a little narrow. The tall cupboard sheltered behind its glass doors many still unstudied treasures, many remnants of ancient life.

And there still remained the great riddle of the shadow of the past. Wasn't that enough for him, a procrastinator, always late, as his professor had said of him? He had been late with Miriam too, hopelessly late. He should have told her there in the Arkarla mountains, in the valley of ringing grasses. Now he would need all his faculties, his whole mind, to win Miriam. Just when the riddle of the past demanded of him so much time and energy. Was he really up to it all? And what made him so sure that Miriam was ready to fall in love with him? What if she loved someone else?

His excitement suddenly left him and he sat down again.

Man's mind cannot fold its wings before the unknown. Unswerving determination before even the most difficult problems is the most extraordinary feature of the human mind. The phantom dinosaur must have some explanation.

Despite himself, Nikitin's thoughts kept returning to the desert expedition. He remembered everything, down to the smallest details, especially those last days before the return to Moscow. His tenacious memory suddenly came up with a vision that had almost vanished from his consciousness.

Nikitin remembered how he had waited for his car in the hotel on the day of their departure from the white city. He had been stretched out on a broad sofa. The windows of the room looked out onto a street flooded with sunshine. The shutters were closed, and a straight narrow sunbeam pierced the half-darkness of the room from a crack between the slats.

Shadows flashed on the wall opposite the window. Unconsciously following their movement, Nikitin suddenly saw a clear inverted image of the opposite side of the street. The naked branches of the poplars, the squat house with the new roof, the palings of the iron gate were all clearly depicted. A man was hurrying by, small, amusing, upside down . . . .

The idea struck Nikitin like a fresh wind. The small shady valley shut in by the overhanging Arkarla cliffs. The narrow cleft of the passage into the broad valley. Directly opposite it the mirror of rosin. This was an enormous natural camera; its focal length could be calculated! Now he knew how the image had been obtained. But he still did not understand the most important thing. How was the photograph developed, and how had the ephemeral play of light and shadow been preserved for thousands of centuries? Though he had been studying photographic manuals for some time, he had no idea how this was possible.

Wait! Nikitin jumped up and began pacing around the room. The image had been colored! He would have to go into the theory of color photography.

Forgetting everything else in the world, Nikitin spent the next day poring over a thick book on color photography. He had already waded through the theory of colors and the analysis of human vision and was now studying the last section, 'Special Methods of Color Photography.' Suddenly he stumbled upon a letter written by Joseph Niepce to Louis Daguerre in the 1830s.

'. . . and it turned out that the emulsion (asphalt rosin) of the plate changed under the action of light. It gave in transmitted light something like the image on a slide, and all the shades of color could be seen clearly,' Niepce wrote.

Nikitin gave a muffled cry and, clutching his temples as if to hold his runaway thoughts in check, read on:

'When the image thus obtained was examined at a definite angle in incident light, a very beautiful and interesting effect was produced. This must have some connection with the phenomenon of Newton's colored rings. It is possible that some part of the spectrum acts on rosin to create very subtle variations in the thickness of the layers.'

The priceless thread explaining the phantom tyrannosaur unravelled through the pages. At first thin and fragile, it gradually became stronger and more reliable.

Nikitin learned that the structure of the smooth surface of such photographic plates is changed under the influence of stationary light waves and that these stationary waves produce definite colored imprints, in contrast to the ordinary black image obtained as a result of the chemical action of light on a silver bromide photographic plate. These imprints of the complex reflections of light waves, invisible even under strong magnification, have limited capabilities—they selectively reflect light of one definite color when the image is illuminated at one strictly determined angle. The sum of these imprints gives a magnificent image in natural color.

In other words, under natural conditions light could act on certain materials to produce an image even without light-sensitive compounds of silver. This was precisely the link that had been missing in his theory.

Nikitin quickened his pace. Melting snow was dripping from the house-tops. The scientist, very much excited, was hurrying to the institute. Three months of work had not been wasted—he knew what to look for, and where to look. The help of opticians, physicists and photographers had contributed greatly to the solution of the problem. Today he would communicate his discoveries to the scientific world for the first time.

The subject of the report and Nikitin's name had attracted a considerable crowd. The paleontologist described his incredible encounter with the phantom tyrannosaur and immediately noted the amused and lively reaction of his audience. Nikitin frowned, but continued in an unhurried and distinct voice :

'This newly uncovered layer of petrified rosin, it seems, preserved a light impression, a photograph, of one moment in the natural history of the Cretaceous period. The sun's rays, reflecting at a definite angle from this black mirror, and acting like a kind of projecting lantern, cast the upright phantom image of a gigantic dinosaur onto certain mirage-producing streams of air. The result was a unique merging of the reflected image with a mirage, resulting in a great enlargement of the original image.

'Without question, the exposure necessary for obtaining light images on rosin was very great. But it's quite possible that the solar illumination was somewhat greater in those times when a tropical climate prevailed. It is also possible that the dinosaurs could stand motionless for hours on end. The large modern reptiles—crocodiles, turtles, snakes, large lizards—can stay for several hours without changing their position. Thus, under conditions of very long exposure, photographs of living sauria are entirely possible, as our dinosaur has clearly proven.

'According to my calculations, the dinosaur must have stood 450 feet from the foot of the two mountain towers.' The scientist pointed to a large map of the area. 'Whether the picture was obtained by powerful lighting, or by a special cloud distribution, or by some other means, it was apparently at once covered by subsequent layers of asphalt rosin and thereby preserved. The shock from our explosion broke off the upper layers and uncovered the image.'

Nikitin paused, trying to overcome his agitation.

'In the final analysis,' he continued, 'the important thing is not the fact, however remarkable, that a few men have seen the living image of a prehistoric animal for the first time in history. Much more significant is the proven existence of light images from the most ancient epochs, imprinted in mountain layers and preserved for tens, perhaps hundreds, of millions of years. These are real shadows of the past from the immemorial depths of time. We hadn't even suspected their existence. No one could have believed that nature is able to photograph itself. Therefore we have not looked for them.

'Of course, photographs of the past demand a multitude of coincident conditions and it is probable that very long time intervals separated each such case. But when one considers the enormity of past time, the number of cases must be very large. After all, the preservation of fossil bones also demands very rare coincidences. Nevertheless we already know many extinct animals, and their number is increasing very rapidly as the techniques of paleontological investigation continue to develop.

'Light impressions, photographs of the past, need not be made and preserved on asphalt rosin alone. We can doubtless look for them in several widely occurring ores—in oxides of iron, manganese, and other metals. Photography by the method of discoloration, in which light destroys an unstable color and produces binary colors, has been known for a long time. Where should we look for these pictures of the past? In ore deposits where we can assume very rapid stratification in the open air or in very shallow water. By carefully exposing the surface of such strata and capturing the light reflections with the help of special sensitive instruments, we should be able to capture these impressions of past ages.

'Finally, we must assume that nature also photographed its past by means other than light. Remember the still unexplained images of the surroundings that lightning sometimes leaves on wooden boards, glass, and the skin of people struck by it. Electrical discharges or invisible radiation, like that from radium, could conceivably also produce images.

'Once we know clearly what we are looking for, we will know where to look, and we will find it!'

The report was finished. The speeches that followed were frankly skeptical. One well-known geologist in particular, noted for his eloquence, characterized Nikitin's speech as absorbing but scientifically worthless 'paleofantasy.' But these attacks did not worry Nikitin. He had long ago decided on his own course of action.

Metallic blows resounded throughout the enormous hall as Nikitin stopped by the entrance. In two showcases standing opposite each other, bulky sauria bared their black teeth. Behind the showcases the floor was strewn with beams, iron pipes, bolts and tools. In the middle of the room, resting firmly on crossbeams, towered two tall vertical posts—the chief supports for the large tyrannosaur skeleton. An intricate framework of iron was already attached to one of them, and two assistants were carefully mounting the enormous bones of the monster's hind legs. Nikitin's eyes followed the smooth curve of pipe which formed the top of the framework and which bristled with copper ferrules. They would support the eighty-three vertebrae along the tyrannosaur's rapaciously curved back.

Near the front support Martin Martinovich, with a wrench in his hand, balanced precariously on the scaffolding. Another assistant, a thin sullen man, clambered along the opposite side of the scaffolding carrying a long iron pipe.

'That won't work!' the paleontologist shouted. 'Be careful! Are you too lazy to move the scaffolding?'

'Why waste time, Sergei Pavlovich?' the Latvian called down cheerfully. 'We know what we're doing. We're from the old school.'

Nikitin smiled and shrugged his shoulders. The gloomy assistant screwed the thread of the pipe, designed to support the massive neck, into the upper tee joint at the end of the main support. Martin Martinovich turned the wrench vigorously. The pipe turned over, carrying the gloomy assistant with it. He collided with Martin Martinovich on the narrow scaffolding and they both tumbled off, one on each side of the frame. The clatter of the falling pipe drowned out the noise of shattering glass and frightened shouts. Martin Martinovich got up somewhat embarrassed, rubbing a fresh bump on his bald head.

'And the fall, was that from the old school too?' Nikitin asked.

'Certainly,' the resourceful Latvian retorted. 'Anyone else would have been crippled for life, but with us—a little broken glass, and not even plate glass at that. We'd better move the scaffolding, it won't reach,' he concluded blandly, as if nothing had happened.

Nikitin put on his lab coat and joined the workers. The slowest part of the work—the preliminary assembling of the skeleton and the construction of the iron framework—had already been completed. Now the framework had only to be assembled and the heavy bones attached to the supports, ferrules, and bolts already screwed or welded to it. The preparation of the bones had also taken several months. The assistants had removed them from the plaster of Paris mold, glued back the broken pieces, and filled in the missing parts with gypsum and wood.

They had done a good job on the framework; and very few adjustments had to be made when the skeleton was mounted. The scientists and their assistants worked enthusiastically, staying till late at night. Everyone wanted to restore the extinct monster to its lifelike, menacing pose as quickly as possible.

In a week the work was finished. The tyrannosaur's skeleton rose to its full height; the hind legs, like the legs of a gigantic predatory bird, were frozen in mid-step; the long straight tail dragged far behind. The enormous skull stood eighteen feet from the floor; the half-open jaws with coarse, sparse teeth resembled a saw bent at an acute angle. The skeleton stood on a low oak platform whose black polished surface shone like the lid of a grand piano.

The slanting rays of the evening sun pierced through the tall arched windows, flashing on the shining glass of the showcase and drowning in the blackness of the polished oak base.

Nikitin stood leaning against the show case. He examined the skeleton with a critical eye, trying to find some hitherto unnoticed violation of the rigid laws of anatomy.

No, it seemed to be quite an accurate reconstruction. The enormous tyrannosaur exhumed from the desert graveyard now stood accessible to the museum's thousands of visitors. Frameworks were already being prepared for other skeletons of horned and armoured dinosaurs. The expedition had accomplished a great deal.

Sunlight flashing on the black base of the showcase vividly reminded the paleontologist of the rosin mirror in the Arkarla mountains. The skeleton had been set up in the same unforgettable pose as the phantom of the living tyrannosaur. The pose seemed completely natural, which was more than one could say about the prehistoric animals in other museums.

'If my respected colleagues knew where I got the idea!' Nikitin smiled inwardly. 'But winners are never criticized.'

And again the scientist's thoughts turned, like the needle of a compass, to the now solved riddle of the shadow of the past. The phantom had become a material phenomenon which the scientist understood. The passionate obsession, the mind's rebellion before an impenetrable mystery of nature, had disappeared. His thoughts now moved in a calm, cold, and deep channel.

He knew very well that he would have to work alone until he could prove to the world the existence of light images from the past. In all probability he would have neither special funds nor extra time. He would have to do all this in addition to his own basic work. An enormous, impossible task.

And geology itself was against him. In the processes which gave rise to mineral strata, that is, to deposits which might be sensitive to light impressions, cases of rapid stratification were extremely rare. He would have to look for layers deposited fast enough to prevent any subsequent action of light. And all this had to coincide with conditions having at least some similarity to a camera, so that the surface was exposed not to ordinary scattered light, but to focussed light. How many pictures must already have been destroyed in the processes of solidification, crystallization and chemical change in stratified rock!

Out of the endless number of such stratifications what were the chances of finding precisely those surfaces which retained pictures of the past? Would the abyss of time really remain forever unresponsive and inaccessible to us?

No. The very infinitude of time was an advantage. Such rare coincidences could happen only once in a thousand years, and there was no chance at all of stumbling upon any particular one. But if millions of millennia had passed, then there were a million such chances, a number quite within the realm of possibility. And the chances were increased many times more by virtue of the earth's enormous surface.

The territory of the Soviet Union encompasses hundreds of millions of square feet composed of a great variety of different types of rock formed under the most varied conditions. Since it was a question of such large numbers, one had to reject narrow concepts born of everyday experience. 'My native land will help me in my search for the past,' Nikitin thought. 'Where could one discover images of the past, if not in its vast expanse?'

Confidence and a zest for new exploration, new struggle, were resurrected in Nikitin's soul.

First of all, he would need an apparatus to capture light reflected from layers of rock. A camera, perhaps, with a very high-powered wide-angle lens. It was essential to determine the angle of reflection accurately. Perhaps a revolving prism.

Nikitin hurried into his office without a backward glance at the skeleton of the tyrannosaur.

'Not that way, Comrade Professor.' A bearded, stern-faced collective farmer stopped Nikitin, who had been walking lost in thought. 'That's a riding path. We go the left, into the ravine.'

'Is it far to the red cliffs?' one of Nikitin's assistants asked.

'Half a mile down the ravine to the river, and about three miles along the bank.' The guide strode forward purposefully. Enormous thick fir trees crowded the path. Between the grayish-green trunks and the slanted moss-covered branches the river sparkled deep below, like scattered fragments of a broken mirror. The air was saturated with the sweetish odor of fir resin, soften and more cloying than the odor of pines. The ravine, overgrown with alders, was like a long closed corridor carpeted with a thick layer of old brown leaves. As they walked on, the leaves got blacker and damper, and water squelched under their feet. The ravine came to an end, and the explorers came out on the steep bank of a swift and cold river. At each bend the river sparkled in bright sunlight, but the rapids lay in shadow and seemed gloomy and forbidding. Not far away they could see cliffs of dark purple clay trimmed with green along their upper edges.

The little group soon reached the cliffs and the workmen got busy. Picks and shovels flashed in sturdy hands. Clay rolled into the river in large grains, like a rain of nuts. Shovelling carefully, they laid bare the smooth shining surface of a layer of clay. It lay at an angle, and Nikitin had to build a platform and mount his camera high above the uncovered layer. Their job done, the workers left. Nikitin's assistants set out along the shore with fishing rods, and the paleontologist was left alone.

Hours passed. Nikitin kept vigil by the camera, from time to time permitting himself to close his weary eyes for a minute or two. He was perfectly calm, almost certain of another failure. Nikitin had set up his camera many times and in many places, and had stared into the lifeless smooth surface of rocks in wearisome suspense. Each time the excitement and anticipation of a new discovery had grown fainter. Hope died, but he stubbornly continued his observations in every likely place.

Now, too, almost without interest, bound only by the duty which he had taken upon himself, Nikitin stared through the camera at the freshly uncovered layer of hardened purple clay. The sun shifted slowly, the tops of the mighty fir trees swayed faintly, water splashed softly in the reeds along the shore. And suddenly in the monotonous even illumination a few dark spots appeared on the clay, became sharper, and soon dotted the whole uncovered surface. Determining the angle of reflection by means of a rotating prism, Nikitin finally brought the image into focus.

Before him lay the bright shore of a remarkably translucent green sea. A smooth beach of silver-white sand shaded almost imperceptibly into emerald water. The long straight crests of little waves froze in their upward flight, streaking the crystal clear surface of the water with vivid bluish green. Further out, the streaks formed triangles and the pointed crests of the waves curved downward in flashes of blinding white and silver foam. Against the pure green water, the horizon appeared to be light blue. One sensed that the air was marvellously transparent and the light extraordinarily bright.

Nikitin looked almost fearfully at this fragment of an unspeakably bright clear world, realizing that the crests of the waves had been caught by rays of the sun more than 400 million years ago. This was the shore of a Silurian sea.

The vision disappeared very quickly as the sun shifted a little. Sunlight, which had produced the image, also snuffed it out. There wasn't even time to adjust the camera.

Nikitin remained to spend the night there, under the platform. Tomorrow at the same time the sun would again bring the phantom shadows to life.

But the scientist shivered from the night dampness and fought off troublesome mosquitoes to no purpose. Northern summers are fickle: the gloomy morning ended in rain. Nikitin watched in despair while the water flowed along the smooth surface of the clay, the streams of rain gradually reddened, and the picture of the marvellous Silurian sea turned to sticky brown mud.

For the second time Nikitin had seen a shadow of the past, for one fleeting moment entranced by the beautiful vision. But if his search had succeeded once, he would have to try again and again!

Nikitin now decided to try looking for images of the past on the walls of caves, which are natural cameras. He would have to look in shallow caves whose calcareous layers might contain light-sensitive substances. There the picture would be protected from the whims of nature and from changes in the position of the sun. And, profiting from bitter experience, he would now prepare the camera in advance. The past would not slip away from him again.

Thin gray fog crept slowly over the oily water. The banks glistened with hoarfrost, but the steep mountain slopes, melted by the rays of the rising sun, were black and gloomy. The blunt nose of a clumsy boat was headed toward a distant sharp rock rising in the middle of the mighty river.

The river flowed swiftly and noiselessly, exhaling piercing cold. A deep thundering roar carried from the distance. On the slippery planks at the helm, Nikitin stood beside the pilot, who was clutching the rudder.

The pilot rubbed his reddened nose with a rough glove.

'That's the Bolloktas howling,' he said hoarsely, moving closer to Nikitin. 'The most dangerous rapids in the river.'

'Beyond that bend?' Nikitin asked slowly.

The pilot nodded gloomily.

'Is that where the cave is?' Nikitin continued. 'On the left bank?'

'Do you really want to land there?' the pilot spoke hoarsely and uneasily.

'Yes, there's no alternative,' the scientist answered firmly. 'You can't reach the cave by land; the cliffs are too steep.'

The surface of the water began to raise long flat waves. The heavy, flat-bottomed boat began to sway and plunge. Water slapped under the bow. The roar drew nearer and grew louder, echoing from the high cliffs. The rocks themselves seemed to be howling threateningly, warning the trespassers of inevitable destruction.

The pilot gave a command, and the crew tugged at the heavy oars. The boat plunged round a bend where the river entered a narrow constricting gorge. Gigantic cliffs, towering haughtily some 1,500 feet in the air, were coming closer and closer. The river bed formed a broad triangle whose apex disappeared behind a bend in the gorge. At the base of the triangle tall foamy billows outlined a large solitary rock. Behind it the triangle was intersected by a row of sharp fanglike stones surrounded by madly whirling water. In the distance the gorge was crowded with tall perpendicular waves, as though a whole herd of rearing white horses had forced their way between the dark vertical walls. On the left a wide semicircular bay jutted out into the stony wall, creating a bulge in the left side of the triangle. There the main stream of the river beat furiously, throwing up sparkling spray.

Nikitin lowered his field glasses and seized the rudder to help the pilot. The large rock in the middle of the river thundered toward them. They had to brave the dangerous left side; otherwise the uncontrollable force of the water would throw the boat against a heap of rocks on the right bank, and it would be a year before they reached the cave. And this would mean that they would never reach it, because the expedition's work was finished, and a hasty departure was imminent.

'Row harder! Harder!' the pilot howled.

The boat flew on the crest of a tall wave, and crashed down into a dark pit of water on the other side of the rock. There was a dull thump as the bottom scraped the rock, and a jerk of the rudder almost threw Nikitin and the pilot overboard. But they braced themselves firmly against the rudder beam and hung on. The boat had turned slightly and was headed toward the shore and the menacing stony tusks. Drenched in water and foam, it tossed desperately on the high waves.

'Row!' the pilot shouted at the top of his lungs.

The rain-soaked, sweat-soaked oarsmen—the expedition's assistants and workmen—tugged at the rebellious oars with all their might. The less experienced, fearfully awaiting destruction, turned to their stubborn chief. His heavily bearded face was grim.

Nikitin stood on the tossing platform, legs spread wide apart, and estimated the distance to the white foamy line marking the border of the back current. The pilot bit his lip and looked in the same direction. The boat slowed for a moment, and then plunged forward again, straight into the boiling foam. There was an impulse to close one's eyes and cringe. A moment more and the boat would surely be smashed to bits against the rocks. But again its speed slackened and it came to a shuddering halt, seized by the back current. Then it entered the quiet black water lapping at the foot of the precipitous granite ledges.

Nikitin sighed with relief. After all, the hazardous exploration of the Boloktas caves was completely incidental to the chief purpose of the expedition. If an accident had occurred while they were pursuing shadows of the past . . . But the boat was bumping gently against the cliff. One of the assistants leaped nimbly onto the ledge of rock and made fast the mooring cable.

'Well, we made it, Comrade Director!' the pilot bowed humorously to Nikitin.

'Nice work!' the scientist answered approvingly.

'Good old Russian know-how!' the pilot declared.

The cliffs towered 500 feet above the boat, then jutted over the bank in a broad semicircular shelf. Above this ledge the mountain sloped evenly, and at its foot gaped the nine black openings of the cave entrances. The whole slope was overgrown with short curly pines and white reindeer moss.

The equipment was hoisted without particular difficulty. Nikitin spent the rest of the day in the caves, and became convinced that his suppositions were correct.

The smooth black wall of the cave was stratified in a series of thin smooth layers of a dark greenish-yellow color. Nikitin hoped that one of the layers of iron and chromium salts might have been changed by the action of light, and might have preserved an image of that era, about 60 thousand years ago, when volcanic activity was still present and hot springs boiled here.

Nikitin's assistants cleared the entrance. The round opening projected light onto the back wall of the cave. It really did look like the inside of a camera.

Nikitin set to work with infinite care and patience. Clearing off layer after layer, he illuminated each surface with a specially constructed magnesium lamp. He changed the position of the lamp and rotated the prism, changing the angles of incidence and reflection, but not the slightest hint of an image appeared in the lenses.

More than ten layers had already been examined and knocked down from the wall. Only one very thin layer remained. Nikitin worked all night, unconscious of time. Angered by his failure, he did not feel tired. But he was bleary-eyed from the glare of the lamp, and the supply of magnesium mixture was running out.

Would this really be another lost summer, now, when he was so well equipped for capturing the shadow of the past?

The eleventh layer seemed to Nikitin smoother than all the others. He lit the magnesium lamp again. A few turns of the screw, and a round hazy image appeared. A vague gray shadow in the right-hand corner looked like a crouching human figure with a slanting line over its shoulder. On the left indistinct spots outlined something round. Nikitin adjusted the camera, but the image wouldn't focus. He realized that he was looking at a new picture of the past, but one so blurred that it would have been difficult even to describe it, let alone photograph it. Nikitin added more magnesium mixture, using the lamp at its full power. There wasn't the slightest doubt— this was the figure of a human being. Everything depended on the amount of light. Although magnesium gives a spectrum similar to the solar spectrum, it was not powerful enough. Only the sun could resurrect the shadows it had itself created. His camera wasn't sensitive enough.

The overheated lamp flared up for the last time and then went out. In the darkness the round opening of the cave entrance stood out clearly. The dawn had caught up with him. The scientist lost his habitual calm. In impotent rage he pounded his fist on the innocent camera.

Nikitin was mad with fury. The narrow cave seemed to be suffocating him. He rushed outside, struck his head sharply against the entrance, and fell to his knees. The blow brought him to his senses, but unquenched fury still boiled inside him. He squinted at the rock overhanging the entrance. So his lamp wouldn't do the job! Then he would see the shadow of the past in sunlight! He always carried explosives, in case he had to uncover layers quickly.

The paleontologist critically examined the roof of the cave and noticed a series of long vertical fissures. It would be child's play to demolish this curtain of rock.

The scientist started to descend to the shore where his companions had camped for the night, but he changed his mind and went back to the cave. There he determined the angle at which the magnesium light had fallen on the calcareous layer, and looked at his compass. Fine! The sun would be in that position between two and three in the afternoon. He would have time for some much-needed sleep. His eyes were so tired that he probably wouldn't have been able to see anything even in sunlight. It looked as though the weather would be good.

As soon as the dust from the explosion settled, Nikitin began to set up the camera, balancing himself on the rocky debris. The smooth greenish wall, undamaged by the blast, glistened moistly in the bright sunlight.

There would be no slip-ups—a loaded film-holder was clutched firmly in his hand. The moment the image appeared in the viewer, he would set the focus and thrust the film-holder into the camera. A successful photograph would prove the existence of the shadows of the past and, more than that, the possibility of preserving and reproducing them. It would be a turning point in a long and hazardous road. Now he would no longer have to work alone. Everyone who has tried to break new paths in science or technology knows very well that the accomplishments of one person working alone are insignificant compared to the concerted effort of many.

Nikitin looked at his watch. It was 2:23. He bent over the viewer, his hand clutching the screw of the prism. Time dragged slowly by, but the suspense did not diminish. Nikitin knew that he would see his shadow of the past.

Slowly, very slowly, the sun changed its position in the sky. Nikitin forgot his surroundings.

Gradually the gray, bent shadow took on the distinct contour of a human figure. The slanting line over his shoulder was a spear.

The man was sitting with his broad shoulders hunched, his muscles taut and bulging. The long spear stuck out in front of him. The broad face, furrowed with wrinkles, was half turned to Nikitin, but the eyes were fixed on the blue wooded hills in the distance. Nikitin noted the thick matted hair, framing a rather high forehead, the jutting cheek bones, and massive jaws. The man's face seemed to reflect worried, tormenting thoughts, as if he were trying to peer into the future. Nikitin did not watch long. In spite of his burning interest in the other details of the picture, he had no time to waste; he had to get a photograph. Nikitin inserted the film-holder and started to remove the shield and expose the film. But he stopped abruptly without making the necessary movement. The light on the smooth wall disappeared suddenly. It grew dark all around. Nikitin turned and saw a massive cloud creeping slowly over the sun. In close ranks behind it, heavy leaden clouds lumbered over the mountain tops—clouds of that ominous violet color which presages heavy snowfall.

Nikitin stared at the sky with despair in his heart. If it snowed, then he would never see the picture again. The faint light impressions would be irretrievably lost.

Nourishing a faint hope, he covered his camera with a raincoat, leaving it in place till the next day, and trudged apathetically back to camp. The new, freakish setback poisoned his mind and numbed his body.

Nikitin's men grew quiet, looking at their tired and dejected chief. They talked in undertones as if by a deathbed.

The wind howled mournfully in the mountains. Large snow flakes came whirling down. Nikitin poured himself a drink, drained it in one gulp, and ordered the men to bring the camera down. His last hope of again seeing the image of the prehistoric man perished. They couldn't postpone their departure by even a single hour. He had to get hold of himself. A delay might mean that the boat would be ice-bound in the frozen river below the rapids, deep in the desolate taiga.

In the morning, when the mountain tops had just begun to be visible in the dark sky, the men started breaking camp.

The mooring cable splashed quietly into the water, and the boat nosed slowly toward the foaming edge of the main current. Suddenly it seemed as though a monstrous soft paw had seized the boat. It tore forward into the gorge and disappeared, bobbing like a chip, into the howling foam of the tall waves.

The table lamp threw a circle of light on a desk cluttered with books. It was half dark in the spacious study. Nikitin sat motionless by the table, deep in thought.

For three years he had known no peace. His former work now seemed to him so tranquil and rewarding that he was tempted to devote himself again exclusively to it. But he could not. He was torn between the old and the new, trying to fulfill his regular duties conscientiously while his whole soul was yearning after the shadow of the past. In these three years the past had been within his reach twice; twice he had seen what no other man had ever seen. And he was just as far from his goal as he had been at that unforgettable moment in the Arkarla mountains. He didn't even have a camera sensitive enough for the job.

He must have been wrong. This was not a job for one person.

Nikitin lit the ceiling light and, squinting, began to gather up his scattered papers. He glanced at the camera standing on a little table. It was battered and scratched from its travels. 'Just as I am,' he thought. Then he laughed bitterly and went out.

The museum was dark. Nikitin's office was at one end of an enormous hall filled with showcases and skeletons of extinct animals. Leaving his brightly lit office, Nikitin stood as if blinded.

He knew all the passageways between the showcases, but he also knew that in some places the horns and bared teeth of skeletons standing on open platforms stuck out into the passages. In the darkness he could easily hurt himself or smash the fragile bones.

The scientist waited until his eyes were accustomed to the darkness. The glass of the showcases gleamed faintly, but the dark bones blended into the night, and the museum seemed empty. Through long habit Nikitin sensed the invisible presence of the museum's lifeless population. A strange feeling possessed him. It seemed to him that the museum teemed with hidden phantoms.

Nikitin moved forward, mumbling at the imperfection of human vision. He knew everything that was here, knew where it stood, but he couldn't see a thing. Just like the shadows of the past. The skeletons were here, yet they had disappeared. There wasn't enough light to . . .

He stopped suddenly, struck by this comparison with the shadows of the past. How stupid he had been, relying only on his own imperfect eyes! How could he have overlooked the fact that these faint images, in an overwhelming majority of cases, reflected only a minute amount of light imperceptible to the naked eye? Therefore artificial lighting could not resurrect even very clear pictures of the past. And how many weaker imprints had been lost!

Nikitin was ashamed. He, a scientist, had designed his camera like a rank amateur, like a dilettante! He had ignored the resources of modern technology, which possessed instruments sensitive to infinitesimal amounts of light.

Stepping carefully, the paleontologist moved through the dark museum, and with each step his conception of the design for the new camera grew clearer. He would once more turn for help to the physicists and technicians. The light reflected from the image would not be perceived directly, but through a combination of sensitive photocells which would transform it into electricity, intensify it, and again transform it into light—into visible light.

The exact reproduction of colors would present some difficulty, but this was not insurmountable. The picture could be intensified, and the color obtained by direct reflection.

Nikitin bumped his shoulder against a showcase and jumped aside. The thing still had to be worked out, but the key to the problem had been found. 'If such a camera can be built,' he thought, 'my worries will be over. In the open I'll rig up a shelter and set up artificial lighting. Underground there'll be nothing to it! Then I'll have the shadow of the past right in the palm of my hand! With the help of a few photocells I can increase or decrease the camera's sensitivity to the different rays of the spectrum.'

The mining engineer was escorting a group of people who had obviously never gone down into the pits before. A blithe young cage operator sidled up to him and asked in a whisper :

'Well, Andrei Yakovlevich, shall I take them down by cable, or shall I use the pneumatic hoist?' He winked expressively at the newcomers.

'What! Have you lost your mind?' The engineer was shocked. 'This man is a famous scientist!' He stole a glance at Nikitin, who was lingering behind. 'And you might wreck their equipment. Just let me catch you . . . !' he broke off threateningly.

Nikitin overheard all of this short conversation, which would have been incomprehensible to the uninitiated. He was quick to intervene.

'Use both,' he shouted to the cage operator. 'The equipment and I can take it. It'll be like old times. And my youngsters will have to get used to it sometime.'

The disconcerted cage operator gaped at Nikitin. Then he grinned broadly and nodded.

The cage began to descend slowly, then suddenly crashed downward as if the cable had snapped. Their feet left the floor, their hearts seemed to leap to their throats, they couldn't breathe. The cage plummeted faster and faster, then slowed down just as suddenly. An enormous weight pinned the men to the floor. It was as though unseen hands had bound each man with a broad, relentlessly tightening belt.

The sensation lasted less than a second, and again the floor dropped out from under their feet. Their bodies became weightless; their hearts seemed to stop beating.

'Wow!' one of Nikitin's men cried out.

But the cage was already decelerating smoothly. It came to a stop at one of the deepest levels in the mine.

'What the hell did you think you were doing?' the man swore, trying to control the trembling in his knees.

Nikitin roared with laughter, much to the annoyance of his frightened subordinates.

The paleontologist descended into the mine extraordinarily confident of success. This confidence was based on his new camera, on the miners' discovery of a layer of petrified rosin like the black mirror in which he had first seen the phantom of the dinosaur, and on a letter which he had just received.

Nikitin smiled as he mentally repeated its brief message. Miriam wrote that she had forgotten neither him nor the shadow of the past. She had gone back to the asphalt deposit a year later. The black mirror had been destroyed, but nothing could destroy the deep impression the phantom of the dinosaur had made on her mind. She had succeeded in interesting the gifted scientist Karzhaev in the project, and they were now searching for shadows of the past.

She hadn't written sooner because there was no point in doing so; here Nikitin sensed a mild reproach. But she had continued to follow his work and felt sure that he would eventually succeed. They had just found an interesting deposit and wanted him to come.

Nikitin had not had time to grasp all the implications of Miriam's letter. He had been too busy during the last days of preparation for the expedition. But he had suddenly become light-hearted as a schoolboy, and his behaviour mystified everyone who knew him.

An acrid smell of burning was wafted from the long mine tunnel. The air, sucked in by a powerful ventilator, rustled softly. Immediately after the charge had been detonated, Nikitin got down to work. It was deserted and quiet here in the old diggings, far away from the rumble of engines and coalcars, and from the flash of lanterns. The impenetrable subterranean gloom, fused with the anonymous blackness of walls of coal, embraced the intruders.

Barely audible, water trickled somewhere. Far to the side the pit-props creaked in unison, reminding the men of the heavy mass of earth above them.

'Who found this remarkable spot?' Nikitin asked his assistant in a low voice.

The latter nodded toward a little old man walking behind them with the engineer.

'He's one of those rare old birds who know every inch of the mine. If it hadn't been for him, we would have spent years searching in this labyrinth.'

Nikitin looked at the old miner in silent gratitude.

Ahead gleamed the clean white colonnade of new pitprops. By their number alone one would have realized that the tunnel ended in a roomy chamber, and the black walls did in fact diverge, revealing a large empty area with tall ceilings.

Nikitin's assistants lagged behind, dragging the heavy equipment through the tunnel. The engineer stepped forward and raised his powerful lantern. A mass of coal shale torn to pieces by the explosion surrounded them on all sides, its innumerable sharp projections gleaming like menacing steel.

Near the entrance, along both sides of the chamber, stood thick corrugated tree trunks. On one side they had grown into a mass of coal and could be distinguished from it only by the diamond-shaped pattern on their bark. On the cleared surface of the floor powerful stumps with forked roots stretched out like enormous spiders. The roots spread along the ancient soil which had supported them in times infinitely long past. The stumps were all of the same height—

the water level of a flooded forest in the Carboniferous age. Large hollows gaped gloomily in the massive trunks.

The tract of dead forest turned to coal and lime seemed to be crushing the men with its antiquity, as if over their heads were suspended not a six hundred-foot mass of earth, but the ponderous depth of the hundreds of millions of years which had passed since these trees died.

At the end of the room a heap of crumbled slate marked the place where the explosion had occurred. An inclined black-brown slab, a layer of hardened bitumen, glistened above their heads. This was the layer under investigation, a layer which had been deposited on the slope of a small hill in the Carboniferous forest.

Soon a magnesium lamp was set up, its bright white beam directed toward the slab. Nikitin set the focus of his camera. Very excited, he coughed and said hoarsely:

'Let's try it.'

What would this surface, so carefully selected, reveal to them? Nikitin switched on the photocells and increased the current. Turning the screw of the prism, he looked into the camera. The layer was already losing its blackness; indistinct vertical lines began to appear on a transparent gray background.

The paleontologist adjusted the camera patiently and carefully until he saw before him the incredibly clear image of the fourth shadow of the past—a shadow which thousands of people would now see.

Nikitin was looking at a flooded forest grove. Pale gray treetrunks, their bark incised with diamond-shaped patterns, surrounded the oily black water. Near its top each tree was bifurcated; the two thick branches disappeared into a deep shadow of dense foliage. One thick scaly trunk lay across the water and rested on a mound of earth on the left. The mound was overgrown with strange plants resembling mushrooms, dotting the moist red soil like tall, slender violet goblets. The fleshy cup of each mushroom was an oily yellow inside.

Behind the mound, above some bent leafless stalks, a clear space filled with turbid pink mist was visible. A bare and crooked branch stuck out of the mist and on it, head tucked in, cowered a weird creature.

Nikitin took a closer look at the picture and started. A broad parabolic head covered with slimy violet-brown skin peered out from under the violet mushrooms which hid its body. Enormous bulging eyes stared straight at Nikitin, mindless, spiteful, ruthless eyes. Enormous teeth set in deep grooves along the snout stuck out from the lower jaw. From the right an opaque pearly light poured into the picture. The air seemed gray, as if seen through smoked glass.

Nikitin stared for a long time through his magic window into the past, into the world of the Carboniferous age. Three hundred fifty million years had gone by since, in a rare play of fate, the light waves had imprinted this picture. The spiteful eyes of the weird creature, the violet mushrooms, the motionless water and the strange gray air focussed with incredible sharpness. In the mine the projector hissed faintly, and the intermittent breathing of the men was clearly audible.

Nikitin was sure he must be losing his mind. He recoiled from the camera. The real, rough-hewn walls of coal, the ancient stumps—perhaps they were the remains of those very same trees which now appeared in his camera, alive and stately! . . . The strained, concentrating faces of the people surrounding him . . . Controlling himself with an effort, the scientist hurriedly adjusted his camera and made several color photographs.

A tall sheaf of copies of Nikitin's article with a colored reproduction of the captured shadow of the past lay on his desk. The paleontologist inscribed the last of the copies to be sent and sighed with satisfaction. He hadn't felt so relaxed and light-hearted for a long time.

Now many younger and perhaps more talented men would follow in his steps. The first page of this mysterious book of nature had been opened. He would no longer be alone on his long and difficult path. But he had never really been alone. Scores of people had helped him in his work, both colleagues and people who had no connection with the scientific world.

A parade of familiar faces marched in review through Nikitin's mind—miners, quarry workers, collective farmers, hunters. They had all helped him generously and selflessly to find and capture the shadow of the past, without questioning his goal, respecting him as a famous scientist.

He owed them a great deal, and now that debt was paid. Small wonder that he felt light-hearted!

Nikitin remembered how, in this same office, he had often been discouraged and had doubted whether he had chosen the right path. He smiled, and quickly wrote a telegram to Miriam telling her that he was coming.

Cor Serpentis
(The Heart of the Serpent)

BY IVAN YEFREMOV

MUSIC burst through the mists of sleep, demanding to be heard. 'Awake! Do not fall prey to dismal entropy! . . .' The familiar air roused memories and set off an endless chain of associations.

Life returned to the huge space ship. It shuddered, but the automatic mechanisms continued to work. The whirlwinds of energy around the dull green metal of the three hive-shaped protective cowls died away. In a few seconds the cowling leapt upwards and disappeared in niches in the ceiling, lost in a complicated maze of pipes, crossbeams and wires.

Two men sat motionless in deep chairs surrounded by the now empty ring supports for the cowling. A third opened his leaden eyes, shook his head cautiously, and got up from the depths of soft insulation. He sat down at the central control panel and leaned forward to read the mass of instruments which studded its illuminated, slanting surface. The panel took up the whole width of the room and stretched to within a half-yard of the seats.

'We're out of the warp!' a firm voice resounded. 'You're always the first one awake, Kari. You have the ideal constitution for an astronaut.'

Kari Ram, electronics engineer and astronavigator for the space ship Tellur, turned at once to meet the still clouded gaze of the ship's captain, Moot Ang. Moving with difficulty, the captain heaved a sigh of relief and went up to the control panel.

'Twenty-four parsecs.* We've gone right past a star. New instruments are never accurate . . or maybe I should say we don't know how to handle them properly yet. You can turn off the music; Tey's awake.'

In the ensuing silence Kari Ram heard distinctly the uneven breathing of his waking comrade.

The central control post occupied a rather large round room

* Parsec equals 3.26 light years.

safely hidden in the bowels of the huge space ship. A bluish screen ran above the instrument panels and hermetically sealed doors, forming a complete circle. Forward, along the ship's central axis, a break in the screen housed the locator disc, almost twice a man's height in diameter. Transparent as crystal, the huge disc seemed to merge with cosmic space, sparkling like a black diamond in the lights from the instrument panel.

Moot Ang gave an almost imperceptible signal, and all three men immediately covered their eyes. An enormous orange sun blazed on the portside screen. Despite the ship's powerful filters, its light was almost unbearable.

Moot Ang shook his head.

'We almost went right through the corona. That's the last time I'll depend on exact courses laid out in advance. It would be much better to go a little out of our way.'

'That's the trouble with these new space warp ships,' Tey Eron, second in command and chief astrophysicist, replied. 'We plot the course, and then the ship whirls along blindly like a bullet in the night. And we're just as blind and helpless inside the protective vortical field. I don't like it, even though it is the fastest means of flight man has so far been able to devise.'

'Twenty-four parsecs!' Moot Ang exclaimed. 'And to us it has seemed no more than a minute.'

'A minute of sleep like death,' Tey Eron objected gloomily. 'While back on Earth . . .'

'It's better not to think about the fact that seventy-eight years have passed on Earth since we left.' Kari Ram stood erect. 'Many of our relatives and friends are dead; there have been many other changes. I wonder what it will be like when . . .'

'That's unavoidable in any long space flight,' the captain broke in calmly. 'It's just that time moves especially fast on the Tellur. And though we're creeping further out into space than anyone before us, we'll return unchanged.'

Tey Eron went up to the computer.

'Everything's in order,' he said a few minutes later. 'There's Cor Serpentis, or, as the ancient Arabian astronomers called it, Unuk al-Xay—Heart of the Serpent.'

'Where's its neighbor?' Kari Ram asked.

'Hidden from us by the main star. See: the K-O spectrum. An eclipse on our side,' Tey answered.

'Take away the receptor shields!' the captain ordered.

The infinite blackness of the cosmos surrounded them, a blackness which seemed still deeper because port and aft the Heart of the Serpent blazed golden orange, putting to rout the Milky Way and the other stars. Far below, one lone white star shone defiantly.

'We're approaching Epsilon Serpentis.' Trying to win the captain's approval, Kari Ram spoke in a loud voice. But Moot Ang said nothing. He was looking to starboard where the distant star blazed with a clean white light.

'That's where my old ship went,' the captain said slowly, conscious of the expectant silence, 'to explore new planets.'

'So that's Alphecca of the Corona Borealis?'

'Yes, Kari. Or, if you prefer its European name, Gemma. But it's time to get to work.'

'Shall I wake the others?' Tey Eron asked.

'What for? We'll make one or two warps if it's all clear ahead,' Moot Ang answered. 'Switch on the optical and radio telescopes, check the tuning of the memory machines. Tey, start the nuclear engines. We'll use them for the time being. Accelerate!'

'Six-sevenths of the speed of light?'

In answer to the captain's silent nod, Tey Eron quickly flipped the necessary switches. The scapeship responded without a tremor, but a blinding rainbow-colored flame lit up the entire circular screen and completely blotted out the pale stars of the Milky Way flickering below.

'We have several hours before the instruments complete their observations and the quadruple check,' Moot Ang said. 'We'll have something to eat, then we'd better all get some rest. I'll relieve Kari.'

Kari Ram, left alone in the control room, moved the swivel chair to the center of the instrument panel and switched off the stern screens. The flame of the rocket engines disappeared.

Reflections of the fiery Cor Serpentis continued to glimmer insolently on the instrument dials. The forward locator remained a black, bottomless well. This was reassuring, for it proved the accuracy of calculations which had taken six years of work by the Earth's finest minds and computing machines.

The Tellur, the first space warp ship ever made on Earth, was moving down a broad corridor of space free of star clusters and dark clouds. This type of ship, which could travel in zero-space, would be able to penetrate much further into the Cosmos than the earlier anameson nuclear rocket ships, whose top speed was only five-sixths or six-sevenths of the speed of light. Warp ships acted on the principle of time compression and were thousands of times faster. But they had one great disadvantage: during a warp the ship was completely out of the crew's control. And men could bear the warp only in an unconscious state, protected by a powerful magnetic field. The Tellur travelled in intermittent bursts, checking carefully to make sure the way ahead was clear before each succeeding warp.

The Tellur was making for a carbon star in the constellation Hercules, hurtling past the Serpent through practically starless space in the upper latitudes of the galaxy. This incredibly distant voyage had as its aim the direct observation of the carbon star's mysterious processes of the transformation of matter. The findings would be invaluable for terrestrial power development. It was suspected that the star had some connection with a dark electromagnetic cloud in the shape of a disc, rotating edgewise to the Earth. Scientists hoped to see a repetition of the birth of our own planetary system here, in relative proximity to the sun. 'Proximity' in this case meant three hundred fifty light years.

Kari Ram checked the safety devices. They indicated that all the connections of the ship's automatic equipment were intact. The young astronaut abandoned himself to his thoughts.

Far, far away, at a distance of 78 light years, life on Earth went on. A beautiful life constructed by man to provide happiness and inspired creative labor. In the classless society, everyone knew his whole planet thoroughly: not just its factories, mines, plantations, and marine industries, its research centers, museums and forest preserves, but also the quiet corners where one could find peace and solitude, or be alone with one's beloved.

But man had left this wonderful world. Responding to the stern demands of his own nature, he had penetrated deeper and deeper into the glacial cosmic abyss in pursuit of new knowledge, new solutions to the mysteries of nature won at a cruel price.

Man had already traveled far beyond the Moon, drenched with deadly X-rays and ultraviolet radiation from the Sun; beyond scorched, lifeless Venus with its oceans of oil, its sticky resinous soil, and eternal fog; beyond cold, sand-flooded Mars with its dim spark of subterranean life. The study of Jupiter had scarcely begun when new ships reached the nearest stars. Space ships from Earth had visited Alpha and Proxima Centauri, Barnard's star, Sirius, Eta Eridani, and even Tau Ceti. Not the stars themselves, of course, but their planets, or their immediate surroundings if they were double stars, like Sirius, which have no planetary systems.

But the Earth's interstellar ships had not yet visited planets where life had reached the highest stage of development—planets inhabited by thinking beings.

From the abyss of space ultrashort radio waves carried news of inhabited worlds; sometimes they reached the Earth a thousand years after they had been sent out. Man was only now learning to decipher these messages and to get some idea of the vast ocean of science, technology and art which surrounded these inhabited islands of our galaxy. Islands still inaccessible to man. And what of those other starry worlds millions of light years away?

All this only increased man's yearning to reach inhabited planets, to find people, perhaps quite different from Earthmen, but people who had also built rational, orderly societies ensuring every man a measure of happiness limited only by the extent of their mastery of nature. It was already known that there existed worlds inhabited by people just like ourselves, and that these were probably in the majority. The laws of development of planetary systems and of life on them are uniform, not only in our galaxy, but in every known part of the Cosmos.

Space warp ships, the latest product of man's genius, made it possible to answer the call of these distant worlds. If the Tellur's flight were successful, then . . . But, like everything else in life, the new invention had two sides.

'And the other side . . .' lost in thought, Kari Ram didn't realize that he had spoken these last words aloud. He started suddenly, hearing Moot Ang's deep, pleasant voice behind him :

> The other side of love—
> Now boundless as the sea,
> Now narrow as a stairwell.
> It's in your blood, you can't get free.

'I didn't know you like old music too,' the captain smiled. 'That love song's at least five hundred years' old.'

'I don't know a thing about old music!' the astronavigator exclaimed. 'I was thinking about this flight, and that when we return . . .'

The captain frowned.

'We've just made the first warp, and you're already thinking about our return?'

'Oh, no! Why would I have bothered to apply for the flight? But I was just thinking that we'll be returning to earth 700 terrestrial years from now. In spite of the doubled life span, by that time our brothers' and sisters' great-grandchildren will already have died.'

'Didn't you know that?'

'Of course I knew it,' Kari continued stubbornly. 'But something else troubles me.'

'I understand. The apparent futility of our flight?'

'Yes! Even before the Tellur was invented, ordinary rocket ships set out for Fomalhaut, Capella and Arcturus. That was fifty years ago, but the Fomalhaut expedition isn't expected back for two years. The ships won't arrive from Arcturus and Capella for forty or fifty years; those stars are forty and forty-five light years away. Now they're already building ships which can reach Arcturus in one warp. Before we get back, man will have completely conquered time, or space, whichever way you look at it. Then our ships will be able to travel much further than the Tellur, and we'll return with a load of obsolete and useless information.'

'We departed from the Earth as dead men depart from life,' Moot Ang said slowly, 'and we'll return as primitive men, survivals of the past.'

'Exactly!'

'You're right, and at the same time completely wrong. Growth of knowledge, and research on the infinite Cosmos must never cease. Otherwise the laws of development would be broken, and development is irregular and contradictory even without that. Suppose the ancient natural scientists, who seem so naïve to us, had waited for, let us say, the invention of the modern quantum microscope. Or that the farmers and builders of ancient times, who drenched our planet with their sweat, had waited for automatic machines. We would still be living in damp mud huts, feeding on crumbs left us by nature!'

Kari Ram burst out laughing, but Moot Ang continued without a smile:

'We have as great an obligation to fulfill our duty as any other member of society. To be the first men to reach hitherto inaccessible depths of the Cosmos, we had to die for 700 years. Those who remained on Earth to enjoy all its blessings will never know the great wonder of peering into the mysteries of the universe.

'As for the return . . . your fears are groundless. In every stage of its history man has retained something of the past, despite the ascending spiral of development. Every century has had unique characteristics, but it has also had features common to all time. Who can say, perhaps that atom of knowledge which we will bring back to Earth may inspire new advances in science, may make man's life still better. It's true that we ourselves will return from the depths of the past, but we will bring lives and hearts dedicated to the future. Will we really be strangers? Can anyone who works to the limit of his ability really be a stranger? Man is not just the sum of his knowledge; he is also an aggregate of very complex emotions. In this respect we who will have known all the rigors of a long journey through space will be no different than the men of the future.'

Moot Ang paused, then ended on a slightly bantering note:

'I don't know about you, but I find it so fascinating to look into the future, that for that alone—'

'You're willing to die for a while!' the astronavigator exclaimed. Moot Ang nodded.

'Go wash up and have something to eat. The next warp is coming up soon. Tey, what are you doing here?'

The second in command shrugged. 'I just wanted to have a look at the course. I'm ready to relieve you.'

Without another word Tey Eron pushed a button in the middle of the control panel. A concave polished cover moved aside soundlessly, and a spiral ribbon of silvery metal slid up from the depths of the instrument. Through it ran a fine black needle indicating the ship's course. Tiny lights sparkling on the spiral like jewels denoted stars of various spectral classes which the Tellur would pass. The needles of innumerable dials began to dance in unison as the computing machines worked out a course for the next warp which would keep the ship as far as possible from stars, dark clouds, and luminous nebulae that could conceal uncharted heavenly bodies.

Absorbed in his work, Tey Eron didn't notice how the time slipped by. The enormous ship continued its flight through the black emptiness of space. The astrophysicist's comrades sat in silence in a deep semicircular sofa near the massive triple door which isolated the control room from the rest of the ship.

The gay tinkle of little bells announced that the calculations were finished. The captain went slowly up to the control panel.

'Excellent! The second warp can be almost three times as long as the first.'

'No, there's a thirty per cent uncertainty factor.' Tey Eron indicated the tip of the black needle which was vibrating almost imperceptibly in time with the indicators connected to it.

'But we'll have complete certainty at fifty-seven parsecs. Decrease it by five to leave a margin for error. That gives us fifty-two parsecs. Stand by for the warp!'

Again the countless mechanisms and connections of the ship were checked over. Moot Ang tuned in on the cabins where the remaining five members of the Tellur's crew were still deep in sleep. The automatic physiological analyzers showed that their organisms were in normal condition.

The captain switched on the protective field around the crew's quarters. Red streams of gas flowing through the pipes concealed behind it ran along the opaque panel on the port wall.

'All set?' Tey Eron, frowning slightly, asked the captain.

He nodded. The three men silently lowered themselves into the deep seats and fastened themselves in with pneumatic pillows. When the last hook was fastened, each one took a hypodermic syringe from a little compartment in the left armrest.

'Well, here goes another 150 years of terrestrial life!' Kari Ram said, plunging the needle into his bared arm.

Moot Ang looked at him sharply. The youth's eyes glittered with the light mockery inherent to a healthy, well-balanced person.

The captain waited until his comrades had leaned back in their seats unconscious. Then he switched on the mechanical robots controlling the warp and the protective field and pulled the levers on a little box near his knee. The massive cowling was lowered from the ceiling as noiselessly and inexorably as fate itself. In the weak blue light the captain took the readings of the control instruments and only then drove the needle into his arm.

The ship came out of its fourth warp. On the starboard, or 'northern', screen the mysterious carbon star to be investigated grew to the dimensions of the Sun as seen from Mercury. The Tellur cruised at a speed less than light some four parsecs from the huge dull star, KNT8oo8.

Stars of this rare class, barely visible from Earth even in the most powerful telescopes, were one hundred fifty to one hundred seventy times the diameter of our Sun, and were characterized by a high percentage of carbon in their atmospheres. At temperatures of two or three thousand degrees the carbon atoms formed unique chain molecules of three atoms each. The atmosphere of stars with such molecules absorbed radiation in the violet part of the spectrum and their light was consequently very weak in comparison to their size.

But the cores of the carbon giants reached temperatures up to 100 million degrees and such stars were therefore powerful neutron generators. They transformed light elements into heavy ones, even into transuranium elements, all the way up to californium and rossium. The latter was the heaviest known element, with an atomic weight of 401, and had first been isolated four centuries ago.

Scientists believed that carbon stars were the factories for the heavy elements of the universe, and that they scattered these elements into space following periodic explosions, thereby enriching the general chemical composition of our galaxy. The space warp ship had finally made it possible for man to study carbon stars and their heretofore unexplained processes of transformation of matter at close range.

The ship's crew regained consciousness, and each man took up the investigations for which he had cut himself off from Earth for 700 years. The ship seemed to be moving very slowly, but no greater speed was necessary.

The Tellur's course bent slightly away from the carbon star toward the south in order to keep the locator screen outside its field of radiation. Its black mirror remained, as it had for weeks, months and years, utterly blank.

The Tellur, or, as it was listed in the register of the Earth's cosmic fleet, IF-1 (Z-685) (the first inverted-field space ship, and the 685th space ship ever built) was smaller than its slower long-range predecessors. Those colossal ships, made obsolete by the invention of the space warp, had carried crews up to two hundred, and new generations born during the flight had made it possible to travel quite far into interstellar space.

Each time such a long-range space ship returned to Earth, it brought with it scores of immigrants from another age, survivals of the distant past. Even though their level of development was very high, the new age seemed alien to them, and often deep melancholy and a sense of isolation became the lot of these cosmic wanderers.

Now warp ships would hurl men still further into space. In what would seem to the astronauts like a very short time, thousand-year-old Methuselahs would appear in human society. Those who set out for other galaxies would return to their native planet millions of years later. This was the negative aspect of distant cosmic flights, the insidious obstacle erected by Nature against her restless sons.

Even though the Tellur was smaller than its predecessors, it was nevertheless an enormous ship with spacious accommodations for its crew of eight. These travellers into the immeasurable depths of space and time were forbidden to have children during the flight, as the crews of earlier ships had been encouraged to do.

The awakening after prolonged sleep called forth, as always, a burst of vital energy. The ship's crew, mostly young people, spent much of their free time in the gymnasium devising strenuous exercises and involved dances, or performing fantastic acrobatic feats in the antigravitational corner of the gymnasium. They loved to swim in the large pool filled with sparkling ionized water that retained the beautiful azure of the cradle of humanity, the Mediterranean Sea.

Kari Ram threw off his working clothes and was rushing toward the pool. A gay voice stopped him:

'Kari, I need your help! This turn just won't work out right.'

Taina Dan, a tall girl in a short tunic of sparkling green that matched her eyes, was the Tellur's chemist and the liveliest and youngest member of the crew. She had often upset Kari's composure by her impetuosity, but he loved dancing no less than she did. Taina was a born dancer. He walked up to her with a smile.

From the high diving board on the left, the ship's biologist, Afra Devi, called down a greeting. She was carefully tucking her mass of black hair into a bathing cap. Tey Eron went up to her, stepping carefully on the springy plastic board. She leaned back on his strong muscular arm, swaying in rhythm to the motion of the board. For a second both stood motionless, strong and confident, their smooth bronze skin gleaming with health. Quick as a flash the girl made a complete turn over Tey's arm and they both plunged into the water, intertwined as if in a dance.

'You've forgotten all about me!' Taina cried, covering Kari's eyes with her fingertips.

'It was beautiful, though, wasn't it?' Kari asked in reply. He drew the girl to him in the first steps of the dance as they entered the sound strip.

Kari and Taina were the best dancers on the ship. They alone were able to give themselves up completely to melody and rhythm, shutting out all other thoughts and sensations. Kari, swept into the world of the dance, felt nothing except the pleasure of light coordinated movement. The girl's hand lay firm and gentle on his shoulder. Her green eyes darkened.

'You're well-named,' Kari whispered. 'I keep remembering that in an ancient language Taina meant the unknown, the mysterious.'

'I'm glad,' the girl replied gravely. 'I thought there were no more mysteries left on earth. There certainly aren't any so far as people are concerned—we're all quite simple and predictable.'

'Do you regret it?'

'Sometimes. I would like to meet someone from the distant past. Someone who had to hide his dreams and emotions from the evil world around him, to temper them till they were as strong and unbending as steel.'

'Yes, I understand. Only I wasn't thinking about people, but about all the unsolved mysteries . . . Like those described in the ancient novels: mysterious ruins, unexplored depths, unscaled heights. And before that all the enchanted forests and springs, forbidden paths and haunted houses bewitched by demons and full of occult powers.'

'Yes, Kari! Wouldn't it be nice to find some hidden corner or secret passage right here on the Tellur?'

'Leading to hidden rooms which concealed . . .'

'What, Kari?'

'I don't know,' the engineer confessed and fell silent.

But Taina was caught up in the game. She tugged at his sleeve insistently, and Kari followed her out of the gym into a dimly lighted side passage. The vibration indicators blinked dully and in unison, as if the ship were fighting off sleep.

Taina took a few rapid, noiseless steps and stopped. A shadow of boredom flashed over her face so quickly that Kari could not have sworn that he had actually seen this sign of weakness. An unfamiliar emotion gripped him painfully, and he took Taina's hand again.

'Let's go to the library. I've got two hours before I have to go on duty.'

She followed him obediently.

As on all space ships the library, or general recreation room, was located directly behind the central control panel. Kari and Taina opened the hermetically sealed door of the third cross-hall and came to the double-doored elliptical hatch of the central passage. Kari's foot had barely touched the bronze plate when the heavy flaps parted soundlessly. The air inside was vibrant with sound. Excited, Taina clutched Kari's hand.

'It's Moot Ang!'

They slipped into the library. A diffuse light seemed to curl like mist under the dull ceiling. Two people were nestled deep in armchairs, half hidden in the shadows between the film cabinets. Taina recognized the doctor Svet Sim and the stocky figure of Yas Tin, the space-warp engineer. The latter's eyes were closed; he was dreaming about something. On the left, under the smooth accoustic shells, the Tellur's captain bent over the silvery case of the EMV.

The EMV, or electromagnetic violano, had long since replaced the harsh-toned, obsolete piano. The EMV combined the piano's complex polyphony and the rich tones of the violin. Sound amplifiers could lend the instrument amazing power.

Moot Ang didn't notice the newcomers. He bent forward a little, raising his face toward the rhombic panels of the ceiling. As in the ancient pianos, shadings of tone were produced by the musician's fingers, although not by striking hammer on string, but with very delicate electronic impulses of almost neutral fineness.

Harmonically interwoven themes of the unity of Earth and Cosmos began to flow and then to recede. The music boiled with contradictions of calm sorrow and cruel distant thunder which increased and then were interrupted by notes ringing like cries of despair. Suddenly the measured, melodious theme disappeared, shattered by an avalanche of dissonances slipping into a dark abyss of discordant mourning for irretrievable losses. Then, unexpectedly, clean, clear notes of transparent joy came to life under Moot Ang's fingers and melted into the quiet sadness of the accompaniment.

Afra Devi, in a white smock, slipped quietly into the library. Svet Sim, the ship's doctor, motioned to the captain. Moot Ang rose and quiet dissipated the spell of the music as the quick tropical night drives away the evening sun. The doctor and the captain went out, followed by the troubled glances of the others.

A very rare misfortune had befallen the second astronavigator on duty—an attack of acute appendicitis. He had evidently not carried out the program of medical preparation for the cosmic journey meticulously enough. Now Svet Sim was requesting the captain's permission to operate immediately.

Moot Ang expressed doubt. Modern medicine possessed methods for regulating the nerve impulses of the human organism, much as electronic impulses are regulated, and could eliminate many diseases. But the doctor insisted, arguing that this would not remove the locus of infection, and that the tremendous physiological strain of space flight might produce a new flare-up.

The astronavigator lay on a wide bed, enmeshed in the wires of the thirty-six electronic devices which followed the condition of his organism. In the darkened room the hypnotizing device blinked rhythmically. Svet Sim glanced at the apparatus and nodded to Afra Devi. She was also the doctor's assistant; each member of the Tellur's crew combined several professions.

Afra brought out a transparent cube filled with bluish liquid in which a segmented metal instrument resembling a large centipede lay immersed. She removed the instrument from the liquid and took from another vessel a conical plug with fine wire hoses attached to it. A slight tap on the clamp and the metal centipede began to move, buzzing faintly.

Svet Sim nodded and the apparatus disappeared into the open mouth of the astronavigator, who continued to breathe peacefully. A semitransparent screen placed at an angle over the patient's stomach began to glow. Moot Ang moved closer. The gray contours of the intestines and the segmented device moving slowly along them were clearly visible in the greenish light. The light flared up a little when the instrument hit an obstruction, the sphincter of the stomach, and entered the duodenum. Then it began to creep along the complicated convolutions of the small intestine and came to rest at the base of the vermiform appendix. Here in the area of inflammation the pain was stronger, and the pressure of the instrument so increased the involuntary contractions of the intestines that sedatives had to be administered.

In a few minutes the diagnostic machine revealed the cause and nature of the inflammation and recommended the necessary mixture of antibiotics and disinfectants. The segmented instrument released long flexible tendrils deep into the appendix. Puss and foreign matter were removed, and the appendix rinsed thoroughly with biological solutions which quickly healed the mucous membrane of the intestines and appendix.

The patient slept peacefully while the remarkable automatic device continued its work. The operation was over and it remained only for the doctor to remove the instrument.

The captain relaxed. However great the power of medicine, in rare cases unforeseen peculiarities of the organism produced unexpected complications, since it was impossible to determine in advance every possible deviation from normal among billions of individuals. Such complications presented no problems in the great medical institutes on Earth, but they could be dangerous on such a small expedition.

Nothing went wrong. Moot Ang returned to the violano in the

now empty library. The captain didn't feel like playing and was soon lost in reflections upon human happiness and the future of man.

This was his fourth trip into the Cosmos. But he had never before even thought of accomplishing such a distant leap across space and time. Seven hundred years! When new achievements and discoveries on Earth were accumulating at such speed, when the horizons of knowledge had already expanded so much. It was difficult now to imagine how little seven hundred years had meant in the epoch of ancient civilizations, when man's aspirations were limited to opening up and settling hitherto uninhabited areas of his own planet. In those ages time, and all human progress with it, flowed as slowly as the Arctic and Antarctic glaciers once had. Whole centuries had been swallowed up in a void of inactivity. What was one lifetime, or a century, or a thousand years, in those distant ages?

How would the peoples of the ancient world have reacted, Moot Ang thought almost with horror, if they could have known in advance how slow their social progress would be, if they could have known that oppression, injustice and chaos would rule their planet for so many more years to come? The passage of seven hundred years in ancient Egypt would only have produced still more brutal oppression in the same slave-owning society. In ancient China the seven hundred years would have begun and ended with the same wars, the same dynasties. In that time Europe would only have fallen from the beginning of the religious night of the Middle Ages into the bloody fires and savage reaction of the Inquisition.

But now the attempt to peer into a future crammed with all the changes, improvements and new knowledge of seven centuries staggered even the boldest imagination.

If real happiness consists in movement, change, progress, then who could be happier than he and his comrades? But it wasn't quite that simple. Human nature is two-sided, like the world which surrounds it and which gave it birth. Even while striving for eternal change, man is always sorry to lose the past, or rather what was good in it. He filters it through his memory and refines it into romantic legends about former golden ages.

Men could not help looking to the good of the past, or yearning for its restoration. Only strong spirits could face the future and foresee inevitable progress and the reorganization of human life. Regret for the past has been etched deep in man's soul, and he has mourned the irretrievably lost, and felt sadness before the ruins and monuments of humanity's past history. Older people, or the reflective and sensitive, especially know this longing for the past.

Moot Ang rose from his seat and stretched his powerful body.

All this had been vividly and fascinatingly described in historical novels. But what could frighten the young people aboard a space ship hurtling into the future? Loneliness, the loss of one's family? The terrible loneliness of a man projected into the future had often been described in the old novels, and it was always depicted as the loss of one's family. But this family was a mere handful of people, connected only by formal ties of blood. But now weren't all men brothers, hadn't the barriers and conventions separating men been destroyed on every corner of our planet?

Yes, Moot Ang thought, this is what he should tell the young people of his crew. We on the Tellur have lost all those dear to us on Earth. But out there in the future, people await us who are no less dear, people who will know more and feel more deeply than the contemporaries we have abandoned forever.

In the central control post Tey Eron had arranged things as he liked them. All unnecessary lights had been turned off, and the large round room seemed cozier in the half-gloom. Humming a simple ditty, he was busy checking and rechecking the calculations.

The ship had almost reached its destination, and today they would have to turn it toward Serpentarius in order to skirt the carbon star under investigation. It was dangerous to approach it too closely. The increasing radiation pressure could deliver a terrible and irreparable blow to a ship travelling at the Tellur's comparatively slow speed.

Sensing someone's presence behind him, Tey Eron turned around. Moot Ang was leaning over his assistant's shoulder, studying the summarized instrument readings in the lower row of little square windows. Tey Eron looked at him questioningly. The captain nodded. Obeying the almost imperceptible movement of the assistant's finger, signals sounded throughout the ship, followed by the familiar metallic words:

'Attention, all hands!'

Moot Ang raised the microphone to his lips, knowing that all over the ship the crew had stopped and turned involuntarily toward the concealed loudspeakers.

'Attention, all hands!' Moot Ang repeated. 'We will begin deceleration in fifteen minutes. All except those on duty should lie down in their cabins. The first phase of deceleration will be over at 18:00 hours, the second phase at 6g's will continue for one hundred forty-four hours. The ship will change course after Collision Danger signal. That is all!'

At 18:00 hours the captain rose from his seat and, fighting off the familiar pain of deceleration in his back and head, announced that he was going to sleep for the whole six days. The Tellur's entire crew sat glued to their instruments; this would be their last chance to observe the carbon star.

Tey Eron frowned at the departing captain's back. The capability and safety of cosmic ships had been improved tremendously, till there was no comparison with the flimsy shells floating on the Earth's seas which had first received the name ships. Nevertheless, this space ship was also little more than a shell in the bottomless depths of space, and it was somehow more reassuring when the captain remained on duty during a difficult maneuver.

Kari Ram started with surprise at the sound of Moot Ang's gay laugh. A few days ago the whole crew had been alarmed by news of the captain's sudden illness. Only the doctor was admitted to his cabin, and everyone involuntarily lowered his voice when passing the tightly closed door. Tey Eron had to carry out the whole maneuver, turning the ship, setting its new course to avoid the area of radiation pressure from the carbon star, and beginning the warp back toward the Sun.

The second in command was walking beside his captain and was smiling constrainedly. It turned out that the captain had cooked up a plot with the doctor, and had intentionally removed himself from command so as to give Tey Eron a chance to carry out the whole operation unassisted. Tey would have admitted to no one the cruel self-doubt that had plagued him before turning the ship about, but he did reproach the captain for alarming the crew unnecessarily.

Moot Ang defended his action with a laugh, and assured Tey that the ship had been perfectly safe in the great void of cosmic space. The instruments were infallible, the quadruple check of each calculation excluded the possibility of error. Belts of asteroids and meteorites could not exist in the area of strong radiation pressure from the carbon star.

'You really don't expect any more surprises?' Kari Ram inquired cautiously.

'Unforeseen accidents are possible, of course. But the great law of the Cosmos, the law of averages, is working in our favor. We can be sure that we'll meet nothing new here in this remote corner of the universe. We'll go back a short distance and go into warp in the direction from which we came, toward the Sun, past the Heart of the Serpent. We've been making toward Serpentarius for several days. It won't be long now!'

'It's strange: there's no joy, no feeling of a job well done, nothing to justify being dead to Earth for 700 years,' Kari said thoughtfully. 'Oh, I know we've made tens of thousands of observations, millions of calculations, photographs, memoranda. New secrets of matter will be uncovered back on Earth. But how intangible and insignificant it all seems! A seed of the future and nothing more!'

'How many battles, struggles, and deaths mankind has passed through—and endless numbers of animals before him on the blind path of evolution—for the sake of these "seeds" of the future!' Tey Eron objected angrily.

'That argument may satisfy the mind. But emotionally only man is important to me, the only rational force in the universe capable of conquering and utilizing the natural development of matter. But man is so alone, always alone! We have indisputable proofs of the existence of many inhabited worlds, but Earthmen have not so much as exchanged glances with other thinking beings. So many dreams, fairy tales, books, songs and pictures have predicted this great event, but still it doesn't happen. The great, brave, shining dream of humanity, born long ago when religious blindness was just being dispelled, hasn't come true.'

'Blindness!' Moot Ang broke in. 'Do you know how our recent ancestors in the first epoch of cosmic flight pictured the realization of this great dream? Military clashes, brutal annihilation of ships, mutual destruction at the first meeting.'

'Incredible!' Kari Ram and Tey Eron exclaimed with heat.

'Contemporary authors don't like to write about the gloomy period of the decline of capitalism,' Moot Ang continued. 'But you know from your school history that humanity at that time passed through a very critical point in its development.'

'Of course,' Kari said. 'When mankind already knew how to control matter and space, but when social relationships and the development of social consciousness lagged far behind the advances of science.'

'Exactly. You have a good memory, Kari. But let's put it another way: man's knowledge and conquest of space conflicted sharply with the primitive ideology of the individualistic property owner. For several years the health and future of humanity wavered on the scales of fate until the new humanity was united into one family in a classless society. In the capitalistic half of the world men could not visualize new solutions. They regarded their society as unshakable and eternal, and saw in the future only inevitable wars and self-annihilation.'

'And they called this a dream?' Kari sneered.

'They did.'

'Perhaps every civilization, wherever human life exists on the planets of other suns, has passed through such critical stages,' Tey Eron said slowly, throwing a fleeting glance at the upper instrument dials. 'We already know of two uninhabited planets with water and

117

an oxygen atmosphere where the winds sweep over dead sand and dead seas. Our ships have photographed . . .'

'No,' Kari Ram shook his head. 'I can't believe that people who already know the infinity of the cosmos and the power of science could . . .'

'. . . reason like animals who have just learned to think? But old societies came into being as a result of elemental forces, without the planning and foresight which distinguish higher forms of human society. Human reason was only in the initial stage of linear, mathematical logic evolved from direct observation of the laws of development of matter and nature. Once humanity had accumulated enough historical experience, and understood the historical development of the world around him, dialectical logic arose as the highest stage in the development of thought. Man began to understand the duality of natural phenomena and of his own life. He realized that, while his life as an individual was as insignificant and transitory as a drop in the ocean or a spark dying in the wind, it was at the same time immensely large, as large as the universe which his reason and emotions embraced in the infinity of time and space.'

The ship's captain fell silent and began to pace up and down in front of his assistants, deep in thought. A shadow of deep concentration lay on their young faces. Moot Ang was the first to break the silence:

'In my collection of book films there is one that is very characteristic for that period. The translation into Modern was not done by machine, but by Sania Chen, a historian who died in the last century. Let's read it.' He smiled at the crew's eager response, and went out to get the book.

'I'll never make a real captain,' Tey Eron sighed regretfully. 'I'll never know as much as Ang does.'

'And I've heard him say that he doesn't make a good captain because the range of his interests is too broad,' Kari replied from the navigator's seat.

Tey Eron looked at his colleague in surprise. They said nothing. The room was quiet except for the low persistent hum of the instruments. The enormous ship hurtled at full speed away from the carbon star toward a group of distant galaxies, four starry islands drowned in the infinite blackness of space. At such a distance they were invisible to the naked eye; only the sensitive instruments could pick up their few quanta of light.

Suddenly something happened. A shining point flashed and danced on the large locator screen. A piercing sound was heard, and the astronauts froze in breathless immobility.

Tey Eron automatically sounded the general alarm ordering all the crew members to their emergency posts.

Moot Ang rushed into the control room and in two strides was at the panel. The black mirror of the locator came to life. A tiny sharply defined ball of light floated in it as in a bottomless lake. The spot wavered up and down and crept slowly to the right. But the robots which gave warning of possible collisions with meteorites did not react. Could this mean that the dancing spot on the screen was not just a reflection of their own beam, but someone else's?

The space ship continued on its course. The spot of light now vibrated in the lower right quadrant of the screen. Conjecture made Moot Ang tremble, made Tey Eron bite his lips, made Kari Ram clutch the edge of the panel till his hand hurt. Something inconceivable was flying to meet them, casting far ahead of it the same kind of powerful locator beam as the Tellur's.

Desire that the conjecture prove right, that the involuntary surge of hope would not end in disillusionment as it had hundreds of times before, was so desperate that the captain was frozen into immobility, afraid to utter a word. And it seemed as though his alarm was communicated to the object hurtling toward them.

The shining point of light went off and on again, flashing at regularly decreasing intervals—four flashes, then two more in rapid succession. Such regularity could be attributed to only one force in the universe—human reason.

There was no longer any doubt; another space ship was coming toward them. Here in the measureless distances of space where no ship from Earth had ever been before it could only be a space ship from another world, the planet of another distant star.

The Tellur's locator beam also began to send out intermittent flashes as Kari Ram fed it signals of the conventional light code. It seemed completely outside the realm of possibility that these simple signals would produce the correct alternation of flashes on the screen of the unknown ship.

Moot Ang's voice on the ship's loudspeakers betrayed his excitement:

'Attention all hands! A strange ship is approaching. We will depart from our course and begin emergency deceleration. Stop all work! Emergency deceleration! To the landing stations!'

There wasn't a second to lose. If the ship coming to meet them was travelling at roughly the same speed as the Tellur, they were approaching each other almost at the speed of light. The locator showed that only a few seconds remained for the crew to take up their posts. Tey Eron whispered something to Kari while Moot Ang was speaking into the microphone. The youth, pale from strain, understood at once and began to manipulate the locator instruments.

'Splendid!' the captain exclaimed, watching the light ray on the control screen focus into an arrow, curve to port and then to starboard, weaving into a spiral.

Not more than ten seconds passed. On the screen a shining arrow of light curved to the right side of the black circle and at once wound itself into a spiral. A sigh, almost a moan, of relief broke simultaneously from the three men in the control room. The strangers flying to meet them from the mysterious depths of cosmic space had understood! And just in time!

The alarm signals rang. Now the solid hull of a space ship, not just a locator beam, was reflected on the main screen. Moving like lightning, Tey Eron switched off the robot pilot and himself turned the Tellur slightly to port. The ringing died away, and the black lake of the screen was empty once more. They caught a mere fleeting glimpse of a light streak flashing past the starboard scanner. The ships parted at incredible speed and hurtled off into the distance.

Several days would pass before they would come together again. Not a moment would be lost; both ships would decelerate, turn, and again approach the place of meeting on a course calculated by precise computers.

'Attention, all hands! We are beginning emergency deceleration! All stations signal readiness!' Moot Ang spoke into the microphone.

A row of green lights above the now dead engine indicators flashed in response. The ship's engines had stopped. The whole ship was taut with expectation. The captain glanced at the control panel and silently nodded toward the seats as he switched on the deceleration robot. The assistants saw Moot Ang frown at the program scale and turn the main switch to the figure 8.

It took but a few seconds for the captain to swallow a heart depressant pill, fling himself into a seat, and turn on the robot.

The ship seemed to brace itself against the emptiness of space and flung its crew into the depths of the hydraulic seats and into temporary unconsciousness, much as the horses of ancient times would stumble and fling their riders over their heads and onto the mercy of fate.

The crew was assembled in the Tellur's library. Only one man remained on duty at the control post. The Tellur had already turned, but was still more than ten billion kilometers from the place where the two ships had passed each other. The Tellur travelled slowly, at one-twentieth of absolute speed, while its computers ceaselessly checked and corrected the course, searching for an infinitesimal speck in the infinity of space. The almost unbearable suspense would continue for eight more days. If all the calculations and the ship's response kept within a reasonable margin of error, and if the strange ship's instruments were just as accurate as the Tellur's, they could expect to come within locator range of one another in that time.

Then, for the first time in all history, man would meet his brothers in thought, power, and aspirations, people from other planets whose existence had long been foreseen and proven by the restless, probing mind of man. The monstrous chasm of time and space separating inhabited worlds had till now remained unconquered. But now people from the Earth would clasp the hands of other thinking beings, and after that of new brothers from other distant stars. A chain of thought and labor would stretch across the abyss of space in a final victory over the elemental forces of nature.

For billions of years tiny clods of living slime had crawled in the dark warm waters of ocean gulfs, evolving after hundreds of billions of years into more complex beings that finally emerged onto dry land. Completely dependent on their environment, struggling bitterly for life and for the preservation of the species, after still more millions of centuries had passed these animals' brains had developed into powerful instruments equipping them for the search for food and the battle for survival.

The tempo of evolution increased constantly, the struggle for existence became fiercer, natural selection was accelerated. There were victims, victims, and more victims; herbivorous animals were devoured; predatory animals died from hunger; the weak, sick, the old perished; countless numbers were killed, battling for mates, defending their young, or swallowed up by natural disasters.

So it was throughout the whole blind course of evolution, until, in the rigorous conditions of the great ice age, some distant relative of the monkey replaced animal instinct with conscious labor in his search for food. Then, aided by the great power of collective effort and rational experience, he became man.

But then followed many thousands of years filled with wars and famine, suffering, oppression and ignorance. In spite of this, man never lost his hope for a better future.

The new generations did not betray that hope. The better future arrived. Humanity, united in a classless society, liberated itself from fear and oppression, reached unheard-of pinnacles of science and art. Even the most difficult thing, the conquest of space, turned out to be within man's powers.

And finally the whole painful ladder of human history, the full might of accumulated knowledge and incalculable labor, reached its culmination in the invention of the long-range space ship Tellur. Through the Tellur the heights of achievement on Earth would touch other heights from another corner of the universe, heights probably scaled by a no less long and difficult path.

In one form or another such thoughts occupied each member of the Tellur's crew. Conscious of the tremendous responsibility, even young Taina became serious. A mere handful out of all the billions of Earthmen—could they be worthy of representing all the Earth's exploits, labor, physical perfection, intelligence and perseverance? How could one prepare for the forthcoming meeting? Only by remembering all the great and bloody struggle of mankind for freedom of body and spirit!

Most important, exciting, and problematic was the question of what the strangers rushing toward them looked like. Would they be ugly or beautiful by human standards?

Afra Devi, the biologist, was the first to express her opinion. A young woman, made even more beautiful by nervous excitement, she kept looking at a picture above the door—a large panorama of Mount Ruwenzori in Equatorial Africa done in three-dimensional paints. The striking contrast of gloomy forest slopes and mountain peaks bathed in light seemed to reflect the play of her thoughts.

Afra said that the once widespread theory that thinking beings can be of any type and of the most varied structure had long since been rejected. Remnants of religious prejudice had forced even serious scientists to the unreasoning assumption that a thinking brain can develop in any body, just as men had formerly believed that gods could take on any physical form. Actually, the human form, the form of the only being on earth capable of rational thought, was by no means accidental. It corresponded to the high level of man's adaptiveness and to the physical demands made by the tremendous load of his brain and his extremely complex nervous system.

'Our understanding of human beauty and of beauty in general,' she said, 'is a product of thousands of years of unconscious acceptance of structural expediency, of forms best adapted to one activity or another. This is why we see beauty in machines, sea waves, trees, and horses, however different they are from the human form. Man, even while still in the animal stage, was liberated, thanks to the development of his brain, from the inevitability of narrow specialization and of adaptation to only one form of life, as is the case with most animals.

'Human legs are not adapted to constant running even on firm ground, but they enable man to cover long distances rapidly, and help him to climb trees and scale mountains. And the human hand is the most universal organ, making it possible for man to carry out millions of tasks. Indeed, it was the hand which transformed the primitive beast into a human being.

'In the very earliest stages of his development man evolved as a universal organism adapted to the most varied conditions. As social life began to develop, this many-sidedness became still greater, and so did man's activities. Man's beauty as compared with that of all other animals lies not only in his physical perfection, but also in his universality, augmented and refined by intellectual and spiritual activity.

'Thinking beings from another world, if they are capable of space travel, must also be highly perfected and universal, in other words, beautiful! There could be no such thing as thinking monsters, human mushrooms, or octopus-men. I don't know how these strangers will look in reality,' Afra concluded, 'whether they will be similar to us in form or have their own beauty, but I am certain that they will be beautiful!'

'It's a nice theory,' Tey Eron said, 'but . . .'

'I know,' Afra interrupted. 'Even the slightest departures from the normal can produce monsters, and here the probability of departure is very great. Slight changes in a human face—the absence of a nose, eyelids or lips—seem repulsive to us, but only because they are departures from the normal human form. The face of a horse or dog is very different from the human face, and yet we do not find it repulsive, but beautiful, because its form is a product of natural expediency. But on a disfigured face natural harmony has been destroyed.'

'You're saying that even if they look quite different from us, they may not seem ugly? What if they resemble us but have horns and a trunk?' Tey persisted.

'A thinking being doesn't need horns, and wouldn't have them. The nose might be drawn out like a trunk, although a trunk is also unnecessary for a creature with hands, and a human being must have hands. A trunk would be a chance phenomenon, not an obligatory condition of the structure of a thinking being. But everything that evolves as a product of natural selection becomes the rule, the median in a whole host of exceptions. Therein lies the beauty of expediency. No, I don't expect to see monsters with horns and tails, there would be no reason for them. Only the lower forms of life are very different from one another. The higher the forms, the more they resemble one another. Paleontology shows us what rigid limits evolution has set for higher organisms—remember the multitudes of different subclasses among the higher vertebrates, the marsupials and placentals, which are externally amazingly alike.'

'You win,' Tey Eron said and looked at the others with evident pride in Afra's logic.

Kari Ram suddenly began to object, blushing a little. He suggested that the strange beings, even if they were quite human in form and beauty, might be infinitely far from human in thought and in their view of life and of the world. And being so different, they might be cruel and terrible enemies.

Moot Ang came to Afra's defense.

'I've been thinking about this recently,' the captain said, 'and I am convinced that at the highest stage of development there cannot be any lack of understanding between thinking beings. Man's thought, his reason, reflects the laws of development of his surroundings and of the whole Cosmos. In this sense man is a microcosm. Thought follows laws of the universe which are the same everywhere. Wherever it appears, thought will inevitably be based on mathematical and dialectical logic. There cannot be any "others" with completely dissimilar thought processes, just as man cannot exist outside of society and nature.'

The enthusiastic response of his audience drowned out the captain.

'Aren't you getting somewhat carried away?' Moot Ang said, frowning.

'No,' Afra Devi contradicted boldly. 'It's always wonderful when the ideas of a whole group of people coincide. It proves that they are correct, and gives a feeling of support . . . especially if it is based on different branches of science.'

'You have in mind biology and the social sciences?' Yas Tin asked. Till now he had said nothing, curled up as usual in a comfortable corner of the sofa.

'Yes! The brightest point in the whole social history of man on Earth was the steady growth of mutual understanding which accompanied the growth of culture and the propagation of knowledge. The higher the cultural level, the easier it was for the different peoples and races of the classless society to understand one another, and the clearer became the common goals of human existence, the need to unite first a few countries, then the whole planet, all mankind. And now, with the level of development achieved on Earth and without doubt by those who are coming to meet us . . .' Afra fell silent.

'That's true,' Moot Ang agreed. 'Two different planets meeting in space should be able to understand one another far more easily than two savage peoples on the same planet.'

'What about the theory that war is inevitable, even in the Cosmos?' Kari Ram asked. 'Our ancestors were convinced of it and they had reached a rather high level of culture.'

'Where is that famous book you promised us?' Tey Eron reminded the captain. 'The one about the two space ships who wanted to destroy one another at their first meeting?'

The captain again set out for his room, and this time nothing stopped him. He returned with a little eight-pointed star of microfilm and placed it in the reading machine. The fantasy by an ancient American author fascinated all the astronauts.

The story, *First Contact,* described dramatically the meeting of a space ship from Earth with a ship from another planet in the nebula of Cancer, more than three thousand light years from the Sun.

The captain of the Earth ship ordered his crew to prepare all stellar maps, records, and course data for immediate destruction and to train all the antimeteorite guns at the strange ship. Then he began to wrestle with a weighty problem: did he have a right to try negotiating with the strange astronauts, or should he immediately attack the ship and destroy it? The captain was terribly afraid that the strangers might succeed in retracing their ship's course and might try to conquer the Earth.

The whole crew accepted the captain's wild fears as irrefutable truth. The meeting of two independent civilizations must, in the captain's opinion, inevitably lead to the subjugation of one, to the victory of the one possessing the stronger weapons. A meeting in space could mean either trade or war; no other alternative occurred to the author.

The Earthmen soon learned that the strangers were very similar to themselves, except that they could see only in infrared light and communicated by means of radio waves. Nevertheless, the Earth people immediately succeeded in deciphering the strangers' language and divining their thoughts. The views on social relations of the strange ship's captain turned out to be fully as primitive as those of the Earth people. He was racking his brain over the problem of how to get out of the situation alive, and was not even thinking about destroying the Earth ship.

This long-awaited event, the first meeting of representatives of different types of humanity, threatened to turn into a terrible disaster. For more than two weeks the ships hung in space about seven hundred miles apart while the astronauts carried on negotiations through a robot. Both captains assured one another of their peaceful intentions and at the same time affirmed their distrust of the other.

There would have been no way out of the situation had it not been for the story's hero, a young astrophysicist. Concealing bombs of terrific explosive powder under their clothing, he and the captain paid a visit to the strangers' ship. They presented an ultimatum: to exchange ships, with part of the crew of the strange space ship moving to the Earth ship, and part of the Earth ship's crew moving to the strangers' ship. As a preliminary all the antimeteorite guns of both ships were to be put out of commission. The boarding parties would learn how to operate the ships, and then all men and supplies would be exchanged. The two heroes with the bombs would remain on the strange ship and would blow it up immediately in case of any trick.

The captain of the strange ship accepted the ultimatum. The exchange of ships and their disarmament proceeded without a hitch. The strange space ship manned by Earthmen and the Earth ship manned by the strangers separated in great haste, vanishing into the feeble glow of the nebula.

A hum of voices filled the library. Even during the reading the young astronauts had shown signs of impatience and violent disagreement. Now they all started talking at once. Everyone addressed the captain, as if he were responsible for this ancient forgotten story.

Most of them pointed out the complete lack of correspondence between the time of action and the psychology of the characters. If a space ship could travel four thousand light years from Earth in just three months, then the time of the story's action would have to be later than the present. No one had yet reached such depths of the Cosmos. But the ideas and actions of the Earthmen were in no way different from those commonly held during the era of capitalism, many centuries ago.

There were also many purely technical mistakes, like the impossibly rapid deceleration of the space ships, and the strangers communicating with each other by radio waves. If, as the story indicated, the atmosphere of their planet had almost the same density as the Earth's, then the development of hearing similar to man's was inevitable, since it required incomparably less expenditure of energy than communication by radio waves or biocurrents. The rapid deciphering of the strangers' language with an accuracy permitting it to be coded into a translating machine was also highly improbable.

Tey Eron pointed out the impoverished description of outer space, a poverty all the more surprising since several decades before the story was written the great ancient scientist Tsiolkovsky had warned mankind that the Cosmos was far more complex than it was believed to be. Despite the work of the great dialecticians, some scientists still believed that the outer limits of knowledge had been reached.

Centuries passed. A multitude of discoveries endlessly complicated our conception of the mutual dependence of phenomena and seemed to set up a barrier against man's knowledge of the Cosmos. But science found an enormous number of circuitous paths for the solution of complicated technical problems. One example was the invention of the warp ship, which seemed to defy ordinary laws of motion. Indeed, the whole might of progress consisted in this conquest of the seeming dead ends of mathematical logic. But the author of 'First Contact' had no conception of the immense knowledge concealed behind the simple formulations of the great dialecticians of his time.

'There's another thing no one has mentioned,' the usually taciturn Yas Tin said suddenly. 'The story is written in English. All the names, nicknames and humorous expressions are English. That's very significant. Linguistics is my hobby, and I've studied the formation of the first world language. The English language was one of the most widespread in the past. The author mirrored an absurd faith in the immutability of the social structure of his time. The slow development of the ancient slave society, or of the epoch of feudalism, the long oppression of ancient peoples was taken as proof of the stability of all forms of social relationships, including language, religion, and the last of the primitive societies, capitalism. The dangerous lack of social equilibrium prevailing during the decline of capitalism was considered unchangeable. Yet the English language was archaic even then, because it was actually two languages, the written and the spoken, and was completely unsuitable for translating machines. It's surprising that the author ignored the fact that language changes faster and more drastically when human relationships are changing rapidly.

'The half-forgotten ancient Sanskrit language turned out to be much more logical and therefore became the basis for the intermediary language used in translating machines. Soon our first world language, which has undergone many subsequent changes, developed from that intermediary language. The western languages proved to be rather short-lived. Still less enduring were people's names borrowed from religious tradition and from completely alien, long-dead languages.'

'Yas Tin has pointed out the most important thing,' Moot Ang joined the conversation. 'This inertia, the stubborn defense of social forms which were inadequate even in the eyes of the author's contemporaries, is much stranger than the scientific or technical errors. Of course, except for a few cases of simple ignorance, this inertia was based on a selfish interest in preserving a social structure which permitted its champions to live far better than most people. So why would they concern themselves about humanity, about the fate of the planet or the health of its inhabitants?

'Senseless waste of minerals, fuel and forests, exhaustion of rivers and soil, dangerous experiments in building murderous atomic weapons—all this taken together determined the actions and world view of men committed, whatever happened, to preserving obsolete social institutions, generating untold suffering and fear for the majority of men. Here were born and developed the virulent concept of exclusive privilege, the fables about the superiority of one group, class, or race of people over others, the justification of violence and war—everything which in ancient times was called fascism.

'Any privileged group will inevitably impede progress, trying to maintain the status quo, while the victims of oppression will struggle against this impediment and against personal privilege. The stronger the pressure was of the privileged group, the stronger became the opposition, the more bitter the struggle and reciprocal cruelty. As a result the moral degradation of all men increased.

'Transfer this from the class struggle in one country to the struggle between privileged and oppressed countries. Remember from history the struggle between the new socialist and the old capitalist societies and you will understand the reason for the birth of the ideology of the inevitability of war and its eventual expansion into the Cosmos. I see in this the very heart of evil, a serpent which will bite however it may be hidden, because it cannot help biting. Remember how the star we passed burned with an evil reddish-yellow light . . .'

' "The Heart of the Serpent"!' Taina exclaimed.

'Yes, the Heart of the Serpent. And the heart of the literature defending the old society, propagandizing for the inevitability of war and of capitalism, is also the heart of a poisonous reptile.'

'Then our fears are also echoes of that ancient serpent's heart,' Kari said sadly. 'And I am probably the most reactionary of us all, because I still have fears, or doubts, or whatever you want to call them.'

'Kari!' Taina exclaimed reproachfully.

But Kari continued stubbornly:

'Our captain described the deadly crises of higher civilizations very well. We all know about planets where life was destroyed because the people on them could not cope with the dangers of war, could not build a new society conforming to the laws of science or quench forever the love of destruction, could not tear out this serpent's heart. We know that our own planet barely succeeded in avoiding such a fate. If the first socialist government had not appeared in Russia, initiating great changes in the life of the planet, fascism would have flourished and murderous nuclear wars with it. But what if they,' the young astronavigator pointed in the direction from which the strange space ship was expected, 'what if they have not yet passed this dangerous peak?'

'That's out of the question, Kari,' Moot Ang answered calmly. 'A certain analogy can be drawn between the evolution of the higher forms of life and the higher forms of society. Man could evolve only under comparatively stable and favorable conditions existing for a long time. This doesn't mean there were no changes. On the contrary, there were drastic changes, but only within the relationships of man, not of nature as a whole. Cataclysms, great shocks and changes would have prevented the development of higher reasoning beings. Even the highest form of society, one which could conquer the infinite depths of space, could do this only after the conditions of life on the entire planet had been stabilized, and, of course, after the catastrophic wars of capitalism were eliminated. No, these strangers who are coming to meet us have also passed the critical point, have also known suffering and death, and have finally built a truly rational society.'

'It seems to me there is a kind of elemental wisdom in the histories of the civilizations of the different planets,' Tey Eron said, his eyes shining. 'Man could not conquer space until he had achieved a higher stage of life without war, where each man had a high sense of responsibility for all his fellow men.'

'Having reached the highest level of development—the communist society—man was able to conquer space, and there was no other way he could have done it!' Kari exclaimed. 'And this applies to any other human race, if we can use this name for all the highest forms of organized, thinking life.'

'We and our ships are the hands of Earth stretched out to the stars,' Moot Ang said seriously. 'And these hands are clean! But this cannot be true only of us. Soon we will touch hands just as clean and powerful!'

The younger crew members could not restrain themselves, and greeted the captain's last words with shouts of triumph. Even the older, more reserved astronauts surrounding Moot Ang were visibly agitated.

Somewhere far ahead a ship from the planet of a strange and distant star was flying to meet them. For the first time in the Earth's long history, her people would come into contact with people from another world. It was therefore not surprising that the astronauts, however they tried to restrain themselves, gave way to feverish excitement. To rest, to remain alone with their burning suspense, seemed out of the question. But Moot Ang, calculating the time it would take for the ships to meet, ordered Svet Sim to issue sedatives to everyone.

'We must meet our brothers in perfect mental and physical condition,' he answered the protests firmly. 'We have an enormous job ahead of us. We will have to find a way of understanding them and of making ourselves understood. To exchange our knowledge for theirs.' He frowned. 'I have never before been so aware of my inadequacy and incompetence.' A worried look had replaced the captain's ordinarily calm expression, the fingers of his clenched fists whitened.

The astronauts, perhaps for the first time, felt the whole weight of the tremendous responsibility which the unprecedented meeting placed on each of them. They swallowed the pills submissively and went to their cabins.

Moot Ang intended to keep only Kari on duty with him. But he glanced at Tey Eron's powerful figure and, changing his mind, beckoned him also to remain in the control room.

The captain stretched out in his chair with a weary sigh, bent his head and covered his eyes with his hands. Tey and Kari kept silent, afraid of disturbing the captain's thought.

The ship was travelling very slowly, at the so-called tangential velocity used on entry into the Roche zone of any heavenly body. The robots piloting the ship held it on a carefully calculated course. It was time for the locator beam of the strange ship to appear. But the screen remained blank and Tey Eron became more and more disturbed.

Moot Ang straightened up with that cheerful but rather sad smile so familiar to the crew members.

'Come, distant friend, to the cherished threshold.'

Staring into the impenetrable blackness of the forward screen, Tey frowned. The captain's song seemed to him out of place at such a serious moment. But Kari took up the refrain still more gaily, glancing slyly at the gloomy second in command.

'Try a sweep with our beam, Kari,' Moot Ang said suddenly, breaking off his song. 'Two degrees on each side and two up and down.'

Tey blushed slightly. He had been mentally reproaching the captain, and had himself overlooked this obvious step.

Two more hours passed. Kari visualized their locator beam, a tremendous distance ahead, sweeping now to the left, now to the right, up and down, covering hundreds of thousands of kilometers of black void. Such tremendous sweeps exceeded even the wildest fancies of the ancient stories about giants on Earth.

Tey Eron was deep in a contemplative stupor. His thoughts flowed slowly and without emotion. He remembered the strange feeling of detachment which had not left him since the take-off from Earth. In primitive times this feeling was probably inherent to man. A feeling of being completely unattached to anything, free of all obligations or worries about the future. Probably such feelings had cropped up in times of great misfortune, war, social upheaval. For Tey Eron the past, everything left behind on Earth, had departed forever, irretrievably lost. An abyss of hundreds of years separated him from a new and completely unknown future. Consequently he had no plans, feelings or desires for the future, save to bring back to Earth the new knowledge wrested from the depths of the Cosmos. And suddenly something had happened which changed all that.

Moot Ang spent the time thinking about the ship coming to meet them. He tried to picture the strangers as being very similar to Earth people, but soon became convinced that it was easier to visualize them as weird improbable figures than to submit his fantasy to the rigid framework of biological law which Afra Devi had discussed so convincingly.

Without raising his head, Moot Ang felt the sudden tension of his comrades and knew that a signal had appeared on the locator screen. He didn't see it; the point of light traced on the black shining disc disappeared too quickly. The signal bell tinkled faintly.

The astronauts leaped up and bent over the control panel, instinctively trying to get closer to the screen. However fleeting the shining dot had been, it signified a great deal. The strange space ship had not hidden itself in the depths of space, but had turned to meet them. It was being piloted no less skilfully than their own; the strangers had been able to calculate the return course accurately and quickly and were now groping for the Tellur with their locator beam.

Two incredibly small particles lost in immense darkness were searching for one another. At the same time these small particles were two enormous worlds full of power and knowledge. Kari moved the beam of the chief locator from 1488 to 375, then still farther down the scale. The point of light returned, disappeared, and flared up again in the black mirror, accompanied by a sound signal which died immediately.

Moot Ang seized the locator verniers and traced a spiral from the periphery to the center of a huge circle in the area from which the space ship was approaching.

The strangers apparently repeated the maneuver. After long effort the point of light settled within the limits of the third circle on the black screen, wavering slightly due to the vibrations of both ships. The bell rang constantly; they had to mute it. There was no doubt that the Tellur's beam had also been picked up by the other ship. The ships were approaching each other at a rate not lower than four hundred thousand kilometers per hour.

Tey Eron read the computer calculations. The ships were about three million kilometers apart; at present speed they would meet in seven hours. In an hour they could begin integral deceleration, which would delay the meeting by a few more hours, provided the strange ship decelerated at a similar rate. The strangers might stop faster, or they might have to pass each other again, which would mean another delay. Should that happen, the suspense would be almost unbearable.

But the strange ship caused no extra delay. It started decelerating faster than the Tellur and then, having determined the latter's rate, adjusted its speed accordingly. The ships drew closer and closer together. The Tellur's crew again gathered in the central control room, watching how the pinpoint of light in the black mirror slowly grew in size. This was the Tellur's own beam, reflected back to the ship from the strange space craft. The spot took on the shape of a tiny cylinder with a thick ring in the middle. The ship didn't even faintly resemble the Tellur. At closer range, dome-shaped thickenings were visible at both ends of the cylinder.

The shining contours spread out until they covered the entire diameter of the black screen.

'Attention, all hands! To your stations! Final deceleration at 8g's.'

The hydraulic seats strained against their supports, blood rushed to the eyes of the crew members, thick sweat broke out on their faces. The Tellur stopped and hung motionless in a void having neither top nor bottom nor sides, in glacial cosmic darkness, three hundred thirty light years from its own yellow Sun.

As soon as they had recovered from the deceleration, the astronauts switched on the direct scanner and a gigantic searchlight. But they saw nothing except a bright fog forward and to port. The searchlight went out and a strong blue light completely blinded the men watching the screen.

'Polarizer grid at 35 degrees. Light filter!' Moot Ang ordered.

'620 wave-length?' Tey Eron asked.

'Yes.'

The blue light was replaced by a powerful orange stream of light which pierced the darkness, turned, caught the edge of a solid structure, and finally lit up the strange ship.

It was only a few kilometers away, a fact which reflected credit on both the Earthmen and the strange astronauts. But from that distance it was still difficult to determine the exact dimensions of the space ship. Suddenly a thick beam of orange light of the same wave length as the Tellur's shot upward from the other ship. The beam disappeared, then reappeared and continued to stand vertical, rising toward an unfamiliar constellation at the edge of the Milky Way.

Moot Ang rubbed his forehead as he always did in moments of intense thought.

'Must be a signal,' Tey Eron said cautiously.

'No doubt about it. I would interpret it this way: the motionless column of light means "Stay where you are, we'll come up alongside you." Let's try answering.'

The Earth craft switched its filter to a wave length of 430 and directed a blue beam toward its stern. The pillar of orange light on the strange ship went out at once.

The astronauts waited, scarcely breathing. The strange ship resembled a spool—two cones united by a cylinder. The base of one of the cones, apparently the forward one, was covered by a dome. A broad funnel on the rear cone opened out into space. In the middle of the ship a wide band of indefinite outline glowed faintly. The contours of the cylinder uniting the cones were visible through the translucent band. Suddenly the band became thick and opaque, whirling around the middle of the ship like the wheel of a turbine. The strange ship grew bigger on the scanning screens; after a few seconds it filled the whole field of view. The Earthmen realized that the ship was much larger than the Tellur.

'Afra, Yas and Kari! I want you on the observation platform with me! Tey will remain at the controls. Switch on the planetary illuminator and the port landing lights!' the captain ordered tersely.

In feverish haste the astronauts put on light space suits used for planetary exploration and for leaving the ship in outer space at safe distances from lethal stellar radiation.

Moot Ang examined everyone critically, checked his own space suit, and switched on the pumps to evacuate the air lock. When the vacuum indicator reached green he turned three handles in rapid succession. The armor plates and insulating sheets moved aside noiselessly, and the round exit hatch flew open. Hydraulic pillars raised the floor of the observation chamber. The astronauts stood four meters above the nose of the Tellur on the round observation platform.

The strange space ship girded with a belt of blue fire was pure white in color. It did not have a mirrored metallic surface designed to reflect all types of cosmic radiation, as did the Tellur, but glistened with the clear whiteness of mountain snow. Only the central ring continued to emit a weak blue light.

The giant hulk of the ship had drawn visibly nearer the Tellur. In cosmic space, far from any gravitational field, the two ships attracted each other, proving that the ship from an unknown world was not made of antimatter.

The Tellur let out from its port side gigantic mooring struts resembling telescoping tubes. The ends of the struts were fitted with cushions of resilient plastic with a protective layer to safeguard the ship from possible contact with antimatter.

The dome-shaped nose of the strange ship was slashed on top by a black gap resembling a mouth opened in an insolent sneer. A balcony enclosed by thin close-set pillars emerged from this gap. Something white moved in the black opening. Afra groaned in disappointment.

Five dead-white, extraordinarily broad figures appeared on the projecting balcony. Roughly the same height as people on Earth, they were much wider, with a ridge of comb-shaped projections down their backs. Instead of the round transparent helmets of the Earthmen, the strangers wore something resembling large sea shells with the concave side facing out. In front large thorns spread out like a fan, forming a kind of awning above coverings which gleamed like black glass.

The first white figure made a sharp gesture from which it became clear that the strangers had two arms and two legs.

The white ship turned its nose toward the side of the Earth ship and extended a telescoping framework of red metal more than 20 meters toward the Tellur. The ships came together with a gentle bump. But there was no blinding lightning of atomic disintegration as the contact was made: the two ships were made of identical matter.

The astronauts on the Tellur's observation platform heard the captain's quiet satisfied laugh in their helmet telephones. They looked at each other in perplexity.

'I just want to assure everyone, and especially Afra,' Moot Ang said, 'that we look just as strange to them! Inflated dummies with jointed extremities and huge round heads, three-fourths empty!'

Afra burst out laughing.

'It's all a matter of what's inside the space suits. The outside isn't important.'

'They have the same number of arms and legs we do,' Kari began.

Suddenly a pleated white covering stretched over the metal framework projected by the white ship, extending out to the Tellur like an empty sleeve. The first figure on the platform, whom Moot Ang by instinct recognized as the captain, began to make unmistakable gestures of invitation, stretching out his arms toward the Tellur and then pressing them to his chest.

The Tellur's crew lost no time in moving the connecting gallery used for communication between ships in space out from the lower part of the hull. But the Tellur's gallery was circular, that of the white ship elliptical. The Tellur's technicians quickly prepared a frame of soft wood which immediately changed its molecular structure and became harder than steel in the cold of outer space.

During this time a cube of red metal with a black front screen appeared on the balcony of the strange ship. Two white figures bent over it, straightened and retreated. The likeness of a human figure appeared on the screen, its upper part expanding and contracting rhythmically. Small white arrows rushed inside the figure and then flew out again.

'Ingenious!' Afra exclaimed. 'That signifies respiration. They're going to show us the composition of their atmosphere. But how?'

As if in answer to her question the respiring model on the screen disappeared, and was at once replaced by another figure—a black spot in a grayish ring-shaped cloud, obviously the nucleus of an atom surrounded by fine orbits of shining electrons. Moot Ang felt his throat tighten; he couldn't have uttered a word. There were four figures on the screen: two in the center, one under the other, connected by a thick white line, and two more on the side connected by black arrows.

Their hearts pounding, the Earthmen counted the electrons. The lower figure, apparently the basic element of their ocean, had one electron around the nucleus—hydrogen. The upper figure, the principal element of their atmosphere and consequently of their respiration, had nine electrons around the nucleus—fluorine!

'Oh, no!' Afra Devi screamed in despair. 'Fluorine!'

'Keep counting!' the captain snapped. 'The one on the upper left has six electrons—carbon; on the right, seven—that means nitrogen. That's clear enough. Give the order to prepare a similar table showing our atmosphere and metabolism. Everything will be the same except that we'll have oxygen, with eight electrons, in the upper middle figure instead of fluorine. What a shame, what a damned shame!'

When the Earthmen projected their table the astronauts saw the first white figure on the balcony of the strange ship stagger and raise a hand to his space helmet in a gesture which made it clear to the Earthmen that he was even more disappointed than they.

This same white figure bent over the railing of the observation platform and made a sharp sweeping motion with his arm, as if he were cleaving something in space. The thorny projections of his helmet bent menacingly toward the Tellur, which stood several meters below the white ship. Then the strangers' captain raised both his arms and brought them down some distance apart, as if he were trying to depict two parallel planes.

Moot Ang repeated the gesture. Then the captain of the strange ship raised one arm high in a gesture of silent greeting, turned, and disappeared into the black mouth. The others followed him.

'We'd better go down too,' Moot Ang said, pushing the descent lever.

Afra had no more than a fleeting glimpse of the magnificent sparkling stars in the black void of space, a sight which always produced in her a peculiar pensive joy. The hatch closed, the light in the air lock flashed on. The pumps hissed faintly, the first indication that the air pressure had returned to normal.

'Shall we build a partition to connect the galleries?' Yas Tin asked the captain as soon as he had removed his helmet.

'Yes. That's what their captain was trying to say. It's a real tragedy: their fluorine atmosphere is deadly poison to us. Oxygen would be just as poisonous for them. Many of our materials, paints and metals which are stable in an atmosphere of oxygen would be destroyed on contact with their breath. Instead of water they have liquid hydrogen fluoride, that same hydrofluoric acid which dissolves glass and attacks almost all silicon-containing minerals. We'll have to set up a transparent partition resistant to oxygen and they'll set up one made of some substance stable against fluorine. Well, let's go, we must hurry. We'll talk it over while we're building the partition.'

The dull-blue floor of the quenching chamber which separated the living quarters from the Tellur's engines was converted into a chemical workshop. A thick sheet of crystal clear plastic was moulded from materials already prepared on Earth, cemented, and left to set.

The white ship showed no sign of life, although it was kept under constant observation in the scanning screens.

The Tellur's library was a beehive of activity. All the crew members were selecting stereofilms and magnetic photo-records of the Earth, and reproductions of its finest works of art. Diagrams and sketches of mathematical functions, schemes showing the crystal structure of the most widely distributed materials on the Earth's crust, on other planets, and on the Sun were being prepared hurriedly. The large stereo screen was adjusted, and the overtone sound unit which reproduced the human voice exactly was enclosed in a fluorine-resistant cover.

During short breaks for food and rest the astronauts discussed the unusual atmosphere of the planet from which their fellow space travellers had come. The unknown planet's cyclical metabolic processes, which made life possible by storing energy radiated by its sun, would necessarily have to follow the same general scheme as that on Earth. A free active gas, whether it was oxygen, fluorine, or something else, could accumulate in the atmosphere only through the metabolic activity of plants; animal life, including human life, then utilized the oxygen or fluorine and combined it with carbon, the basic element of all plant and animal bodies.

The strange planet must have hydrofluoric acid oceans. Splitting hydrogen fluoride with the help of the sun's radiant energy, just as we on earth split water, the plants of the strange planet would store carbohydrates and give off free fluorine. People and animals breathed a mixture of fluorine and nitrogen, getting their energy from the combustion of carbohydrates in fluorine, and exhaling carbon tetrafluoride and hydrogen fluoride.

This type of metabolism would give one and a half times more energy than the Earth's oxygen-based metabolism, and it was therefore not surprising that the planet had developed the highest forms of life. But the greater activity of fluorine in comparison with oxygen would also demand stronger solar radiation. To split a molecule of hydrogen fluoride in the photosynthesis of plants, the yellow-green rays used to split water would be ineffective; it would require the more powerful blue and violet rays. Evidently the energy source of the unknown planet must be a very hot blue star.

'There's a contradiction there,' Tey Eron broke in, returning from the shop. 'Hydrogen fluoride is very volatile.'

'Yes, it boils at plus 20 degrees,' Kari answered, checking a manual.

'What's the freezing point?'

'Minus 80.'

'In other words their planet would have to be rather cold. That doesn't jibe with a hot blue star.'

'Why not?' Yas Tin objected. 'It could be some distance from the star. The oceans may lie in the temperate or polar zones. Or . . .'

'Undoubtedly there are many possible explanations,' Moot Ang said. 'Whatever they are, the fact is that a ship from a fluorine planet is right here before us, and we will soon learn all the details of its life. What is more important to understand right now is the fact that fluorine is very rare in the universe. Although recent research has moved it up from fortieth to eighteenth place in terms of total number of atoms, oxygen occupies third place in the universe, after hydrogen and helium and followed by nitrogen and carbon. Or, using another system of calculations, oxygen is two hundred thousand times more prevalent than fluorine. This can only mean that there are very few planets in the universe that are rich in fluorine, and the number with vegetation which could release free fluorine into the atmosphere must be infinitesimal.'

'Now I understand their captain's gesture of despair,' Afra Devi said thoughtfully. 'They are searching for men like themselves, and their disappointment was very great.'

'If it was very great that means they have been searching for a long time, and have already encountered other thinking beings.'

'And they were oxygen-breathing beings like ourselves,' Afra rejoined.

'But there may be other types of atmosphere,' Tey Eron objected. 'Chlorine, for example, or sulfur, or even hydrogen sulfide.'

'They wouldn't be able to support the highest forms of life!' Afra exclaimed. 'Their metabolism would only give from a third to a tenth as much energy as oxygen.'

'Not sulfur,' Yas Tin grumbled. 'It's energy is equal to that of oxygen.'

'You are presupposing an atmosphere of sulfuric anhydride and an ocean of liquid sulfur?' Moot Ang asked. The engineer nodded in assent.

'But in that case sulfur would replace not oxygen, but hydrogen,' Afra frowned. 'And hydrogen is the most widely distributed element in the universe. Sulfur is so rare that it could hardly replace hydrogen. Such an atmosphere would be even rarer than a fluorine atmosphere.'

'And could only exist on very warm planets,' Tey answered, leafing through the manual. 'An ocean of sulfur would be liquid only at temperatures from 100 to 400 degrees.'

'I think Afra is right,' the captain interjected. 'All these hypothetical atmospheres are too rare compared with our standard atmosphere made up of the most common elements in the universe. The composition of our atmosphere is no chance phenomenon.'

'Of course not,' Yas Tin agreed. 'But there could be many chance phenomena in the infinity of the Cosmos. Let's take our "standard" Earth. She and her neighbors, the Moon, Mars and Venus, all contain large quantities of aluminium, which is in general quite rare in the universe.'

'Nonetheless, to find repetitions of such rare phenomena in the infinity of space could take tens, hundreds, or thousands of years,' Moot Ang said gloomily. 'Even with warp ships. If they have been searching for a long time, I understand how they must feel.'

'It's a good thing our atmosphere is composed of the commonest elements of the universe, and that we can expect to find a great many planets like ours,' Afra said.

'And yet the first people we met were not the least bit like us,' Tey retorted.

Afra was getting ready to object heatedly when the ship's chemist came in to announce that the transparent screen was ready.

'But can't we just board their ship in space suits?' Yas Tin asked.

'We can, just as they can visit ours. There will probably be many such exchanges of visits, but we'll first get acquainted from a distance,' the captain answered.

The astronauts mounted their transparent wall at the end of the connecting sleeve, and the white figures on the other ship began to set one up in their gallery. Then the Earthmen and the strangers met in space, helping one another to buttress the connecting frame. Pats on the sleeve or shoulder were exchanged in easily recognizable gestures of friendship.

Shaking the horny projections on their head shells, the strangers tried to peer through the smoky helmets at the Earthmen whose faces were fairly visible. The slightly convex front shields under the thorny awning of the strangers' helmets completely concealed their features. But instinct told the Earthmen that the attentive eyes examining them were curious and friendly.

When invited to board the Tellur, the white figures answered with gestures of refusal. One of them touched his space suit and then quickly flung up his arms as if he were scattering something.

'They're afraid their space suits will disintegrate in oxygen,' Tey guessed.

'No. They want, just as we do, to meet in the gallery first,' Moot Ang said.

The two space ships, now joined together, hung motionless in the infinity of space. The Tellur switched on its powerful heaters so that its crew could enter the uniting gallery in ordinary work-clothes—close-fitting blue overalls of synthetic wool.

On the other side of the gallery a blue light sparkled like the sunlit mountaintops of Earth. With the difference in lighting on the two sides of the transparent partition it looked aquamarine, as if it were made of clear solidified seawater.

The silence was broken only by the quickened breathing of the excited Earthmen. Tey Eron brushed against Afra's shoulder and felt the young woman trembling. He embraced her firmly and she answered with a quick, grateful glance.

A group of eight strangers appeared in the connecting gallery. Strangers? The Earthmen couldn't believe their eyes. Deep in his soul each one had expected something extraordinary, unheard-of. The close resemblance of the strangers to Earth people seemed miraculous. But this was only at first glance. The longer the Earthmen examined the strangers, the more differences they found in the parts of the body not concealed by their clothing.

The blue light went out and terrestrial lighting was switched on. The transparent partition lost its green tint and became almost colorless. Human beings were standing behind this almost invisible wall! Was it really possible that they breathed a gas lethal to the Earthmen, and bathed in corrosive hydrofluoric acid? Their physical proportions were normal; their height corresponded to the average height of Earthmen. Their skin was a strange iron-gray color with a silvery sheen and an inner blood-red gleam like polished hematite.

The round heads were overgrown with thick, pitch-black hair. But the most remarkable feature was their eyes. Incredibly large and long, with sharply slanting lids rising toward the temples at the outer corners, they took up the whole width of the face, and were set higher in the head than the eyes of Earthmen. The whites were deep turquoise in color and seemed disproportionately long in relation to the black iris and pupil.

Straight, fine black brows grew into the hair high over the temples and almost met over the narrow bridge of the nose, forming a wide angle. The hair dropped from the center of the forehead toward the temples in a clean straight line in perfect symmetry with the brows, giving the forehead the shape of a horizontally drawn-out diamond. The short blunt nose had nostrils opening downward like the Earthmen. The small mouth with purple lips revealed rows of straight teeth of the same pure turquoise as the whites of the eyes. Below the eyes the face narrowed sharply into an angular chin, making the upper half of the face seem very broad. The structure of the ears remained a mystery—they were covered by headbands of gold braid.

The strangers were of both sexes. The women had long graceful necks, softer facial features, and luxuriant masses of hair cut short. The men were taller and broader, with wider chins. The differences between them were in general the same as those between men and women on Earth.

It seemed to Afra that they had only four fingers on each hand, and the fingers didn't seem to have joints, since they bent freely without forming angles.

They couldn't see the strangers' feet because they sank deep into the soft floor covering. In terrestrial light the clothing, short wide jackets and long loose trousers much like the ancient clothing once worn on Earth, seemed dark red, almost the color of bricks.

As the astronauts continued to look, the faces of the newcomers from the fluorine planet began to seem less odd. More than that, the unique exotic beauty of the strangers came through to the people from Earth. Their charm lay mostly in the enormous alert eyes, which radiated warm intelligence and friendliness.

'What eyes!' Afra couldn't help exclaiming. 'It's easier to become human with eyes like that than with ours.'

'Why is that?' Tey whispered.

'The larger the eye, the greater the number of rods and cones in the retina, the more details from the surrounding world it can assimilate.'

Tey nodded his understanding.

One of the strangers stepped forward and made a gesture of invitation. Immediately the terrestrial lighting on their side of the gallery went out.

'I didn't think of that!' Moot Ang groaned.

'I did,' Kari retorted calmly. He switched off the normal lighting and turned on two powerful lamps with 430 filters.

'We'll look like corpses,' Taina complained.

'Don't worry,' Moot Ang said. 'Their spectrum of maximum visibility extends far into the violet region, maybe even into the ultraviolet. This should mean that they see many more shades and much warmer tones than we do, but I can't imagine what they're like.'

'We'll probably seem much yellower to them than we really are,' Tey said **thoughtfully.**

'That's a lot better than blue corpses. Just look at us!' Taina persisted.

The Earthmen took several photographs and pushed the osmium-crystal overtone loudspeaker through a small airlock. The strangers set it up on a tripod. Kari directed a narrow band of radio waves at the cup-shaped antenna, and the speech and music of Earth pealed forth in the space ship's fluorine atmosphere. A device for determining the temperature, pressure and composition of the atmosphere of the unknown planet was passed through in the same way. As might have been expected, the internal temperature of the white space ship was lower than that of the Earth ship, no higher than seven degrees. The atmospheric pressure was greater than on Earth, and the force of gravity practically the same.

'Their body temperature is probably higher,' Afra said, 'just as ours is higher than the average atmospheric temperature. It should be about 14 degrees.'

The strangers passed their own instruments through, encased in two little mesh containers that gave no hint as to their function.

One of the containers emitted high intermittent clear sounds that seemed to vanish into the distance. From this the Earthmen realized that the strangers heard notes of higher frequency than they did. If their hearing range was roughly the same as that of Earthmen, part of the low notes of human speech and music must have been lost to the inhabitants of the fluorine planet.

The strangers again turned on the terrestrial lighting and the Earthmen switched off the blue light. Two of the strangers, a man and a woman, approached the transparent wall. They calmly threw off their dark-red clothing and stood motionless, hand in hand. Then they began to turn slowly, showing the Earthmen their bodies, which were even more similar to those of the people of Earth than their faces. The harmonious proportions of the figures were in complete accordance with the Earth's concepts of beauty. The somewhat more angular lines and sharper transitions between the various parts of the body produced a clean sculptured effect that was enhanced by the gray color and darker shadows of the skin.

Their heads sat proudly on long necks. The man's broad shoulders, the shoulders of a worker and fighter, and the broad hips of the woman, the child-bearer, took away nothing from the impression of intellectual power of these envoys from an unknown planet.

When the strangers retreated with the familiar gesture of invitation, and extinguished the yellow terrestrial light, the Earth people didn't hesitate. At the captain's request, Tey Eron and Afra Devi stood hand in hand before the transparent partition.

Despite the weird lighting, which gave their bodies the cold tint of blue marble, the astronauts gasped in admiration at the naked beauty of their comrades. Even the strangers understood it. Dimly visible in the unlighted gallery, they exchanged glances among themselves and made short incomprehensible gestures. Afra and Tey stood free and proud, electric with tension.

The strangers finally finished photographing and turned on their own lights.

'Now I have no doubt that they know what love is,' Taina said. 'Real, beautiful, warm human love. Their men and women are so beautiful and so intelligent!'

'You're quite right, Taina, and this is all the more wonderful, since it means they will understand us in everything,' Moot Ang answered.

'Yes! Look at Kari! Kari, don't fall in love with a girl from the fluorine planet. That would be a real tragedy.'

The astronavigator came out of his trance and reluctantly tore his eyes from the inhabitants of the white space ship.

'I could,' he smiled sadly. 'I really could, in spite of all the differences in our bodies and the monstrous distances separating our planets. Now I understand the power of human love.' The young man turned back toward the smiling face of the woman from the strange planet.

Now the strangers pushed forward a green screen. Small figures began to move in procession on it, carrying heavy objects up a steep incline. On reaching the flat top of the incline, each figure dropped his burden and fell face downward. Like a terrestrial animated cartoon, the picture conveyed the idea of weariness and a desire to rest. The Earthmen too were exhausted from the many hours of tense anticipation and from the first impressions of the meeting.

The inhabitants of the fluorine planet had apparently expected to meet other people, and had prepared for it by making such pantomime films. Although the Tellur's crew had not been prepared for the meeting, a way out of the difficulty was found. They moved a drawing screen up to the partition and the Tellur's artist, Yas Tin, began to sketch a series of pictures. First he portrayed the same tired figures, then he drew one large face with such an obviously inquiring expression that the strangers became as animated as they had at the appearance of Tey Eron and Afra Devi. Then the artist depicted the Earth circling the Sun and divided the orbit into twenty-four parts, blackening half of them.

The strangers quickly responded with a similar scheme. On both sides metronomes helped to determine the duration of the units of time. The Earthmen learned that the fluorine planet made a complete revolution around its axis in fourteen terrestrial hours, and circled its blue sun in nine hundred days. The break for rest which the strangers suggested equalled five terrestrial hours.

Still stunned by their experiences, the Earthmen left the connecting gallery. The lights in both galleries went out; even the external illumination of the ships was extinguished. The two space ships hung side by side, dark and motionless, as if everything alive in them had perished, turned to ice in the monstrous cold and deep gloom of outer space.

But inside the ships fervent, energetic life went on. The inexhaustibly inventive human brain was seeking new means of transmitting the knowledge and aspirations of thousands of years of labor, danger, and suffering to their brothers in thought from the planet of a distant star. This knowledge had first liberated man from the power of ruthless nature, then from savage and arbitrary social structures, from disease and premature old age, and had raised him to the boundless heights of the universe.

The second meeting in the gallery began with a display of stellar maps. Neither the Earthmen nor the inhabitants of the fluorine planet recognized the constellations which the others' ship had charted. (Only later, back on Earth, did astronomers succeed in establishing the exact position of the fluorine planet's blue sun: it lay in a small star cluster of the Milky Way, near Tau Ophiuchi). The strange ship had been heading toward a star cluster in the northern region of Ophiuchus, and had first met the Tellur near the southern border of the constellation Hercules.

In the stranger's gallery a screen made of red metal slats about the height of a man was erected. Something was spinning behind it, visible in the empty spaces between the slats. Suddenly the slats turned edgewise and disappeared, revealing an enormous empty space with blinding blue spheres representing the satellites of the fluorine planet spinning in its depths. The planet itself drew slowly nearer. A broad blue band of impenetrable cloud enveloped its equator. At the poles and near the polar zones the planet gleamed grayish-red. The temperate zones resembled the hull of the strange space ship in their immaculate whiteness. Here the atmosphere was less cloudy, and the contours of seas, continents, and mountains could be dimly made out. The planet was larger than Earth. Its rapid rotation gave rise to a powerful electric field around it. A violet radiance stretched out in long tongues along the equator into the blackness of space.

In breathless attention, the Earth people sat hour after hour, eyes glued to the transparent wall. Amazingly realistic pictures of the fluorine planet continued to unfold. The Earth people saw the violet waves of a hydrofluoric acid ocean washing shores of black sand, saw red cliffs and ridges of craggy mountains shining with a blue lunar radiance.

Closer to the poles the atmosphere became bluer, and the dark blue light of the violet star around which the fluorine planet revolved became deeper and purer. The mountains here rose in round domes, billows, and flat bulges with a bright opalescent luster. Blue twilight lay on the deep plains, stretching from the polar mountains to the scalloped strip of sea in the south. Large gulfs smoked with opalescent blue cloud. Gigantic structures of red metal and grassy-green stone lined the seashore and crept in endless rows along the steep valleys toward the poles. These gigantic aggregations of buildings, visible from enormous heights, were broken up by broad strips of thick greenish-blue vegetation, or by the flat domes of mountains which glowed from within like the opals and moonstones on Earth. The round caps of frozen hydrofluoric acid at the poles sparkled like sapphires.

Dark blue, light blue, azure, and violet colors predominated. The air itself seemed permeated with bluish radiance. The strange planet seemed cold and indifferent, like a vision seen through crystal— clean, distant, and unreal. It was a world totally lacking in the caressing warmth and variety of the Earth's red, orange and yellow colors.

Chains of cities could be seen in both hemispheres of the planet, in areas corresponding to the Earth's polar and temperate zones. Toward the equator the mountains became sharper and darker. Toothed peaks jutted out from the steaming surface of the sea, and ribs of mountain ranges stretched in a latitudinal direction along the border of the tropical regions.

There blue vapor curled in solid masses. In the heat from the blue star the highly volatile hydrogen fluoride saturated the atmosphere, approached the temperate zones in colossal walls of vapor, condensed, and poured in torrents back into the warm equatorial zone. Gigantic dams kept these violent torrents in check. Channeled into aqueducts and pipes, they served as a source of energy for the planet's power stations.

Fields of enormous quartz crystals dazzled the eye. Here silicon apparently took the place of our salt in the waters of the hydrofluoric acid sea.

The cities on the screen drew nearer, standing out sharply in the cold blue light. The whole area of the planet's inhabited zone, except for the mysterious equatorial regions, drowned in milky blue, had been built up, changed, and improved by the hands and creative mind of man. Much more so than our Earth with its enormous tracts of virgin forest, ancient ruins and abandoned fields.

The labor of countless generations and of billions of people rose higher than the mountains and covered the entire surface of the fluorine planet. Life had triumphed over the stormy waters and the dense atmosphere pierced by lethal radiation from the blue star and by incredibly powerful electrical discharges.

The Earthmen could not tear their eyes away. Their consciousness was split, for visions of their own native planet arose simultaneously in their minds. They did not see it, as their distant ancestors had, in a limited perspective depending on their place of birth and residence. They did not see it as some particular stretch of broad field and damp forest, as rocky melancholy mountains, or as transparent sea shores sparkling gaily in warm sunlight. They saw the whole Earth in all the variety of its climatic zones; cold, temperate and hot countries passed before the mental view of each astronaut. They remembered the endless beauty of the silvery steppes, home of free blowing wind; the mighty forests of dark firs and cedars, white birch, broad-leaved palms and gigantic bluish eucalyptus. They remembered the shores of the north with its walls of moss-grown cliffs; the whiteness of coral reefs in radiant blue tropical seas; the frigid, piercing sparkle of snowy mountain ranges; the unreal, shifting haze of the desert. They remembered majestic rivers, slow and wide or galloping fiercely along steep ravines like herds of white horses. They remembered the wealth of color; the immense variety of flowers; the Earth's blue sky with clouds like white birds; the sun's heat and the gloom of rain; the eternal changing of the seasons. And amid all this richness of nature a still greater variety of people in all their beauty, with their aspirations, exploits, dreams, sorrows, songs and dances, tears and laughter.

The same power of intelligent labor, with its incredible inventiveness and artistry, displayed its beauty everywhere; in buildings, factories, machines and ships.

Perhaps the strangers with their enormous slanted eyes saw much more than the Earthmen in the cold blue colors of their planet. Perhaps they had gone much further than the children of Earth in transforming their more monotonous nature.

We who are creatures of an oxygen atmosphere which is hundreds of thousands of times more common in the universe have found a large number of planets with conditions suitable for us, and would find and unite with brothers from other stars. But would they be so fortunate—offsprings of rare fluorine, with their unusual fluoric proteins and bones, with their blue blood corpuscles that absorb fluorine as our red ones absorb oxygen?

These people were imprisoned in the confined space of their planet and had probably been searching for a long time for beings like themselves, or at least for planets with a fluorine atmosphere suitable for them. But how could they find such a rare pearl in the abyss of space, how could they reach it through distances of thousands of light years? It was easy to understand their great despair at meeting oxygen people, probably not for the first time.

The landscapes of the fluorine planet in the strangers' gallery were replaced by a view of colossal buildings. The slanting walls reminded one of Tibetan architecture. There were no right angles or horizontal planes; transitions from vertical to horizontal followed flowing spiral or screw-shaped lines.

In the distance towered a dark opening similar in outline to a contorted oval. As it drew nearer, one could see that the lower part of the oval was an ascending spiral road which disappeared into the gigantic black entrance of a building the size of a whole city. Large blue signs mounted on red were visible above the entrance. From a distance they looked like the ripples of a wave. The entrance drew still closer, revealing in its depths a huge dimly lit hall with walls that shone like fluorescent fluorspar.

Suddenly, without forewarning, the picture disappeared. The astronauts, who had expected to see something extraordinary, felt literally stunned. The gallery on the other side of the transparent wall was now illuminated with an ordinary blue light. The strange astronauts reappeared, but this time their movements were hurried and abrupt.

A series of pictures flashed on the screen in rapid succession, so rapid that the Tellur's crew could barely follow them. Another white space ship identical to the one which now lay beside the Tellur, was moving somewhere in the darkness of space. Its central ring whirled and flashed, throwing out rays in all directions. The ring suddenly stopped rotating and the ship hung in space not far from a blue dwarf star.

Thin flashing pencil-rays of light streamed out from the ship toward a second ship exactly like it on the left side of the screen. The second ship was hanging motionless beside a ship from Earth which the Earthmen recognized as their own Tellur. The white space ship picked up the message of its twin and at once moved away from the Tellur into the black distance.

Moot Ang sighed so loudly that his subordinates turned to him with a mute question.

'That means they'll leave soon. They have a second ship travelling somewhere very far away and the two have somehow communicated, although how they can do it at such distances is beyond me. Something has happened to the other ship, and they are signaling to our friends.'

'Perhaps it hasn't been damaged, but has found something important?' Taina suggested quietly.

'Perhaps. Whatever it is, they'll be leaving. We must work at top speed to take more pictures and record as much information as possible. The most important things are their maps, their course, the things they have seen on their voyage. I have no doubt that they have met oxygen people like ourselves before.'

Exchanges with the strangers revealed that they could remain for one more terrestrial day. The Earthmen, stimulated by special drugs, worked with an energy no less frenzied than that of the gray inhabitants of the fluorine planet.

The scientists photographed whole books with pictures and words, and recorded the sounds of the strange language. They exchanged collections of minerals, liquids, and gasses in stable transparent containers. The chemists of both planets tried to decipher the symbols depicting the composition of organic and inorganic compounds. Afra, pale from fatigue, pored over diagrams of physiological processes, genetic schemes and formulas, and a chart showing the stages of embryological development of the inhabitants of the fluorine planet. The endless chains of the molecules of fluoride-resistant protein were amazingly similar to our protein molecules, providing the same energy filters, the same barriers in the struggle of living matter against entropy.

Twenty hours passed. Tey and Kari, nearly dead with fatigue, appeared in the gallery carrying rolls of stellar maps which traced the Tellur's entire route from the Sun to the place where the ships had met. The strangers hurried even more. Photomagnetic tapes of the Earthmen's memory machines recorded the position of unknown stars with unfamiliar signs for distance, astrophysical data, the complex zigzag routes of both white ships. All this would have to be deciphered later by means of tables of explanation provided by the strangers.

And finally, five stars with planets whirling around them appeared on the screen. The Earthmen gasped in admiration. The picture of the awkward, pot-bellied space ship was replaced by a whole fleet of more graceful ships. Human beings in space suits stood on oval platforms lowered from their hulls. The symbol for oxygen crowned the picture of the planets and the ships. But only two of the planets had lines connecting them with the space ships. One stood near a large red sun; the other revolved around a bright golden star of the spectral class F. Apparently life on the remaining three planets with an oxygen atmosphere had not yet reached the high level required for space flights, or perhaps thinking creatures had not yet developed on them.

The Earthmen didn't find out. But they now had invaluable information about the location of these inhabited worlds many hundreds of light years from the place where the two space ships had met.

The time for parting was at hand.

The crews of the two space ships were lined up facing each other on both sides of the transparent wall. The pale-bronze Earthmen and the gray-skinned fluorine people (the name of their planet remained a mystery) exchanged friendly but sad smiles and mutually understood gestures of farewell.

Unspeakably sharp sadness took possession of the Tellur's crew. Even the flight from Earth, made in the knowledge that they would not return for seven hundred years, had not produced such a painful feeling of irrevocable loss. They could not reconcile themselves to the thought that in a few minutes these beautiful, strange, good people would disappear forever into the cosmic void in their lonely and hopeless search for intelligent life similar to their own.

Only now, perhaps, the astronauts understood with their whole being that the most important thing in all their searches, aspirations, dreams, and struggles is man. For any civilization, any star, for all the infinite universe, the chief thing is man, his mind, emotions, strength and beauty—his life!

The primary task of the future lay in promoting the happiness, and development of man—now that the victory over the Heart of the Serpent, over the mad, ignorant, malicious squandering of vital energy in lower stages of human society was complete.

Man is the only force in the universe capable of acting rationally and of overcoming the monstrous obstacles blocking the way to a rational world, to the triumph of intelligent life and generous, noble feelings.

The strangers' captain made a sign with his arm. At once the young woman who had demonstrated the beauty of the inhabitants of the fluorine planet rushed up to the partition to face Afra. Flinging her arms wide, she pressed against the partition as if to embrace the beautiful Earth woman. Afra, unconscious of the tears streaming down her cheeks, flattened herself against the transparent wall like a trapped bird beating its wings against glass. Then the strangers' light went out, and the blackened glass became a void which swallowed all the yearnings of the Earth people.

Moot Ang ordered them to switch on the terrestrial lighting, but the gallery on the other side of the partition was empty.

'Outside group, put on your space suits and disconnect the gallery!' Moot Ang's voice burst authoritatively into the mournful silence. 'Engine crew—to your stations! Navigator—to the control room! All hands prepare for take-off!'

The crew left the gallery, carrying the instruments with them. Only Afra remained behind, standing motionless in the dim light from inside the Tellur, as if frozen by the glacial cold of interstellar space.

'Afra, we're closing the hatch!' Tey Eron called from somewhere inside the ship. 'We want to watch them take off.'

The young woman came to suddenly and shouted: 'Wait! Tey, wait!' She ran up to the captain. The second in command stood perplexed, but Afra returned very quickly with Moot Ang by her side.

'Tey, bring the projector into the gallery! Call the technicians. Put the screen back!' the captain ordered on the run.

People hurried as if trying to avoid a collision. A powerful beam flashed in the gallery at the same intervals as the Tellur's locator when the ships had first met. The strangers, interrupting their work, reappeared in the gallery. The Earthmen switched on the blue light. Trembling, Afra bent over the drawing board and began to make hurried sketches. The double spiral chains of the heredity patterns should be roughly the same for Earthmen and for the fluorine people. Afra sketched them and then drew a diagram of the metabolism of the human organism, beginning with the utilization of radiant energy stored by plants. She glanced at the motionless gray figures and crossed out the fluorine atom with its nine electrons, replacing it with oxygen.

The strangers started. Their captain stepped forward and brought his face close to the transparent partition, staring at Afra's clumsy sketches with his enormous eyes. Suddenly he raised clasped hands above his forehead and bowed low before the Earth woman.

They had understood the glimmer of an idea born in Afra's mind at the last moment under the sadness of parting. Afra had conceived the bold plan of changing the very chemical processes which give life to the entire complex organism of man. Replace fluorine with oxygen in the metabolic cycle by influencing the patterns of heredity! Preserve all the inherited characteristics of the fluorine people, but force their bodies to work on a different energy basis! This tremendous task was still so far from realization that even the seven centuries of the Tellur's separation from Earth—centuries of uninterrupted scientific progress—would not even begin to approach its solution.

Yet how much the combined efforts of both planets might accomplish! And if still other thinking beings were to join them, fluorine humanity would not be lost in the depths of the universe like a shadow which leaves no trace.

When the peoples of many planets of innumerable stars and galaxies united, and they inevitably would unite, the gray-skinned inhabitants of the fluorine planet would not be outcasts simply because of the accident of their anatomical structure.

Perhaps the grief of inevitable separation and loss was exaggerated. Infinitely far apart in the structure of their planets and their bodies, the fluorine people and the Earth people were quite similar in thought and emotion. It seemed to Afra that she could read all this in the enormous slanted eyes of the captain. Or was this merely a reflection of her own thoughts?

But the strangers apparently possessed that same faith in the power of human reason inherent to the people of Earth. No doubt because of this timid spark of hope lit by the biologist of the Tellur, their friendly gestures no longer seemed like signs of farewell, but clearly spoke of future meetings.

The space ships parted slowly so as not to damage one another by the blasts of their auxiliary engines. The white ship was soon wrapped in a cloud of blinding flame. When the flame died, there was nothing behind it save the blackness of space.

Then the Tellur set out cautiously and went into a warp, bridging once insurmountable interstellar distances. Safe inside protective casings, the crew slept as the light quanta flying toward them were compressed, and as the distant stars changed from blue to deeper and deeper violet. The ship plunged into the impenetrable gloom of zero space, toward the warm life of Earth throbbing and waiting below.

Flying Flowers

BY MIKHAIL VASILYEV

(I)

THE mountain stream plunged down a three-hundred-foot precipice. Gaining the edge in a tearing hurry it made its first madcap leap; from a distance it seemed that a bluish-green ribbon hung from a grey rock. The other end of the ribbon was lost in a white cloud of spray where the stream smashed against the gargantuan boulders.

All in a lather of white foam now and generously tossing it to either side, the stream leapt on impatiently from level to level as it hurried down the slope. After a final dash into the gray murkiness of the gorge it joined a bigger stream and together they continued their journey to the sea.

Zavyalov half-lay on a narrow ledge of rock just above the place where the spray shot from below met the bluish column of water. Occasional gusts of wind drove spray against his face. The ledge was wet and slippery and not exactly a safe place to linger.

Zavyalov pressed his right cheek against the cold roughness of the rock. The waterfall was right in front of him. From so close it no longer seemed a bluish-green ribbon, but what it was: a torrent of water, mighty and furious, in veins of foam and dirt, eager to snatch up and batter to death anything that got within reach of its cold embrace. He turned his head gingerly and pressed his left cheek against the rock. His glance traveled along the bare basalt. No, there was no hope of climbing that wall. A seasoned mountaineer, he had realized this when he was standing at the foot of the cliff, appraising, some forty minutes before. But he thought he would try all the same. And he had, seeking precarious purchase in every crumbly bit of weather-worn rock, every cleft produced by roots of some plant. It had taken him forty minutes to get to that ledge, forty minutes of tremendous risk. He ought not to have indulged himself, not really, he thought now.

Again Zavyalov moved his head cautiously, glancing up this time. His goal was quite near. About sixty feet higher and across the fall, where there were human figures carved in the cliff face, some aiming their bows, kneeling on one knee, others throwing spears, still others rowing.

Just below the group of carvings gaped the dark mouth of the cave. A big black cross topped it, running through the whole group and badly damaging some of the figures; obviously a later addition.

It was those primitive ornaments that had first roused his interest. Quite a find at this altitude too, almost next to the snow line, and he thought that many an archaeologist or ethnologist would have given much to be in his place. Of course a party of geologists, only four of them at that, including their guide, a local hunter, could not be expected to do archaeological investigations. But then what actually interested him at the moment was something different. How did the people who had left behind eternal marks of their presence manage to get to the cave? Did they use other, easier means of access? Or, perhaps, the waterfall, which was in his way, appeared at a later stage, cutting off access to the cave from this side?

And, indeed, across on the other side he could pick out a few likely footholds. By stepping on that fawnish knob one could reach as far as a small bush, which should mask a cleft of some sort. From there, placing one's left foot on that black slab, one could pass into a fifteen-foot-long chimney. That would be easy to scale. And above it there was something in the nature of a ledge, barely noticeable from this distance. Yes, the way to the cave continued just beyond the waterfall. By no means easy, but certainly climbable.

On their way up, two fat green caterpillars crawled busily past Zavyalov's cheek. It's easy for them, he thought, they've got eight legs, and I only four, legs and arms together.

Zavyalov moved a bit. His body felt numb. Pressing his side to the rock, he eased one leg for a few moments, then the other. Then, finding the best position, he reached out his left hand for his field glasses. They felt extremely heavy: the arm seemed to outweigh his whole body. For one fleeting moment he felt he was losing balance and falling. Vertigo swooped on him. With a great effort he steadied himself, chin pressed against wet rock, drew the hand with the glasses up to his face and again turned his head. The other side of the cliff face was so close in the lenses that it seemed he could touch it with his hand. And it was definitely climbable, right to the cave mouth, as he was able to ascertain, picking out the way with an eager eye. But how could one get there over that fifteen-foot-wide quivering ribbon of water?

Zavyalov lowered the glasses; the wall he had been examining leapt back into place. Even as it did so the stone his right hand had been gripping dislodged, ready to fall. Automatically his left hand dropped the field glasses and clutched at the rock for support. As he recovered his balance, his glasses disappeared in the spray below.

'Must climb down, I'm dead tired,' he told himself aloud and never heard his own voice for the roar of the falling water. It was only then that, for the first time, he became aware of that mighty roar. He shouted as loud as he could, but still could not hear himself.

Snake-like, he inched his way forward along the cold slippery stone. At a point where the ledge was almost petering out he finally stopped and looked at the foamy fringe of the water column right next to his face. The main mass of water curved out from the cliff, it was a leap, not a glide. A few large drops struck his cheek. Hugging the wall, he began the descent.

He stopped for a breather on a flat rock. He had not yet reached the bottom, but what remained was not so difficult. He sank down with his back propped against a rock and stretched his legs. His knees were shaking, all the strength was drained out of his arms, so that he would not even have been able to undo a button.

He felt fear. . . .

The sun emerged from behind a mountaintop; the slope was decked out with yellow, blue and red flowers, pastel-tinted and fragile-looking, but really quite tough and well adapted to fight stern nature. Their subdued beauty made them especially dear to him. For a long time he watched a large velvety bumblebee making rounds of the flowers. He would cling to the edge of a flower, plunge head first into the calyx until almost nothing was seen of him, then reappear in a little while, clean his front legs matter-of-factly and, yellow with pollen, buzz on to the next.

A large, exceptionally beautiful butterfly alighted on Zavyalov's damp shirt. Settling down comfortably, it opened and closed its wings as if fanning itself. Zavyalov sat quite still. Another butterfly perched on his knee, a freak with one wing much smaller than the other. A third one fluttered down on his forearm. Its body was noticeably bigger than the bodies of the other two. They all opened and closed their gaily coloured wings in unison, as if keeping common time.

(II)

Nikolai and Olga lingered just outside the circle of light from the camp-fire. Zavyalov guessed why: Nikolai had been carrying both rucksacks and now one of them was changing hands.

Their job for the day had been to explore the western branches of the valley. Zavyalov was a bit surprised when Nikolai, a tall lithe boy, showed him their route on the map: he had never expected they would be able to cover so much.

'Well, and what have you got to show?'

Nikolai produced the specimens: a few chips of granite and quartz, several kinds of rock crystal, and an assortment of pebbles picked up on the banks of mountain streams. Pebbles were useful as an indication of the type of rock one could expect upstream.

Zavyalov took out the Geiger counter and, putting on the earphones, checked the specimens for radioactive content. (Uranium prospecting was the purpose of their expedition.) The granites and gneisses gave the usual two to three clicks, while the rest did not yield a sound.

'My luck's been no better,' he said, 'the mineral's lying low. And plenty of it too, believe me, I can smell it. My nose has never let me down yet. Well, we'll talk business tomorrow. Let's have our meal.'

While they ate Zavyalov told them about the cave, omitting the climbing part of it as pedagogically unsound. Foolhardy risk should not be encouraged in budding geologists. There is enough danger in a prospector's work as it is.

His story, however, failed to evoke any response in the two students, tired after the day's exertions. But it did in the fourth member of their team, their guide, who went by the somewhat familiar, though affectionate, nickname of Dad.

'That place's called Gamayun's Cross, and the cave Gamayun's Cave. But there's no path to it. Nobody has ever been in it. Only the mountain spirits can carry you inside there. You've got to know the magic word for it.'

'You say nobody has been there, but who carved those figures and the cross then?'

'Oh, that's a different story. Gamayun did it.'

'Tell us about Gamayun,' Olga wanted to know.

'Gamayun was a rich hunter, they say. A greedy and evil man he was, would never do a good turn to anybody. He had an only daughter who was called Din. Beautiful as a picture she was. There was not a lad in the village who wasn't gone on her. The richest men in the district offered huge bride prices for her. But she fell in love with Gits, her father's herdsman. They decided to run away and get married. "The world is big," Gits would say to her, "there must be other places where I can fetch a mountain ram with an arrow or spear a bear." Gamayun learned about this plan—he was a wizard and nothing could be kept secret from him—and on the night when his daughter was to run away he gave her a sleeping potion. Then he called the mountain spirits and with their help took her to a hiding place which even Gits, who knew all the paths in the mountains, would never find. Gamayun had his own plans for Din: he wanted to marry her off to a rich old man from a neighboring village and get a really big bride price. The old geezer already had three wives but was eager to marry Din. And she was fifteen at the time—best age for the bride in our parts.

'All that night Gits waited for Din with a pair of horses at the end of the village. When dawn came he decided she had betrayed him, swung into saddle and galloped off into the mountains. His horse was quite winded when he dismounted at midday near a mountain spring. He sat down and thought what was to be done. Meanwhile Din woke up in the cave where the mountain spirits had carried her. In the very same cave you saw today, Sergei Andreyevich. Dripping wet she was, for the spirits had dipped her into the stream. She got up from her grass bed, went up to the cave mouth and saw a sheer wall of rock and a waterfall roaring away at her feet. No way out! What could she do? And suddenly she heard a few thin blades of grass that hugged the cliff speak to her in human voices.

' "Do you want us to tell Gits where to look for you?" they asked her.

' "Oh, yes," said Din.

' "What will you give us for it?"

' "What do you want?"

' "Your beauty and your strength."

' "What do you need them for?" Din asked, surprised.

' "We need your strength the better to cling to rock and fight the wind. We need your beauty to be admired by everybody. Look how weak and ugly we are now."

' "And what will remain for me if I give you my beauty and strength?"

' "You will have your love. Why, surely that is your proudest possession."

'Indeed what is there in strength and beauty when there is no love, thought Din and agreed.

'And that very moment the most beautiful flowers blossomed forth everywhere she could see. The bluebells took the blue of her eyes, the carnations the scarlet of her lips, and the violets the whiteness of her arms and shoulders. Din did not know it all had been taken from her, only she felt a sudden weakness all over her body and sank down on the granite. And when she looked at her arms she saw that they had become gray, coarse, and flabby like an old woman's. But even that did not make her feel sorry, because there was nothing but love in her heart now.

' "But when will you do what you promised?" she asked.

'Then one of the flowers broke off its stem and, flapping its petals, flew away. It rose higher and higher, so high that it could at last see

Gits sitting beside a spring. Then it dropped on his shoulder and told him where to look for Din.

'Gits sprang into the saddle and galloped off. He was strong and brave. But nobody could get to Gamayun's cave without the help of the mountain spirits. Gits climbed half the way and knew he could get no farther. So he hung on to the cliff, Din sat in the cave and the waterfall roared between them.

'Then Gits struggled upright, found a foothold in a cleft and shouted so loud that Din could hear him above the torrent's roar.

' "Jump over to me!" he shouted.

'The former Din could have jumped over the stream straight into Gits' arms, but, having given all her strength away, she only jumped halfway. The waterfall seized her and swept her down, but Gits stretched his arm and caught his beloved, though they both nearly perished as he did so. With Din in his arms, Gits got down the cliff, mounted his horse and galloped away.

'Gamayun came back to his cave and could not find Din. He understood it was Gits who had taken her away and was so angry he decided they both must die. To cast an evil spell on them he had to draw those who were to fight Gits. But he had nothing to draw with. So he seized a rock and began hewing figures with it in the cliff face. He first sent a bowman against Gits. The bowman shot his arrow but Gits caught it in the air, turned it, and hurled it back. And it flew and pierced the bowman's chest. That night Gits was stronger than all the enemies Gamayun sent against him. Nothing is stronger than true love in this world.

'When the lovers had galloped so far away that Gamayun's magic could no longer reach them, Gits dismounted and made a fire. He laid Din down beside it because she was so weak she could not even sit up. There was only love in her heart, and one cannot live by love alone. And so she died, her head in Gits' lap, her arms around his neck.

'They say Gits died soon afterwards. How could he live when every flower reminded him of Din—the roses, of the gentle color of her cheeks, the bluebells, of her blue eyes? . . .'

'And Gamayun,' Olga asked softly, 'what happened to him?'

'Gamayun? When Gamayun learned about his daughter's death remorse began tormenting him, they say. He took a rock and hewed a cross in the cliff above the cave. And the mountain spirits left him, for a cross strikes fear in them. Then he disappeared. Whether he died in the cave or threw himself into the waterfall, nobody knows. . . .'

'How long ago did all this happen?' asked Zavyalov.

'My grandfather told me this story, and he heard it from his grandfather, who used to say that *his* grandfather, when he was quite young, knew an old man who, as a small boy, saw Gamayun.'

'You told it beautifully, Dad,' said Olga. 'Do you think it's a true story?'

'Hard to say. Tales aren't all lies, I s'ppose, nor all truth either. But there's always a bit of wisdom in them. It's wise people who tell them in our parts.'

'What splendid, all-powerful love,' Olga said, gazing at the dying embers. 'And what a wise philosophy: love is stronger than anything in this world but man cannot live by love alone. How beautiful and how true. . . . So the alpine flowers' loveliness is the beauty of the dying Din. . . . But what could that flying flower symbolize? I have never met the metaphor before. Have you, Sergei Andreyevich?'

Zavyalov started. He, too, was under the spell of the hunter's tale, but his train of thought had been different. He had remembered things from his past, things that were gone but not forgotten. How he longed for the girl to call him Sergei, and not Sergei Andreyevich. She was at once like and unlike the other one. Yes, of course, she was better than the other one, if for no other reason than because she was here with him at the campfire. The other one would never dream of going away from the comforts of the city unless she went to a fashionable seaside resort. How he longed—But Olga would never know about it. He was past thirty and she just twenty. Besides Nikolai was obviously attracted by her. They'd make a perfect match. And he, as head of the team, really had no business going about courting a student on her field work with him.

'Why don't you say something? Have you fallen asleep too?'

'No, I was thinking.'

'But tell me, have you ever heard of flying flowers in some folk legend or other?'

'Not that I know of.'

'Must be a local image then. They usually stand for something quite concrete.'

(III)

'To think that you could fall asleep in the middle of such an absolutely wonderful legend! No, you're not human, Nikolai. Not a live spark in your heart.'

'I'm a geologist. Legends interest me to the extent they have some bearing on my job. Had there been mention of an abandoned quarry or some such thing in it, I'd have pricked up my ears. But there was the usual rigmarole: beautiful daughter, tyrannical father, and, of course, poor but valiant suitor.'

'But what about flying flowers? Even Sergei Andreyevich says he hasn't heard about this image.'

'Flying flowers might interest botanists, but I'm a geologist.'

'Stop repeating that you're a geologist. Sergei Andreyevich is also a geologist, but look how wide his interests are. Archaeology, ethnography, Chinese medicine. . . . And d'you know what he's most keen on?'

'No.'

'Prospecting on other planets. Going as a geologist with the very first space expedition. He has even written poetry about space flights.'

'How do you know?'

'They still remember his verses at the Institute from the time he was a student. Want me to recite them?'

'Fire away.'

Zavyalov made a wry face. The youngsters were apparently not aware he had returned and could hear them from the tent. But how had that inquisitive girl laid her hands on his rhymes? He had written them, and he had wanted to become the first astro-archaeologist. For that matter he was still very active in the astronautics section.

But he wrote no poetry any more. Ever since that time. . . . Rita had been married for five years now, yet he still felt stunned. Working like a beaver, lecturing, doing research—anything to help forget. Perhaps he shouldn't have done it? After all it was he who gave up Rita because she wouldn't go his way. Perhaps he should have gone her way? Then Rita wouldn't have become the wife of that fellow . . . 'that accountant fellow,' as he had called him at their last meeting. What did she say to that? Trotted out a proverb: she believed in proverbs, particularly in the type coined for the specific use of the well-fed and satisfied. Something like 'A bird in the hand is worth two in the bush.' He was the bush part of it— telegraph operator-gunner in the war years, later honors graduate, then research student at the Geological Prospecting Institute, until he gave up his post-graduateship in the second year for field work. That was what had caused the break.

'You don't know how to get on in life, as people do,' she told him. Yes, he did know how to get what he wanted, but he wasn't looking for the same things in life as she was, their ideas of happiness were different. But what *was* happiness? Last night Dad had said that man can't live by love alone. But can man live without love? He had—for five years. But could that be called life?

Yes, of course, work you like was the main thing in life and the choice he had made was right. But then why all these memories? And now this young girl, Olga. . . . And again somebody else's. . . .

Outside, the howling of the wind in the ravine added to the rattle of the mountain torrent rushing along in its stone bed. This made a fitting background to the tale of space conquest that a girl's voice was reciting with great feeling and utter conviction.

A thrilling journey! Though terrestrial skies
Seem blue and clear, yet on our way through space
Uncounted obstacles and dangers will arise:
Magnetic storms, tremendous meteors, cosmic rays. . . .
But we shall triumph! Yes, we shall! And there, afar,
Beyond the reach of any poet's dream,
There, luring us, our goal—another star
Through endless night mysteriously shall gleam.
Our trajectory nearer as we trace,
Upon our radar's palpitating screen,
A strange and lovely planet's clearing face
Adorned with streaks of lightning, will be seen. . . .
With chains of islands scattered there and here,
And weird contours of unearthly sea and land,
Before our gaze, fantastic and austere,
A new world will arise—and then expand. . . .

The voice stopped, as if snapped at the highest pitch of emotion. There was a few moments' silence. Then the dialogue started afresh.

'He spreads himself thin, your Sergei Andreyevich. Fewer rhymes would have got him his doctorate long ago. And here he is, climbing rocks with us. Is that your idea of life—tent, fire and all?'

'Stop it, Nikolai!' Olga nearly screamed. Zavyalov visualised a wrathful face with a pair of deep, burning eyes, now a much darker shade of blue than usual.

'Oh, what a rotten thing to say! Why, he's had several invitations from his Institute and from the Academy of Sciences. . . . His articles are quoted in textbooks. And you—you're just a schoolboy compared to him.'

'Tut, tut, my dear girl, I should have thought you could spare my silver-haired head that avalanche of wrath.' Nikolai sounded somewhat taken aback by Olga's outburst. 'All right. They invited him and he said no. He's a genius, and I'm a schoolboy. But all I was trying to say was that he spreads himself thin over too many undertakings. And that goes for you too. Take today's butterflies. What's in them for you? See my point? Catch *me* saying no to a readership at the Institute.'

It was high time he put an end to this involuntary eavesdropping. Zavyalov coughed. The voices stopped abruptly.

He stepped outside and went over to the shed.

'Well, what're you doing?'

'I'm sorting out the specimens and Olga's amusing herself with butterflies.'

Nikolai's reply was a patent challenge but Zavyalov chose to ignore it. He looked through Nikolai's entries in the team's logbook, making a few casual remarks. The young man knew his job well. Then he turned to the girl, who was bent over an empty food box topped by a piece of glass. A few fair curls had escaped from under her kerchief onto her knitted brow. She was peering into the box. Under the glass there was a colorful collection of luxuriant butterflies such as those Zavyalov had seen by the waterfall.

'Aren't they absolutely lovely,' the girl said. 'If I'm not mistaken this is a species not described before.'

'But you are. That is an ordinary species, though changed a lot through certain environmental conditions.'

'These being?'

'Radioactivity. Look at all these mutations, in color and form and size. Incidentally, where did you catch this lot?'

'By the waterfall. I went to have a look at Gamayun's Cave. But you know it's not as untrodden by man as it looks. People have been there before and not so long ago.'

'What makes you think so?'

'Here's what I have found there.' Olga showed him a badly battered metal binocular casing that seemed to have passed through a crusher. There was anxiety in her eyes.

'Stop worrying, Olga, those were my field glasses. I broke them accidentally and threw them in the water, which did the rest. But what is it that interests you in those butterflies?'

'I was crazy about collecting all kinds of insects when I was a kid. It's very interesting, really. It's a world apart, full of its own mysteries. Do you know, for instance, that a butterfly can locate another at a distance of a little under a mile even without seeing it?'

'Yes. They say butterflies have an acute sense of smell.'

Olga shook her head.

'No, I don't think that's the answer. How could a sense of smell, however acute, help a butterfly amidst a flower-field full of the most different aromas of the greatest intensity? Is it possible to single out a faint smell from that riot of scents? It's something else, I'm sure. I did a bit of an experiment today. I placed a butterfly under a tumbler downwind from another butterfly—in case a little of the smell got out—'

'And what did you find?'

'I repeated the experiment several times and every time the second butterfly was soon fluttering around the tumbler.'

'How do you explain this remarkable communion? By telepathy?'

'I don't know. . . . Of course, butterflies don't think, but they might emit some radio waves. And locate one another as if by a radio beacon.'

'I was struck yesterday by the way they opened and closed their wings, basking in the sun—all in time, like a company of soldiers at drill. Of course they could see one another. I don't think telepathy has anything to do with it, really.'

'Well, let's see.'

Olga turned over the pane of glass covering the box. There were a few butterflies on it. One of these fluttered away. The others, comfortable where they were, began moving their wings in unison. Though well apart, they seemed to operate as identical components of a single mechanism.

Olga took a piece of cardboard and put it vertically on the glass, cutting the group of butterflies in two. Wing movements in both groups remained synchronous.

'There you are, Sergei Andreyevich, it's not sight, you see, it's something else.'

Zavyalov was obviously interested. And he liked the neat and clever way in which Olga had done that little experiment. So it was not sight. What was it then? Radio waves? Some kind of tiny oscillations, not detectable, or, perhaps, not detected by anybody? And if so, was it endemic or common to all lepidoptera?

These questions merited further study. For all he knew, nature might have employed some novel principle here that man could benefit from. It wouldn't be such a bad thing, for instance, to develop a one-mile-range receiver-transmitter the weight of a butterfly. That would presumably be a hundred times lighter than existing types.

(IV)

Again Zavyalov was on the narrow ledge above the waterfall. Again alone. Over the past two days he had progressed from surmise to conviction, but he felt the evidence he had was too slim to share with others. So he had gone out alone for a final check.

The sun shone brightly aloft and there was a brilliant rainbow arched over the quivering silver-specked mass of water. The drops that reached the warm granite evaporated quickly; fine wisps of vapor curled up and disappeared. Taking every precaution Zavyalov stood upright, facing the wall. His left hand clutched at the cliff wall almost at the water's edge, whence he now proceeded to inch his way, very slowly, until his face felt a cooler current of air caused by the precipitous fall of water. But this wasn't the main stream, this was just its left flank, and he had counted on its not being very thick.

Zavyalov felt no fear this time. On the contrary, he was buoyed up and sure of success. Presently, finding a secure foothold, he ran his left hand along a crevice into the stream and beyond it. The impact on his arm of that accelerated mass of water was terrific, but he knew he could just make it. Then his foot followed, and, surprisingly enough, quickly found firm purchase. He made a dash and emerged—after a cold shower—behind the greenish-blue curtain of water.

As soon as his eyes got accustomed to the quivering twilight he saw that, despite the wetness of the rock and the water sluicing down in places, ascent was possible.

Then to his great surprise Zavyalov noticed an iron hook sunk into the wall not far from his face. It was ruinously rusty but it resisted the tug he gave it. So that was the mountain spirit that had helped Gamayun to get into his cave. If Gamayun had done it, surely he could do it. Soon he was at the cave mouth.

There was a small flat space in front of it, which had escaped his eye. The despotic father must have been standing on it while he hewed the figures meant to bring peril to his daughter and her lover. But was it really Gamayun who had carved them? The explorer's heart gave a leap. He noticed that some of the figures were worn smooth by time, others half-obliterated through cracking and the fall of weather-worn rock. That could not be the work of two or three centuries. Twenty to thirty millenniums, more likely. That was the estimate that his experience as a geologist suggested to him.

But if the Gamayun legend was an invention, pure and simple, a whole chain of circumstantial evidence would fall to the ground. No, that could not be so. It was Gamayun—a filicide and an unintentional suicide—who had sunk that hook into the rock and provided himself with a hiding place that was to become his tomb.

He would of course take pictures of the figures and then make a detailed sketch of them in his notebook—in case his camera failed. In any case they would appear in *Problems of Archaeology* not later than next spring. They had waited for so many centuries that a few more months would be of no importance.

Zavyalov swung into the cave. The entrance was lit brightly by the rays of the sun. His first few steps inside the cave felt as though he were treading a deep-pile carpet; an accumulation of cocoons of countless butterfly generations, he guessed. This soon gave place to rock floor. Here it was darker, and Zavyalov halted for a moment to allow his eyes to accommodate themselves. Suddenly there was a hollow thud behind him, the floor rocked slightly, stones rattled down from the vault, and he found himself in complete darkness. Zavyalov broke out in cold sweat. Cut off! Trapped in a cave where a few hours' stay spelt death. In that same cave that had robbed Din of strength and beauty, and her father of life.

Zavyalov switched on his torch. The subsidence was not extensive and apparently only involved a single slab of granite. But it was big, and had slid squarely across the entrance, all but sealing off the cave so that Zavyalov could only force an arm through in one place. Enlarge the hole? What a hope! That'd take him three to four days, which he didn't have. He could not even wait till the next day when his companions would start a search for him. They would tumble to his going out to explore this cave, of course. But would they guess where he was? No, they'd more likely decide he'd fallen into the torrent and look for his body downstream. He might shout all he could, they wouldn't hear him above the roar of the waterfall even if Nikolai climbed up to that ledge.

He ought to get a grip on himself and think coolly.

It wasn't so much the thought of death, he reasoned. He'd faced it before as he hovered over towns looking like gigantic fiery hedgehogs, a target for searchlight beams and tracer flak. But he hated the idea of meeting his end in this way and shelving the riddle of Gamayun's Cave for many, many years. Though, in fact, he wasn't as yet quite sure he himself held the solution.

Playing the beam of his torch about him, Zavyalov went deeper into the cave. It gradually widened, though not much, while its ceiling receded sharply, making the cave a narrow cleft in the massif of granite. Suddenly shivers ran down his spine: picked out by the fitful light of his torch, a man appeared in front of him, eyes ablaze, lips stretched in a malevolent grin, displaying a set of glittering teeth highlighted by little tongues of bluish flame. In fact, the very time-honored image of a ghoul or one of the Devil's own minions.

Plucking up his courage, Zavyalov took a couple of steps forward and trained the torch beam on the ghost's face. It was the dead face of a mummy half-seated in the shallow recess in which the cave ended.

The man who had been thus mummified must have been a real giant in his lifetime: hunched as he was his head was level with Zavyalov's. He had to be, thought the geologist, to be able to drag his daughter all the way up to the cave. So this was Gamayun—clad in a linen shirt over trousers of the same material and a leather belt. . . .

And that solved the riddle of Gamayun's Cave beyond a shred of doubt. The cave was indeed made up of minerals bearing fantastic, unheard-of radioactive concentrations. How big the valuable deposits were had yet to be explored, but their high grade was a certainty even now.

He retraced his steps back to the cave mouth. What could he do? Write a message, it occurred to him. By the vague light from the hole he jotted down a few lines about his discovery on a page torn from his notebook, made a dart with it and threw it outside. He repeated the motions nine times—the number of blank pages in his notebook.

This done, he thought hard. What else could he do? In his place Din had sent her lover a flower. Perhaps she had just used it to scratch her message on? It didn't sound right, though. Why a flower, when it was easier to scratch her message on a leaf or a piece of cloth torn from her dress?

The youngsters back in camp must still be unaware of anything. Dad was cooking their meal and Nikolai sorting the specimens. And Olga? Well, Olga would most likely be studying the mysterious mechanism of butterfly communication.

A flying flower. . . . Could Din not have written her last love-letter on a butterfly's gaudy wings? Supposing he tried. . . . No, what utter rubbish. . . . And yet—who knows—what if it succeeded?

An idea was struggling in his mind, which he had first dismissed as utter rubbish, then took up tentatively again, then— After all, as one condemned to death he had nothing to lose, he told himself. And his life was the stake.

(V)

'You think he overheard the little conversation we had this morning, do you? That might mean a failure for me in my field practice. What the devil made me blabber my opinion of him!'

'How disgusting you are, Nikolai!'

'Why are you so rattled? I'm doing my job well, aren't I, and always will, all my life, be on top of my job whatever it is. And all the rest is just a damned nuisance that gets on one's nerves— Anyway I don't quite see what's biting you this time.'

'It's just that doing your job well still doesn't make a man out of you.'

Nikolai offered no reply. For a few minutes both went on with their work.

'Look, Nikolai!' Olga exclaimed all of a sudden. 'What's that?'

'Butterflies,' Nikolai said nonchalantly, stepping over to her.

'But look at the way they're moving their wings. . . .'

'The usual way. All together. You've already admired the fact together with your darling Sergei Andreyevich.'

'Look at them,' Olga was saying, disregarding his words, 'they've always moved their wings at even intervals before. Now they're uneven—longer and shorter.'

'Using Morse code, eh?'

'No, impossible . . . wait . . . give me your pencil.'

On a scrap of paper she began hurriedly putting down dots and dashes for shorter and longer wing movements. Soon she had a few lines ready.

'Now for the decoding,' said Olga.

'Can you do it?'

'Yes.'

'Where did you learn?'

'I went to a radio ham circle at school.'

'Whatever for? Too much time to spare?'

'For this particular occasion. Just for this once. There you are Just read it aloud.'

' "Am in cave. Need help. Zavyalov." '

(VI)

In the evening they gathered around the campfire as usual.

'You see, geologically this place looked like a typical uranium-bearing area. There's no point in going deeper: you know all that stuff. But to strike uranium was an entirely different matter. There might not have been any at all in the first place, or it might have been dispersed in minute quantities in granite. It's the butterflies that gave me my first inkling of an open deposit somewhere near. You know that radioactivity causes mutations in insects. And I'd never before seen so many mutations as at the confluence of the two streams. That was why Olga could not recognize an ordinary butter-fly.

'Soon I managed to locate the rough boundaries of their habitat. It was in the area of the waterfall. The mutation butterfly was extremely rare farther upstream and plentiful downstream——carried there by the wind, I thought, which always blows in the same direction here. So I began exploring the area.

The water and pebbles proved only slightly more radioactive than normal; so if there was any uranium about it had no direct contact with the water. Yet it was obvious that the local butterflies were exposed to high levels of radioactivity in the chrysalis stage. That prompted me to search for a deep crevice in the rock where the chrysalises might mature.

'Then it was that I stumbled on Gamayun's Cave.

'Its remarkable qualities must have been known to the stone-age men. Possibly the cave and the whole cliff were held sacred in those days and used for pagan rituals. That must also have been the purpose of the figures carved in the cliff face.

'All this was very circumstantial, of course, and I hesitated to bring it up. I tried to reach the cave on my own and failed. The climb was much too risky. I ruined my field glasses in the attempt and decided to stay content with taking pictures of the cliff face with a telephoto lens.

'However, the tale Dad told us gave a new fillip to my speculations. A cave where a girl loses her strength and beauty could only have been a radioactive one. The same could have killed Gamayun. But in a legend deeply rooted in folklore fact is inseparable from fantasy. In this one, for instance, Gamayun is credited with carving figures which had existed for tens of millenniums before his time. So could the rest of it have been just fantasy, for that matter. And though personally I was almost convinced, I again said nothing to you and ventured out alone. Which nearly cost me my life.

'The final proof that the cave was a radioactive treasure-house was furnished by the mummy. The whites of its eyes, its teeth and nails were phosphorescent due to prolonged radioactive exposure. There were no signs of decomposition because radiation killed all the microbes. But I had this proof only when I myself became a prisoner and was beginning to expect a place next to Gamayun.

'I wrote my message to you, threw out a few copies of it in the hope somebody might pick it up, and prepared for the inevitable. . . . But then an idea occurred to me. . . . You remember the legend mentions a flying flower. Now a butterfly could be that. I even seemed to remember I'd come across a similar metaphor in a Persian epos I once read.

'You remember how amazed we were at the butterflies beating their wings in unison and even wondered who their drill-sergeant was. I'm not affirming anything, but I'd like to advance the idea that wing movements cause the impulse by means of which they manage to communicate. They are their own drill-sergeants, as it were. So why shouldn't I take over the job for a while, I thought.

'I knew that Olga would be studying her butterflies just then. So I caught a most gorgeous butterfly as it was about to flutter outside and stretched down at the hole. The rest I did with the help of two needles. Imagine my joy when I saw a butterfly basking outside open and close its wings in time with the one whose wings I was manipulating. Apparently quite a few butterflies in the locality must have been doing their setting-up exercises at that time in Morse.

'I'm not at all sure what learned lepidopterists will have to say on the matter. They might even say that nothing of the kind happened. And any experiments they made would probably bear them out. But the fact is that here we're dealing with a unique case of mutation, going back countless generations. And perhaps this feature, which can be observed with the ordinary cabbage butterfly, has, to my good fortune, reached a high level of development with this particular mutation.

'I replaced the tortured butterfly after a while by another one. There are millions of cocoons in the cave; it's an enormous nursery. And in about two hours I felt somebody tugging at the rope I'd payed out through the hole. That was Nikolai, and just about time too. I pulled it in and found the stick of dynamite at the end. The rest was easy.

'As the senior member here I'd like to stress one point. Geology is by no means a narrow science. A geologist should know a thousand and one things which might appear to have nothing to do with his job. But this goes for other sciences too. Nowadays new developments are taking place increasingly in the border regions between two and more sciences, as Academician Zelinsky once put it. Without knowledge entirely optional for me as a geologist we could have missed our uranium deposits and I might have lost my life.

'And one more thing. For a scientist knowledge and opportunity to increase it should be the two most important things. And, believe me, the post he occupies, the string of letters he has after his name, the fees he gets—all that is secondary.'

That night Zavyalov and Olga were the last to leave the campfire. The geologist was jotting down notes in the logbook; the girl, sitting with her arms around her knees, was peering into the dying embers of the fire.

'Sergei Andreyevich, would you mind if I asked you a personal question?'

'A question? Why, you're welcome.'

'Why are you not married?'

Zavyalov had expected anything but that. He was not aware that a woman can detect a man's love for her on infinitely more slender evidence than he had used in unearthing the uranium deposits. A little embarrassed, but looking straight into her eyes, he said softly:

'If you wish I will tell you about it. You and nobody else. . . . But not here—in Moscow when our field practice is over.'

(VII)

Zavyalov dialed a number. It was a number he knew by heart but for the last five years had never dialed more than once a year. And out of five times he had heard her voice only once. Hearing to the end all those 'Hello, press the button, use another line,' he had hung up in silence. That had been two years ago. Now he answered at once.

'Rita, this is Sergei. You have not forgotten me completely, have you? I'd like to see you. For a minute, or for an hour, I don't know. But alone and immediately.'

In ten minutes he saw her in the opening door. She had changed. She had filled out and was even more beautiful. But he knew at once she no longer had any sway over him. . . .

He could go now: after all, that was what he'd wanted to be quite certain about.

Meanwhile Rita searched in her mind for something to say. Weather was trivial, how-are-you and all that, too general. . . . She thought she knew what had brought this man here. But he never said a word and suddenly she noticed something.

'You have two new medals?' she said in astonishment and envy, looking at his chest with those blue innocent eyes of hers whose purity he had so loved. 'My husband hasn't got a single one. And probably never will have, the imbecile. He doesn't know how to get on in life. . . . But where're you going, Sergei dear?' she said and stretched her plump, marble-white, beautiful arms to him.

Never saying a word, he turned on his heel and went away.

In the evening he told everything to the other woman.

The Maxwell Equations

BY ANATOLY DNIEPROV

(I)

IT all began on a Saturday evening when tired from my mathematical pursuits I took up the local evening paper and came across this advertisement on the last page :

> Kraftstudt & Company Ltd. accept orders
> from organizations and individuals
> for all manner of calculating,
> analytical and computing work.
> High quality guaranteed. Apply :
> 12 Weltstrasse

That was just what I needed. For several weeks I had been sweating over Maxwell equations concerning the behavior of electromagnetic waves in the heterogeneous medium of a special structure. In the end I had managed by a series of approximations and simplifications to reduce the equations to a form that could be handled by an electronic computer. I already pictured myself traveling up to the capital and begging the administration of the Computer Center to do the job for me. For begging it would have to be, with the Center working full capacity on military problems and nobody there giving a damn for a provincial physicist's dabblings in the theory of radiowave propagation.

And here was a computer center springing up in a small town like ours and advertising for customers in the local paper !

I took up the receiver to get in immediate touch with the company. It was only then I realized that apart from the address the advertisement gave no particulars. A computer center not on the telephone ! It just didn't make sense. I called the editors.

'Sorry, but that was all we received from Kraftstudt,' the secretary told me. 'There was no telephone number in the ad.'

Kraftstudt and Co. was not in the telephone directory either.

169

Burning with impatience I waited for Monday. Whenever I looked up from those neatly penned equations concealing complicated physical processes, my thoughts would turn to Kraftstudt Co. Men of vision, I thought. In our time and age when mankind endeavors to clothe its every idea in mathematical garb, it would be hard to imagine a more profitable occupation.

Incidentally, who was this Kraftstudt? I had been a resident of the town quite a long time but the name rang no bell. As a matter of fact, I did vaguely recollect having heard the name before. But I couldn't remember when or where, no matter how hard I jogged my memory.

Came Monday. Pocketing the sheet of equations, I started out in search of 12 Weltstrasse. A fine drizzle forced me to take a taxi.

'It's a goodish way off,' said the cabby, 'beyond the river, next door to the lunatic asylum.'

I nodded and off we went.

It took us about forty minutes. We passed through the town gates, went over a bridge, skirted a lake and found ourselves in the country. Early green shoots could be seen here and there in the fields along the dirt road, and the car stuck in muddy ruts every now and then, its back wheels spinning furiously.

Then roofs appeared, then the red brick walls of the lunatic asylum, standing in a little depression and jocularly referred to in town as the Wise Men's Home.

Along the tall brick wall bristling with bits of broken glass ran a cinder-paved lane. After a few turnings the taxi pulled up at an inconspicuous door.

'This is Number Twelve.'

I was unpleasantly surprised to find that Kraftstudt Co.'s premises were in the same building as the Wise Men's Home. Surely Herr Kraftstudt hasn't ganged up the loonies to do 'all manner of mathematical work' for him, I thought—and smiled.

I pressed the doorbell. I had to wait long, the better part of five minutes. Then the door opened and a pale-faced young man with thick tousled hair appeared and blinked in the daylight.

'Yes, sir?' he asked.

'Is this Kraftstudt's mathematical company?' I asked.

'Yes.'

'And you advertised in the newspaper? . . .'

'Yes.'

'I have some work for you.'

'Please come in.'

Telling the driver to wait for me, I bent my head and slipped through the door. It closed and I was plunged in complete darkness.

'Follow me, please. Mind the steps. Now to your left. More steps. Now we go up. . . .'

Holding me by the arm and talking thus, the man dragged me along dark crooked corridors, up and down flights of stairs.

Then a dim yellowish light beamed overhead, we climbed a steep stone staircase and emerged into a small hall.

The young man hurried behind a partition, pulled up a window, and said:

'I'm at your service.'

I had a feeling of having come to the wrong place. The semidarkness, the underground labyrinth, this windowless hall lighted by a single naked bulb high at the ceiling, all added to a thoroughly odd impression.

I looked around in confusion.

'I'm at your service,' the young man repeated, leaning out of the window.

'Why, yes. So this is the Kraftstudt and Co. computer center?'

'Yes, it is,' he cut in with a trace of impatience, 'I told you that before. What is your problem?'

I produced the sheet of equations from my pocket and handed it through the window.

'This is a linear approximation of those equations in their partial derivatives,' I began to explain, a little uncertainly. 'I want them solved at least numerically, say, right on the border line between two media. . . . This is a dispersion equation, you see, and the velocity of radiowave propagation here changes from point to point.'

Snatching the sheet from my hand the young man said brusquely:

'It's all clear. When do you want the solution?'

'What do you mean—when?' I said, surprised. 'You must tell me when you can do it.'

'Will tomorrow suit you?' he asked, his deep dark eyes now full on me.

'Tomorrow?'

'Yes. About noon. . . .'

'Good Lord! What a computer you've got! Fantastic speed!'

'Tomorrow at twelve you will have your solution, then. The charge will be four hundred marks. Cash.'

Without saying another word I handed him the money together with my visiting card.

On our way back to the entrance the young man asked:

'So you are Professor Rauch?'

'Yes. Why?'

'Well, we always thought you'd come to us sooner or later.'

'What made you think so?'

'Who else could place orders with us in this hole?'

His answer sounded fairly convincing.

I barely had time to say good-bye to him before the door was shut on me.

All the way home I thought about that strange computer center next door to a madhouse. Where and when had I heard the name of Kraftstudt?

(2)

The next day I waited for the noon mail with mounting impatience. When the bell rang at half past eleven I jumped up and ran to meet the postman. To my surprise I faced a slim pale girl holding an enormous blue envelope in her hand.

'Are you Professor Rauch, please?' she asked.

'Yes.'

'Here's a package for you from Kraftstudt's. Please sign here.'

There was only one name—mine—on the first page of the ledger that she held out for me. I signed and offered her a coin.

'Oh, no!' She flushed, murmured good-bye and was gone.

When I glanced at the photo copies of a closely written manuscript I couldn't believe my own eyes. From an electric computer I had expected something entirely different: long columns of characters with the values of the argument in the first column and those of the solution in the second.

But what I held in my hand was a strict and precise solution of my equations!

I ran my eye through page after page of calculations that took my breath away with their originality and sheer beauty. Whoever had done it possessed an immense mathematical knowledge to be envied by the world's foremost mathematicians. Almost all the modern armory of mathematics had been employed: the theory of linear and nonlinear differential and integral equations, the theory of the functions of a complex alternating current, and those of groups, and of plurality, and even such apparently irrelevant systems as topology, number theory and mathematical logic.

I nearly cried out in delight when at the end of a synthesis of countless theorems, intermediate calculations, formulae and equations the final solution emerged—a mathematical formula taking up three whole lines.

And to add a touch of the exquisite, the unknown mathematician had given himself the trouble of resolving the long formula into a simpler one. He had found a brief and precise form containing only the more elementary algebraic and trigonometric expressions.

At the very end, on a small inset, there was a graphic representation of the solution.

I could wish for nothing better. An equation which I thought could not be solved in the final form had been solved.

When I had recovered a little from my initial surprise and admiration I went through the photo copies again. Now I noticed that he who had solved my problem had been writing in great hurry and very closely as though trying to save on every˙ scrap of paper and every second of time. Altogether he had written twenty-eight pages and I pictured mentally what a titanic work that had been! Try and pen a letter of twenty-eight closely written pages in one day or just copy, without following the meaning, twenty-eight pages out of a book, and you will surely find it a hellish job.

But what I had in front of me was not a letter to a friend or a chapter copied out of a book. It was the solution of a most intricate mathematical problem—done in twenty-four hours.

For several hours I studied the closely written pages, my surprise mounting with each hour.

Where had Kraftstudt found such a mathematician? On what terms? Who was he? A man of genius nobody knew? Or perhaps one of those wonders of human nature that sometimes occur on the border line between the normal and the abnormal? A rare specimen Kraftstudt had unearthed in the Wise Men's Home?

Cases have been recorded of brilliant mathematicians ending their days in a lunatic asylum. Maybe my mathematician was one of those?

These questions plagued me for the rest of that day.

But one thing was clear: the problem had been solved not by a machine, but by a man, a mathematical wizard the world knew nothing about.

The next day, a little calmer, I reread the whole solution for the sheer pleasure of it this time, just as one will listen again and again to a piece of music one loves. It was so precise, so limpid, so beautiful that I decided to repeat the experiment. I decided to give Kraftstudt Co. one more problem to solve.

That was easy, for I was never short of challenging problems, and I chose an equation which I had always thought impossible to break down so that it could be handled by a computer, let alone be finally solved.

This equation, too, dealt with radiowave propagation, but it was a specific and very complex case. It was an equation of the type that theoretical physicists evolve for the fun of it and soon forget all about because they are much too complex and therefore of no use to anybody.

I was met by the same young man blinking in the daylight. He gave me a reluctant smile.

'I have another problem—' I began.

Nodding briefly he again led me all the way through the dark corridors to the bleak reception hall.

Knowing the routine now, I went up to the window and handed him my equation.

'So it's not computers that do these things here?'

'As you see,' he said without looking up from my equation.

'Whoever solved my first problem is quite a gifted mathematician,' I said.

The young man did not say a word, deep as he was in my equation.

'Is he the only one in your employ or have you several?' I asked.

'What has that to do with your requirements? The firm guarantees—'

He had no time to finish, for at that moment the deep silence of the place was shattered by an inhuman scream. I started and listened. The sound was coming from behind the wall beyond the partition. It was like somebody being tortured. Crumpling the sheets with my problem, the young man, throwing a side glance and seizing me by the hand, dragged me to the exit.

'What was that?' I asked, panting.

'You'll have the solution the day after tomorrow, at twelve. You'll pay the bearer.'

With those words he left me by my taxi.

(3)

It is hardly necessary to say that after this event my peace of mind was completely gone. Not for one moment could I forget that terrible scream which had seemed to shake the very stone vaults sheltering Kraftstudt and Co. Besides I was still under the shock of finding such a complicated problem solved by one man in one day. And finally I was feverishly waiting for the solution of my second problem. If this one, too, was solved, then. . . .

It was with shaking hands that two days later I received a package from the Kraftstudt girl. By its bulk I could tell that it must contain the solution to the monstrously complicated piece of mathematics. With something akin to awe I stared at the thin creature in front of me. Then I had an idea.

'Please come in, I'll get the money for you.'

'No, it's all right.' She seemed frightened and in a hurry. 'I'll wait outside. . . .'

'Come on in, no point in freezing outside,' I said and all but dragged her into the hall. 'I must have a look first to see whether the work's worth paying for.'

The girl backed against the door and watched me with wide-open eyes.

'It is forbidden . . .' she whispered.

'What is?'

'To enter clients' flats. . . . Those are the instructions, sir. . . .'

'Never mind the instructions. I'm the master of this house and nobody will ever know you've entered.'

'Oh, sir, but they will, and then . . .'

'What then?' I said, coming nearer.

'Oh, it's so horrible. . . .'

Her head drooped suddenly and she sobbed.

I put a hand on her shoulder but she recoiled.

'Give me the seven hundred marks at once and I will go.'

I held out the money; she snatched it and was gone.

Opening the package I nearly cried out with astonishment. For several minutes I stood there staring at the sheaf of photo paper unable to believe my own eyes. The calculations were done in a *different* hand.

Another mathematical genius! And of greater calibre than the first. The equations he had solved in an analytical form on fifty-three pages were incomparably more complicated than the ones I had handed in the first time. As I peered at the integrals, sums, variations and other symbols of the highest realms of mathematics I had a sudden feeling of having been transferred into a strange mathematical world where difficulty had no meaning. It just didn't exist.

That mathematician, it seemed, had no more difficulty in solving my problem than we have in adding or subtracting two-digit numbers.

Several times I tore myself away from the manuscript to look up a thing in a mathematical manual or reference book. I was amazed by his skill in using the most complex theorems and proofs. His mathematical logic and methods were irreproachable. I did not doubt that had the best mathematicians of all nations and ages, such as Newton, Leibnitz, Gauss, Euler, Lobachevsky, Weierstrass and Hilbert, seen the way my problem had been solved they would have been no less surprised.

When I finished reading the manuscript I fell to thinking.

Where did Kraftstudt get those mathematicians? I was convinced now he had a whole team of them, not just two or three. Surely he couldn't have founded a computer firm employing only two or three men. How had he managed it? Why was his firm next door to a lunatic asylum? Who had uttered that inhuman scream behind the wall? And why?

'Kraftstudt, Kraftstudt . . .' hammered in my brain. Where and when had I heard that name? What was behind it? I paced up and down my study, pressing my head with my hands, tasking my memory.

Then I again sat down to that genius-inspired manuscript, delighting in it, rereading it part by part, losing myself to the world in the complexities of intermediate theorems and formulae. Suddenly I jumped up because I recalled that terrible inhuman scream once more and with it came the name of Kraftstudt.

The association was not fortuitous. No, it was inevitable. The screams of a man tortured and—Kraftstudt! These naturally went together. During the Second World War a Kraftstudt served as investigator in a Nazi concentration camp at Graz. For his part in the murders and inhuman treatment he got a life sentence at the Nuremberg trials.

I remembered the man's photo in all newspapers, in the uniform of an SS Obersturmführer, in a pince-nez, with wide-open, surprised eyes in a plump goodnatured face. People wouldn't believe a man with such a face could have been a sadist. Yet detailed evidence and thorough investigation left no room for doubt.

What had happened to him since the trials? Maybe he had been released like many other war criminals?

But what had mathematics to do with it all? What was the connection between a sadistic interrogator and the solutions of differential and integral equations?

At this point the chain of my reasoning snapped, for I was powerless to connect those two links. Obviously there was a link missing somewhere. Some kind of mystery.

Hard as I beat my brains, however, I could think of nothing plausible. And then that girl who had said, 'They will know.' How scared she had been!

After a few days of tormenting speculation I finally realized that unless I cracked the mystery I would probably crack up myself.

First of all I wanted to make sure that the Kraftstudt in question was that same war criminal.

(4)

Finding myself at the low door of Kraftstudt and Co. for the third time, I felt that what was to happen next would influence my whole life. For no reason I could understand then or later, I paid off the taxi and rang the bell only after the cab had swung round the corner.

It seemed to me that the young man with his crumpled old-manish face had been waiting for me. Without saying a word he took me by the hand and led me through the dark subterranean maze into the reception hall where I had been on the two previous occasions.

'Well, what brings you here this time?' he asked in what seemed to me a mocking tone of voice.

'I wish to speak to Herr Kraftstudt personally,' I demanded.

'Our firm is not satisfying you in some way, Professor?' he asked.

'I wish to speak to Herr Kraftstudt,' I insisted, trying not to look into his prominent black eyes, which now shone with malicious mockery.

'As you wish. It's none of my business,' he said after a long scrutiny. 'Wait here.'

Then he disappeared through one of the doors behind the glass partition.

He was gone over half an hour and I was dozing off when a rustle came to me from a corner and out of the semidarkness stepped a white-smocked figure with a stethoscope in hand. 'A doctor,' flashed through my mind. 'Come to examine me. Is this really necessary to see Herr Kraftstudt?'

'Follow me,' the doctor said peremptorily and I followed him, having no idea what was to happen next and why I had ever started it.

Light filtered into the long corridor in which we now were through a skylight high up somewhere. The corridor ended with a tall massive door. The doctor stopped.

'Wait here. Herr Kraftstudt will see you presently.'

In about five minutes he opened the door wide for me.

'Well, let's go,' he said in the tone of a man who was regretting what was going to happen.

I obediently followed him. We entered a wing with large bright windows and I shut my eyes involuntarily.

I was brought out of my momentary stupor by a sharp voice:

'Why don't you come up, Professor Rauch?'

I turned to my right and saw Kraftstudt in a deep wicker chair. He was the very man whom I remembered so well from the newspaper pictures.

'You wished to see me?' he asked, without greeting me or rising from his desk. 'What can I do for you?'

I controlled myself with an effort and went right up to his desk.

'So you have changed your occupation?' I asked, looking hard at him. He had aged in those fifteen years and the skin on his face had gathered into large flabby folds.

'What do you mean, Professor?' he asked, looking me over carefully.

'I had thought, Herr Kraftstudt, or rather hoped that you were still. . . .'

'Ah, I see.' And he guffawed.

'Times have changed, Rauch. Incidentally, it's not so much your hopes I am interested in at present as the reasons that brought you here.'

'As you can probably guess, Herr Kraftstudt, I have a fair knowledge of mathematics, I mean modern mathematics. I thought at first you had organized an ordinary computer center equipped with electronic machinery. However I'm now convinced that this is not the case. In your establishment it's men who solve the problems. As only men of genius would solve them. And what is most strange—with monstrous, inhuman speed. As a matter of fact, I took the liberty of coming to meet your mathematicians, who are indeed extraordinary men.'

Kraftstudt first smiled, then began to laugh quietly, then louder and louder.

'I don't see the joke, Herr Kraftstudt,' I said indignantly. 'My wish appears ridiculous to you, does it? But don't you realize that anybody with an interest in mathematics would have the same wish on seeing the kind of solution I got from your firm?'

'I'm laughing at something quite different, Rauch. I'm laughing at your provincial narrowmindedness. I'm laughing at you, Professor, a man respected in the town, whose learnedness has always boggled the imagination of immature maidens and old spinsters, at the way you hopelessly lag behind the swift strides of modern science!'

I was staggered by the insolence of that ex-Nazi interrogator.

'Listen, you,' I shouted. 'Only fifteen years ago your speciality was applying hot irons to innocent people. What right have you to prattle about swift strides of science? Come to that, I wished to see you to find what methods you use to force the brilliant people in your power to perform work which would take men of genius several years or perhaps all their life to do. I'm very glad I have found you. I consider it my duty as a scientist and citizen to let all the people in our town know that a former Nazi hangman has chosen as his new trade to abase men of science, men whose duty has always been to work for the good of humanity.'

Kraftstudt got up from his chair and, frowning, approached me.

'Listen to me, Rauch. Take my advice and do not provoke me. I knew you would come to me sooner or later. But I never imagined you would be such an idiot. Frankly speaking, I thought I would find in you an ally, so to speak, and a helper.'

'What?' I exclaimed. 'First you explain to me by what honest or dishonest means you are exploiting the people who bring you profit.'

Before my very eyes his face shrank into a lump of dirty yellowish skin. The pale-blue eyes behind the pince-nez turned into two slits that bore into me acidly. For a fleeting moment I had a feeling of a thing being examined by a prospective buyer.

'So you want me to explain to you how honestly our firm operates? So you're not satisfied with having your idiotic sums done for you as they should be done in the twentieth century? You want to experience for yourself what it means to be solving such problems?' he hissed, his vile face a mask pulsating with rage and hate.

'I don't believe everything is above board here. Your reputation is proof enough. And then I overheard one of your men screaming—'

'That's enough,' Kraftstudt barked. 'After all I never asked you to come. But since you are here—and in such a mood—we'll make use of you whether you like it or not.'

I had been unaware that the doctor who had brought me there was standing all the time behind me. At a signal from Kraftstudt a muscular hand closed on my mouth, and a piece of cotton soaked in something pungent was thrust under my nose.

I lost consciousness.

(5)

I came to slowly and realized that I was lying stretched on a bed. Voices of men in a heated argument crowded in on me. For a while all I knew was that their subject was scientific. Then, as my head cleared a little, I could understand what it was about.

'I can tell you this: your Nichols is no example. The coding of stimulation is highly individual, you know. What stimulates will-power in one man might stimulate something quite different in another. For instance, an electrical impulse that gives Nichols pleasure deafens me. When I get it I have a feeling two tubes have been thrust into my ears with a couple of aircraft engines revving up at the other end.'

'All the same the activity rhythm of neurone groups in the brain doesn't differ much from man to man. That's what our teacher's taking advantage of, really.'

'With not much success, though,' a tired voice said. 'Nothing beyond mathematical analysis so far.'

'It's all a matter of time. No short cuts here. Nobody would introduce an electrode into your brain to examine the impulses, because that would damage the brain and consequently the impulses. Now a generator allows for a wide range of change in coded impulses. And that makes for experiments without damage to the brain.'

'That's as may be,' the tired voice demurred. 'The cases of Gorin and Void don't bear you out. The Gorin died within ten seconds of being put inside a frequency-modulated field. Void screamed with pain, so the generator had to be switched off immediately. You seem to forget the principal thing about neurocybernetics, my friends, and that is that the network of neurones in the human body effects immense numbers of synapses. The impulses these transmit have their own frequency. As soon as you are in resonance with this natural frequency your circuit gets tremendously excited. The doctor's probing blindfolded, so to speak. And that we are still alive is pure chance.'

At that moment I opened my eyes. I was lying in a room that looked like a large hospital ward with beds lining the walls. In the middle stood a big deal table piled high with remnants of food, empty tins, cigarette stubs and scraps of paper. The scene was lit dimly by electric light. I rose on my elbows and looked round. Immediately the conversation stopped.

'Where am I?' I whispered, looking over the faces staring at me.

A voice whispered, 'The new fellow's come to.'

'Where am I?' I repeated, addressing them all.

'So you don't know?' asked a young man in his underwear, sitting upright in the bed to my right. 'This is the firm of Kraftstudt, our creator and teacher.'

'Creator and teacher?' I mumbled, rubbing my leaden forehead. 'What do you mean—teacher? He's a war criminal.'

'Crime is relative. It all depends on the purpose. If the end is noble, any action is good,' trotted out my neighbor on the right.

This piece of vulgar Machiavellianism made me look at the man with renewed curiosity.

'Where did you pick up that bit of wisdom, young man?' I said, letting my feet down and facing him.

'Herr Kraftstudt is our creator and teacher,' they suddenly began to chant in chorus.

So I have landed in the Wise Men's Home after all, I thought.

'Well, friends, things must be very bad for you to say a thing like that,' I said, looking them over again.

'I bet the new boy has his maths in a frequency band between ninety and ninety-five cycles!' a stout fellow shouted, half rising from his bed.

'And he'll squeal with pain at no more than 140 cycles in the uniformly accelerated pulse code!' bellowed another.

'And he'll be forced to sleep by receiving a series of eight pulses per second with a pause of two seconds after each series!'

'I am certain the new boy will develop ravenous hunger if stimulated at a frequency of 103 cycles with a logarithmic increase in the pulse power!'

The worst I could imagine had happened. I was indeed among madmen. The strange thing, however, was that they all seemed to have the same obsession: the possible influence of some kind of codes and pulses on my sensation. They thronged round me goggle-eyed, shouting out figures, giving modulations and powers, betting on how I would act 'inside the generator' and 'between the walls' and what power I was likely to consume.

Knowing from books that madmen should not be contradicted, I decided not to start any arguments but to try to behave like one of them. So I spoke in as inoffensive a tone as possible to my neighbor on the right. He seemed just a bit more normal than the others.

'Would you please tell me what you're all talking about? I must admit I'm completely ignorant of the subject. All these codes, pulses, neurones, stimulations—'

The room shook to a burst of guffaws. The inmates reeled with laughter, holding their sides, rocking and doubling up. The laughter became hysterical when I rose in indignation to shout them down.

'Circuit Number Fourteen. Frequency eighty-five cycles! Stimulation of anger!' somebody shouted and their laughter crescendoed.

Then I sat on the bed and resolved to wait till they calmed down.

My neighbor on the right was the first to do so. Then he sat on my bed and fixed his eyes on mine.

'Do you mean to say you really don't know anything?'

'Word of honor, not a thing. I can't make head or tail of what you were saying.'

'Word of honor?'

'Word of honor.'

'All right. We'll believe you, though you're certainly a rare case. Deinis, get up and tell the new boy what we're here for.'

'Yes, Deinis, get up and tell him all about it. Let him be as happy as we are.'

'Happy?' I asked, surprised. 'Are you happy?'

'Of course we are, of course we are,' they all shouted. 'Why, we know ourselves now. Man's highest bliss is to know himself.'

'Didn't you know yourselves before?' I asked.

'Of course not. People don't know themselves. Only those who are familiar with neurocybernetics know themselves.'

'Long live our teacher!' someone shouted.

'Long live our teacher!' they all shouted in automatic unison.

The man whom they called Deinis came up and sat down on the bed next to mine.

'What education have you?' he asked in a hollow tired voice.

'I am a professor of physics.'

'Do you know anything about neuropsychology?'

'Nothing at all.'

'Cybernetics?'

'Almost nothing.'

'Neurocybernetics and the general theory of biologic regulation?'

'Not the vaguest idea.'

An exclamation of surprise sounded in the room.

'Not a chance,' Deinis muttered. '*He* won't understand.'

'Go on, please, I'll try my best to follow you.'

'He'll understand all right after a dozen generator sessions or so,' a voice said.

'I understood after five!' someone shouted.

'A couple of turns between the walls will be even better.'

'Anyway, explain things to me, Deinis,' I insisted, fighting down a terrible premonition.

'Well, do you understand what life is?'

For a long time I said nothing, staring at Deinis.

'Life is a complex natural phenomenon,' I uttered at last.

There was a snigger. Then another. Then many more. The inmates of the ward were looking at me as though I had just uttered some obscene nonsense. Deinis shook his head disapprovingly.

'You're in a bad way. You've a lot to learn,' he said.

'Tell me where I am wrong.'

'Go on, Deinis, explain to him,' they all shouted in unison.

'Very well. Listen. Life is constant circulation of coded electrochemical stimulations along the neurones of your organism.'

I thought that over. Circulation of stimulations along neurones. I seemed to remember hearing something like that before.

'Well, carry on.'

'All the sensations that go to make up your spiritual ego are nothing but electrochemical impulses that travel from receptors up to the brain to be processed, and then down to effectors.'

'Yes, well?'

'All sensations of the outer world pass along the nerve fibres to the brain. Each sensation has its own code, frequency, and speed. And these three parameters determine its quality, intensity, and duration. Understand that?'

'Let's assume I do.'

'Hence life is nothing more nor less than the passage of coded information along your nerve fibres. And thought is the circulation of frequency-modulated information through the neurone synapses in the central regions of the nervous system, that is, in the brain.'

'I don't quite understand that,' I confessed.

'It's like this. The brain is made up of nearly ten thousand million neurones similar to electric relays. They are linked up into an elaborately interconnected system by fibres called axones. These conduct stimulation from neurone to neurone. It is this wandering of stimulation along the neurones that we call thought.'

My premonition grew to fear.

'He won't understand a thing until he's been inside the generator or between the walls,' shouted several voices at once.

'Well, let's assume you're right. What follows from that?' I said to Deinis.

'That life can be shaped at will. By means of pulse generators stimulating the corresponding codes in the neurone synapses. And that is of enormous practical importance.'

'Meaning?' I asked softly, sensing that I was about to get an insight into Kraftstudt and Co.'s activities.

'That can be best explained by an example. Let us consider the stimulation of mathematical activity. Certain backward countries are at present building what are called electronic computers. The number of triggers, or relays, such machines have does not exceed five to ten thousand. The number of triggers in the mathematical areas of the human brain is in the order of one thousand million. Nobody will ever be able to build a machine with anywhere near that number.'

'Well, what of it?'

'Here you are: mathematical problems can be solved much more efficiently and cheaply by a mechanism created by Mother Nature and lodged here,' Deinis passed his hand across his forehead, 'than by any expensive junk built for the job.'

'But machines work quicker!' I exclaimed. 'A neurone, so far as I remember, can be excited no more than 200 times per second, whereas an electronic trigger can take millions of pulses. That is precisely why fast-working machines are more efficient!'

The ward rocked with laughter again. Deinis alone retained a straight face.

'You're wrong there. Neurones can be made to take impulses at any speed provided the exciter has a sufficiently high frequency. For example, an electrostatic generator operating in the pulsed condition. If you place a brain in the radiation field of such a generator it can be made to work at any speed.'

'So that is the way Kraftstudt and Co. make their money, is it!' I said, jumping up from the bed.

'He is our teacher!' they all chanted again. 'Repeat it, new boy. He is our teacher!'

'Leave him,' Deinis ordered suddenly. 'He will understand in time that Herr Kraftstudt is our teacher. He doesn't know anything yet. Listen to this new boy. Every sensation has its own code, its own intensity and duration. The sensation of happiness—55 cycles per second with coded series of one hundred pulses each. The sensation of grief—62 cycles with a pause of 0.1 second between pulses. The sensation of joy—47 cycles with pulses increasing in intensity. The sensation of sadness—203 cycles, pain—123 cycles, love—14 cycles, poetic mood—31, anger—85, fatigue—17, sleepiness—8, and so on. Coded pulses in these frequencies move along the neurones and thus you experience all the sensations I've mentioned. They can all be produced by a pulse generator created by our teacher. He has opened our eyes to the meaning of life.'

These explanations made me giddy. I didn't know what to think. The man was either as mad as a hatter or really giving me a glimpse into mankind's future. I was still dizzy from the after-effects of the drug I'd been given in Kraftstudt's study. A wave of weariness swept over me, I lay back and closed my eyes.

'He's under frequency 7 to 8 cycles! He wants to sleep!' someone shouted.

'Let him have his sleep. Tomorrow he'll start learning life. They'll take him inside the generator tomorrow.'

'No, he'll have his specter recorded tomorrow. He might have abnormalities.'

That was the last thing I heard. I slid into deep sleep.

(6)

The man I met the next day at first appeared to me quite pleasant and intelligent. When I was led into his study a floor up in the firm's main building he came forward to meet me, smiling broadly, hand stretched out in greeting.

'Ah, Professor Rauch. I'm indeed pleased to meet you.'

Returning his greeting with restraint I inquired after his name.

'My name is Boltz, Hans Boltz. Our chief has given me an embarrassing commission—that of extending apologies to you in his name.'

'Apologies? Is your chief really subject to pangs of conscience?'

'I don't know. I'm sure I don't know, Rauch. Anyway, he's extending his most sincere apologies to you for all that has happened. He lost his temper. He doesn't like being reminded of the past, you know.'

I smiled wrily but said, 'Why, I did not come with any intention of raking in his past. My interest lay elsewhere. I wanted to meet those who so brilliantly solved—'

'Pray be seated, Professor. That is exactly what I was going to speak to you about.'

I settled in the proffered chair and studied the broadly smiling face behind the large desk. Boltz was a typical north-country German with an elongated face, fair hair, and large blue eyes. His fingers were playing with a cigarette case.

'I'm in charge of the math department here,' he said.

'You? Are you a mathematician?'

'Yes, in a way. At least I have a smattering of it.'

'That means I can meet some of them through you?'

'You've already met all of them, Rauch,' Boltz said.

I stared at him blank-eyed.

'You've spent a day and a night with them.'

I remembered the ward and its inmates with their nonsense about impulses and codes.

'Do you expect me to believe those crackpots are the brilliant mathematicians who solved my equations?'

Not waiting for a reply I burst into laughter.

'And yet they are, indeed. Your last problem was solved by a certain Deinis. So far as I know, the same individual who last night gave you a lecture on neurocybernetics.'

After a few moments' thought I said:

'In that case I don't understand anything. Perhaps you would explain it all to me?'

'With pleasure. But after you've seen this.' And Boltz offered me the morning paper.

I unfolded it slowly and suddenly jumped up. Looking at me from the first page was . . . my own face framed in black. Over it was the banner caption: 'Tragic death of Dr Rauch.'

'What's the meaning of this, Boltz? What sort of farce is this?' I expostulated.

'Please calm yourself. It's all quite simple really. Last night when crossing the bridge over the river on your way home from a walk near the lake, you were attacked by two escaped lunatics from the Wise Men's Home, killed, mutilated, and thrown into the river. Early this morning a corpse was discovered at the dam. The clothes, personal belongings, and papers helped to identify the corpse as yours. The police called at the Home this morning and have pieced together a complete picture of your tragic death.'

It was only then that I looked at my clothes and realized that the suit I had on was not mine; I dived into my pockets; all the things I'd had on me were gone.

'But this is preposterous—'

'Yes, of course, I quite agree. But what can be done, Rauch, what can be done? Without you Kraftstudt and Co. may suffer a serious setback—go bust, in fact. I don't mind telling you that we are up to our eyebrows in orders. They're all military and extremely valuable. And that means round-the-clock computing. Since we completed the first batch of problems for the Defense Ministry, business has just snowballed, you might say.'

'And you want me to become another Deinis for you?'

'Oh, no, Rauch. Of course not.'

'Then why that farce?'

'We need you as an instructor in mathematics.'

'Instructor?'

I jumped up again, staring wildly at Boltz. He lighted a cigarette for himself and nodded at my chair. I sat down, completely bewildered.

'We need new mathematicians, Professor Rauch. Either we get them or we'll very soon be on the rocks.'

I stared at the man, who did not seem to me half so pleasant now as he'd done before. I seemed to discern traits of innate bestiality in him, faint, but coming to the fore now.

'Well, what if I refuse?' I asked.

'That would be just too bad. I'm afraid you'd have to join our—er —computer force then.'

'Is that so bad?' I asked.

'It is,' Boltz said firmly, standing up. 'That would mean you'd finish your days in the Wise Men's Home.'

Pacing up and down the room, Boltz began to speak in the tones of a lecturer addressing an audience:

'The computing abilities of the human brain are several hundred thousand times those of an electronic computer. A thousand million mathematical nerve cells plus the aids—memory, inhibition, logic, intuition, etc.—place the brain high above any conceivable machine. Yet the machine has one essential advantage.'

'Which is?' I asked, still not understanding what Boltz was driving at.

'If, say, a trigger or a group of triggers is out of order in an electronic machine, you can replace the valves, resisters, or capacitors and the machine will work again. But if a nerve cell or a group of nerve cells in the computing area is out of order, replacement, alas, is impossible. Unfortunately we are obliged to make brain triggers work at an increased tempo here. As a result, wear and tear, if I may call it so, is greatly accelerated. The living computers are soon used up and then—'

'What then?'

'Then the computer goes into the Home.'

'But that's inhuman—and criminal,' I said hotly.

Boltz stopped in front of me, placed a hand on my shoulder and, with a broad smile, said:

'Rauch, you've got to forget all those words and notions here. If you won't forget them yourself we'll have to erase them from your memory for you.'

'You will never be able to do that!' I shouted, brushing away his hand.

'Deinis' lecture was wasted on you, I see. Pity. He spoke sense. Incidentally, d'you know what memory is?'

'What has that to do with our subject? What the hell kind of crazy business are you up to here? Why—?'

'Memory, Professor Rauch, is prolonged stimulation in a group of neurones due to a positive reverse connection. In other words, memory is the electrochemical stimulation that circulates in a given group of nerve cells in your head. You, as a physicist interested in electromagnetic processes in complex media, must realize that by placing your head in the appropriate electromagnetic field we can stop that circulation in any group of neurones. Nothing could be simpler! We can not only make you forget what you know, but make you recall what you have never known. However it's not in our interests to resort to these—er—artificial means. We hope your common sense will prevail. The firm will be making over to you a sizable share of its dividends.'

'For what services?'

'I've already told you—for teaching mathematics. We sign up classes of twenty to thirty people with an aptitude for math—this country has an abundance of unemployed, fortunately. Then we teach them higher mathematics in the course of two to three months—'

'But that's impossible,' I said, 'absolutely impossible. In such a short time, I mean. . . .'

'It's *not* impossible, Rauch. Don't forget you'll be dealing with a very bright audience, uncommonly intelligent and possessing a wonderful memory for figures. We will see to that. That is in our power.'

'Also by artificial means? By means of the pulse generator?' I asked.

Boltz nodded.

'Well, do you agree?'

I shut my eyes tightly and thought hard. So Deinis and the others in the ward were normal people and had been telling me the truth yesterday. So Kraftstudt and Co. had really developed a technique of commercializing human thought, willpower and emotions by means of electromagnetic fields. I sensed Boltz's searching eyes on

me and knew I must hurry with my decision. It was devilishly hard
to make. If I agreed I'd be speeding my students on their way to the
Wise Men's Home. If I refused I'd do the same to myself.

'Do you agree?' Boltz repeated, touching me on the shoulder.

'No,' I said, my mind made up. 'No. I can be no accomplice to
such abomination.'

'As you wish,' he said with a sigh. 'I'm very sorry, though.'

After a minute's silence he stood up briskly, went over to the door
and, opening it, called out:

'Eider, Schrank, come in here!'

'What are you going to do to me?' I asked, also getting up.

'To begin with we'll record the pulse-code specter of your nervous
system.'

'Which means?'

'Which means we'll record the form, intensity, and frequency of
the pulses responsible for your every emotional and intellectual
state and make them into a chart.'

'But I won't let you. I will protest. I—'

'Show the Professor the way to the test laboratory,' Boltz cut in
indifferently and turned his back on me to look out of the window.

(7)

As I entered the test laboratory I had already formed the decision
which was to play a crucial role in the events that followed. My line
of reasoning was this. They are going to subject me to a test that
will give Kraftstudt and his gang complete information on my inner
self. They need this to know what electromagnetic influence to bring
to bear on my nervous system to produce any emotion or sensation
they want. If they are fully successful I'll be in their power beyond
hope of escape. If they are not I'll retain a certain amount of free
play. Which I might soon badly need. So the only hope for me is
to try to fool those gangsters as much as possible. That I could do so
to a degree I deduced from what that slave of Kraftstudt's had said
yesterday about pulse-code characteristics being individual, except
where mathematical thought is concerned.

I was led into a large room cluttered up with bulky instrumenta-
tion, the whole looking like the control room of a power station.
The middle of the laboratory was taken up by a control console with
instrument panels and dials. To its left, behind a screen of wire mesh,
towered a transformer, several generator lamps glowing red in
white porcelain panels. Fixed to the wire mesh which served as a
screen grid for the generator were a voltmeter and an ammeter.
Their readings were used, apparently, to measure the generator's

output. Close by the control console stood a cylindrical booth made up of two metallic parts, top and bottom.

As I was led up to the booth two men rose from behind the console. One of them was the same doctor who had taken me to Kraftstudt the day before, the other a wizened old man whom I didn't know, with sparse hair disciplined into perfect smoothness on a yellow cranium.

'Failed to persuade him,' the doctor said. 'I knew as much. I could see at once that Rauch belonged to the strong type. You will come to a bad end, Rauch,' he said to me.

'So will you,' I said.

'That's as may be, but with you it's definite.'

I shrugged.

'Will you go through it voluntarily or do you want us to force you?' he then asked, looking me over insolently.

'Voluntarily. As a physicist I'm even interested.'

'Splendid. In that case remove your shoes and strip to the waist. I must examine you first and take your blood pressure.'

I did as I was told. The first part of 'registering the specter' looked like an ordinary medical check-up—breathe, stop breathing and the rest of it.

When the examination was over the doctor said:

'Now step into the booth. You've got a mike there. Answer all my questions. I must warn you that one of the frequencies will make you feel an intense pain. But it will go as soon as you yell out.'

In my bare feet I stepped on to the porcelain floor. An electric bulb flashed on overhead. The generator droned. It was operating in the low-frequency band. The tension of the field was obviously very high. I felt this by the way waves of warmth swelled and ebbed slowly through my body. Each electromagnetic pulse brought with it a strange tickling in the joints. Then my muscles began contracting and relaxing in time to the pulses.

Presently the frequency of the warmth waves was increased.

Here it goes, I thought. If only I can bear it.

When the frequency reached eight cycles per second I would want to sleep. If only I could fight it. If only I could fool the blackguards. The frequency was slowly increasing. In my mind I counted the number of warm tides per second. One, two, three, four, more, still more. . . . Then sleepiness was on me with overwhelming suddenness. I clamped my teeth together, willing myself into wakefulness. Sleep was pushing me under like an enormous clammy weight, bearing me down, loading my eyelids. It was a miracle I was still on my feet. I bit my tongue, hoping pain would help me throw off the nightmarish burden of sleep. At that moment, as if from afar, a voice came to me:

'Rauch, how do you feel?'

'Not bad, thank you. A bit cold,' I lied. I didn't recognize my own voice and bit my lips and tongue as hard as I could.

'Don't you feel sleepy?'

'No,' I said, though I thought I would drop into sleep the next moment. And then, abruptly, all sleepiness was gone. The frequency must have been increased beyond the first terminal threshold. I felt fresh and cheerful as after a good snooze. Now I must fall asleep, I thought, and, shutting my eyes, snored away. I heard the doctor say to his assistant:

'Odd. Sleep at 10 cycles instead of 8½. Write it down, Pfaff,' he told the old man. 'Rauch, your sensations?'

I didn't reply, still snoring loudly, my muscles relaxed, knees stuck against the side of the booth.

'Let's go on with it,' said the doctor. 'Increase the frequency, Pfaff, will you.'

In a second I 'woke up.' The frequency band through which I was now passing made me experience a whole gamut of emotions and changes of mood. I was sad, then gay, then happy, then utterly miserable.

'Time I yelled out,' I suddenly decided.

At the moment the generator's roar increased I screamed at the top of my lungs, whereupon the doctor immediately ordered:

'Cut the tension! It's the first time I've met such a crazy type. Write down: pain at 75 cycles per second when normal people experience it at 130. Go on.'

That frequency is still in store for me, I thought in dread. Will I be able to cope with it?

'Now, Pfaff, try 93 on him.'

When the frequency stabilized something entirely unexpected happened to me. I suddenly remembered the equations which had brought me to Kraftstudt and with perfect clarity visualized every stage of their solution. This is the frequency which stimulates mathematical thinking, I thought fleetingly.

'Rauch, name the first five members of the Bessel function of the second order,' the doctor demanded.

I rattled off the answer. My head was crystal clear and my whole being was permeated with a wonderful feeling of knowing everything and having it all on my tongue's tip.

'Name the first ten places of π.'

I named them.

'Solve a cubic equation.'

The doctor dictated one with unwieldy fractional coefficients.

In two or three seconds I had the solution ready, naming all the three roots.

'Let's go on. He's quite normal in this department.'

Slowly the frequency increased and I felt maudlin. There was a lump in my throat and tears welled in my eyes. But I laughed. I roared with convulsive laughter as if being vigorously tickled. I laughed, while the tears rolled down my cheeks.

'Some idiotic idiosyncrasy again. In a class of his own, you might say. I at once knew him for a strong nervous type subject to neuroses. When will he start bawling, I wonder?'

I 'bawled' when weeping was farthest from my mood, when all of a sudden my heart was overflowing with buoyant happiness as a nuptial cup with good wine. I wanted to troll and laugh and dance for joy. All of them—Kraftstudt and Boltz and Deinis and the doctor —seemed to me capital fellows, the jolliest chaps I had ever met. It was then that, with great effort, I started to whimper and blow my nose loudly. Though hideously inadequate, my weeping soon elicited the now familiar comments of the expert:

'What a type! All upside down. Nothing even remotely resembling the normal specter. This fellow will give us a lot of trouble.'

How far is one hundred and thirty? I thought, in abject terror, when the happy and carefree sensation had given way to a feeling of worry, ungrounded anxiety, the presage of impending doom. . . . I started humming a tune. I was doing it mechanically, with a great effort, while my heart pounded away in premonition of something terrible, something fatal and inevitable.

I at once knew when the frequency approached the one stimulating the sensation of pain. At first there was just a dull ache in the joints of the thumb on my right hand, then a sharp pain seared through an old wartime wound. This was followed by a terrible toothache spreading at once to all the teeth. Then a splitting headache was added.

Blood pulsed painfully in my ears. Shall I be able to stand it? Shall I have enough willpower to overcome the nightmarish pain and not show it? People have been known after all to be done to death in torture chambers without groaning once. History has recorded cases of people dying on the faggots mute. . . .

The pain went on increasing. Finally it reached its peak and my whole body became one knot of gnawing, stinging, racking, throbbing, excruciating pain. I was all but unconscious and saw purple specks revolving before my eyes, but I remained silent.

'Your sensations, Rauch,' the doctor's voice penetrated to me.

'A sensation of murderous rage,' I muttered through clenched teeth. 'If I only could lay my hands on you. . . .'

'Let's go on. He's completely abnormal. Everything's backwards with him.'

And when I was on the verge of passing out, ready to scream or groan, all pain was suddenly gone. There was sweat, clammy and cold, all over my body. My every muscle trembled.

Later some frequency made me see a blinding light which was there even when I shut my eyes, then I experienced wolfish hunger, heard a scale of deafening noises, felt cold as if taken out into the frost without a stitch on. But I persisted in giving the doctor wrong answers until he fumed with rage. I knew I still had coming to me one of the most terrible tests mentioned in the ward the day before: loss of willpower. It was will that had seen me through so far. It was this invisible inner force that had helped me fight the sensations created artificially by my tormentors. But they would get at it eventually with their hellish pulse generator. Now, would they be able to find I had lost it? I waited for that frequency in dread. And it came.

Suddenly I felt indifference. Indifference to being in the hands of the Kraftstudt gang, indifference to him and his associates, indifference to myself. My mind was a complete blank. The muscles felt flabby. All sensations were gone. It was a state of total physical and moral spinelessness. I couldn't force myself to think or make the slightest movement. I had no will of my own.

And yet, surviving in some remote corner of my consciousness, a tiny thought insisted: *You must . . . you must . . . you must.*

You must what? Why? Whatever for? 'You *must . . . you must . . . you must,*' kept on insisting what seemed to me a single nerve cell by some kind of miracle impervious to the all-powerful electromagnetic pulses that held sway over my nerves, bidding them to feel whatever those hangmen wanted.

Later, when I learned about the theory of the central encephalic system of brain activity, according to which all the nerve cells in the cortex are governed by a single, master group of nerve cells, I realized that this supreme psychic authority was impervious even to the strongest outside physical and chemical influences. That must be what saved me then.

Suddenly the doctor ordered:

'You will collaborate with Kraftstudt.'

I said:

'No.'

'You will do all that you are told to do.'

'No.'

'Run your head against the wall.'

'No.'

'Let's go on. He's abnormal, Pfaff, but mind you we'll get at him yet.'

I shammed loss of willpower just when a sensation of the strongest will flooded my whole being and I felt I could make myself do the impossible.

Checking on my 'abnormalities' the doctor put me a few more questions.

'If the happiness of mankind depended on your life, would you give it?'

'Why should I?' I asked dully.

'Can you commit suicide?'

'Yes.'

'Do you want to kill the war criminal, Obersturmführer Kraft-studt?'

'What for?'

'Will you collaborate with us?'

'Yes.'

'Damned if I can make anything out of him! I hope it's the first and the last time I have such a case to deal with. Loss of willpower at 175. Write that down. Let's go on with it.'

And they went on for another half-hour. Finally the frequency chart of my nervous system was complete. The doctor now knew all the frequencies by means of which I could be made to experience any sensation or mood. At least he thought he did. Actually the only genuine frequency was the one which stimulated my mathematical abilities. And that was just what I needed most. The point was that I had evolved a plan of blowing the criminal firm sky-high. And mathematics was to be my dynamite.

(8)

It is an established fact that hypnosis and suggestion work best on weak-willed individuals. That was how the Kraftstudt personnel instilled in the calculators—their wills generator-treated—awed obedience and reverence towards their 'teacher.'

I, too, was to pass through an obedience course, but because of my 'abnormal' specter this was postponed for a time. I required an individual approach.

While a working place was being especially set up for me I had comparative freedom to move about. I was allowed to go out of the ward into the corridor and glance into the classrooms where my colleagues studied or worked.

I was not allowed to join in the common prayers held between the walls of a huge aluminum condenser for half an hour every morning, during which Kraftstudt's victims paid homage to the firm's head. Devoid of will and thought, they dully repeated words read to them over a closed-circuit broadcast system.

'Joy and happiness lie in self-knowledge,' announced the relayed voice.

'Joy and happiness lie in self-knowledge,' the twelve men on bended knees repeated in chorus, their will-power destroyed by the alternating current field 'between the walls.'

'By understanding the mysteries of the circulation of impulses across neurone synapses we achieve joy and happiness.'

'. . . joy and happiness,' repeated the chorus.

'How wonderful that everything is so simple! What a delight it is to know that love, fear, pain, hatred, hunger, sorrow, joy are all nothing but the movement of electrochemical impulses in our bodies!'

'. . . in our bodies.'

'How miserable he who does not know this great truth!'

'. . . this great truth,' repeated the slaves dully.

'Herr Kraftstudt, our teacher and savior, gave us this happiness!'

'. . . happiness.'

'He gave us life.'

'He gave us life.'

I listened to this monstrous prayer, peeping through the glass door of a classroom.

Inert and flabby, with eyes half closed, the men repeated the nightmarish maxims in expressionless voices. The electric generator hardly ten paces away pumped submission into their minds robbed of resistance. Something inhuman, vile to the extreme, bestial and at the same time exquisitely cruel was being done to them. Boggled for comparison at the sight of that herd of miserable creatures with no will of their own, my mind could only suggest dipsomania or drug addiction at their worst.

The thanksgiving over, the twelve passed into a spacious hall with rows of desks. Suspended over each desk was a round plate of aluminum forming part of a mammoth condenser. A second plate was apparently sunk in the floor.

This hall reminded me somehow of an open-air café with shaded tables. But the idyllic impression was swept away as soon as I looked at the men under the plates.

A sheet of paper setting out the problem awaited each one of them. At first the calculators looked at these in dumb incomprehension, still under the influence of the will-destroying frequency. Presently the frequency of 93 cycles was switched on and a crisp order to begin work relayed.

And all the twelve, snapping up pad and pencil, pitched into feverish scribbling. This could not be called work. It was frenzy, a kind of mathematical epilepsy. The men writhed and squirmed over their pads; their hands shuttled to and fro till they blurred; their faces turned deep purple with the strain; their eyes started out of their sockets.

This lasted for the best part of an hour. Then, when their hands started moving jerkily, heads were lowered almost to the tabletops and livid veins swelled rope-like on their extended necks, the generator was switched to 8 cycles. All the twelve at once dropped asleep.

Kraftstudt saw to it that his slaves got some rest!

Then it all began afresh.

One day, while watching this horrible scene of mass mathematical frenzy I saw one of the calculators break down. Suddenly he stopped writing, crazily turned to one of his furiously writing neighbors and stared at him blankly for a while as if at great pains to remember something.

Then he gave a terrible guttural cry and began tearing his clothes. He bit himself, gnawed at his fingers, tore skin off his chest, battered his head on the table. Finally he passed out and slumped down on the floor.

The rest paid not the slightest attention, their pencils still working feverishly.

I was so enraged that I started pounding on the locked door. I wanted to call out to the poor devils, tell them to have done with it, to break out and fall on their tormentors. . . .

'Don't get so worked up, Herr Rauch,' I heard a calm voice beside me. It was Boltz.

'You are criminals! Look what you're doing to those people. What right have you to torture them?'

He smiled his bland intellectual smile and said:

'Do you remember the myth about the Greek hero? The gods offered him the choice between a long but quiet life and a short but turbulent one. He chose the latter. So did these men.'

'But they were not offered any choice. It's you and your pulse generator that chose to stampede them toward self-annihilation for the sake of dividends!'

Boltz laughed.

'Haven't you heard them say they are happy? And so they are. Look at the way they're working in happy abandon. Does not bliss lie in creative labor?'

'I find your arguments revolting. There is a normal tempo in human life and it is criminal to try to accelerate it.'

Bolt laughed again.

'You're not exactly logical, Professor. There was a time when people traveled on foot or horseback. Nowadays they fly by jet. News used to spread from mouth to mouth, taking years to snail-pace round the globe; now radio brings events right into your home even as they happen. Present-day civilization accelerates the tempo of life artificially and you don't think it's a crime. And the host of all sorts of artificial amusements and delights, aren't they too accelerating life's tempo? So why should you consider artificial acceleration of the functions of a living organism a crime? I'm certain that these people, were they to live a natural life, would not be able to do a millionth part of what they can do now. And the meaning of life, as you know, is creative activity. You will fully appreciate that when you become one of them. Soon you will know what joy and happiness are! In fact, in two days' time. A separate room is being set up for you. You will be working there alone, because, you will excuse my saying so, you are somewhat different from normal people.'

Boltz slapped me amiably on the shoulder and left me alone to ponder his inhuman philosophy.

(9)

In accordance with my 'specter' they started my obedience training at a frequency which gave me enough willpower to achieve a feat of defiance. My first feat was easy: again I shammed loss of willpower. Kneeling down and staring ahead as vacuum-eyed as I possibly could, I repeated dully the now familiar thanksgiving balderdash. In addition a few truths about neurocybernetics were inculcated in me as a novice. They boiled down to remembering which frequencies stood for what human emotions. Out of these, two were particularly important for my plans: the one stimulating mathematical thinking and another, which, luckily, was not far from the 93 cycles.

My training lasted for a week, after which time I was deemed obedient enough to be put to work. The first problem I was given was analyzing the possibility of intercepting an ICBM.

It took me two hours to do. The result was not cheerful for the Ministry: it couldn't be done under the conditions indicated.

The second problem, also of a military nature, was calculating a neutron beam powerful enough to set off an enemy's nuclear warheads. The answer was again cheerless. A neutron cannon as calculated would have to weigh several thousand tons.

It was indeed a delight for me to solve those problems and I must have looked as possessed as the other calculators, with the difference, however, that the generator, instead of making me an obedient tool, was infusing me with confidence and enthusiasm. A joyous feeling of being on top of the world did not leave me even during the sleep breaks. I pretended to sleep but in reality I was working out my plans of appropriate punishment.

When I was through with the Defense Ministry problems I began to solve in my mind (so that nobody would know) the problem most important for me, how to blow Kraftstudt and Co. sky-high.

I meant the phrase metaphorically, of course, having no dynamite and no chance of obtaining any in that prison-like madhouse. Anyway blasting was no part of my plan.

Since the pulse generator could stimulate any human emotion, why not try to use it, I reasoned, to rouse human dignity in its victims and make them rebel against the ex-Nazi criminals? If this were possible they would require no outside help to smash this scientifically-minded gang. But was there a way to do it? Was there a way, that is, to exchange the frequency stimulating mathematical thinking into one that unleashed anger and hatred in man?

The generator was operated by its aged creator, Dr Pfaff, an able engineer but apparently witn a strong sadistic streak. As he obviously delighted in the perverse way his creation was used, I could not count on any help from him. Dr Pfaff was absolutely out. The generator had to work on the frequency I required, without his help or knowledge.

Now if a pulse generator is overloaded, that is, if more power is taken off than its design allows, the frequency drops. That means that by adding an extra load in the form of a resistor, a generator can be made to operate on a frequency lower than shown on the dial.

Kraftstudt and Co. exploited mathematical thinking at a frequency of 93 cycles per second. Anger is produced by 85. That meant the frequency had to be cut down by a total of eight cycles! I started calculating an extra load to do that.

During my visit to the test laboratory I had noted the readings on the voltmeter and ammeter of the generator. Their product gave me its power. Now for the mathematical problem of an extra load. . . .

I first traced in my mind the way the gigantic condensers, inside which those poor devils slaved, were connected to the generator. Then, in forty minutes, I solved the pertinent Maxwell equations and did all the other, most complex calculations.

It appeared that Herr Pfaff had an excess of power of only $1\frac{1}{2}$ watts!

This was sufficient to calculate how a frequency of 93 cycles could be changed to one of 85. All I had to do was to ground one of the condenser plates through a resistor of 1,350 ohms.

I nearly shouted with joy. But where could I get a length of wire of that resistance? I thought next. It had to be very exact, too, or the desired effect would not be achieved.

I feverishly cast my mind about for substitutes but could think of none. A feeling of impotence swept over me when a black plastic cup suddenly appeared in my field of vision in the act of being placed on my desk by a small trembling hand. I looked up and could barely suppress an exclamation of surprise: standing in front of me was the thin girl with frightened eyes, the one who had delivered the Kraftstudt mail to me.

'What are you doing here?' I asked under my breath.

'Working,' she answered, hardly moving her lips. 'So you're alive.'

'Yes. I need you.'

Her eyes darted about.

'Everyone in town thinks you were killed. So did I.'

'You go to town?'

'Yes. Almost every day, but. . . .'

I caught her tiny hand and held it in mine.

'Tell everybody in town, especially at the University, that I'm alive and kept here by force. Tell them this tonight. My friends here and I must get help to get out.'

There was terror in the girl's eyes.

'What are you saying?' she whispered. 'If Herr Kraftstudt gets to know, and he can find out anything . . .'

'How often are you interrogated?'

'Next time will be the day after tomorrow.'

'You've got a whole day. Screw up your courage. Don't be afraid. Do as I tell you, please.'

The girl snatched her hand away and hurried out.

There were pencils in the black cup. Ten of them altogether, of different colors for different purposes. Mechanically I took the first that came to my hand and fingered it: it was marked '2B,' a very soft pencil. It had plenty of graphite, a fair conductor. Then came '3B' and '5B' pencils, then those of the 'H' range, hard ones, for copying. As I fingered them my mind seethed in a turmoil of speculation. Then all of a sudden, like a flash of lightning, I remembered the specific resistances of pencil graphites: A '5H' pencil has a resistance of 2,000 ohms. The next moment I had a '5H' pencil in my hand. The problem was solved now not only mathematically but practically. There in my hand was a length of wood-enclosed graphite with the help of which I could bring punishment to a gang of modern barbarians.

I secreted the pencil in an inner pocket as carefully as a priceless treasure. Then it occurred to me where I could get two pieces of wire, one to connect to the condenser plate over my desk, the other to the radiator in the corner, with the pencil graphite in between.

I remembered the table lamp in the ward where I lived with the other calculators. It had a flexible cord which, being about five feet long, could be unwound into a forty-foot length of thin wire, which would be more than enough for the job.

I had just finished my calculations when the relayed voice announced dinner time for the calculators.

I left my solitary cell in high spirits and made for the ward. Glancing back in the corridor, I saw the doctor look with obvious displeasure at the solutions of the problems I'd been given. Apparently the fact that there was no way of intercepting an ICBM or setting off the enemy's atomic bombs by a neutron cannon was not to his liking.

He had no premonition though of what *could* be done with ordinary graphite from a copying pencil!

(10)

The table lamp I had in mind had apparently not been in use for a long time. It stood in a corner on a high stool, dusty, fly-specked, its cord coiled tight round the upright.

Early in the morning when the inmates filed out to wash, I cut off the cord with a table knife and put it in my pocket. At breakfast I pocketed a knife and when everybody went out for the prayer I locked myself in the toilet. In a matter of seconds I had skinned off the insulation sheath and exposed numerous strands of thin wire, each about five feet long. Then I split the pencil gingerly, took out the graphite core and broke off three-tenths of its length. The remaining part should have the resistance I required. I made tiny notches at either end of the graphite where I secured the wires. The resistor was ready. All that remained to be done was to connect it to the condenser plate and then ground it.

That I could do during my work.

The calculators had an eight-hour working day with ten-minute breaks after each hour. After the lunch break, at 1 p.m., the hall where they worked was as a rule visited by the Kraftstudt and Co. executives. The head of the firm used to linger in the hall for some time, obviously enjoying the sight of twelve men writhing in mathematical throes. I decided it was the best time to change the frequency.

I went to my place of work that morning with the resistor all ready in my pocket. I was walking on air. At the door I met the doctor. He had brought my problems for the day.

'Hey, sawbones, wait a minute,' I called out to him.

He stopped in his tracks and looked me over, astonished.

'I'd like a word with you.'

'Well, what is it?' he grunted.

'It's like this,' I began. 'It occurred to me while I was working yesterday to return to a conversation I had with Herr Boltz. I think I was rather rash. I wonder if you would let Herr Boltz know that I agree to teach math to the firm's new recruits.'

'Good for you,' he said with sincerity. 'I told them that your specter being what it is you should be set up as an overseer over that mathematical manure. We badly need an efficient overseer. Your working frequencies are all different. You could just walk among them and drive the lazy or those who have slipped out of resonance.'

'Why, of course, doctor. But I think I'd better stick to teaching. God knows I don't feel like bashing my head against a tabletop as I saw a fellow do the other day.'

'Very sensible,' he agreed. 'I'll be speaking to Kraftstudt. I think he will agree.'

'When will I know his decision?'

'By one o'clock, I expect, when we make our round of the premises.'

'Good. If it's all right with you I'll approach you then.'

He nodded and walked off. On my desk I found a sheet of paper which gave me conditions for the calculation of a new pulse generator four times more powerful than the existing one. So Kraftstudt thinks of expanding his business, I thought. Yoking to it fifty-two calculators instead of the thirteen he has now. Almost lovingly I touched the pencil graphite with bits of wire in my pocket to make sure it hadn't broken.

The conditions of the problem showed me that my calculations in connection with the existing generator were correct. My hopes for success soared. I began looking forward to lunch break. When the clock on the wall showed a quarter to one I took my device and connected one end to a bolt on the aluminum plate above my desk. The other end I lengthened with more pieces of wire until it was long enough to reach the radiator in the corner of the room.

The last minutes dragged painfully. At last the minute hand touched twelve. I quickly connected the wire to the radiator and strode into the corridor. Advancing towards me was Kraftstudt with Pfaff, Boltz and the doctor in attendance. At the sight of me they broke into smiles. Boltz motioned me to join them. I did so and we all stopped at the glass door of the room where the calculators worked.

Pfaff and Kraftstudt were in front and I couldn't see what was going on inside.

'That was a wise move,' Boltz whispered to me. 'Herr Kraftstudt has accepted your offer. You won't regret it—'

'What's the matter?' Kraftstudt asked suddenly, turning on his retinue. Engineer Pfaff cowered, looking through the door with an odd expression on his face. My heart missed a beat.

'They're not working! They're staring about, damn 'em!' Pfaff growled.

I pressed forward and looked through the glass panel. What I saw surpassed my wildest hopes. The men who before had bent so obediently over their desks were sitting upright now, looking about them boldly and speaking to one another in loud, resolute voices.

'It's time we put an end to it, boys. D'you realize what they're doing to us?' Deinis was saying aggressively.

'Of course we do. They've been drumming into us that we achieve happiness through their pulse generator, the bastards. I've a mind to help 'em achieve theirs!'

'What's happening there?' Kraftstudt queried threateningly.

'I've no idea,' Pfaff mumbled, rolling his faded eyes. 'They act as if they were normal! Why don't they go on with their work?'

Kraftstudt was livid by now.

'We won't be on time with at least five defense orders,' he said through clenched teeth. 'See that they start working immediately!'

Boltz snapped the lock open and our party trooped in.

'Stand up to greet your teacher and savior,' Boltz said loudly.

A pregnant silence was the answer. Twelve pairs of eyes full of anger and hatred blazed in our direction. A spark was enough now to set it off. My heart sang with joy. Kraftstudt Co. was about to bust! I stepped forward.

'What are you waiting for? The hour of delivery has come. Your happiness is in your own hands. Go on, smash this criminal gang who wanted to see you all in the madhouse!'

No sooner had I finished than the calculators rushed from their places and fell on the petrified Kraftstudt and his party. They bore Boltz and the doctor down and started throttling them. They cornered Kraftstudt, punching and kicking him. Deinis straddled the prone Pfaff and seizing his bald head by its ears drummed it against the floor. Some tore the aluminum awnings down, others smashed windowpanes. The loudspeaker, torn down by a calculator, crashed to the floor, followed by the desks. The floor was strewn with sheets of calculations torn to bits.

I stood in the centre of that battlefield, issuing commands:

'Now don't let Kraftstudt get away! He's a war criminal! He's the kingpin of this hell on earth where you've been worked to madness! Hold tight that scoundrel Pfaff! He designed that pulse generator! Give Boltz what he deserves! He recruited you and planned to recruit many more!'

And the men, splendid in their righteous wrath, punched, kicked, and throttled their enemies.

Though no longer under the influence of the generator they could not stop now in the noble indignation of people breaking free from thraldom. Kraftstudt and his party, torn and bleeding, were dragged into the corridor and to the exit.

I led the agitated men, hooting and jeering and cursing their former masters, through the windowless reception hall where I'd handed in my problems, through the narrow subterranean maze to the back door where we finally emerged into the open.

We were blinded momentarily by a hot spring sun and we stopped short. But not only because of the sun. In front of the door leading to Kraftstudt's apartments pressed a huge crowd of people. They had been shouting something but at the sight of us suddenly went silent. Then I heard somebody call out:

'Why, it's Professor Rauch! So he *is* really alive!'

Deinis and his colleagues kicked forward the battered executives of Kraftstudt and Co. One after another they struggled to their feet and glanced with cowardice from us to the crowd pressing threateningly round them.

A thin, pale girl broke from the crowd. So she had found courage to do what I asked her!

'That's him,' she said, pointing at Kraftstudt. 'And him,' she added, jerking her head at Pfaff. 'They started it all. . . .'

A murmur came from the crowd. Voices were raised in anger. The people surged forward. Another moment and the criminals would have been torn limb from limb. But Deinis raised his hand.

'Friends, we're civilized people,' he said. 'We mustn't take justice into our own hands. The interests of humanity will be better served if we let the world know about their crimes. They must be brought to trial and we will all stand as witnesses. Within those walls heinous crimes have been committed. Taking advantage of the progress of science, those monsters were reducing men to slavery and exploiting them to the last spark of life.'

'Bring the criminals to trial!' everybody shouted. 'Bring 'em to trial!'

The crowd headed for town. The criminals were in a tight circle. Elsa Brinter, the thin girl, walked at my side. She clutched my hand as she spoke to me:

'I thought hard after our last conversation. Then I somehow felt strong and brave. And very angry for you and your friends and myself too.'

'That's what always happens to those who hate their enemies and love their friends,' I said.

Kraftstudt and his associates were handed over to the town authorities. The Burgomaster made a long speech studded with biblical references. He ended by saying: 'For crimes so subtle in their cruelty Herr Kraftstudt and his colleagues will be tried by the Federal Court of Justice.'

Then they were taken away in police vans, and have not been heard of since. Nor have there been any reports in the press. But it has been rumored that Kraftstudt and his colleagues entered government service and were entrusted with setting up a large computer center for the Defense Ministry.

I always boil with indignation now when looking through a newspaper I find on the last page this perennial advertisement:

WANTED

for work at a large computer center, men aged 25-40 and having knowledge of higher mathematics. Write to Box***

The Astronaut

BY VALENTINA ZHURAVLEVA

'What can I do for these people?' shouted Danko in a
voice that drowned the thunder.
Suddenly, he clutched at his breast, tore it open, plucked
out his heart and held it high above his head.

Maxim Gorky

I THINK I should begin by explaining in a few words the reason that
brought me to the Central Astronautics Archives. My story might
otherwise seem incomplete.

I am a spaceship physician with three astroflights to my credit.
My subject is psychiatry, or rather astropsychiatry, as it is called
nowadays, The problem which I am working on at present first arose
years back—in the 1970s. In those days flights to Mars took over a
year, to Mercury just under two years. The engines only worked at
take-off and landing. No astronomical observations were carried out
in flight—sputnik-mounted observatories did that. So what could
the crews do during those long months? Practically nothing. Forced
inactivity led to tension, to nervous breakdowns and mental dis-
orders. No amount of reading or listening in could make up for
what the first spacemen lacked on board ship. For what they lacked
was work—the hard, creative work to which they were accustomed.
It was then that the principle of hobby-minded personnel selection
was first advanced. The nature of the hobby, it was thought, was
entirely immaterial, so long as it gave the astronaut something to
do during the flight. And thus we got pilots who had a passion for
mathematics, navigators keen on ancient manuscripts, poetry-
writing engineers, etc.

There was a new entry in the astronaut's certificates, the famous
item 12: 'Interests other than professional.' However, a breakthrough in rocket technology soon provided a new solution of the
problem. Ion engines cut travel between planets to a few days. Item
12 was dropped.

Some years later, however, the problem reappeared with a

vengeance. Mankind had mastered interstellar travel. Yet though the speeds of ion rockets were eventually stepped up to suboptical, journeys to even the nearest stars took up to twenty years. . . .

Item 12 was back in the flying certificates. In terms of actual rocket control crews were occupied no more than 0.01 percent of flight time. TV faded away a few days after blast-off, radio lasted another month. And there were still years and years ahead. . . .

Rockets were manned by crews of six to eight in those days, not more. Tiny cabins and a 150-foot-long greenhouse were all the living space they had. It is difficult for us who fly in interstellar liners to imagine how people in those days did without all these gyms, swimming pools, stereo theatres and promenade galleries.

But I have digressed without beginning my story.

I don't know, haven't yet had time to find out who it was that designed the Archives buildings. But he was obviously a highly gifted architect. Gifted and daring. The buildings rise on the shore of a Siberian reservoir sea which was formed twenty years ago when they dammed the Ob. The main building stands on a high shore. I don't know how it was done, but it seems to soar above the water, a white pile looking like a schooner under a full press of sail.

Altogether there are fifteen people at the Archives. I have already met some of them. Most of them are here for short spells. An Australian writer is collecting material about the first interstellar flight. A scholar from Leningrad is studying the history of Mars. The diffident Indian is a famous sculptor. Two engineers—a tall strong-faced young man from Saratov and a small polite Japanese—are working jointly on some project. What kind I don't know. The Japanese smiled politely when I asked him about it. 'Oh, it's an absolute trifle. Not at all worthy of your high attention.'

But I am digressing again, when I should really be beginning my story.

I came to the Central Astronautics Archives to look into the history of the 12th item, which I needed for my research.

I spoke to the director the first evening. He's a man still in his prime, who all but lost the sight of both his eyes in a fuel tank explosion aboard a rocket. He wears glasses of some special make —triple-lensed and blue-tinted. His eyes are not visible and it seems the man never smiles.

'Well,' he said, having heard me out, 'I think you should start with Sector 0-14. Oh, excuse me, that's a system we use here; it doesn't mean anything to you, of course. I meant the first expedition to Barnard's Star.'

To my shame I knew next to nothing about that expedition.

'Your flights were in different directions,' he said with a shrug.

'Sirius, Procyon and 61 Cygni. And all your research so far has been on flights to those stars, hasn't it?'

I was surprised that he should know my record so well.

'The story of Alexei Zarubin, commander of the expedition,' he went on, 'will provide the answers to some of your questions. You will have your materials in half an hour. Good luck.'

The eyes were invisible behind the blue-tinted lenses. His voice sounded sad.

The materials are on my desk. The paper is yellow with time; the ink on some of the documents (they wrote with ink in those days) has faded. But their meaning is not lost: there are infra red copies of all the documents. The paper has been laminated, and the sheets feel hard and smooth.

Through the window I can see the sea. Its breakers roll in ponderously; the water rustles up the shore like pages being turned. . . .

An expedition to Barnard's Star in those days was a hazardous adventure. The star is six light-years away from the Earth. The rocket was to fly half that distance under acceleration, and half under deceleration. The journey there and back was expected to take just under fourteen years.

For those aboard the rocket the time would be slowed down to only forty months. Not too long, it seemed. But the danger was that for thirty-eight out of those forty months the rocket engine was required to work at full blast.

The rocket had no fuel reserve—an unwarranted risk, one would think nowadays, but there was no alternative then. The ship could take no more than what the tightly calculated fuel tanks carried. Therefore any delay en route would be fatal.

I read the minutes of the selection committee. One after another the candidates for captain were turned down. And no wonder. The flight was to be exceptionally hard, the captain had to be an excellent engineer and combine a level head with reckless courage. Then suddenly everybody was unanimous.

I turn a page. The service record of Captain Alexei Zarubin.

A few minutes and three pages later I realize why Alexei Zarubin was selected captain of the *Polus*. In a truly amazing way the man combined 'ice and fire,' the calm sagacity of a scholar and the fiery temperament of a fighter. That was probably why he had been entrusted with the most daring ventures. He seemed to have the knack of overcoming insurmountable obstacles.

The committee selected the captain. As tradition decreed, the captain picked his own crew. But what Zarubin did could hardly be called picking. He just contacted five astronauts who had crewed with him before and asked whether they were prepared to under-take a risky flight. With him, yes, they said.

There are photographs of the crew in the materials. Black and white, two-dimensional. Captain Zarubin was twenty-six then, but he looks older in the photo. A rather full face with high cheekbones, tightly pressed lips, a prominent aquiline nose, wavy, soft-looking hair and unusual eyes—calm, seemingly lazy, but with a daredevil flicker lurking in the corners.

The others were even younger. Two engineers, a married couple, photographed together because they always flew together. The navigator with the meditative look of a musician. A stern-faced girl doctor and an astrophysicist, his eyes stubborn in a face patchy with deep burns, the results of a crash landing he had made with the captain on Dione, a satellite of Saturn.

Now for item 12. I thumb the pages and see the pictures have told the truth. The navigator is a musician and composer. The stern-faced girl is keen on microbiology, a serious subject. The astrophysicist is learning languages; he has already mastered five and now thinks of tackling Latin and Ancient Greek. The engineers are fond of chess, the new kind—with two white and two black queens and an 81-square board.

The captain's hobby strikes an odd note. It's unusual, unique, I have never heard of anything like it. He's been keen on oil painting since he was a boy. That is understandable for his mother was a professional painter. But the captain seldom takes up his brush, he's interested in something else. He yearns to rediscover the lost secrets of the medieval masters—the composition of their oils, the way they mixed and used them. He carries out chemical research as he does everything he undertakes—with the devotion of a scholar and the ardor of an artist.

Six different people, six different personalities and backgrounds. It's the captain who welds them together. They love him, they trust him, they even imitate him. So all of them know how to be freez-ingly calm and recklessly risky.

The blast-off for Barnard's Star. The atom reactor works without a hitch, letting out an even, invisible stream of ions. The ship flies under acceleration. It is hard at first to work, even to move about. The girl doctor makes everybody stick to a fixed regimen. Gradually the astronauts settle down to the flight conditions. The greenhouse is assembled, then the radiotelescope. Normal life begins. Control of the reactor and other mechanisms takes up very little time. Everyone has to devote four hours a day to studies in his own field. The rest they spend as they think fit. The serious-minded girl is devouring monographs on microbiology. The navigator has com-posed a song which is quite a hit. The engineer couple sit for hours over the chessboard. The astrophysicist wades through Plutarch in the original.

There are brief entries in the ship's log: *The flight is proceeding normally. The reactor and mechanisms operate faultlessly. Spirits are high.* Then suddenly an anguished entry: *Telecommunication has gone dead. The rocket is beyond reach now. Yesterday we watched the last telecast from the earth. How hard it is to see one more link severed!* Days later two more lines: *Have perfected the reception antenna of the radio. Hope to be able to carry on reception for another seven or eight days.* And they were happy as could be when the radio actually worked for another twelve days.

Building up speed, the ship swept towards Barnard's Star. Months went by. The atom reactor worked with utmost precision. The fuel was consumed strictly as precomputed, not an iota above.

The catastrophe came unannounced.

One day, when they were over seven months out, the reactor's operating condition changed. A side reaction had sharply stepped up fuel consumption. There was a brief entry in the log that day: *Have no idea what has caused the side reaction.* They did not know in those distant days that infinitesimal admixtures in the atomic fuel could sometimes make all the difference between a controlled and uncontrolled reaction.

The sea grumbles outside the window. The wind has picked up and the breakers no longer rustle but hiss angrily as they pound the shore. A woman's laughter wafts in to me. But I mustn't let myself be distracted. I can almost see those six in the rocket. I know them —I can imagine what they were going through. I may be wrong in some details—what does it matter? But no, I am even right in those. I feel certain everything happened as I see it.

A brownish liquid boiled frothily in the retort. The brownish steam passed through a coil pipe into the condenser. The captain was peering at the dark-red powder in a test-tube. The door opened. The flame wavered and danced. The captain turned his head. Framed in the doorway was the engineer.

He kept control of himself but his voice betrayed him. It was loud, unnaturally firm and altogether not as usual.

'Take the load off your feet, Nikolai,' the captain said and pushed a chair forward. 'I did those calculations yesterday with the same result. Come on, sit down.'

'What shall we do?'

'Do?' The captain glanced at the wall clock. 'Fifty-five minutes to supper. Enough time to discuss it. Please let everybody know we'll be having a conference, will you.'

'Very well,' the engineer replied distractedly. 'I'll let them know. Yes, of course.'

He couldn't understand why the captain dawdled. The ship's speed was increasing with every passing second; some kind of decision was imperative and urgent.

'Look at this,' the captain said, passing him the test tube. 'You might be interested. It's cinnabar. Makes a devilishly attractive oil. But tends to darken when exposed to light.'

He explained to the engineer at some length how he had managed to produce a light-resistant cinnabar. The engineer shook the test tube impatiently. There was a clock empanelled above the desk, which the engineer couldn't help glancing at: half a minute, the speed was a mile and a quarter per second greater, another minute, another two and a half miles per second. . . .

'I'll be going,' he said finally. 'I must tell the others.'

Going down the steps he suddenly realized he was no longer counting the seconds or at all hurrying.

The captain shut the door tightly and put the test tube casually back into the rack. He allowed himself a faint smile. Panic is after all a chain reaction. Which all things extraneous tend to slow down, he thought as he went back to his chair. The humming of the reactor cooling system filled his ears. The engines were busy accelerating the *Polus* flight.

Ten minutes later the captain went down to the messroom. The five astronauts rose in greeting. All of them were in astronaut's uniform, worn only on special occasions, and the captain realized there was no need for him to explain the situation.

'Well,' he said. 'It seems only I forgot to don the uniform.'

Nobody smiled.

'Please be seated,' the captain said. 'A council of war. Well now, let the youngest begin, as is the custom. You, Lena. What do you think we should do?'

He turned to the girl. She solemnly said:

'I'm a doctor, Alexei Pavlovich. And the problem under discussion is strictly technological. I will give my opinion later, if I may.'

The captain nodded:

'As you like. You're the cleverest among us, Lena. And, as a woman, the shrewdest, too. I'll bet anything you like you've got an opinion ready.'

The girl said nothing.

'Well,' the captain went on. 'Lena will speak later. Your turn, Sergei.'

The astrophysicist spread his arms in a gesture of indecision.

'This isn't up my alley either. I've got nothing pat. But I do know there's enough fuel to last us all the way to Barnard's Star. So why should we turn back when we're only halfway out?'

'Why?' the captain repeated. 'Just because once we're there we won't be able to come back at all. But we can now, when we're only halfway out, as you say.'

'I see your point,' the astrophysicist said thoughtfully. 'But, you know, we might be able to return after all. Not by ourselves, of course. By a relief rocket. They'll see we're not coming and they'll send one. Surely astronautics is developing.'

'So it is,' the captain smiled wrily. 'With the passage of time. So fly on? Is that it? Good. Now you, Georgi. If it's up your alley, of course.'

The navigator sprang up, pushing his chair aside.

'Sit down,' the captain said. 'Sit down and speak calmly. Don't jump.'

'There can be no question of returning!' the navigator almost shouted. 'We can only go forward. Forward in face of the impossible. Why, how can we even speak of returning? Didn't we know from the outset the expedition was hazardous? And here we are, ready to turn tail at the first difficulty. I say, forward and only forward!'

'Well,' the captain drawled. 'Forward in face of the impossible. Beautifully said. Well, what do the engineers think? You, Nina? And you, Nikolai?'

Nikolai glanced at his wife; she nodded and he began. He spoke calmly as if thinking aloud :

'The purpose of our flight to Barnard's Star is exploration. But if we six make some discovery it won't in itself have any value. It will have that only if and when mankind learns about it. If we reach Barnard's Star and have no means of coming back, what earthly use will there be in our findings? Sergei says a relief rocket will come eventually. I, too, think that is feasible. But those who come will themselves have made all the discoveries. What shall we have accomplished? What shall we have contributed to man's knowledge? Actually we shall only have brought harm. Yes, I mean it. Back on Earth they will be waiting for our return. And in vain. If we turn back now only a minimum of time will be wasted. A new expedition will immediately set out. In fact we ourselves will. A few years may be lost, but then the data we've so far gathered will have been safely brought to the Earth. As things stand now there's no chance of that. So why go on? We two are against it. We must turn back. And now.'

A long silence descended. Then the girl asked :

'And what do you think, Captain?'

The captain smiled wistfully.

'I think the engineers are right. Beautiful words are still words. But the engineers appeal to common sense and calculation. We set out to discover. If we do not pass on our discoveries, they might as well not have been made. Nikolai is absolutely right. . . .'

Zarubin got up and ponderously paced the messroom. Walking was difficult. The 3G load brought about by the rocket's acceleration impeded movement.

'The relief rocket variant is out,' he went on. 'But there are still two possibilities. The first is to turn back to the Earth. The second, to fly on to Barnard's Star—and still return to the Earth. Return in spite of fuel shortage.'

'How?' asked Nikolai.

Zarubin went back to his chair, sat down and said :

'That I don't know. Not yet anyway. But there are another eleven months of flight ahead. If you decide we should turn back now, we will. But if you will trust me to think up something in those eleven months that would pull us through, well then . . . forward in face of the impossible! That is the way I see it, friends. What do you say? You, Lena?'

The girl screwed her eye at him.

'Like any man, you're very cunning. I'd bet you've already thought up something.'

The captain laughed.

'You'd lose. I haven't thought up anything. But I will. I certainly will.'

'We believe in you,' Nikolai said. 'We do believe in you.' Then, after a pause, he added : 'Though, frankly, I don't quite see how anything could pull us through. There will be 18 percent of propellent on the *Polus*. Eighteen instead of fifty. But you said you'd think up something. So let's fly on. As Georgi says, forward in face of the impossible.'

The window shutters creak softly. The wind leafs through the pages, scours about the room, filling it with the damp smell of the sea. Smell is a wonderful thing. You don't have it on board ship. The conditioners purify the air and keep up the required humidity and temperature. But conditioned air is as vapid as distilled water. All sorts of artificial smell devices have been tried, but with no success. The aroma of ordinary, earthly air is much too complex to imitate. Even now I smell the sea and the damp, autumn leaves, and, vaguely, some perfume, and sometimes, on a gust of wind, the earth. And wet paint, too.

The wind is leafing through the pages. . . . What could it be the captain counted on? When the *Polus* had reached Barnard's Star her fuel reserve would be down to only 18 percent. Eighteen instead of fifty. . . .

In the morning I ask the director whether I may see Zarubin's pictures.

'We'll have to go upstairs,' he says. 'But . . . tell me, have you read it all?'

He listens to my answer, nodding.

'I see. I thought so, too. Yes, the captain took upon himself a great responsibility. . . . Would you have believed in him?'

'Yes.'

'So would I.'

He is silent for quite a while, his lips quivering slightly. Then he gets up and goes through the motions of adjusting his spectacles.

'Well, let's go.'

He limps. We walk slowly through the long corridors. 'You will read about it yet,' the director starts. 'Volume Two, starting from page 100, if I remember rightly. Zarubin wanted to unravel the secrets of the Italian Renaissance masters. You see, oil painting deteriorated starting with the 18th century—I mean its technique. A lot was thought to have been lost beyond hope of recovery. The painters could no longer mix oils that were at once bright and stable. The brighter the oil, the quicker it darkened. Especially the blues. Well, Zarubin. . . . But you will see for yourself.'

The pictures hang in a narrow, sunlit gallery and the first thing that strikes me is that each is executed in one primary color.

'These are studies,' says the director. 'To try out the technique, nothing more. This is "A Study in Blue".'

Flying side by side in a blue sky are two frail human figures, with strapped-on wings, a man and a woman. All is done in blue, and never have I seen such an infinity of shades. It is a night sky, raven black on the left horizon and a melting, midday blue in the opposite corner. The winged humans shimmer from the lightest blue to the deepest violet. The colors are brilliant, almost vibrant in some places, and subdued, transparent in others.

There are more pictures. 'A Study in Red': two suns above an imaginary planet, a chaos of chiaroscuro ranging from blood red to salmon pink. 'A Study in Brown': a fairy-tale forest.

The director is silent. I wait, looking at the blue-tinted, impenetrable glasses.

'Read further,' he says softly. 'Then I shall show you more pictures. Then you'll understand.'

I am reading as fast as I can. As fast as I can without losing the thread. . . .

The *Polus* hurtled on toward Barnard's Star. The speed reached the maximum and the engines began to brake. Judging from the scant entries in the log everything was normal. No breakdowns, no sick aboard. Nor did anyone remind the captain of his pledge. And the captain was calm, confident, and cheerful as always. He went on with his research and had done more studies.

What were his thoughts when he was alone in his cabin? Neither the ship's log nor the navigator's diary gives any answer. But here is an interesting document. The engineers' report. About the malfunctioning of the cooling system. Crisp, concise language bristling with technicalities. But between the lines I read, 'If you have changed your mind, friend, this is where you can turn back. With no loss of face. . . .' And the captain's verdict across it, 'We'll do repairs on a planet of Barnard's Star,' which means, 'No, friends, I haven't changed my mind.'

After nineteen months of flight the ship reached her destination. The dim red star had only one planet, almost the size of the Earth, but completely icebound. The *Polus* tried to land. But the jet of ions melted the ice and the first attempt failed. The captain chose another site, again the ice melted. Only at the sixth attempt did they manage to strike rock floor under a thin sheath of ice.

From that day the entries in the log book were done in red ink. That was how discoveries were traditionally recorded.

The planet was a dead world. Its atmosphere was almost pure oxygen but not a trace of animal or plant life was found. The thermometer read 58° F. below zero. *A wretched planet*, the navigator wrote in his diary, *but what a star! Discoveries galore!*

And it was indeed so. Even today, when our knowledge of the structure and evolution of stars is increasing by leaps and bounds, the discoveries made by the *Polus* expedition have retained much of their value. The study of the gaseous envelope of the red dwarfs of the Barnard's Star type is still a classic.

The logbook. . . . The scientific report. . . . The astrophysicist's paper setting out a paradoxical hypothesis of star evolution. . . . And, at last, what I have been looking for—the captain's order for departure. Still it comes as a surprise, almost a shock. Unable to believe my eyes, I hastily turn the pages. An entry in the navigator's diary. I see it all.

One day Zarubin said:

'That's all. Prepare for departure.'

The crew of five stared silently at their captain. The wall clock ticked away. . . .

The five stared silently at the captain. And waited.

'Prepare for departure,' the captain repeated. 'You know we've only got 18 per cent of propellent. But there is a way out. First of all we must reduce the rocket's weight. All the heavy electronic gear will have to go, except for the controllers.' He saw that the navigator wanted to say something and waved him to silence. 'We've got to do it. Also all the partitions in the empty tanks, and some of the greenhouse sections. But that's not all. Fuel consumption is particularly heavy during the first months of flight—due to low acceleration, as you know. Comfort will have to be dispensed with: the *Polus* will depart to full 12 G's instead of three.'

'Flight control is impossible under that load,' Nikolai demurred. 'The pilot will not be able—'

'I know,' the captain cut him. 'I know. For the first months control will be done from here, from this planet. One of us will stay behind to do it. Keep quiet! Remember—there's no other way out. It's got to be done. Now, listen to this. You two cannot stay behind because you expect a child. Yes, I know. You are a doctor, Lena, and your place is with the crew. Sergei's an astrophysicist and will also fly. Georgi is too excitable. That leaves me. Don't argue. Everything will be done as I say.'

I look through Zarubin's calculations. I am a doctor and out of my depth in the maze of mathematics. But one thing is immediately obvious: the calculations were done to absolutely no tolerance, as it were. The rocket was stripped to a bare minimum and the take-off G-load was pushed up to a crushing maximum. The bigger part of the greenhouse was left on the planet and that carved deep into the astronauts' rations. The emergency power supply system with its two microreactors was also dismantled. As was almost all electronic equipment. If something untoward happened en route the rocket would be unable to regain Barnard's Star. *The risk is cubed*, the navigator wrote in his diary. And below, *But for the one who stays behind it's risk raised to the tenth, hundredth power.* . . .

Zarubin would have to wait for fourteen years. To wait for the relief rocket. Fourteen years on an alien, icebound planet. . . .

More calculations. Power was the prime thing. It had to last out the ground control period and the fourteen long years after. And again no allowance for emergency.

A photo of the captain's quarters, made out of the greenhouse sections. The transparent walls permit a view of the two microreactors and miscellaneous electronic equipment. The ground control antenna is on the roof. All round lies an icy waste. Aloft Barnard's Star shines coldly in a gray, murky sky. It is four times bigger than the Sun in diameter but little brighter than the Moon.

I turn over pages in the logbook hastily. My eye runs through it all: the captain's parting advice, the arrangements for radio communication in the first days of flight, the list of things the captain would need. . . . Then, suddenly, one word, *Blast-off*.

After that a few odd-looking lines as if scrawled by a child: lines uneven, letters angular, broken. That was 12 G's.

With difficulty I make out the words. The first entry: *Everything's fine but for the cursed G-load. Vision heavily veiled.* . . . Two days later: *Accelerating as calculated. Can't walk, just crawl.* . . . A week later: *It's tough, very* (crossed out). . . . *The reactor operates as calculated*.

Then two blank pages follow, while on the third, smeared with ink, a diagonal entry: *Ground control weakening. There's some obstacle in the beam's path. This* (crossed out). *This is it.* And below, on the same page, in a firm hand: *Ground control restored. The power indicator stands at four. The captain is giving away all the power he's got but we can't stop him. This means help won't reach him in time.* . . .

I close the logbook. I can only think about Zarubin now. I imagine the fading of ground control came quite unexpectedly. Suddenly the indicator rang and. . . .

The indicator was ringing shrilly. The needle went down, quivering. The power beam had met an obstacle and control was slipping rapidly.

The captain stood at the transparent wall. The dim sun was sinking behind the horizon. Brownish shadows sped across the icy waste. The wind drove snow dust, whipped it along, carried it aloft into the murky, reddish-grey sky.

The indicator was ringing insistently. What little power was getting through was not enough for control. Zarubin was looking at the setting Barnard's Star. Behind him lamps flashed wildly on the panel of the electronic navigator.

The purplish-red disc was rapidly sinking below the horizon. For a fleeting moment a myriad of scarlet pin-points flickered on as the last rays were refracted by the ground ice. Then there was darkness.

Zarubin went over to the instrument board, switched off the indicator's signal. The needle was not moving any longer. Zarubin turned the wheel of the power regulator. The greenhouse was filled with the drone of the motors of the cooling system. He went on turning the wheel until it would turn no more. Then he went to the other side of the board, removed the safety lock and gave the wheel two more full turns. The drone rose to a shrill, vibrant, earsplitting roar.

The captain shuffled back to the wall, sank down on the bench. His hands were shaking. He took out his handkerchief and dabbed his brow. Then he pressed his cheek against the cool glass.

It was wait now, wait till the new, superpowerful signals reached the rocket and bounced back.

And he waited.

He waited, losing all awareness of time, while the microreactors roared away at bursting point and the cooling system motors shrieked and groaned. The flimsy walls shuddered.

The captain waited.

Finally something forced him up and over to the instrument board. The needle on the indicator was back to normal. There was enough power now to control the rocket. Zarubin smiled wanly, said, 'There,' and glanced at the consumption dial. The consumption was 140 times greater than the precomputed.

That night the captain did not sleep. He was compiling a new programme for the electronic navigator. All the side effects of the power failure had to be eliminated.

The wind whipped up seas of snow on the plain. A subdued aurora borealis glowed over the horizon.

The microreactors screeched as if run amok, pouring forth into space what had been carefully husbanded to last for fourteen years. . . . Having fed the programme into the electronic machine the captain made a tired round of his quarters. Stars shone high above the transparent roof. Somewhere out there the *Polus* was accelerating earthwards.

It is very late but I decide to call on the director nonetheless. I remember he has mentioned some other pictures by Zarubin.

The director is sitting up.

'I knew you would come,' he says, putting on his spectacles hastily. 'Let's go, it's next door.'

In the adjacent room lit up by fluorescent lamps hang two middle-sized pictures. The first thought that crosses my mind is that the director has made a mistake. Zarubin couldn't possibly have painted these. They have nothing in common with what I saw in the morning: no color experiments, no fantastic subjects. They are two ordinary landscapes. A road and a tree in one, and the edge of a wood in the other.

'Yes, this is Zarubin,' the director says as if reading my thoughts. 'He stayed behind on the planet—as you already know, of course. Well, it was a desperate way out, but still, it offered them a chance. I say this as an astronaut—as a former astronaut,' the director adjusted his spectacles, then went on, 'But then Zarubin did what— Well, you know about it. In four weeks he gave off the power stored for fourteen years. He restored ground control and brought the *Polus* back to her course. Well, when the rocket reached suboptical speed, braking began at normal G-load, and the crew could take over.

By that time there was next to no power in Zarubin's microreactors. Nor could anything be done about it. . . . That was when he started on these pictures. In them his love for life and the Earth. . . .'

A country road topping a rise. A mighty rugged oak tree by its side. It is done in the manner of Jules Dupré of the Barbizon school: sturdy, gnarled, full of life and vigor. The wind drives along small shaggy clouds. A boulder lies by the ditch, and it seems that only a moment ago a weary traveller has been sitting on it. . . . All the details are executed carefully, lovingly, with an amazingly rich color and light shading.

The other picture was never finished. It's a wood in spring. Everything is soaked in air, light, warmth. . . . Wonderful golden hues. . . . Zarubin was a perfect colorist.

'I brought these pictures to the Earth,' the director says softly.

'You?'

'Yes.'

His voice is wistful, almost apologetic.

'The materials you have been looking through have no end. That is part of other expeditions. When the *Polus* returned, a rescue expedition was immediately equipped and sent out. All that could shorten the flight was done. The crew agreed to fly under 6 G's. They got to the planet—and did not find the greenhouse. They took tremendous risks and returned empty-handed. Then—many years later—I was sent. We had a breakdown on the way. There,' he put a hand up to his spectacles. 'But we got through. And found the greenhouse and the pictures. . . . And a note from the captain.'

'What was in it?'

'Just one line: "Forward in face of the impossible." '

We look silently at the pictures. It suddenly occurs to me that Zarubin painted them from memory. There was ice all round him, lit up by the evil reddish glow of Barnard's Star. And on his palette he was mixing warm, sunny colors. . . . In item 12 he could in all truth have written: 'Am interested in, passionately love the Earth, its life, its people.'

The deserted corridors of the Archives are still and quiet. The windows are open, the sea breeze stirs the heavy curtains. The breakers roll in in stubborn cadence. They seem to whisper: forward in face of the impossible. A pause, another wave and a whisper: Forward. . . . And another pause. . . .

I want to reply to the waves: 'Yes, forward, only forward, always forward.'

A New Year's Fairy Tale

BY VLADIMIR DUDINTSEV

I LIVE in a fantastic world, in a fairy-tale land, in a city created by my own imagination. Surprising things happen to people there, and a few of these adventures fell to my lot. I will tell you some of them, taking advantage of the fact that men are inclined to listen to all kinds of fables at New Year's time. My story will be about the tricks that time plays on us. Time, of course, is limitless, and exists everywhere. In a fairy-tale world clocks are just as dependable as official Moscow time. So I will risk beginning the story: perhaps some curious person will be interested in my fable, and in its locale, which may intersect his serious, day-to-day existence.

A mysterious bird flew into our city—an owl. Several persons were made happy by its visit. My immediate superior, the director of the Solar Research Laboratory where I work, was the first. The second was a neuropathologist, a school friend of mine. The owl selected me to be the third. This bird was remarkable. It would not have been a bad idea to study its habits, and to include its picture in a Book of Birds.

I had already published scientific papers on certain properties of solar light. I had a degree in science, had been made a consultant on several committees, and was eager to get ahead. Emulating the behaviour of our venerable older men, I had learned to hold my head high, as they did, to ponder deeply over a question addressed to me, and to express my esteemed, considered opinion with a drawl, and with raised eyebrows. There was another important habit—I had begun to take great care of my expensive overcoat. Like the older men, I hung it in my own closet on a wooden hanger marked with my initials.

Being endowed with certain modest talents, I followed the advice of an academician, and taught myself to jot down whatever thoughts popped into my head. It's a well-known fact that our most valuable ideas don't come while we worry over them for hours at a desk. They fly in like a gust of wind, usually when we are walking along the street. I would write down these ideas, and then forget about

218

them. Our janitress was very well aware that the drawers of my
desk contained magic papers which burned like gunpowder. She got
into the habit of cleaning out my desk and using the papers to light
all the stoves in the laboratory.

Under a cloak of maturity there dwelt in me a naive child. (The
same thing was true of my boss, who was a doctor of science.) This
rosy-cheeked child sometimes came to the surface, especially in the
evening hours when we bachelors settled down at home in front of
the television set. For hours, with wide eyes, numb as if in a drunken
stupor, we watched the legs of the soccer players flashing on the
little screen.

As you see, I do not spare myself at all. I am displaying many
sides of my character, and will display still more, for your considera-
tion. I understand the thing completely and will be my own most
severe judge. My eyes were opened some time ago, when the owl
first paid me a personal visit. The owl opened my eyes, and I am
grateful.

For example, I took a new view of my running quarrel with a
certain S., a corresponding member of one of the provincial aca-
demies of science. In an article published five years ago, he had
called one of my publications the 'fruit of idle fantasy'. I had to
retaliate. In a follow-up article, I casually refuted S.'s fundamental
theses, and added, appropriately I think, these words: 'This is just
what Candidate of Science S. is unsuccessfully trying to prove.' (I
knew very well that, although he is a corresponding member, the
degree he holds, like mine, is only candidate.) S. immediately
answered my thrust with a pamphlet where he said, as if in passing,
that I was adjusting my results to fit my theory. He put the word
'theory' in quotation marks. Soon after this I printed a long article
on my latest solar observations, which confirmed my 'theory' and
smashed S.'s calculations to smithereens. 'The battleship took a
torpedo broadside,' my friends commented on the exchange. I
didn't mention S.'s name in my article—I knew that my foe would
not survive this second torpedo. I simply said 'certain authors.' But
the battleship survived, and answered. . . .

And so on. This war, which lasted five years, completely ruined
my nerves, and not only mine.

But let me get back to my story. One morning we all gathered in
the laboratory, hung out coats on hangers, and engaged in a free-
wheeling conversation, as we often did to put ourselves in the mood
for work. Our esteemed director, the Doctor of Science, started the
conversational ball rolling. In his free time he studied ancient lore
and collected stone axes, old coins, and books. In my opinion this
hobby, rather than our work, embodied for him the whole meaning
of his tranquil life.

'Here's something strange!' he said, in a bid for our attention. 'Not long ago, studying an inscription on a stone slab, I found this depicted.'

He showed us a sheet of white paper bearing an India ink picture of a large-eared owl.

'I managed to decipher the inscription.' The director spoke with pride. 'There was a name, and the words: "And the years of his life were nine hundred." '

'Ye-es,' one of my friends, who loved clothes and practical jokes, said. 'I'd settle for four hundred.'

'What for?' a broad-shouldered, dry, middle-aged man, who usually said nothing, broke in sharply. He was different from all of us because of his accentuated carelessness in dress, his silence, and his unheard-of capacity for work. 'You don't need four hundred years,' he said. 'You're in no hurry.'

'I would like to call your attention. . . .' The director raised his voice, making us understand that we had interrupted him in the middle of a sentence. 'May I have your attention? Owls like this have been found in many countries at different times. There is one desert with a huge granite owl. This is the first such find in our area. I have a right to brag.' Here the director broke into a smile. 'This owl and this inscription are my personal discovery. I dug up this stone in my own garden.'

We congratulated the lucky man, took another look at the owl, and proceeded each to his own task.

'I simply must learn the meaning of this picture,' the chief said. 'Then I'll publish it.'

'Perhaps this hieroglyph denoted a person who was able to make the best possible use of his time?' I suggested.

'It's possible, but it must be substantiated.'

'But a life lasting nine hundred years!' I exclaimed, unable to control myself. 'Was such a long life really ever possible?'

'Everything is possible!' shouted my busy broad-shouldered neighbor, without looking up from his work.

'What are you trying to say?' the director asked politely.

'Time is a riddle,' was the even more enigmatic answer.

'Yes, time is a riddle,' the director pounced on the intriguing idea. He took an hourglass from the wall, turned it over and set it on the desk. 'Time flows,' he said, watching the sand. 'And look what comes of it: each brief moment of our lives is like a tiny grain of sand, like an infinitely small dot. . . . It disappears in an instant.'

I suddenly felt a pain deep in my breast. There had been a few months of rare, unexpected love in my life, and these months, which I now looked back upon with pain, merged into a single instant, a grain of sand falling to the bottom of the hourglass. Gone without a trace, as if it had never been! I heaved a sigh. If only one could reverse the flow of the sand!

'Excuse me, chief,' our personnel director interrupted my thoughts. 'According to your theory, if I may call it that, since time is a mere dot, does that mean we have neither our heroic past, nor a sunny future?'

He loved to ask pointed questions in a loud voice, as if he had caught a person in some terrible crime.

'I'm sorry if I said something wrong,' answered our amicable director. 'But I don't think I've succeeded in formulating any theory. This is all a joke, a play of the imagination.'

'A strange kind of play. After all there are limits.'

'My friend!' our shaggy, ever-busy eccentric shouted suddenly. We all turned around. 'All that which is new, that which we are searching for, is almost always found beyond the limits.'

His mouth open (it was a habit of his), he began to laugh silently into the stern face of the personnel director. Thus we discovered a new aspect of our colleague's character.

We had been sitting in the same room with him for two years, but we didn't know him. We only knew that he shaved rarely and was in the habit of tossing his overcoat, from which half the buttons were missing, on a chair. And we knew he did the work of four men. But we didn't really know him at all.

'You know, I think now is the time for me to tell you an interesting story,' again we heard the voice of our colleague, bent over his work as usual.

Everyone was surprised. This was the first time the man had generously decided to waste time conversing with us. I had no idea that our remarks about longevity would have such an effect on him.

'But right now I have to run down cellar and set the instruments going, so that no time will be wasted,' he went out quickly.

'He's as dry as dust, isn't he?' someone asked.

'I don't think so,' the practical joker objected. 'A woman comes to see him sometimes. I live next to him. She's rather young. I bumped into her once on the stairs, but she didn't even notice me. Blinded by love.'

'You know he has a unique old watch. Amazingly accurate, and it only has to be wound once a year,' the director said.

'There you have it, my friends!' Our graying, touseled, new friend (we had just gotten to know him that day), our workhorse, entered, took his place and picked up a slide rule. 'Nine hundred years, you say. . . . But don't you know that time can stand still or fly very swiftly? Have you ever had a date, and had to wait and wait?'

'Yes, time can creep very slowly,' the director said.

'It can stand still! Do you remember hearing that scientists have germinated lotus seeds which had been lying in a stone grave for two thousand years? Time stood still for those seeds. Time can be stopped or pushed forward.'

As he spoke he manipulated the slide rule and jotted something down. Even during a conversation he managed to keep working.

'I'll explain these words with a story which, irrespective of its moral, will interest you.'

As he began the story it seemed to me that he turned toward me —as if the words were meant exclusively for me.

'Several years ago in a certain kingdom, in a certain land, in our city, to be exact, an extraordinary thing happened. On a Sunday, in one of the shadiest corners of the Park of Culture, sixty, perhaps even a hundred, well-dressed men assembled for a discussion which they had decided to conduct in the open air. It later became known that a two-hour symposium, so to speak, had been held in our park —a symposium of thieves and bandits, held to form a "legitimate" brotherhood. The group had its own stern rules. Breaking them was punished by death. To be accepted as "legit," a man had to be recommended by several sponsors. A motto was tatooed on the chest of each new member: a few words which could immediately identify a person as one of the gang.'

'What bearing does this story have on our discussion about time?' the director asked in a quiet voice. 'Or perhaps you haven't finished yet?'

'No, I haven't finished. It has the most direct bearing. I am about to get to the point. The convention of "legitimate" bandits imposed six death sentences. Five were carried out. They couldn't catch the sixth condemned man, because his case was more complicated. First, I will tell you what kind of man the sixth was, and what his guilt consisted of. He was the chief, the president, or, as they called him, the "pakhan" of the whole "legitimate" society, the oldest and cleverest of all the bandits. He was locked up in a far-off jail, and there in solitude the thought must have come to him that in his whole life he had actually not accomplished anything nor gained anything, and that he had little time left to live. He reasoned that the whole purpose of a bandit's life is to appropriate the wealth of other people as easily as possible—their gold and other valuables. But the value and power of material things in human society are declining catastrophically.'

'So he was a theoretician—your bandit?' the ironic voice of the personnel director was heard.

'Yes, he was a serious man,' our eccentric agreed. I felt ever more sympathetic toward him. 'This criminal, who had done so much harm, quieted down in the last years and began to read books. Books have immense power! He read a great many books. He was in no hurry to leave prison—it was a convenient arrangement for him to read and meditate in his stone cage, and the members of the brotherhood obtained for their leader any book he wanted, even though it might be kept in the cellars of the government treasury under seven locks. Yes . . . now he saw that the power of expensive things was falling catastrophically. There was a time in the distant past when rich people, princes, had partitioned off reservoirs in the sea gulfs and had bred sharks in these reservoirs. The sharks were fed on human flesh—slaves thrown into the sea. To serve these sharks at a banquet was considered the height of fashion. Now we cannot even think about these amusements of our ancestors without shuddering. There was a time when gold was a nameless metal sleeping in the ground. Then man gave it a name and value. It was considered very elegant to wear clothing, or to carry weapons, sparkling with gold. But now none of us would think of appearing with a gold chain across his stomach or even with a gold pin on his necktie. The prestige of gold is dropping. And precious fabrics? I assure you that even our present-day expensive fabrics are already going out of fashion. To show off expensive things today is a sign of spiritual backwardness.'

'Just look how this bandit did away with material values! I'd like to know what will take the place of things?' the personnel director asked. This story upset him a little because he himself was currently displaying a very expensive woollen suit with padded shoulders, and his wife had once come to the laboratory carrying a heavy silver fox fur on her arm.

'It all depends on the things we are talking about. There are things and things. The bandit realized this, and began to think. He understood that only the beauty of the human soul can replace material things, and that you can't buy or steal that. You can't make anyone love you by force of arms. The soul's beauty is free. It came to the forefront just as soon as gold and velvet lost their pre-eminence. Now Cinderellas in chintz dresses triumph over princesses draped in silk. Because the whole value of a cheap dress lies in the beauty of the design, and this it not a material value. The design of a dress reflects taste, the character of those who created and selected this pattern. It's no accident that many princesses who still possess a soul have begun to dress like Cinderellas. And if we meet someone draped in furs and expensive material, we don't go into raptures over her rich clothing. We avoid such a spiritual monster who thus betrays herself for everyone to see.

'My bandit saw this. And suddenly he realized that in all his life he had never possessed such "things" as the approval of men, friendship, true love, but had instead aspired all his life to something which has no value. Something in the nature of a fiscal reform occurred. Yes. . . .' The storyteller's voice became hoarse. He coughed. 'But the people, the love and friendship which he needed, did exist. He knew them. . . . There was a woman. But he couldn't even show his face before her. He didn't dare open up to her.

'So this man expressed all his ideas in a long letter to the brotherhood and announced that he was "abdicating" and intended to enter the society of everyday, working people and by some kind of outstanding accomplishment to win those things which he had never known in his life, but to which he suddenly felt drawn with all his being. The prison administration printed his letter in a special pamphlet. You understand, of course, that the document was tremendously effective; it had to be exploited.

'Now look at the tight squeeze our "pakhan" was in. During his life he had amassed in various courts sentences totalling two hundred years and hadn't even begun to serve them. He knew that the government would not reduce his sentence. On the other hand, knowing better than anyone else the rules of the brotherhood, he was fully aware that his comrades would never forgive his treachery and that somewhere a sharpened knife was already waiting for him. But he had to go on living for a few more years, at least, to accomplish what he had set out to do. So before the sentence of his "brothers" could be carried out, he fled for the last time. He had enough money and, as it happens in fairy tales, he found doctors to replace all the skin on his face, hands, and head, and also his hair. They even changed his voice. They were great masters.

'The bandit got hold of irreproachable documents and became a new man. He graduated from two institutes in three years. Now he was winding up his affairs. He had conceived a very great project; he wanted to present a gift to the human race. . . .'

'That's all very fine.' I interrupted him because he had been looking at me the whole time. 'But what bearing does this have on our conversation? On the fact that time can stand still or fly, on what was inscribed on the stone: "And the years of his life were nine hundred"?'

'A very direct bearing. The executors of the sentence are hunting down this man, stubbornly tracking him. He has very little time left. Time—do you understand? This man intends to live his whole life over again in one or two years. What would have happened if he had lived his whole life in this way? His life would have been perhaps, longer than nine hundred years.'

'You mean, of course, the content of his life and not its duration?' the chief asked.

'It's plain to see that you are not very economical with time!' My neighbour was angry. 'Yes, yes, yes! The content. What we fill the vessel of time with. We should fill it only with the most intense pleasures, the greatest joys. . . .'

'Well, he's really carried away!' Again the personnel director's voice was heard. 'This is a sermon of pure egotism. Everything must give you joy and pleasure. But I think one should work for the people. Eh? How do you feel about that?'

'You are behind the times, that's how I feel about it. We'll have to take you in hand. You are implying that joy and pleasure are sins, to which you secretly devote yourself within your own four walls. Working for people is your public duty. Compared with you, my bandit is a man of progress. He has tasted all your joys and is fed up with them. Now he recognizes only one joy—the joy which you consider stern duty.'

'Tell me,' the director began after a moment of silence, 'How do you know all these details? This man changed his name, his face. . . . He is undoubtedly no fool, and wouldn't reveal himself to just anyone he met.'

'I am not just anyone to him.'

'You must turn him in, if you are a man of conscience,' the personnel director remarked suddenly. 'You should report him. He has committed so many crimes, and has escaped from prison.'

'Not for anything,' our comrade said. 'Not for anything! He is no longer a bandit. He isn't dangerous now; he is even useful. When he has finished his work he will give himself up.'

Then he took his famous watch from his pocket, a heavy sphere on a steel chain.

'Excuse me. I have to go take the instrument readings.'

And he started to leave. At the door he stopped.

'You should all think about this story. And you especially.' He looked straight at me. 'I think that perhaps you are able to profit from the experience of certain people, and will stop playing games and put an end to your fruitless polemic with this corresponding member. . . .'

How could I have guessed then that life would also involve me in this story, make me its second hero; his double!

To verify a suspicion which suddenly occurred to me, about half an hour later I went down into the cellar. The door to the room where this man sat, surrounded by instruments sparkling with glass and copper, creaked slightly. The sound was barely audible, but he jumped up so abruptly that he smashed several flasks.

'Pardon me,' I said.

'You are checking a suspicion?' he asked, growing calmer.

'You're careless,' I answered.

'I'm not afraid of you.' He turned back to the instruments.

Now that I was sure of what I had only suspected before, certain other things also became clear to me. (I had so far kept quiet about them.)

Not long before these events I discovered that I had become the object of someone's interest. A certain shadow continually followed me from a distance along the city streets. I never succeeded in seeing the face of my pursuer, although he made no particular effort to hide. He (or she) selected dark archways or doorways for his observation point. He would steal out into the sunlight, but as soon as I reached into my pocket for my glasses my companion would sneak off quietly into the archway. Several times I went up to the door or archway where this person who seemed so much in love with me was hiding, but I found no one.

Not long ago the first soft, pure snow fell. I was walking along an empty street late at night, and heard footsteps behind me. Even before I turned around I realized that it was he (or she). I turned, and saw something resembling a cloak or the tails of a dress suit flashing around the corner. I took off in mad pursuit, but when I wheeled around the corner I saw a completely empty white alley. I examined the snow and found no tracks. Later, though, I recalled that there were a few cross-shaped imprints like the tracks of an enormous chicken, melting in the light, airy snow.

In the cellar I whispered all this to my friend. He gripped my hand and said:

'Thank you. I have noticed something myself. Now go. I must hurry. As you see, time is rushing me. It wouldn't hurt you to step up your pace either. A lot can happen. . . .'

We were both working on the same problem, but using different approaches. One of us was right, one was wrong. But the problem was even worth being wrong about if that could show the correct path to others. We were searching for ways to condense sunlight. The product which we hoped to obtain would ensure months, even years of bright sunlight and warmth for that distant continent whose inhabitants don't know what the sun is. One side of our planet is never illuminated by the sun. Here night and winter are eternal. The fact that my friend seized on this most vital of all problems was for me one more proof that he was the extraordinary leader of the bandits, in a great hurry to live. Would he be able to complete his project in a year, or even in two years?

You see, I am a person who appraises things soberly—I mark time from year to year and always think carefully how I should begin, just because beginning a research project means putting other things aside, burying oneself in work for ten good years. If only the whole laboratory could have worked on the project! But thank God they at least permitted the two of us to work on it. We had plenty of opposition. Nearly all the members of the scientific council regarded us as daydreamers. So it would take ten years. How could he even get started in only two years?

But it turned out that this man did not have two years at his disposal, but only a few hours. Next morning they called me from the hospital. The night before, near our doorstep (we lived in the same house), my extraordinary bandit had been found, blood gushing from several deep knife wounds in his back. The whole institute was upset; famous doctors were called in from other hospitals. But it was too late. By noon the institute officials had already called the bureau of funeral arrangements.

His death, which he himself had predicted, as it were, affected us strongly. For several days when we met in the morning at work, we all exchanged expressive glances. I turned out to be quite a coward. First I was in a panic and even lost weight. I couldn't listen to extraneous conversations which had no relation to the work, and I worked intensely for a week. But after a week, when I received a new issue of our scientific journal and read in the table of contents the name of the corresponding member S., I immediately flared up and forgot everything in the world except this paper covered with printed symbols. I leafed through the journal nervously and immediately saw a footnote set in fine print (the most biting statements are always set in fine print). There was my name, in a setting of politely venomous words. My life returned to its old groove. Paper, paper, whoever invented you! I abandoned my work, and spurred on by all my supporters, wrote an article containing not one, but three, footnotes. They should have demolished my enemy. The whole department had a hand in composing these footnotes. To give you an idea what we looked like while doing this, I suggest that you go to the Trediakovsky Museum and look at Repin's painting 'The Zaporozhians writing to the Sultan.' Our entire department is depicted in this painting—with our director guffawing and holding his stomach, and me, wearing glasses, sitting at a table with a pen in my hand.

Back in the old familiar rut, I completely forgot about the person who had been shadowing me, hiding behind corners, arches and entranceways. After those depressing days which culminated in the funeral, the dark coattails did not appear. I was sure that one of the bandits who had executed the condemned man had been following me.

But not long after I received the printed copy of my answer to my primordial enemy S., or, to be more exact, when I was leaving the editorial office where they had ordered one more article from me, I felt with all my being that someone was looking at me fixedly from behind. I looked around, and saw no one. But, staring hard, I did manage to catch a glimpse of a shadowy figure in a dark gap on the second floor of a half-demolished house which was being torn down. It immediately slipped aside, and disappeared behind the wall.

On that very day it was my 30th birthday. I intended to invite my friends to help celebrate this round number. And now, as you see, in broad daylight, the first shadow settled over my holiday.

I went home and climbed the stairs to my floor. In the lounge where we all watched television in the evenings, one of my friends, who loved clothes and practical jokes, was waiting for me.

'Well, are we going to celebrate today?'

'I don't feel too well,' I answered. 'Let's postpone it.'

'One must not be out of sorts on such a momentous day. Thirty years—the best age for a man!'

Then he presented me with a bright necktie.

'Shall we celebrate after all? I'll drink you under the table!' he whispered. 'By a lucky chance I got some rare wine!'

While I was speaking with him I noticed a woman, a stranger, sitting in the corner. She must have been waiting for me for a long time—in some strange way I sensed this. Now she rose and took a step toward me. I no longer heard anything my friend said to me. She was about thirty, very beautiful, with sloping shoulders. Her beauty lay in the unique, charming imperfections of her face and figure, and especially in her sad, direct gaze. The same beauty unexpectedly revealed itself also in her low-pitched, quiet voice. I immediately remembered that other golden grain of sand which had long ago settled to the bottom of the hourglass. That one lay forgotten, extinct, but this one was moving toward me.

'I was asked to give you this on your birthday.' She spoke in an almost official tone, and handed me the familiar onion-shaped watch, big, heavy, on a steel chain. 'And this too.'

She took an envelope from her purse and handed it to me.

I asked: 'Is it from him?'

'Yes,' the woman answered.

I wanted to learn whether the man who had died had known real love, a love which it was impossible to buy or steal. But she gave me no time to ask. She guessed the question by my facial expression, and stopped me with a movement of her hand.

'I loved him. I did,' she whispered, 'and I still do. And I will continue to love him. But he wasn't sure . . . never knew for sure. . . . I played games with him. Do you understand what I mean? And when they let me see him at the hospital I kept crying out to him: "Yes, yes, yes!" But he didn't hear me.'

I bowed my head. My poor friend! I knew how it must have been.

I put the watch in my pocket, saw the woman to the door, and then came back.

'That's the same woman,' our dandy whispered to me. 'She came to visit the bandit. She didn't notice anyone else. If you met her in the doorway, she would walk straight on as if she were going to walk right through you. Blinded by love.'

And he added, laughing:

'But she did notice you. Watch out!'

I went to my room and tore open the envelope.

'You will receive this letter if I have been murdered,' my deceased friend wrote. 'You are a gifted person. I am writing to you because you know more about me than the others, and perhaps you value time more than they do. Life is given once and we must drink it unceasingly. In huge swallows. One must grasp at what is most precious. I have already told you what is most precious. Not gold or rags. I want you to live so as to attain great joy. You must never forget the eclipsed continent where millions of people now live. Let the day you receive this letter be the day of your real birth. . . .'

I didn't finish reading the letter. I was interrupted by a sudden, immense and happy thought. 'I am more fortunate than he,' popped into my mind. 'I still have half my life ahead of me, maybe even two-thirds. I don't have to hurry. There is time for everything.'

At that moment a dark solid mass covered my window. The painters must be dragging their scaffold up to the fourth floor. I turned the paper over to read further, and went up to the window, closer to the light. 'But why would painters be working outside in the middle of winter?' I suddenly wondered. I lifted my head and started violently. On the other side of the window, on an iron railing under the sill, sat an enormous owl with shaggy ears and gray side-whiskers and—what was strangest of all—greatly distorted, as if it had been sculptured by a primitive, prehistoric man. It was my owl. This was the first time I had seen it in the flesh. I shook the letter at it threateningly, and cried: 'Shoo!' The owl paid no attention whatsoever.

An answer to the riddle came in a piercing flash. I even broke into sudden perspiration from pain and fear. 'Phew!' I caught my breath with difficulty and wiped my forehead. The owl sat motionless in its place, erect, as all owls sit. I took another breath, wiped my forehead and stealthily left the room. I don't remember how I got out into the wintry street. To whom should I turn now? Ah, yes, to my schoolmate, an experienced neuropathologist, a man with a creative turn of mind. He would be interested in my case, and would help me.

I stepped rapidly through the evening purple of the boulevard and at once heard a strange hopping gait behind me. I looked around. Someone was standing behind the nearest tree. I saw clearly a shaggy ear and protruding wing. The owl was just about my size!

The doctor was busy. I sat for a long time near the white doors of his office and heard rapid, measured footsteps inside. Finally the door swung open, and my friend appeared in a white coat, wearing a white cap pulled down to his brows, emaciated and pale from work without sleeping.

'Well, how did it go?' someone called out somewhere.

'Just the same!' he shouted, twitching nervously, looking at me without seeing me. 'Again nothing came of it.'

I got up. The doctor slowly came to himself. He noticed me, recognized me, stretched out his hand.

'If this is a social visit, you've come at a bad time.'

'It's not a social visit.'

'Come in, then.' He took my hand and examined the tips of my fingers. 'How old are you?'

'Thirty.'

'I had forgotten we're the same age. Well, what's troubling you? Are you being followed by someone?'

'If you only knew what someone! Someone weird. You'll burst out laughing.'

'I know who it is. Shall I show you? Come with me.'

He led me into the office, and turned his face toward the window.

'My owl!' I whispered.

It was sitting outside the window.

'Not just yours,' the doctor said. 'Mine too. Let me see your hands. Ye-e-es.'

He went to the table and turned his back to me. Then he turned around.

'You're bound to find out sooner or later. It might as well be sooner: you have one year to live.'

The floor suddenly gave way under my feet, and I would have fallen if my friend hadn't caught me and seated me in a chair.

I know that some people are not afraid of death. Such brave souls have nothing to protect and feel responsible for. I confess to you: I shook with fear. When I finished my work, yes, then I could die. But not now!

'I don't believe it,' I whispered.

'You'd better get up and start running,' the doctor said, raising his brows, visibly nervous. 'You have a whole year left to live.'

'I don't believe it!'

'Get out of here!' he shouted suddenly. 'You're stealing time from me! I'm ill myself; I have only a year and a half left.'

Nevertheless at the door he held me back and quickly, almost in a running patter, said:

'This is an old disease. Gifted people suffer from it most of all, and in its most acute form. More prosaic beings get sick quietly and die slowly.'

'And you haven't discovered anything yet?'

'We have, a great deal. But we still don't have the cure. And yet, we do know something. . . .'

And he uttered these incomprehensible words:

'If a person can see the owl clearly, he is already half cured.' And he slammed the door after me.

'Do I see it distinctly? I'll have to check,' I thought.

Then in the quiet I heard a clear ticking: the watch, the bandit's gift, was doing its job, counting off the seconds accurately. Hearing its resounding ticking, I took out the heavy steel watch, inserted the figured key and wound the spring. The key turned twenty times and would turn no longer. That was all! The watch was wound for one year.

'I must hurry! I must think through everything,' I said to myself. For the first time in my life I hurried in earnest, that is, dispassionately.

The clear, frosty evening greeted me with gay lights, automobile noises and the distant twinkling of stars.

'I will think, and I will look at the stars,' I decided. The starry sky seemed to descend over me so that I could see its vast infinity better.

'So be it. The flesh dies. Let it die. But thought, thought! Will it really disappear?' I closed my eyes.

'I shall not disappear,' my thought replied out of the darkness. Unlike my feelings, it was calm. 'Look,' thought continued. 'The world of civilization has existed for several thousand years. But see how short-lived are things made by man. Machines, furniture, clothes—all turn to dust in a matter of two-score or three-score years. We have accumulated knowledge: the secrets of the smelting of metals and the hardening of cement, the formulae of medicines. Burn the books, destroy the secrets of various crafts, allow a few decades for them to be forgotten completely, and humanity will have to begin all over again on its old road up from the Stone Age. And your son—not your grandson, mind you, but your son—will dig up from the earth a cogwheel that you made in your youth and pray to it as if it were a miracle created by God.'

A waltz, loud and pure, poured out over the city from an invisible loudspeaker. I didn't know who had written it. It was as though it wasn't music that I heard—it wasn't an orchestra; the horns weren't horns, the violins weren't violins, but the voices of my emotions. And when the woodwinds introduced their song, when the wood itself began to sing, it all became clear—singing quietly in their crowded box were my irrevocably imprisoned desires, confined within the limits of my short life.

'You want to live,' the unknown composer spoke to me. 'Take a look at what a few notes did to you, those few notes which I put down a hundred years ago, after a brief and miserable sojourn among people. Listen: that man to whom little time is allotted, loves life more passionately, more deeply. It is better not to have and to yearn than to have and not to yearn! I loved life intensely and I pass on this love to you.'

He went on, his voice lowered:

'Listen to me. Even in my short life I experienced the peak of happiness. You know well what I'm talking about. But you? Has anyone ever shaken your hand in gratitude, shaken it hard enough to dislodge your heart from its place? Have you ever looked into eyes filled with tears of love?'

I was stunned. I had never known any of this! I had loved, yes, but I had never seen such eyes. I had never experienced a great friendship, nor earned men's gratitude. My head lowered, I stopped listening to the music, and the lights of the city grew dim around me. My ears caught only one sound—a cheerful ticking. This was the watch, the bandit's gift, doing its work, counting off seconds— my seconds. 'You have a whole lifetime before you! A whole year! You have just been born! You are now younger than you were! Run faster to your place of work. Everything is there—friendship and love!'

I started running, leaped into a taxi. 'To the laboratory—faster, faster!' The driver, shifting into third, turned around in amazement, to take a look at his strange passenger.

Leaving the taxi at the entrance, I ran in and hurried up the stairs. In the corridor near a red-hot stove, her head down, the old stove-tender was sleeping on a chair. I woke her up.

'Let me have all my papers! Quickly! The ones I gave you in the morning. The whole basketful!'

'My dear boy, you're too late!'

I groaned and rushed to poke among the glowing ashes in the stove.

'I burned everything, everything. What a beautiful fire—only your papers burn that way. See how warm it got—I even fell asleep!'

'Tick-tick-tick,' said the bandit's watch in my pocket. With jaw set, I unlocked my office and began to carry boxes of equipment out onto the street, to the taxi. I had decided to open a branch laboratory at home and to work at night. Perhaps I would indeed earn man's highest gratitude, but so far I hadn't even begun!

When I entered our bachelor apartment, holding a box in each hand, I found several persons near the television set in the lounge. These were the "regulars."

'So, it's been decided, I see, to postpone the celebration,' the practical joker said to me.

He twirled the knobs of the television set. The legs of the soccer players flashed on the screen. All the watchers froze. Their eyes were unnaturally large, motionless. I heard the ticking of my watch and realized that if our television set had worked uninterruptedly for two thousand years these five men would have sat there in exactly the same pose, never tearing themselves away, and would have been preserved for posterity, like the lotus seed.

I asked a few people to move their chairs, to be out of my way when I carried the boxes through; I placed the equipment in my room and let the cab driver go.

My owl was sitting in its place behind the window. It no longer upset me. It was clearly outlined by the bright light from the room. Did I see it clearly? I went up to the window. We looked at one another for a while. Then the owl began to move back and forth along the iron railing, exactly as it might have walked back and forth along a tree branch at the zoo. It bent over, raised its three-clawed foot, which looked as though it had been dipped in wax, and with rapid movements, like a chicken, scratched its beak with a claw. Then it became quiet again, sat upright, and fixed upon me the two tinny circles of its eyes. I saw my owl very clearly!

I took hold of myself and quickly began to open boxes and set up equipment. In five minutes my room was sparkling with glass and nickel—it became a laboratory.

'What can I accomplish?' I thought. 'I'll need at least ten years!'

I tried to recapture some of the ideas which I had at various times burned in the laboratory stoves. I tried to write them down again, but nothing came of it.

'It would have cut my work in two!' I even beat my fist against the table.

Then I caught sight of the bandit's note which I had thrown on the floor during the day. I had not finished reading the last few lines, and these lines were now staring up at me from the floor.

'I can be of some use to you. Did you understand the story about the bandit? If so, ask the woman who now stands before you, and she will give you the notebook in which I secretly jotted down all your ideas, the ones which you kept throwing into the stove for two years. I wanted to make use of them myself—you didn't seem to need them.'

'How can I find her now?' I shouted, again not finishing the note. Just then I saw the words: 'Her telephone . . .'

In a few seconds I was standing, as if in a fairy tale, among the men hypnotized by the television set. They breathed evenly, their eyes wide open. Setting the telephone on the shoulder of one of them, I dialed the number. A few buzzes sounded, and then her voice.

A new chapter in my new, short life began that moment. It began with a misunderstanding, which I myself precipitated.

'You should answer immediately!' I shouted before I realized how rude I was. 'Where is the notebook? Why didn't you hand it to me?'

'You didn't ask,' she replied. 'You didn't even read through the letter. It said: "If you . . ."'

'It's obvious that time means nothing to you!' I burst out again. The receiver suddenly became silent.

'Why don't you say something?' I roared again. 'The notebook, the notebook!'

'I'm coming,' the low, caressing voice answered.

When I heard her footsteps I suddenly realized that I hadn't been waiting for the notebook alone. From the very first moment I had seen this woman, I had felt drawn to her, quietly, imperceptibly, as a chip of wood is drawn by the current toward a distant waterfall. Had this second golden grain of sand reached the neck of the hourglass, ready to fly through it in an instant? 'Well, go ahead and fly,' I thought. 'This doesn't exist for me now. Don't all beautiful women love to be pursued—pursued persistently and for a long time? They should, and you, of all women, because you still haven't forgotten the man to whom you cried out, 'Yes, yes, yes!' And you will hardly forget him—could a nonentity like me crowd out the memory of that exotic, improbable man with the face of a stranger? I am dead to love; it doesn't exist for me.'

Then she opened the door and came in—small, quiet, beautiful, with sloping shoulders. 'I love you!' shouted everything that was alive in me. I understood that the childhood of my new life had already passed, and that adolescence had set in. But then I heard a chilling knock against the window pane. I didn't even bother to turn around. Everything was clear to me at once.

Barely taking time to greet the woman, I snatched the notebook from her hand, turned my back to her, opened the notebook and saw the sketches, diagrams and calculations—the very ones which for several years I had thoughtlessly thrown away to be burnt. I leafed through the notebook. Aha! Now I'd need, not ten, but eight years. I would set up the experiments so that they would proceed in several directions at once. Day and night.

'Why are you in such a hurry?' the woman asked, seeing the

haste with which I connected the wires and set up the apparatus.

'There's very little time left,' I said abruptly. 'Life is short and there is much work to be done. I am in a great hurry.'

I turned on all the equipment and lit cheerful fires under the flasks and retorts. Clear boiling streams ran through the glass pipes and the rare earths in the crucibles began to melt.

My owl was sleeping behind the window, its head tucked under a wing. I decided to test the thing once more, in order to remove the last doubt.

'What is that outside the window?' I asked the woman suddenly, pointing at the owl.

At this, the enormous bird raised its head and blinked the yellow lenses of its eyes rapidly. The woman went to the window, stooped, and shielded her eyes from the light with both hands.

'There's no one there,' she said smiling. And suddenly she became silent. She began to stare fixedly at me, and bit her lip as if struck by some discovery. 'There's no one there,' she repeated. 'Did you see anyone? Is someone following you?'

'Nobody there? Fine,' I said evasively.

And suddenly she asked me a question. Now it was her turn to surprise me, to leave me speechless. She asked:

'Why did you move to another room?'

I was dumbfounded. I stiffened, but didn't answer her—I was already the slave of a new discipline. I began to turn the handle of my old adding machine. I had some calculations to make. The woman didn't tear her eyes away from me.

After about an hour she couldn't hold back; she began to laugh quietly.

'At least tell me where you are going in such a hurry.'

'Where? One man, you know whom I mean, has probably already told you where he was hurrying.'

'He did. . . .'

'That's exactly where I am hurrying. I have spent a lifetime without accomplishing anything. But I am capable of doing something for humanity. I won't have any rest on this earth until a grateful person shakes my hand hard enough to jolt my heart from its place. I will work for that person. He will come, and that will be my day of happiness.'

These words must have pleased her. She became silent and then started all over again.

'Why are you wasting time? This is so unlike you. Why don't you make use of your wonderful calculating machine?'

Never heard of it! What kind of machine? Again I did not respond. Finally she took me by the hand and led me to the door.

'What now?' I stopped.

'Don't waste time,' she said mocking me. 'Don't worry; I'll help you gain time.'

She dragged me into another apartment, the one where my extraordinary colleague, the bandit, had lived. She fetched a key, opened the door to his room, and put on the light. Then she turned away from me, hiding a smile. But I positively beamed with joy. The latest and most expensive equipment, just what I needed, occupied the room. I began to examine it, to move it around, and forgot all about my companion.

'Shame on you!' she broke in suddenly. 'Pretending you've never seen these things before!'

Again she was back on the same tack.

'What are you trying to say?' I asked sharply.

'Well, you must have at least dropped in on your friend,' she answered evasively. 'Don't tell me you didn't even see this?'

In an aquarium on the windowsill, an unfamiliar large white flower was growing, filling the air with its strong fragrance. The woman led me to it. She seemed to be testing me. And suddenly I remembered.

'This is the lotus grown from a seed which lay in a tomb for two thousand . . .'

'Ye-es,' she said triumphantly. 'You get an A+ for that. And do you recognize this?'

And she pointed to a computing machine of the latest model, one which I hadn't even dared to dream about. Such a machine could do the work of a whole bureau of statisticians equipped with simple adding machines.

'May I take it with me?' I couldn't keep myself in check any longer.

'You're wasting time!' she raised her voice, mimicking the bandit, or me. 'Yes! Yes! Yes! It's all yours. All the equipment. Even the lotus.'

She seemed to be offended at something.

'Well, it's understandable,' she said, sunk in thought. 'You changed your face and your voice, so you had to change your room, too. So that no one would know, or report. . . . Not even your friends. . . .'

I should have given thought to these words right there and then! But, as I've said, I was the slave of a new discipline which gave a new turn to everything. I let her words slip by as chatter.

That night I made immense progress in my work. I became convinced of the validity of my most conjectural assumptions. If the work progressed at the same rate, I would have the first results in eight months, and then I could involve the whole institute in the project. All the skeptics would beat a retreat.

In the morning, without noticing anything around me, full of the wildest hopes, I went to the laboratory. Even before I entered the room I heard a gay bustle. It turned out that my eternal foe S. had already printed an answer to my article.

'What agility!' our director exclaimed ironically, and after each of his words a mock-threatening noise rose and subsided in the circle of my supporters.

They all stood around my desk. The chief laughed, holding his belly, and only the scribe with a pen behind his ear, that is, myself, was missing from the famous picture.

'Now, dear warrior, it's your turn,' the director said, and spread the newspaper clipping on my desk.

But I surprised them. I didn't even look at the latest production of S., who now seemed to me merely a naïve, but in no way dangerous, eccentric. He no longer made my blood boil; another fire was burning in it. I ignored him like a mosquito. But, getting ahead of my story, I ought to mention that this S. went on for a long time to write articles especially for me. In one footnote he said that I had been shamed into silence, in another that I had donned a muzzle and retired to the bushes, hiding my head like an ostrich. He crowed like a rooster and flapped his wings from afar, trying to provoke me into continuing the battle.

Seeing that I laid the newspaper clipping aside, my colleagues exchanged glances.

'Is it really you?' the practical joker asked, astonished. 'Look, he hasn't even shaved. Friends, he has thrown his overcoat on a chair! Well, well! There are two buttons missing from it. Don't you think he is someone else? There is some resemblance to that man . . . the one who used to sit beside him. . . .'

And he looked pointedly at the bandit's desk.

He was right—I had changed greatly. I had become a different person. Overnight I had dropped all the mannerisms of the great scientist, stopped drawing out my words and deliberating over silly questions. I was soaring constantly in a kind of incandescent half-sleep. A thirst for life awakened in me, and my conceptions of pleasure were strangely altered.

What did I take pleasure in? I constantly looked at her. She had set herself up securely in my room, installed a folding bed, and worked at the instruments day and night. I don't even know when she slept. I took pleasure in watching her from a distance as she sat at the table, and I admired the particular curve of her head and neck, like a young mother bending over her child.

And, watching the line of her head, neck, and sloping shoulders, this tender, waving arc by which I would have recognized her anywhere, I dreamed. I wanted her to turn around, to look at me. She always obeyed my wordless commands—she would turn around, her chin resting on her shoulder. But some question always troubled her, and she would look at me fixedly and turn back to her work.

This question tormented her. She decided to arrange one more test for me. We had an established rule: if there was a break in the work, we would always go somewhere for an hour or two—to an exhibit, to the opera, or to a concert. So one evening, setting the automatic controls and switching on the instruments, she took me by the arm.

'We have some free time. A whole hour. Make me a gift of it?'

I thought it over.

'All right. It's yours.'

We went out into the street. She was leading me until we found ourselves walking along a dark alley.

Suddenly the woman asked:

'Is it possible that you don't remember this path?'

I was bored by now, and didn't bother to hide my annoyance.

'I beg you to drop this strange game. You've been playing it for two months now, I do not understand it at all, and it's robbing us of time.'

'Why are you in such a great hurry all the time?'

At precisely that moment, in the shadows behind a street light, I saw the dark outline of my owl, and its shining, rapidly blinking eyes. I stopped. I wanted to ask my companion to look at these eyes, and then remembered that she wouldn't see them anyway.

'Why am I in a hurry?' I decided to tell her everything right there and then. 'I'll tell you why. I have less than a year to live.'

My words had a powerful effect on her, as though I had uttered that final word she needed to hear to burst out with her question. She stopped me, walked in front of me, and, holding her hands together, cupped my face in them. Her eyes were very close to me, and they were full of tears.

'If you are certain of this, then why are we deceiving each other here?' she whispered.

I was about to say something, but she sealed my lips with her fingers.

'I know it's you, you!'

Only then did I realize what had troubled her.

'You think that I'm this . . . your . . . ?'

'You've tortured me enough. Remember how you tried to hide from me the first time. What have I done to deserve such punishment?'

'But I am not he! I'm someone else!' I shouted. 'Look—I have different hair, a different face. I haven't changed my appearance at all. I don't have any scars from skin grafts. Everything you see is me!'

'You didn't have scars the first time either. But I guessed, I guessed immediately. Tell me, when I brought you your notebook and the watch, why did your expression suddenly change, why did you want to ask whether there was love between me and him? You wanted to know very badly. I saw through your naïve caginess.' She burst out laughing. 'Do you realize how happy you made me at that moment?'

'I'll soon part with you for good,' I said.

'We'll never part. I'll find you, even if you run away from me again, even if you change your height, in addition to getting a new face.'

'I have less than a year to live. There's no getting around that.'

'I don't believe that. You've been saying it for many years.'

'He said it, and they killed him.'

'They didn't kill him! You're clever, you've thought it all through. You left orders to give everything to your double. To yourself. You're a sly one! They'll never catch up with you!'

'What the devil! This is absurd.'

He, that other man, must have used the same words to cut her off. She burst out laughing.

'I won't talk about it anymore. Even then you didn't like it. I won't. You're gentler now than you ever were before. Your character has become milder, you smile so! You talk so well about the gratitude that will come. . . . I've wasted so much time! Why did I let myself play games with you like a seventeen-year-old? Do you want me to shout the word you had pleaded for? Yes! Yes! Do you hear? Tell me that you hear.'

'I hear,' I whispered. I couldn't fight the current any more. The chip was borne to the waterfall. 'Which me do you love more,' I asked, 'the one who was killed or the one who is here beside you?'

'The one who is here!'

I was loved. I could see the eyes. I had only to turn my head slightly to the right and I saw two stars shining with tears.

I took the place of the bandit who had departed from us. My adolescence now passed into mature youth.

Just as the doctor had predicted, my health took a turn for the worse five or six months after my visit to him. One bright day in midsummer I had to take to my bed.

I guiltily told my loved one, who was gentle and bewildered: 'You know, my dear, it's difficult for me to walk. You'll have to carry on alone; I'll stay in bed today. Turn on the radio.'

She turned it on, and immediately the voice of our dark continent was heard, now loud and howling, now dropping to a rumble of static. They were working there, mining coal, raising cabbage under artificial light.

'We must act more energetically,' I said. 'We'll have to hurry.'

And the boiling streams ran still more swiftly in the glass tubes, the fires grew ever brighter.

One rainy September day we finished work on an installation. I lay in bed, so weak that I couldn't lift my head.

'Open the first lead cowl,' I said.

She opened it.

'An error,' she said in her quiet voice. 'There's only a small reddish coal.'

'No, it is no error,' I replied calmly. 'This is only a variant. Everything has been accounted for on the other installations. But this piece of coal can be demonstrated. . . . Call the staff. Call the director.'

They came in on tiptoe, as one should enter a sickroom. I hadn't allowed them to come to see me before, and now, entering my room converted into a laboratory, they stopped at the door and began to look around. Surprised by everything they saw, they didn't know what to think: the walls were covered with scribbled formulas, the furniture was scratched with a nail—I even wrote on that—and the sparkling instruments sent forth light streams of heat toward them.

Then they saw me. My appearance must have been a shock to them; they became still quieter. Only the practical joker, whose eyes were glued to my beloved, whispered something to the director.

'Tell them,' I said.

In the manner of a trained scientist, she made a ten-minute report on our work and showed them the piece of coal which stubbornly refused to cool off.

This coal amazed everyone, especially the director. He was the first to come up to me, and solemnly shook my hand. Then the rest of my colleagues came rushing noisily, tripping over each other, to shake my weak, emaciated hands, and I felt as though my heart would move from its place at any moment.

'Today we all join you in the work,' the chief said. 'The entire laboratory!'

From that day on two men were on duty in my room day and night. In addition, we kept receiving data from the laboratory by telephone. We began to progress by leaps and bounds.

On a cold December day, in the director's presence, my beloved removed the second lead cowling.

'Another error,' she whispered to the director. 'This one is even worse—the coal is completely black!'

But I overheard her.

'This error, too, was calculated.' My lips barely moved. 'Keep going! Faster!'

My sense of hearing was extraordinarily developed. Although the director covered his mouth with his hand, I heard him whisper:

'A third failure will kill him.' Then he added in a loud voice: 'Hm. I think it would be better to move the third installation to our laboratory. There we can carry out the experiment with greater speed and precision.'

'I entrust it to you,' I said.

Now I was alone with my wife in the quiet, empty room. Just the two of us and the owl, who one day had managed to squeeze its way into the room through the glass vent and either dozed on the windowsill or paced under the table, rapping its beak against the floor. My wife—she really was that—sat near me, and we quietly reminisced about our short-lived youth.

On the third or fourth day I felt worse, and asked her to open the window.

'Dear, it's very cold outside. Should I?'

'Yes, open it, open it,' I whispered.

My wife went up to the window.

'What's happened? Spring in December! Can you feel it? The snow is melting in the streets, and a fly, fully awake, is buzzing against the glass!'

'Open the window!'

She opened it slowly, felt the air, and then flung the window wide open. Together with the warm spring breeze a wonderfully pleasant distant music burst into the room. It streamed over the city, now quietly, now pouring out in a mighty wave. I took in the music, but did not know that it came from the telephone wires which were carrying all over the world the news of man's victory over cold and darkness. Every now and then a majestic sound would blend with the music and disappear into the distance—the sound of airplanes flying over the city with a precious cargo; they were carrying the first spring to the dark continent. But, ignorant of this, very ill and utterly weak, I kept listening for my colleagues in the hope they would bring the good news. Besides, I was frightened by my owl, for it kept pacing around my bed in a strange state of excitement, shaking itself and flapping its wings violently. Nothing is more trying than having to part with life when you haven't completed your task, a task that must be accomplished for the sake of man, and one only you can achieve.

And then I fell asleep. A staircase creaked somewhere, doors slammed, hurried footsteps scuffled. But I wasn't aware of all this. I heard only the voice of the doctor, my old schoolfriend:

'He's still alive!'

He sat down at the head of my bed and began to unscrew a lead cartridge with trembling hands.

'Quickly, quickly, tell me the news!' I wanted to shout.

And I did shout, because I was no longer ill.

A blinding drop shimmered in the doctor's hand, flooding the whole room with sunlight. I had known about the drop all along. I had dreamed about it. Time and again, I would close my eyes and see it, even when I had first begun to set up the instruments. And now I couldn't look at this tiny sun—it was too bright. I got out of bed, staggering on my weak legs. My beloved rushed up to help me, but I waved her aside and walked around the room without support. I even stamped my feet. My wife leaned against the wall, radiant, incredulous.

'Thank you, doctor,' she whispered.

'Do not thank me. It was he who conquered his own death. He created his own cure. This sunlight is his.'

Again the staircase creaked, the door slammed, and a whole crowd burst into the room—my colleagues, and many other people whom I didn't know. They surrounded me; someone shook my hand. The director made his way to me.

'So, you managed to condense time, after all!' he congratulated me. 'In ancient times they would have painted an owl beside your name! You once voiced the theory that this hieroglyph . . . Do you remember?'

'And, you know, it's been confirmed,' I said. Then I thought: 'I really did condense my own time! I have lived a lifetime in one year. And so many such years are ahead of me—a whole ocean of time!'

Whom should I thank for this? I looked at the windowsill where my owl always sat, but it wasn't there. Only an aquarium, with a lotus growing in it. And beyond the window, far, far away in the pale-blue sky of that spring day, a large bird was flying toward the horizon, flapping its wings heavily.

An ocean of time lapped at my feet. I stood on its shore, ready to begin life anew, and the mysterious waves of the future kept splashing over my feet, then receded, enticing me. Tomorrow I would sail far beyond the horizon. At the same time, I was a little frightened—in that year I had become accustomed to the constant presence of the owl. How could I live without that reminder? Wouldn't the mighty ocean spreading in front of me turn into a mere trickle which I would scarcely notice as I stepped over it?

Then I remembered the watch, the bandit's gift. And I instantly turned cold with fear—I couldn't hear the watch!

I seized the chain. Of course! It had stopped! A year, a whole year, had passed. It was time to wind it again!

I took out the watch, inserted the key, and turned it twenty times. Now the key stopped turning, the watch was running again. Running into the New Year!

Appendix

On the Moon

BY KONSTANTIN TSIOLKOVSKY

(1)

I WOKE up and lay thinking about the dream I had just had. I had been swimming, and it was especially pleasant to dream about the summertime here in the dead of winter.

But it was time to get up. I stretched and got out of bed. How easy it was to sit down and to stand up. What had happened? Perhaps I was still asleep. I moved without any effort at all, as though I were standing up to my neck in water. My feet seemed scarcely to touch the floor.

There was no water; when I waved my arms I felt no resistance. I must still be sleeping. I rubbed my eyes, but nothing changed. Strange!

But I had to get dressed. I moved the chair aside, opened the closet door, and took out my suit. As I began to lift things . . . I couldn't understand it at all!

Maybe I had become stronger. Why was everything so light, why could I now lift objects which I couldn't even budge before?

These couldn't be my legs and arms, my body, which had been so heavy and done everything so laboriously. Where had this new strength come from?

Perhaps some force was drawing me and everything around me upward, thereby lightening my work. If that were the case, it must be a powerful force indeed. I felt as though at any moment I would be lifted up to the ceiling.

Why was I now leaping, instead of walking? Something was pulling against the force of gravity. It strained my muscles and forced me to jump.

I couldn't resist the temptation. I jumped.

I seemed to rise and fall rather slowly. I jumped a little higher and got a bird's eye view of the room. Ouch! My head bumped the ceiling. This ceiling was fairly high; I hadn't expected a collision. In the future I would be more careful.

246

The shout woke my friend. He tossed around on the bed, and soon he too leaped up. His amazement was no less than mine. I was able to see what I myself had looked like a few minutes ago. I was delighted with the spectacle of my friend's wide-eyed stare, his amusing poses, and the unnatural animation of his movements. His exclamations of surprise, so like my own, were very amusing.

When my physicist friend had no further surprises to offer me, I asked him what had happened. Had our strength increased or had the force of gravity become smaller?

Either supposition would have been equally surprising, but there is nothing on earth which a man cannot regard dispassionately once he has become accustomed to it. My friend and I had not yet reached this stage, but we were already anxious to determine the cause of these strange phenomena.

My friend had a very logical mind and he quickly analyzed the whole situation, which I found completely incomprehensible and confusing.

'We can measure our muscular strength with a spring balance,' he said, 'and find out whether or not it has increased. I'll brace my feet against the wall and pull on the spring. You see—180 pounds. My strength hasn't changed. You do it, and you too will be convinced that you haven't become a superman.'

'I can't agree with you,' I objected. 'The facts are against it. How could I lift this bookcase? It weighs nearly a ton. At first I thought it was empty, but I looked inside, and there's not a single book missing. And explain to me how I can jump 12 feet in the air?'

'You can't lift heavy weights or leap high into the air, your body doesn't feel so light, because your strength has increased. The spring balance has already disproved that assumption. The fact is that the force of gravity has decreased. We can easily confirm this with the spring balance, and even determine exactly how much it has decreased.'

He picked up the first weight which came to hand—a 12-pound weight—and hung it on the spring balance.

'Look,' he continued, reading the scales. 'A 12-pound weight shows 2 pounds. So the force of gravity has decreased by a factor of 6.'

Then he added thoughtfully:

'That is exactly the gravitational force which exists on the surface of the Moon, due to its small volume and low density.'

'Maybe we're on the Moon?' I burst out laughing.

'If we're on the Moon,' the physicist laughed, going along with the joke, 'it's no great misfortune. If such a miracle is possible, it can also be reversed, and we'll be able to return home again.'

'Wait! Let's be serious for a minute. If we put some object on an

ordinary beam balance, would the decrease in gravity be noticeable?'

'No. The counterbalance would decrease in weight just as much
as the object itself, and the equilibrium would not be destroyed,
despite the change in gravity.'

'Yes, I understand.'

Nonetheless I tried to break a stick in two, still hoping to show
that my strength had increased. But I didn't succeed, despite the
fact that it was a small and brittle stick.

'You're really stubborn. You might as well give up,' my friend
said. 'Just think of all the changes which must be taking place
throughout the world.'

'You're right,' I answered and threw the stick down. 'I had forgotten everything. I had forgotten the very existence of humanity.
But I am as anxious as you are to communicate with them.'

What had happened to our friends? What upheavals had
occurred?

I drew back the curtain (we lowered it at night because the
moonlight prevented us from sleeping), and was getting ready to
exchange a few words with my neighbor. Instead I recoiled in
horror. The sky was pitch-black!

What had happened to the city and its inhabitants? What I saw
was a wild incredible place brightly lit by the sun.

Had we really been moved to some deserted planet?

I couldn't say a word, but only bellowed incoherently.

My friend rushed toward me, thinking that I must be having a
fit. But I pointed to the window. He stuck his head out and also
became speechless.

If we did not faint it was only because the small gravitational
force prevented an increased blood-flow to the heart.

We looked around the room. The curtains blocked the extraordinary sight from view, and the familiar objects in the room
reassured and calmed us.

A certain residue of fear made us huddle close together. First we
raised the edge of one curtain; then we raised them all a little;
finally we decided to go outside to have a look at the funereal sky
and the changed surroundings.

Although we were preoccupied with the forthcoming expedition,
we managed to make a few observations. As we walked through
the large, high-ceilinged rooms, we had to treat our coarse muscles
extremely carefully. If we didn't, our heels slid helplessly along the
floor. There was no danger of falling, as there would have been on
snow or ice, but our bodies would jump considerably. When we
wanted to move ahead rapidly, we first had to lean forward like a
horse forced to draw an overloaded cart. But the analogy was not

complete—actually all movement was extremely easy. To descend a staircase step by step, to walk one pace at a time, was too slow and boring. Such ceremonies might be appropriate on Earth, but were simply laughable here. We learned to move at a gallop and soon could easily take ten or more stairs at a time, like boisterous schoolboys. Sometimes we leaped clean over the staircase or out a window. In a word, circumstances transformed us into leaping animals, like grasshoppers or frogs.

So we ran through the house, leaped outdoors and galloped off toward one of the nearest mountains.

The sun was dazzling and looked bluish. Shielding our eyes from the sun and from the glare reflected by nearby objects, we observed the stars and planets. Most of them also had a bluish tint. They did not twinkle, and therefore looked like silver-headed nails pounded into the black sky.

The moon, in its last quarter, was a great surprise to us, because it seemed three or four times larger than the moon we were accustomed to seeing. And it was much brighter than it is on Earth during the day, when it looks like a white cloud.

Quiet. Clear weather. Cloudless sky. No plants or animals to be seen. A wilderness with a black, monotonous sky and a lifeless dark blue Sun. No lakes or rivers: not a drop of water. If the horizon had at least looked whitish, this would have shown the presence of vapor, but it was just as black as the zenith.

There was no wind, no grass or trees, no chirping of grasshoppers, no birds or colorful butterflies. Only mountains and more mountains, terrifying, high mountains which did not glisten with snow. Not a single snowflake anywhere. There were valleys, plains, plateaus. Huge piles of rocks, black and white, large and small, but all of them sharp and glittering. There were no smooth, rounded rocks softened by waves, because there were no waves to play on them with noisy good humor or to wear them down.

There were smooth, undulating places without a single pebble. Only black fissures, which crawled on all sides like snakes. Hard, rocky ground; no soft loam, no sand, no clay.

Not a cheerful picture. Even the mountains were bare, shamelessly naked, since the transparent hazy blue veil which the atmosphere throws over mountains and other distant objects on Earth was missing here. Harsh, extraordinarily sharp landscapes. Incredibly dark shadows. Transitions from darkness to light were abrupt, with none of the soft modulations which we are so used to, and which require an atmosphere. Even the Sahara would have seemed a paradise compared with what we saw. We would have welcomed the scorpions and locusts and the scorching sands raised by dry wind, not to speak of the sparse vegetation and palm groves.

It was time to go back. The ground exuded a cold that made our legs tremble but the sun was hot. The overall sensation was one of unpleasant coldness. It was not unlike the feeling a person has when he tries to warm himself before a blazing fireplace and cannot because the room is very cold. Pleasant warmth streams along his skin but cannot vanquish the chill.

On the way back we kept warm by leaping, like gazelles, over piles of stone fifteen feet high. They were made of granite, porphry, syenite, mountain crystal, and several transparent and opaque quartzes and silicates—all volcanic rocks. We noticed other signs of volcanic activity.

We arrived home. It felt good to be indoors; the temperature was more constant. We felt disposed to conduct new experiments and discuss everything we had seen.

Obviously we were on another planet, a planet which had no air or atmosphere of any kind. If there had been, the stars would have twinkled. In air the sky would have been blue and the distant mountains would have looked hazy. But we didn't understand how we could breathe or hear one another.

Many things pointed to the absence of air or of any other gas. For example, we could not smoke and foolishly wasted a whole pile of matches trying. A sealed, airtight rubber bag was compressed without the slightest effort, proving that it contained no gas of any kind.

Scientists have proved that the Moon has no atmosphere.

'Are we on the Moon?'

'Have you noticed that the Sun looks the same size as it does from Earth? Such a phenomenon could be observed only from the Earth or her satellite, since they are almost the same distance from the Sun. On other planets it would seem either larger or smaller. From Jupiter, for example, the sun would seem five times smaller than from Earth. From Mars it is about 1½ times smaller, while from Venus it would look 1½ times larger. On Venus the Sun is twice as bright as on Earth; on Mars it is only half as bright. On Jupiter the Sun's intensity is 25 times less than on Earth. We have observed nothing like that here.

'Yes, we must be on the Moon. Everything points to it. Even the size of the satellite, which looks like a cloud to us, and which is apparently the planet we left against our will, testifies to the fact. It's too bad we can't examine her terrain and determine exactly where we are. We'll have to wait for nightfall.'

'How can you say,' I objected, 'that the Earth and the Moon are the same distance from the Sun? The difference is considerable—about 240 thousand miles, if I remember correctly.'

'I said "almost the same distance", since this 240 thousand miles is only one four-hundredth of the total distance to the Sun,' the physicist replied. 'An insignificant fraction.'

(2)

I was exhausted, not so much physically as mentally, and was in great need of sleep. What time was it? We had got up at 6:00; it was now 5:00. Eleven hours. Judging by the shadows, the sun had scarcely moved during that time. The mountain's shadow had not advanced the least bit toward the house; the shadow from the weather vane lay on the same rock. One more proof that we were on the Moon.

The Moon rotates very slowly. Here one day would equal 360 terrestrial hours, and the nights would be just as long. This was most inconvenient; the Sun disturbed our sleep. I remember that I had the same experience when I once spent several summer weeks in polar countries. The sun never left the horizon and it was terribly monotonous. But there was a great difference from the present situation. Here the sun moved slowly, but regularly; there it moves rapidly and describes a circle near the horizon every twenty-four hours.

The remedy is the same in both places—we closed the shutters.

But were our watches right? Why was there such a discrepancy between our watches and the pendulum wall clock? Our watches said 5:00, the wall clock said 10:00. Which was right? Why did the pendulum swing so slowly? Obviously the wall clock was slow.

Our wrist watches were not affected, since they did not move by gravity, but by the resilience of a steel spring, and this resilience was the same here as it is on the Earth.

We could check it by taking our pulse. Mine is normally 70 per minute. Now it was 75, but the slight increase could be explained by nervous excitement resulting from the unusual surroundings and strong impressions.

There was still another way to check the time. At night we would be able to see the Earth, and it would make a complete rotation in twenty-four hours. This would be even more reliable than an accurate watch.

Despite our sleepiness, the physicist could not rest until he had adjusted the wall clock. He took down the long pendulum, measured it, and made it six times shorter. The stately wall clock was transformed into a stump. But the short pendulum also swung regularly, and the wall clock now agreed with our wrist watches.

Finally we lay down and covered ourselves with blankets which we scarcely felt. The pillows and mattresses seemed light as air. Here one could have slept on boards.

I could not help feeling that it was too early to go to bed. The Sun, time itself, seemed to have frozen, like all lunar nature.

My friend stopped answering me, and I fell asleep too.

We awoke cheerful, optimistic, and with wolfish appetites. Till now excitement had robbed us of any desire for food.

I was thirsty. I unstoppered the flask, and . . . what was this? The water was boiling! Sluggishly, but boiling. I touched the flask. It should have burnt my hand, but was barely warm and not very pleasant to drink.

'My friend, how do you explain that?'

'We are in an absolute vacuum, and the water boils because it is not held back by atmospheric pressure. Let it boil for a little while, and don't stopper it. In a vacuum boiling is followed by freezing. But we won't let it reach the freezing point. . . . That's enough. Pour some water into a glass and cork the flask—otherwise we'll lose a lot.'

Liquids flow slowly on the moon. The water in the flask stopped boiling, but in the glass it continued to bubble sluggishly. The longer it bubbled, the more sluggish it became. The rest of the water in the glass turned to ice, then even the ice evaporated. How would we manage dinner? Bread and other solid food could be eaten without difficulty, although it dried up quickly when the hermetically sealed box was opened. The bread turned to stone. Fruits shrank and also became rather hard, but their skins helped retain some moisture.

The habit of eating hot food is a strong one, and it was impossible to light a fire. Wood, coal, even matches, would not burn.

'Why don't we put the sun to work? They cook eggs on the burning sands of the Sahara.'

We fixed the pots and pans so that their lids fitted tightly. Their contents were prepared according to all the rules of culinary art, and they were placed all together in the Sun. Then we gathered up all the mirrors in the house and set them up to reflect the sunlight directly onto the pots and pans.

In less than an hour we were able to eat well-cooked food.

What can I say? You've heard about Mouchez?* His highly perfected solar cooking was now obsolete. You think I'm bragging? Perhaps. Our voracious appetites may explain these presumptuous words—appetites which would have made any mess seem like a gourmet dish.

There was one bad feature : we had to hurry, and often choked

---

* Amedée-Ernest-Barthélémy Mouchez (1821-1892), French astronomer and author of science-fiction short stories. (R.M.)

or swallowed wrong. You will understand this when I tell you that the soup boiled and then cooled rapidly not only in the bowls, but even in our throats and stomachs. If we got lost in thought for a moment, the soup turned to a lump of ice. It's amazing that our stomachs are still intact. The pressure of the boiling liquid stretched them considerably.

In any case, we were full and reasonably calm. We could not understand how we could live without air, or how we, our house, yard, garden and supplies of food and drink had been transferred from the Earth to the Moon. We even began to have doubts, and wondered whether we were asleep and dreaming, or whether this was some kind of witchcraft. Then we got used to the situation and reacted with curiosity, sometimes with indifference. The unexplainable no longer surprised us, and the danger of a lonely death from starvation didn't even enter our heads.

After dinner we went for a walk. I couldn't have gone to sleep, I was afraid of a stroke.

We went out into the yard, which had exercise bars in the center and a fence and outbuildings on the sides.

What was this rock doing here? We could hurt ourselves on it. In the yard the ground was of ordinary soft earth. We started bravely toward the gate. Size didn't bother us: working together, we lifted the rock, which weighed more than a ton, and rolled it over the fence. We could hear a dull thud as it struck the moon's rocky surface. The sound didn't reach us through the air, but underground. The blow shook the soil, then travelled through our bodies, and made our eardrums vibrate. In this way we heard the sounds which we made ourselves.

Is that how we heard one another? Hardly. Our voices would not have sounded as they do in air.

The ease of movement aroused a strong desire to jump and climb. The joys of childhood! I remembered how pleasant it had been to clamber on trees and rooftops like a cat or a bird. And the contests leaping over ropes and ditches, and racing for prizes. I had been an ardent devotee of such pastimes.

Who can forget the old days? I was not very strong, especially in my arms. I could jump and run fairly well, but had great trouble climbing. I had dreamed of great physical strength: I would have taken revenge on my enemies and rewarded my friends. There is little difference after all between a child and a savage.

Now these dreams of physical strength seemed merely amusing. Nevertheless the burning desires of childhood came true here on the Moon. Thanks to the Moon's insignificant force of gravity, my strength had increased sixfold.

What did that fence mean to me? Nothing more than a doorstop or a footstool which on Earth I could have just stepped over. As if to test this thought, we leaped up and flew over the fence without a running start. And how pleasant it was to run without feeling your feet under you. We decided to have a race.

Each time our heels struck the ground we flew forward for yards. We covered the whole yard like galloping horses—thirty-five hundred feet in less than a minute.

Your earthly 'giant steps' couldn't possibly cover such distances.

We took measurements; at an easy gallop we rose about ten feet off the ground. In a longitudinal direction we covered thirty-five feet or more with each step, depending on the speed at which we were running.

Barely tensing our muscles, using only the left hand, we clambered up a rope in the exercise area of the yard. It was frightening. We were twenty-eight feet from the ground. Imagining that I was still on the clumsy Earth, my head began to spin. I lost my nerve and decided to jump down. Ouch! I hurt my foot.

I should have warned my friend, but instead I maliciously urged him to jump, shouting to him:

'Jump! There's nothing to it. It doesn't hurt.'

'You're wasting your time. I am very well aware that a leap from here is equivalent to a five foot leap on Earth. Obviously your feet are going to feel it a little.'

My friend started to fly. His flight was slow, especially at the beginning. He stayed aloft for 5 seconds.

'Well, how goes it, my friend?'

'My heart is beating fast, that's all.'

We reached the garden, climbed through the trees, and ran along the avenues. Why weren't the leaves dried out? Fresh green, a shield against the sun. Tall lindens and birches. We jumped and climbed along the slender branches like squirrels, but they didn't break. Of course not—here we were no heavier than fat turkeys.

We crawled over bushes and between the trees, and our movements were like flying. It was very easy to keep one's balance. Suddenly I stumbled on a knot and expected to fall. But the loss of balance was so slow that the slightest movement of an arm or leg was enough to restore it.

The large yard and garden began to seem like a cage, and we headed for the open spaces. At first we ran along level places, coming upon shallow trenches seventy feet wide.

With a running start we sailed over them like birds. But now the ground began to slope, mildly at first, then steeper and steeper. I was afraid I would soon be out of breath.

My fears were groundless. We climbed effortlessly with large rapid strides. But it was a high mountain, and one tires easily on the Moon. We sat down. The ground felt light, as if the stones had become softer.

I picked up a large rock and struck it against another one. It gave off a shower of sparks.

We rested and started back to the house.

'Is it very far?'

'No. Only about fourteen hundred feet.'

'Could you throw a stone that far?'

'I don't know. Let's try.'

We each took a small sharp stone. Mine went clear over the house. It was a good thing—watching it, I was afraid it might break the glass.

'Yours went even farther!'

It should be interesting to try shooting here. Bullets and shells would fly hundreds of miles horizontally or vertically.

'But would gunpowder explode here?'

'Explosive substances should have even greater force in a vacuum than in air, since air only restricts their expansion. They don't need oxygen, because the compounds themselves contain enough of it.'

(3)

We arrived home.

'I'm going to pour out some gunpowder on the windowsill where the sunlight will hit it,' I said. 'Focus the burning glass on it. . . . You see—it's caught fire. . . . It has exploded, even though we can't hear it.' The familiar odor of gunpowder disappeared almost immediately.

'You'll be able to shoot. Just don't forget to set the percussion cap. The burning glass and the sun will replace the action of the trigger.'

'Let's aim the rifle straight up so that we'll be able to find the bullet afterward.'

A flash, a faint noise, a slight tremor underfoot.

'Where is the cartridge case?' I exclaimed. 'It should be right around here.'

'It flew off with the bullet and will travel almost as fast. On the Earth it's only the atmosphere which prevents it from keeping up with the bullet. Here even a feather would rise or fall as fast as a stone. Take one from the pillow and I'll take a little iron ball. You can throw your feather and hit even a distant target as accurately as I can throw the iron ball. Given this force of gravity, I can throw the ball about fourteen hundred feet, and you can throw the feather the same distance. It's true, you won't kill anyone, and will scarcely

255

be aware that you're throwing anything. Let's aim our missiles at the same target . . . that piece of red granite over there.'

The feather outstripped the iron ball slightly, as if it were carried along by a strong wind.

'But what has happened to the bullet? It's been three minutes since we shot it, and it still hasn't returned,' I said.

'Wait two more minutes and it will probably return,' the physicist answered.

As a matter of fact, in just about that time we felt a slight tremor, and saw the shell not far away.

'But where's the bullet? Surely this shell didn't make the ground shake?' I asked in amazement.

'The bullet probably melted, and the spray flew in all directions.'

Looking around, we did find a few tiny pellets, apparently bits of the vanished bullet.

'It certainly flew a long time! How high did it go?' I asked.

'About forty-five miles. The low gravitational force and the absence of air friction make this possible.'

Our minds and bodies were exhausted and demanded rest. Being on the moon had its fascination but the unrestrained climbing and jumping took its toll. Especially during long flights, we didn't always manage to land on our feet, and often hurt ourselves. During flights of four to six seconds we not only had a good view of our surroundings; we were able to carry out certain maneuvers in space. At first we could not turn somersaults in the air at will, but soon we could do three of them in succession. It was a curious sensation, and a most curious thing to watch. So I followed my friend's movements for a long time as he carried out many such experiments without any support from the ground. It would take a whole book to describe them.

We slept eight hours, and it was getting warmer when we woke up. The sun had risen higher. This was not so evident on the relatively small surface of the body, but the soil began to lose its scalding coldness.

But it was time to take some precautions, since it was clear that there was a good possibility we might be roasted alive long before noon came.

What should we do? We devised several plans. We could live in the cellar for a few days, but we could not be sure that in the evening, that is, two hundred fifty hours, the heat would not reach us there, since it wasn't very deep. Anyway it would be boring to be cooped up without any conveniences.

You might think it would be preferable to be bored and uncomfortable than to be roasted alive. But wouldn't it be still better to select a rather deep ravine, and spend the time in pleasant coolness? It would be much gayer and more poetic. So we decided to look for a ravine, and to descend into it gradually as the sun became more scorching. A depth of several yards would be adequate.

We seized umbrellas and provisions sealed in boxes and casks, and threw fur coats over our shoulders. They would be equally useful in extreme heat or extreme cold, and they weighed almost nothing on our shoulders.

We spent a few more hours eating, resting, and discussing gymnastics on the moon and the remarkable feats which acrobats from Earth could have performed here.

The heat became infernal; it was dangerous to delay any longer. Outside, in the sunlit places, the rocky soil was so hot that we had to tie thick wooden slabs under our boots.

In our haste we carelessly dropped glass and earthenware dishes, but they didn't break—the force of gravity was too weak.

I almost forgot to mention the fate of our horse, who was transported to the moon with us. When we tried to hitch it to a cart, the unfortunate beast somehow broke away and raced off faster than the wind. Tumbling head over heels and injuring himself, he failed to adjust to the force of inertia, collided with a pile of rocks which got in his way, and was smashed to bits. The flesh and blood at first froze and then shrivelled up.

I should also mention the flies. They were unable to fly, but instead leaped at least a foot into the air.

We lifted all our provisions in enormous loads to our shoulders. This was very amusing, since everything seemed light and empty. We closed the doors, windows, and shutters so that the house would suffer less from the high temperature, and set out to find a suitable ravine or cave.

During our search the sharp changes in temperature surprised us very much. Places which had been bathed in sunlight for a long time were like red-hot stoves. We passed over them quickly and rested in the shade thrown by large rocks or cliffs. This was so refreshing that if we had lingered there we might very profitably have put our fur coats to use. But these places were not very reliable. The sun would pass to the other side of the rock and beat down on the place which had been shady and cold. We were aware of this, and were looking for a ravine where the sun would shine only for a short time, not long enough to heat the rocks.

We found a ravine with almost perpendicular walls. Only a few feet of it were visible; the rest was black and apparently bottomless. We found a sloping descent which seemed to lead to hell itself. The

R

first few steps presented no difficulty, but then the darkness became thicker and we could see nothing at all ahead of us. The prospect of going farther seemed frightening and even dangerous, till we remembered our flashlight. We turned it on, and the beam at once lit up a ravine one hundred fifty feet deep. It seemed safe to descend.

The complete darkness was caused in the first place by the fact that the ravine lay in the shade. The rays reflected from the high mountains didn't penetrate there because it was too narrow and deep. Secondly, there was no sunlit atmosphere above it, as there would have been on Earth. As a result, the ravine was blacker than any pit.

As we descended lower, sometimes clutching the walls for support, the temperature dropped, but never lower than 15 degrees Centigrade, which was apparently the average temperature for this latitude.

Selecting a convenient level place, we spread out our fur coats and settled down comfortably.

But what was this? Has the night descended? We gazed at the strip of dark sky and the innumerable stars shining above our heads. But according to the chronometer only a short time had passed. The sun couldn't have disappeared that quickly.

An awkward movement smashed our flashlight, but the carbon filament shone even more brightly. On Earth it would have burned up in the air and died out at once.

Out of curiosity I touched the filament. It broke and everything was plunged into darkness. We couldn't see each other. Only the edges of the ravine were visible high above us, and in the long narrow strip of black sky an even greater number of stars gleamed.

It was hard to believe that the day was at its height. I couldn't bear it, and groped for the spare flashlight. Switching on the electric current, I climbed upward. It became lighter and warmer. The sunlight was blinding; it completely eclipsed the flashlight.

It was still daytime; both the sun and shadows were unchanged. How hot it was! I quickly clambered down again.

(4)

Having nothing else to do, we slept like bears. Our lair did not become hotter.

Sometimes we went out, found a shady place, and watched the course of the sun, stars, planets, and our own big moon, which surpassed our Earth's pitiful moon as much in size as an apple does a cherry.

The sun moved at almost the same rate as the stars, lagging

behind them very slightly, a phenomenon which is also observed from the Earth. The moon was completely motionless and was not visible from our ravine. This grieved us very much, since the darkness would have allowed us to observe it as well as though it were night, and the night was still a long time away.

Noon was approaching. The shadows no longer became shorter. The moon, resembling a thin sickle, turned paler and paler as the sun drew closer to it.

The moon is an apple, the sun a cherry. The cherry hid behind the apple and produced a solar eclipse.

This is a frequent and grandiose phenomenon on the moon. On the Earth it is rare and insignificant. A small shadowy spot, barely the size of a pinhead (it may be several miles long, and still merely a pinhead compared with the size of the Earth), streaks the planet, and under favorable conditions passes from city to city and spends a few minutes in each of them. Here the shadow covers either the whole Moon or a significant part of its surface, and the total darkness lasts for many hours.

The sickle became still thinner, and was barely visible alongside the sun. Then it disappeared altogether. We crawled out of the ravine and observed the sun through a dark glass. It looked as though someone had flattened one side of its shining mass with an invisible gigantic finger.

Now only half the sun was in view.

Finally it disappeared completely and everything was sunk in gloom. An enormous shadow blanketed us.

But the blindness was quickly dissipated, and we saw the moon and a myriad of stars.

Not the sickle moon. This one was a dark circle enveloped in a magnificent blood-red radiance, particularly bright, although somewhat pale, on the side where the last of the sun had disappeared. The surroundings were flooded with crimson.

At this moment thousands of people on Earth were watching a total lunar eclipse. Perhaps our own families were among them.

While we were lost in melancholy the red wreath became more even and more beautiful. Then it outlined the whole periphery of the moon. This was the middle of the eclipse. The opposite side from that where the sun had disappeared grew lighter and paler, then more and more brilliant, till it looked like a diamond set in a red ring.

Night turned to day and our torpor vanished. Familiar surroundings reappeared before our eyes.

I have told you that we selected a shady place and made our observations. You might well ask how we could observe the sun from a shady place.

Well, not all the shady places were cold, and not all the places lit by the sun were hot. The temperature of the ground depends mainly on the length of time the sun has warmed it. Some places were sunlit for only a few hours, and had been in shadow before that time. Obviously their temperature must be extremely low. Where cliffs and steep mountains threw shadows there were areas illuminated so that the sun could be observed from them, even though they were cold. It's true that they were not always near at hand, and before you found them you might be thoroughly roasted.

For convenience, and partly for exercise, we decided to drag some of the large, still-cool rocks out of our ravine in order to build up a little platform which would protect our bodies from the heat.

No sooner said than done. Now we could always go up to the surface and, perched on the heap of stones, solemnly make our observations.

But the stones got warm, and we dragged out new ones. We had an inexhaustible supply of rocks in the ravine, and no lack of strength here on the moon.

Immediately after the eclipse we also set about determining the latitude of the part of the moon where we were located. This was easily done by keeping in mind the time of the equinox (it was evident because of the recent eclipse) and the position of the sun. The place turned out to be in the fortieth degree of northern latitude. So we were not on the equator of the Moon.

Noon, seven terrestrial days since the sunrise, which we had not witnessed, passed. The chronometer showed that we had been on the moon for five terrestrial days. In other words we had arrived early in the lunar morning, in its forty-eighth hour. This explains why the ground had been so cold when we woke up. It had not yet warmed up after the terrible cold of the preceding 360-hour night.

We slept, and each time we woke up we saw above us more and more new stars. They were the same familiar stars we had seen on Earth, but the narrow cleft from which we watched permitted us to see only a few of them at once. They did not twinkle in the black field but flowed twenty-eight times more slowly than on Earth.

Jupiter came into view. Here we could see its satellites with the naked eye, and watch their eclipses. Then Jupiter disappeared and the polar star came into view. The poor thing doesn't play an important role here.

Only the moon never peeped into our ravine, and would not have even if we had waited a thousand years. It did not appear because it is forever motionless. Only the movement of our bodies on this planet could animate it. Then it could fall, rise, and vanish again.

It's impossible to sleep all the time. We started making plans.

We decided to leave the ravine at night. Not immediately after sunset, because the ground would be extremely hot, but several hours later. We wanted to visit our little house to see what was happening there, to see what the sun had been up to. After that we would admire the view of the Moon's moon. Up to now we had seen it as a cloud. At night it would be revealed in all its beauty and luster, and from all sides, since it would make one complete rotation in twenty-four hours, which is but a small fraction of the lunar night.

Our own large moon, that is, the Earth, has phases just like the moon at which we formerly gazed with dreamy curiosity.

In our latitude there is a new moon, or a new Earth, at noon. The first quarter is at sunset; the half-moon at midnight; the last quarter at sunrise.

We were in a locality where the days and nights last for a month. This was all right, but only when we were in the hemisphere visible from the Earth. As soon as we would move to that unhappy and mysterious hemisphere which is not visible from the Earth we would immediately be deprived of nocturnal illumination. This half is mysterious because the Earth never sees it, and it is therefore very intriguing to scientists. It is unhappy because its inhabitants, if it has any, never see the heavenly bodies, and thereby miss a magnificent spectacle.

Are there any inhabitants on the Moon? What are they like? Do they resemble us? So far we had not met any, and it would have been rather difficult to do so, since we had spent almost all our time in one spot and had occupied ourselves more with gymnastics than with selenography.

Especially interesting was that unknown half of the moon where the black skies are always covered with a mass of tiny stars whose delicate radiance is not destroyed by refractions in the atmosphere, nor drowned by the coarse light of the enormous moon.

Don't hollows perhaps exist on the moon where gasses, liquids and a lunar population could accumulate? These are the things we talked about while we were waiting for sunset and for the night. We were not impatient or bored.

We conducted several interesting experiments with olive oil, and succeeded in obtaining drops of enormous dimensions. Drops of oil from a horizontal plane reached the size of an apple as they fell. Drops from a narrow opening were much smaller, and the oil flowed about two and a half times more slowly than it would have on Earth under identical conditions. The phenomenon of capillarity on the Moon was six times stronger, and consequently oil along the edges of a vessel rose above the median level six times higher than on

Earth. Oil in a small wine glass had the form of a compressed sphere.

We did not neglect the demands of our stomachs, and fortified ourselves with food and drink every six to ten hours. We had a samovar whose lid could be closed tightly, and quite often sipped a brew made from Chinese tea leaves. Of course, the samovar did not function in the conventional way, since there was no air for burning coal or wood. We simply carried it out into the sun and covered it with very hot stones. It sang animatedly without boiling. Vapor escaped through the open vent with considerable force, since there was no counterbalancing atmospheric pressure.

It was no real treat to drink this tea. There was a good chance of scalding oneself badly, because the water burst out on all sides, like gunpowder.

For this reason we first placed the tea in the samovar, let it get very hot, and then took away the hot stones and waited until it had cooled. Then we were able to drink the tea without burning our lips. But even this comparatively cold tea escaped with considerable force and bubbled like seltzer water in the glasses and in our mouths.

(5)

Sunset was approaching. We watched the sun touch a mountain peak. On Earth we could have done this with the naked eye. Here it was impossible, because there was no atmosphere or water vapor to reduce the power of the sun's heat and light. Without dark glasses we could look at it only for a second.

The sun sank from view, but very slowly. A half hour had passed since it first touched the horizon, and more than half of it was still visible.

In Petersburg or Moscow the sunset is over in three to five minutes. In tropical countries it lasts only two minutes. Only at the pole does it continue for several hours.

Finally, the last of the sun, resembling a bright star, sank behind the mountains. But there was no play of colors at sunset. Instead we saw around us many mountain tops shining with a bright reflected light. This light, which lasted for several hours, was enough to keep us from being submerged in gloom, even if there had been no moon. One distant peak gleamed like a lantern for thirty hours. Then it too died away, and only the moon and the very faint stars were left.

Immediately after the sunset, and for some time later, the reflected sunlight drowned out the light of the moon. When the last mountain peak had been extinguished the moon, lord of the night, reigned supreme.

Our moon's surface was fifteen times larger than the surface of the Earth's moon, and its light intensity exceeded the light of the Earth's moon fifteen or sixteen times. We could read without straining our eyes. It did not seem at all like night, but like some fantastic daylight.

We sent mute greetings to the Earth. Our hearts throbbed with a bittersweet longing. Reminiscences flooded our souls.

How dear and mysterious this once berated and banal Earth now seemed. The Earth's ocean of air made it look like a picture covered with blue glass.

We saw Africa and part of Asia, the Sahara, the Gobi, Arabia—countries with no rain and with cloudless skies. Clouds appeared as white formless tufts and strips. The dry land looked dirty yellow or dirty green. The seas and oceans were dark, but of different shades, probably depending on whether they were agitated or at rest. Perhaps it was breakers playing on the water that made the sea look whitish in one spot. In some places the waters were covered with clouds, most of them snow white, although a few were grayish, probably due to bright upper layers of icy crystalline dust.

The two opposite ends of the planet shone especially brightly because of the polar snows and ices. The whiteness in the north looked cleaner and had a larger surface than in the south.

If the clouds had not been moving it would have been difficult to distinguish them from the snow. But the snows lay deeper in the airy ocean and the blue color covering them was therefore darker than that covering the clouds.

Snowy points of light were scattered over the whole planet, even on the equator. These were mountain tops, so high that even in tropical countries the snowy caps never disappear from them.

We saw the shining heights of the Alps, the Caucasus, the Himalayas.

In the telescope we could see even the finest details. The moon, or, rather, the Earth, was in the first quarter. The dark half of the Earth, weakly lit by the Moon, could just barely be made out, and was much darker than the ashen sections of the Moon visible from Earth.

We were hungry, but before we went back into the ravine we wanted to find out whether the soil was still hot. We removed the paving of stones which we had set up and replaced several times, and it was as though we were plunged into an incredibly hot bath. The heat quickly penetrated our shoes, and we retreated in haste; the ground would not be cool for a long time.

We ate dinner in the ravine, going out every two or three hours to observe the moon.

We could have watched it for about twenty hours had it not been for its cloudiness. In certain places the stubborn clouds would not depart. We were impatient but did not give up hope and actually did see these places as soon as good weather set in.

For five days we hid in the bowels of the Moon and went out only to nearby places, and for a short time.

The ground cooled off, and after five terrestrial days, or the middle of the night by lunar time, it had cooled enough for us to undertake a trip around the Moon to explore its plains and mountains.

The huge, dark hollows of the Moon are usually called seas, but the name is completely incorrect, since water has never been detected there. Perhaps we would find in these 'seas,' and in still lower places, traces of Neptunian activity—traces of water, air and organic life, which some scientists thought had disappeared from the Moon in ages long past. There is a theory that all this had once existed on the Moon, and that it even might exist now, somewhere in the crevices and abysses. According to this theory, there had once been water and air, which in the course of centuries had been swallowed up by the soil, forming chemical combinations with it, and there had also once been organisms—some low order of vegetation—since wherever there is water and air, there are also fungi, and fungi are the beginning of at least the lowest forms of organic life.

My friend thinks, and there is some basis for it, that there has never been life or water or air on the Moon. If there were water and air, they would have been at such a high temperature that no organic life could have existed there.

I hope the reader will forgive me for expressing the personal views of my friend, which have so far not been proven. When we complete our circle of the moon, we will know which theory is correct.

So we seized our packs, considerably lightened by the large amounts we had eaten and drunk, and left our hospitable ravine. By the light of the stationary moon we set out for the little house.

The shutters and other wooden objects had blackened and crumbled on the surface from the prolonged action of the sun. In the yard we found splinters from a sealed barrel of water which we had carelessly left in the sun and which had burst under the pressure of the steam. There was, of course, not a trace of the water; it had evaporated completely. Near the porch we found fragments of glass from the lantern, whose metal mounting had melted. We found less damage in the house; the thick stone walls had protected it. In the cellar everything was intact.

We collected enough supplies from the cellar so that we wouldn't die of hunger or thirst and set out on our long journey to the polar region of the Moon and to the mysterious hemisphere which no human being had ever seen before.

'Why don't we run along behind the sun, westward,' the physicist suggested, 'and bend our course a little toward one of the poles? In that way we can kill two birds with one stone: we will reach the pole and the dark hemisphere, and at the same time avoid the extreme cold. If we do not lag too far behind the sun, we will be traveling in areas which have been warmed for a definite time, and which consequently will have a constant temperature. We can even change the temperature whenever we like. If we go closer to the sun the temperature will rise. If we lag behind it will drop. This will be especially helpful since we will be approaching the pole, whose average temperature is low.'

'Is it possible to do that?' I questioned my friend's strange theories.

'Entirely possible,' he replied. 'Just keep in mind how easy it is to run on the Moon and the apparent slowness with which the sun is moving. As a matter of fact, the longest lunar orbit is about sixty-six hundred miles. In order not to drop far behind the sun, we will have to cover this distance in thirty days, or seven hundred hours, expressed in terrestrial language. This means we will have to run at a speed of ten miles per hour.'

'Ten m.p.h. on the Moon!' I exclaimed. 'Nothing to it.'

'There you are.'

'We can easily run twice that fast!' I continued, remembering our gymnastic exercises. 'And then every twelve hours we can sleep the same length of time. . . .'

'Remember that we will be in a different latitude,' the physicist pointed out. 'The closer to the pole, the smaller the parallels, and since we will be moving toward the pole, we would be able to decrease our speed gradually and still keep the same distance from the sun. But the cold of the polar region won't permit this. As we approach the pole we will have to come closer to the sun so as not to freeze. In other words, we should run along places which are subjected to more prolonged illumination by the sun. The polar sun does not rise high above the horizon, and therefore the heating of the ground is incomparably weaker, so that even by sunset it will only be warm.

'The closer we are to the pole, the closer we should come to the sun, in order to insure relative constancy of temperature.'

We slipped westward like shadows, like ghosts, noiselessly touching the pleasantly warm ground. The moon was almost full and therefore shone very brightly, creating the effect of an enchanting picture covered with blue glass which seemed thicker and darker toward the edges. At the very edge it was impossible to distinguish dry land from water or clouds.

We were seeing the hemisphere rich in dry land. Within twelve hours we would see the watery side of the Earth, the Pacific Ocean covering almost the whole hemisphere. It reflected the sun's rays poorly, so that if it had not been for the brightly shining clouds and ice, the moon would not have looked as bright as it did now.

We climbed the hills easily, and ran down still more easily. At times we sank into shadow, and at once saw many more stars. At first we encountered only small hills. But even the highest mountains presented no obstacle, because here temperature is not a function of height, and the mountaintops were as warm and free from snow as the low plains. Hilly expanses, ledges, and precipices were not at all frightening on the Moon. We leaped over hilly places from seventy to a hundred feet high. If they were impassably high we ran around them or clung to the steep slopes and projections with the help of fine string, sharp sticks with hooks, and spiked soles. Because of the small gravitational force we did not need heavy ropes for support.

'Why don't we run to the equator, since we've never been there?' I asked.

'There's no reason why we shouldn't,' the physicist agreed.

We immediately changed course. Since we were running extremely fast, the ground rapidly became warmer and warmer. Finally, as we drew nearer the equator, it was impossible to run because of the heat.

'What would happen,' I asked, 'if, in spite of the heat, we continued to run at this speed in the same direction?'

'After seven days we would first see the mountaintops illuminated by the sun and then the sun itself rising in the west.'

'Do you really mean that the sun would rise where it normally sets?' I asked incredulously.

'That's right, and if we were fairy-tale salamanders, immune to fire, we could see it with our own eyes.'

'What would happen, would the sun just appear and again disappear or would it rise in a normal way?'

'If we were running along the equator at a speed somewhat greater than ten miles per hour, the sun would move from west to east, and would set in the east. But as soon as we stopped it would immediately move in the normal way, and would again sink behind the horizon in the west.'

'And what if we ran neither faster nor slower than ten miles per hour, what would happen then?' I asked.

'Then, as in the time of Joshua, the sun would stand still in the sky and the day or night would never end.'

'Could the same thing happen on Earth?' I persisted.

'It could, but only if we were able to move at a speed equal to or exceeding 1016 miles per hour.'

'Fifteen times faster than a hurricane?! No, thank you, that is not for me!'

'So you see, what can be done here easily, is completely unthinkable there on the Earth.' The physicist pointed toward our moon.

So we perched on rocks and talked, since it was impossible to run because of the heat. We were exhausted, and soon fell asleep.

A marked coolness awakened us. We jumped up nimbly, leaping about ten feet into the air, and again ran toward the west, toward the equator.

The reader will remember that our house was located in the fortieth degree of latitude, so that we were still a considerable distance from the equator. But do not make the mistake of thinking that a degree of latitude on the Moon is the same as on the Earth. Do not forget that the size of the Moon compared to the size of the Earth is like a cherry compared to an apple. One degree of latitude on the Moon is therefore less than twenty miles, while on Earth it is over sixty-eight miles.

We knew that we were approaching the equator, because the temperature of the deepest crevices, which represented the average temperature of the region, gradually increased to a constant high point of 50 degrees Réaumur. Then it began to decrease, which meant that we were in another hemisphere. We determined our position with greater accuracy astronomically.

But before we crossed the equator we encountered many mountains and dry 'seas.' The shape of lunar mountains is very well known to the inhabitants of Earth. They are for the most part round, with a hollow in the middle.

The hollow is not always empty; sometimes another whole mountain rises in its center, with a new crater which is, however, almost never active.

Probably in times long past these volcanoes had thrown out the rocks which were present here in such large numbers. No other origin seemed credible. Out of curiosity we ran around the volcanoes, along their very rims, and, peering inside the craters, twice saw flowing, gleaming lava. Once we even noticed an enormous tall shaft of light over the top of a mountain, probably from a large number of rocks heated to incandescence. They shook the ground as they fell.

Because of the lack of oxygen on the moon, or for some other reason, we found only unoxidized metals and minerals, most frequently aluminum.

The low, level spaces, the dry 'seas,' despite the physicist's convictions, were covered with faint but unmistakable traces of Neptunian activity. We loved these places. They crumbled somewhat from the touch of our feet, but we ran so fast that the dust settled immediately. We loved them because they cushioned our heels along the stony places and took the place of soft rugs or grass. This alluvial layer could not interfere with our running; it was too shallow.

The physicist pointed into the distance and I saw red sparks spraying like a campfire off to the right. Some of the last ones described red arcs. By mutual agreement we made a detour to determine the cause of this phenomenon.

When we reached the place we saw scattered pieces of red-hot iron. The smaller pieces had already cooled, the larger ones were still glowing.

'That's meteoric iron,' the physicist said, picking up one of the cooled pieces. 'It also falls on the earth,' he continued. 'I have often seen them in museums. These meteoric rocks are called aerolite, but the name is not a good one. It is particularly inappropriate here on the moon where there is no air. Here you cannot see them until they strike the granite soil and incandesce as a result of the transformation of kinetic energy into heat. On Earth they are visible almost from the moment of their entry into the atmosphere, since they are heated by friction with the air.'

Having crossed the equator, we again decided to travel toward the northern pole.

The cliffs and piles of rocks were amazing. They stood out in bold outline. We had seen nothing like it on Earth. They assumed fantastic forms, and on Earth would unquestionably have crashed down with an awful roar. Here the force of gravity was not strong enough to hurl them down.

We rushed on, drawing closer and closer to the pole. The temperature in the fissures dropped lower and lower. On the surface we were not aware of this because we were gradually overtaking the sun. Soon we would witness its miraculous rise in the west.

We didn't run fast—there was no need for it—and we no longer descended into the crevices to sleep because they were too cold. We rested and ate wherever we stopped. We even slept on our feet, abandoning ourselves to disconnected dreams. This was not surprising; the same thing could happen on Earth. It is all the more possible here, where in terms of weight standing is the same as lying down.

(6)

The moon dropped lower and lower, casting on us and on the

lunar landscape a light alternately weak and strong, depending on the side which it turned to us—water or dry land—and on the degree to which the atmosphere was saturated with clouds.

In time it touched the horizon and began to set behind it. This meant that we had reached the other hemisphere, invisible from the Earth.

After four hours it had completely disappeared, and we saw only its reflection on a few mountaintops. Then they too died away. The gloom was remarkable. A sea of stars, which on Earth only a powerful telescope could have revealed.

But their lifeless immobility was unpleasant, the black background oppressive.

What was that shining so brightly in the distance? Half an hour later we discovered that it was a mountaintop.

As we ran up the mountain, half of it was shining in the sunlight. But even while we were running it sank into darkness and the sun was no longer visible from it. Obviously this was the place of the sunset.

We descended more quickly, flying like arrows shot from a bow. There was no need to hurry. We would have seen the sun rising in the west even if we had run at a speed of three miles per hour, that is, even if we had not run at all. But it was impossible not to hurry. How wonderful! The star rising in the west began to sparkle. It grew rapidly larger. Now a whole section of the sun came into view, then the whole sun. It rose higher and higher, standing out from the horizon distinctly.

And all this was only for us, as we ran. The mountaintops behind us died out one after the other. If we had not seen the oncoming shadows the illusion would have been complete.

'That's enough! We're worn out!' the physicist exclaimed in a joking tone, addressing the sun. 'You can go in peace.'

We sat down and waited until the sun, setting in its normal way, hid itself from view.

The show was over. We turned back and were soon fast asleep.

When we woke up we again pursued the sun at a leisurely pace, merely for the sake of warmth and light. We didn't let it out of our sight again. It rose and sank, but never left the sky, and continued to warm us. When we fell asleep the sun was rather high. We woke up. The rascal sun made a feeble attempt to set, but we curbed it and forced it to rise again.

Now we were drawing near the pole. The sun was so low and the shadows were so enormous that we shivered with cold while crossing them. The extremes of temperature were striking. Some projecting places were so warm it was impossible to approach them closely. Other places had lain in shadow for fifteen days or more and you couldn't cross them for fear of catching rheumatism. Keep in mind that here the sun, even though it lies almost on the horizon, warms the surface of the stones turned toward it twice as powerfully as when it is directly overhead on Earth. Of course such a situation cannot exist in the polar countries of Earth because a large part of the sun's rays are absorbed by the atmosphere, and because on Earth it does not shine so obstinately *at* the pole—the sun circles the stone every 24 hours.

But you will say: 'What about heat conductivity? The cold ground should draw heat from the rocks.' It does sometimes, when the rock forms a solid mass with the ground itself. But many of these granite boulders, despite their size, are simply on the surface and touch the ground only at three or four points. The heat is conducted through these points extremely slowly, imperceptibly. And the radiation is so weak that the mass becomes hotter and hotter.

However, it was not these rocks, but the very cold valleys lying in the shade which troubled us most. They hindered our approach to the pole because these shady expanses became wider and more impassable the closer we came to it.

For all practical purposes, seasons of the year did not exist here. In summer the sun at the pole does not rise more than five degrees, while on earth the increase is five times larger. When summer did come here it would just barely have permitted us to reach the pole.

Continuing to follow the sun, and describing a circle, or, more correctly, a spiral, around the Moon, we again left this region, frozen in places, with hot stones scattered everywhere.

We had no desire to freeze or to roast. As we went farther and farther away from the pole, it got hotter and hotter, and we were forced to abandon the sun. We had to drop behind in order not to be fried alive. We ran on in darkness at first relieved a little by the bright summits of the mountain ranges. Then even they disappeared. It became easier to run; we had consumed a large part of our supplies.

The moon, which we had forced to move, would soon appear. We were overjoyed to see it. It could not be otherwise—we had been away so long.

Many more hours dragged by. Although we had never seen these places and mountains before, they did not excite our curiosity, but only seemed monotonous. We were fed up with all these wonders. Our hearts ached. The sight of our beautiful but inaccessible Earth only sharpened the pain of reminiscences, the wounds of irretrievable loss. If we could at least reach the house soon. That, after all, was not a dream. But even there, what awaited us? Familiar but lifeless objects, which could stab and wound the heart still more.

What was the source of our grief? We hadn't felt it at first. The novelty of our surroundings had overshadowed it. We hurried toward the house, so that at least we would not have to look at these dead stars and the funereal sky.

The house couldn't be very far away. We knew by astronomical calculations that it must be here, but in spite of this we not only couldn't find the familiar yard, we couldn't even recognize a single feature of the landscape. We walked on, searching everywhere. It was nowhere to be found. Sick with despair, we finally stopped and fell asleep. Awakened by the cold, we ate some of the little remaining food. Our only defense from the cold was running. As ill luck would have it, we didn't find a single crevice where we might have escaped from the cold. We were again forced to run after the sun, to run forever, like slaves hitched to a chariot. But not forever—there was only enough food left for one meal. Then even that was gone.

Sleep closed our eyes, and the cold forced us to huddle against one another. What had become of all those ravines which we had found everywhere when we didn't need them?

We didn't sleep long. The cold, which had become still more piercing, waked us unceremoniously and without pity. We couldn't sleep more than three hours in a row.

Weak, worn out by grief, hunger, and the advancing cold, we could not run with our former speed. We were slowly freezing to death.

I was sleepy, but my friend kept me awake. Then he became drowsy and I kept him from sleeping, from fatal sleep. He had taught me the terrible significance of this last sleep.

We supported and strengthened one another. As I remember it now, the idea of abandoning one another didn't even occur to us.

The physicist fell asleep and began to rave about the earth. I embraced him, trying to warm his body with my own.

Seductive dreams—dreams of a warm bed, a fire in the fireplace, food and wine—took possession of me. My family surrounded me, took care of me, felt sorry for me. Served me. . . .

Dreams, dreams! A blue sky. Snow on the neighboring roofs. A bird flying by. Faces, familiar faces. The doctor . . . what is he saying?

'Lethargy, prolonged sleep. . . . His condition is dangerous. . . . Marked drop in weight—he's emaciated. . . . But his breathing has improved; he's coming to. . . . He's out of danger!'

Happy, tear-stained faces surrounded me.

I had been ill and unconscious, but had now awakened. I had

gone to sleep on Earth, and I woke up on Earth. My body remained here, while my thoughts had flown away to the Moon.

But I was delirious for a long time. I kept asking about the physicist, talked about the Moon, and was surprised that all my friends were now there with me. The Earth and the heavens were all mixed together. One moment I thought I was on the Earth; the next moment I had again returned to the Moon.

The doctor forbade everyone to argue with me or to irritate me, fearing that I might lose my sanity.

I returned to consciousness very slowly and was slower still in regaining my health.

It goes without saying that the physicist was very surprised when I told him this whole story after my recovery. He advised me to write it down and to fill it in with explanations of my own.

THE END